THE
GALLERY
ASSISTANT

Also by Kate Belli

Opulence and Ashes
Treachery on Tenth Street
Betrayal on the Bowery
Deception by Gaslight

THE GALLERY ASSISTANT

A Novel

Kate Belli

EMILY BESTLER BOOKS
ATRIA
New York   Amsterdam/Antwerp   London
Toronto   Sydney/Melbourne   New Delhi

EMILY BESTLER BOOKS

ATRIA

An Imprint of Simon & Schuster, LLC
1230 Avenue of the Americas
New York, NY 10020

For more than 100 years, Simon & Schuster has championed authors and the stories they create. By respecting the copyright of an author's intellectual property, you enable Simon & Schuster and the author to continue publishing exceptional books for years to come. We thank you for supporting the author's copyright by purchasing an authorized edition of this book.

No amount of this book may be reproduced or stored in any format, nor may it be uploaded to any website, database, language-learning model, or other repository, retrieval, or artificial intelligence system without express permission. All rights reserved. Inquiries may be directed to Simon & Schuster, 1230 Avenue of the Americas, New York, NY 10020 or permissions@simonandschuster.com.

This book is a work of fiction. Any references to historical events, real people, or real places are used fictitiously. Other names, characters, places, and events are products of the author's imagination, and any resemblance to actual events or places or persons, living or dead, is entirely coincidental.

Copyright © 2025 by Sarah C. Gillespie

All rights reserved, including the right to reproduce this book or portions thereof in any form whatsoever. For information, address Atria Books Subsidiary Rights Department, 1230 Avenue of the Americas, New York, NY 10020.

First Emily Bestler Books/Atria Books hardcover edition October 2025

EMILY BESTLER BOOKS/ATRIA BOOKS and colophon
are trademarks of Simon & Schuster, LLC

Simon & Schuster strongly believes in freedom of expression and stands against censorship in all its forms. For more information, visit BooksBelong.com.

For information about special discounts for bulk purchases, please contact Simon & Schuster Special Sales at 1-866-506-1949 or business@simonandschuster.com.

The Simon & Schuster Speakers Bureau can bring authors to your live event. For more information or to book an event, contact the Simon & Schuster Speakers Bureau at 1-866-248-3049 or visit our website at www.simonspeakers.com.

Interior design by Davina Mock-Maniscalco

Manufactured in the United States of America

1 3 5 7 9 10 8 6 4 2

Library of Congress Cataloging-in-Publication Data has been applied for.

ISBN 978-1-6680-9365-8
ISBN 978-1-6680-9367-2 (ebook)

For Celeste,
who was with me on that day, has been there every day since,
and I imagine will be for all the days to come.

PART ONE

CHAPTER ONE

Williamsburg, Brooklyn
Mid-November, 2001

How did I get home last night?

The thought hit, abrupt and bracing, along with the near-firehose pressure stream of scalding water from the showerhead above. I jumped out of the way, reaching to adjust the temperature, though it didn't do much good. The pipes were as old as the rest of the building, and finicky; the water was either near boiling or icy cold.

I managed to find a tolerable warmth and quickly scrubbed myself, trying to avoid the messy mound of hair piled on the top of my head. I was already so late for work, there was no time to wash and dry it, and it was too cold out to let it air-dry. The foul scent of cigarette smoke mixed with the steam from the shower, intensifying it. Funny how I loved the taste of cigarettes so much, but the later smell on my clothes and in my hair was disgusting.

How did I get home?

I paused, taking an extra moment I didn't have to let the water blast my shoulders, and gingerly pressed my lips with damp fingertips.

They stung slightly.

The rest of me seemed fine, other than the usual symptoms of a raging hangover. My stomach roiled slightly at every movement and my head pounded in a steady, sickening rhythm.

I placed my hands against the slick tile wall and rested my forehead between them for a beat, mentally scanning the rest of my body, feeling if the water stung anywhere in particular, if I had any unusual aches or pains.

Nothing.

"Chloe."

I started at the unexpected voice, then poked my head out from the shower curtain. My roommate, Vik, was barely visible in the steam, but I could still make out his frown.

"You said to make sure you were out after five minutes. It's been seven." He took a deep drink from the chipped "I HEART NY" mug we fought over. "It's already nine o'clock."

"Is that coffee?" I was pretty sure it wasn't, but hope sprung eternal.

"Chai. You were going to get coffee yesterday, remember? You forgot, I guess."

Right. I had planned to pick up a can of Bustelo after work on my way to Inga's party but had stopped at Rosemary's Tavern for a beer instead. One beer had turned into a few, and I'd wound up arriving at the party close to ten. An image emerged: Vik with his arm slung around Ben in a haze of smoke, his head thrown back and laughing.

Poof. There and gone.

"How late did we stay? I can't remember." I injected a little laugh into the question. *Silly Chloe, drank so much she can't remember getting home!*

I turned the water off and stuck my arm around the curtain.

I waited for a response, which was slow in coming.

A towel arrived before an answer.

"Benny and I left around one," he said cautiously. Ben was Vik's boyfriend. I dried myself with the towel. It was one of a set of two I'd had since my freshman year of college, a pale-green-and-white-striped Laura Ashley that was pretty threadbare now.

"I don't know what time you got back," Vik continued.

"Well, I made it home somehow." I infused as much nonchalance into the statement as I could. Vik stepped out of the bathroom as I swept the curtain back, towel wrapped around me. He stayed in the hallway, sipping his chai and studying me over the rim of the mug. "What is it?"

He shook his head. "Nothing. You're going to be so late."

"The price we pay," I said. "What a party, huh?"

"Yeah, what a party. You were getting awfully friendly with some guy when we left," he said with a shrug. I froze for a second, then reached for my body lotion. "We offered you a ride, but you didn't want to leave. I don't blame you; he was cute."

Some guy? *What guy?*

I tried to remember but came up blank. I'd woken up naked, but that was indicative of nothing. I usually slept naked.

"Is Benny still here?"

"He's been at work for an hour already. Okay, it's 9:10 now." Vik turned, businesslike, toward the kitchen. "Want some chai?"

"Nope. Thanks, though." The smell of the spices coming from Vik's mug was making my stomach turn even more. What I really needed was a giant, icy fountain Coke and a greasy bodega egg sandwich. I headed off to get dressed, lotion in hand, and tried to calculate if I'd have enough time to pick up breakfast. It wasn't looking good.

I closed the door and paused, surveying my room. Everything seemed in its usual place: The salvaged kitchen chair piled high with clothes, the old dining table I'd borrowed from an ex and never given back that I used as a desk. My ancient Mac sat atop it, surrounded by coffee cups rimmed with dried residue, prompting the immediate thought, *I need to soak those*, even though I knew I wouldn't. My bed was so rumpled it was impossible to tell if I'd had a guest or not. Our tabby, Groucho, was curled up in the middle of it, right in the warm spot where my sleeping body had been less than thirty minutes ago. The stack of books off to the side wasn't disturbed, nor was my dresser top full of knickknacks: The fading half stubs of concert tickets, one rainbow-striped glove missing its mate, the bottle of Chanel No. 5 I hoarded and only wore on special occasions.

Nothing was different from the day before.

So why did everything feel off?

I pushed open the cheap folding closet door. Shoved in the back behind a tangle of summer shoes, I could just make out one corner of the blue-gray archival box. It looked undisturbed, resting, as always, under a wrinkled plastic bag containing what had once been my best dress.

I swallowed hard and pulled the towel tighter around myself.

"Nine-sixteen." Vik's voice floated through the door, full of disapproval.

Shit.

I dropped my towel to the floor and rummaged through the clothes pile on the chair until I found a dark denim skirt and a red, collared jersey top that didn't reek too badly of a bar and wasn't coated in cat hair. The top was a little more fitted than I liked to wear to work—I'd developed a decent-sized bust good and early and had been self-conscious of it since middle school—but beggars couldn't be choosers. I pulled them on, unwound my hair from its knot, and spritzed it with a spray that was supposed to neutralize the smoke scent. It did a decent job, though I kind of smelled like a car air freshener. I shoved aside the mystery of how I got home as I lost myself in the minutiae of getting out the door: quick tooth brush, bag, boots, coat.

Four blocks later, I stopped to take one more drag and then stomped out my half-finished cigarette before entering the subway. The cigarette had calmed my stomach a little but my head was still pounding, desperate for caffeine. The whole world seemed muted today. The sky was a heavy, leaden gray, the sort that threatened sleet. The buildings that lined Bedford Avenue were shades of tan and light ochre, washed out and dull. I closed my eyes, steeling myself for the onslaught of noise and smells and motion that awaited me down the subway steps.

"Chloe."

I turned, opening my eyes and blowing the smoke from my last inhale. Gio had come outside from his store holding a blue-and-white paper cup toward me, a bright and welcome splash of color. "You want a coffee?"

"Uh, yeah," I said in surprise. "How did you know?"

He cupped his hand around the tip of a match to light his own cigarette, his brown eyes squinting. "Vik called, said to slip you one if you passed by," he said out of the corner of his mouth before inhaling deeply. "Said to give you a breakfast roll, too, but we ran out a while ago."

This was not a surprise. The sweet rolls at Ricci's were the best in the neighborhood, maybe the whole city, and usually sold out before nine.

A strong wind gusted from the river but the coffee was hot and strong and sweet, just how I liked it. "Well, let me pay you." I began digging in my bag for a single, but Gio held up his hand and shook his head.

"Nah, I put it on Vik's tab," he said, grinning.

I grinned back. I liked Gio, everyone did. He had a narrow, handsome face, with high cheekbones and expressive brown eyes so dark they were nearly black. His family's bakery was a neighborhood fixture, one of the old-school places that had been on Bedford for decades, back to the 1930s maybe. Sometimes I caught him watching me as I passed its plate-glass front window and thought maybe he liked me more than he should, but he never made a move.

Not even when he could have.

The ghost of a sensation arose, of Gio's thin, muscular arms wrapped tightly around me, and for a second I could feel them, warming me despite the increasing wind.

I stomped the memory down.

I didn't like to think about that night.

"You must be freezing," I said instead. He wasn't wearing a coat, just his dark green apron emblazoned with Ricci's in white embroidery on the chest over a spotless white T-shirt. "Go back inside."

He shrugged one shoulder, half a smile curling around his cigarette. "Nah, a little cold don't bother me."

"Hey, can I bum one?" I heard him before I saw him, and the familiar voice caused an instant eye roll. Bo was pretty high on the list of people I didn't think I could handle this morning. But here he was, ambling toward us, one hand thrust deep in his pocket, the other holding a large Styrofoam cup. The sheepskin-lined collar of his jacket was turned up, and his shoulders hunched up by his ears from the cold. Didn't any of these guys ever wear a hat?

"God, Bo, already?" I eyed his Styrofoam cup, surely from Rosemary's Tavern across the street. "It's not even ten."

Gio gave a curt nod, taking a deep drag but pulling his pack out of his back pocket for Bo. I itched for another cigarette myself, but resisted.

"Still going from last night. Went out after the show, wound up here, haven't made it home yet."

Bo was trying to finish a novel and worked a variety of odd jobs, including as a freelance stagehand occasionally. He was currently working for *The Producers* and kept wonky theater hours. We slept together sometimes.

Okay, a lot.

Or we used to. I'd pulled back recently.

Bo flipped his lank coppery bangs off his forehead, accepting a light from Gio too. "You had quite a time last night, huh?" he said to me.

"What?" It was suddenly hard to speak. I dredged my brain, pictures and sounds from the night before jostling one another, but they were fragments and nothing formed a whole. Vik and Ben laughing in the smoke. A huge painting, splashed with color. And Inga, her eyes widening in what? Surprise? Fear?

I shook my head. The gesture felt a little furious. "You weren't there."

Was he?

Bo didn't know Inga.

He jerked his head toward the bar. "Heard all about it."

I stared at the windows of Rosemary's, my favorite neighborhood dive and frequent hangout. Gaudy, glittering paper turkeys pressed against the glass—Rosemary herself decorated for every holiday—but it was impossible to see inside from this side of the street. Who was in there?

How the fuck did I get home?

"Don't let Mike catch you with that." Gio frowned at Bo's beer, referring to the beat cop who walked Bedford during the day. Bo raised a brow and drained his cup.

"With what?"

Gio turned to me, mouth tight. "Vik also told me to tell you that you're really late."

"Yeah, he's right." Nausea surged again and I swallowed hard. It was on the tip of my tongue to press Bo, who was giving me a calculating sideways look, about what he'd heard, but the words died in my mouth.

Suddenly every nerve was tingling. I couldn't bear standing on that sidewalk another second. I needed to get away, far from Bo's knowing smirk, from Gio's wary concern.

From whoever was in Rosemary's.

"Better head off, then," Bo drawled, crushing his cup into a ball with one fist.

"Thanks for this, Gio." I raised the paper cup in a little salute and hurried to the subway stairs. I didn't look back.

CHAPTER TWO

"He's already asked about you," Carmen said as I rushed into the gallery. The jarring noise of the buzzer she'd pressed to let me in hung in the air.

"Shit, really?" I yanked off my hat and glanced at the red plastic watch on my wrist. It was almost 10:30, an hour past when I was supposed to arrive.

"Mm-hmm." Carmen's huge brown eyes, lined with the longest lashes I'd ever seen, swept over me. I knew I looked as bad as I felt, and I resisted the urge to check my hair, which was surely flying in a million different directions now that my hat was off.

"He called up about fifteen minutes ago, asked if you'd phoned in." She shrugged, one black-turtleneck-clad shoulder brushing a giant gold hoop earring, making it sway.

"Thanks," I said.

Carmen raised one perfectly arched eyebrow at me and answered the shrilly ringing phone. Her voice filled the sleek marble space, echoing into the tall ceilings and bouncing off the hard white walls, following me as I made my way toward the stairs. "Fletcher & Sons," she said, followed by a pause. "Who should I say is calling?"

I forced myself to walk, not run, through the main gallery space. Even though my boss was waiting, I couldn't help but pause for a beat at the top of the stairs in front of my favorite work in the current exhibition. It was a gorgeous drawing by Picasso, part of a show on nineteenth- and twentieth-century representations of dance. Delicate black lines of pastel swooped and dove, just a few strokes, capturing the energetic lift of the dancer's leg. She had one arm extended forward, another reaching back. Broader swaths of color, white and yellow and the prettiest shade of blue, somehow conveyed the dancer's motion, her tutu. It was simple and complex at the same time.

Something about the ease of the dancer's body, the way she was about to take flight, made me feel a little lighter. Not entirely easy, but that ease and freedom were possible, if I could just find the right position. Most days, I took a few minutes in front of the drawing to soak it in.

Every day, I marveled that I got to walk by a Picasso.

Carmen cleared her throat noisily behind me, a clear signal to hurry up.

I wound down the circular staircase into the lower level of the gallery. Here, the decor diverged from the open, gleaming, bright rooms of the upstairs galleries, where the front windows of the old brownstone let in glorious light, to a cramped warren of small offices created from the original lower-floor rooms of the nineteenth-century structure, what had probably once been the servants' quarters, an irony not lost on me. The only windows were placed high; small, barred rectangles that permitted a bare amount of sunlight to enter.

I wove through the bigger of the offices, past Olive, the gallery's bookkeeper, and Sebastian, the registrar, the former who offered a cheerful good morning and the latter who gave the clock on the wall a pointed, disbelieving look.

Lou didn't look up from his typing when I slunk into the narrow office we shared, unwrapping my scarf and shoving it into my coat sleeve. I slid into the chair at my tiny desk and fired up my computer.

"Do me a favor," Lou said, his voice low and doleful, his long face matching his tone. I flinched and waited, listening to the hum of the machine as it woke up. Lou still hadn't looked my way, his rotund frame hunched forward as he kept his eyes on his screen. "Do me a favor," he repeated. "Get here on time."

I hunched over my own keyboard in response. "I know. I'm sorry, I—"

"They're going to be mad," Lou interrupted, shoving back from his desk and swiveling to face me as he pushed his longish salt-and-pepper hair off his forehead. It was something he only did when stressed. I turned in his direction, overwhelmed with guilt. There was no need to clarify who "they" were. Lou was talking about Henry Fletcher and his daughter, Sloane, the eponymous Fletchers of Fletcher & Sons.

Or daughter, as the case was these days.

Lou deserved better. He'd taken a chance on me, pushed Henry and Sloane to promote me to his assistant from my old position as receptionist, Carmen's job, when his former assistant, who had been a total flake anyway, finally quit after 9/11. I wasn't sure if the Fletchers agreed because they, like Lou, seemed to sense some promise in me or because they felt guilty, but I was grateful all the same. The promotion had meant a big jump in pay, and far more interesting work than answering phones and scheduling meetings. Now I got to research museum-quality works of art, like the Picasso. It was exhilarating.

"I stayed at the party too late," I admitted. "I'm really sorry." My stomach tangled again. Lou had been at the loft last night too. Had I done or said something stupid in front of my boss? Embarrassed myself somehow? Did Lou see me make out with that guy, the one Vik mentioned? Heat rose to my cheeks at the thought. How could I have been so stupid, to get wasted at a work party, risk the first job I'd ever really liked?

Lou heaved a gusty sigh and gave me an appraising look. I remembered my reflection before I left the apartment this morning: dark circles under my eyes no amount of concealer could cover, sallow skin, my face puffy and exhausted from too much alcohol and not enough sleep. Normally I considered myself moderately attractive, dark blond hair and light blue eyes in a heart-shaped face, but today, with my cracked lips and stupefied expression, I knew I looked only haggard and hungover.

"You want some coffee? Let's get some coffee."

I nodded a meek acceptance and followed him to the kitchen on the other end of the floor. A pot had just finished brewing, and Willa, the housekeeper, turned a beady eye in my direction.

"This pot is fresh, Mr. Lou," she said in the light, musical accent that revealed her Caribbean background. "Looks like you need some, girl." Willa snorted in laughter, shaking her neatly braided head.

Lou pulled two mugs from a cupboard, smiling. "Thanks, Willa. We were at a party at that new artist's loft last night. Inga Beck? Guess Chloe stayed kind of late."

Willa pulled out the milk and sugar, arranging them on the counter. "Those big paintings, all the swirly colors?" Her mouth turned down. "They're not to my taste, those."

"A new direction for the gallery, that's for sure." Lou doctored his coffee with lots of milk and sugar, until it was so light it looked more like weak tea. I stirred a generous heap of sugar into my own, watching it disappear.

"You need anything else, Mr. Lou?"

"We're good, Willa, thanks."

"All right then." Willa swept from the kitchen, but not before giving me a warning glance. I knew the look; it was to put the kitchen back to rights before we left. Willa was a stickler about her domains.

Lou leaned back on the counter. The way he eyed me over his mug reminded me of Vik this morning, equal parts censure and concern. I turned away and took a deep, grateful slug. Willa made good coffee.

"So how late did you stay?"

I mimicked Carmen's one-shouldered shrug. "Late." I didn't dare tell him I actually had no idea how late, because I couldn't remember getting home.

He gave a neutral nod. "Seemed like it was getting kind of wild when I left."

"A little."

Lou waited a few beats. I waited, too, anxiety taking root in my brain and starting to swirl.

Wild? What did he know that I didn't? Was he gearing up to have a talk about something I'd done, something he'd seen?

But he didn't say anything else about the party. Instead, he fished a clean spoon out of a drawer and stirred his coffee again. "You doing okay, kid?"

I sipped my own coffee, relieved he wasn't going to press. "Yeah. I drank a little too much is all."

Another few beats. Lou's look shifted, his face softening into an expression I'd come to recognize and dread.

"It's okay if you're not," he started.

I held a hand up. "Lou, come on. I don't want to hear it." He didn't need to clarify that he wasn't talking about Inga's party anymore. I knew what he meant. His expression gave it away.

Pity. A welcome stab of anger joined the other feelings roiling inside my chest.

"I know you don't, but I'm gonna say it anyway." His Brooklyn accent intensified, as it always did when his emotions ran high. "You need to talk about it," Lou insisted.

He meant the day the towers fell.

"There's nothing wrong with talking to someone," he said. "A professional. I've done it, lots. In my marriages, by myself. It can really help."

I gave him a look, forcing the anger back down. Lou was only trying to help.

"I know." Lou sighed. "Didn't help the marriages. But it helped *me*."

"I don't have insurance, Lou."

"I bet they'd pay—"

"No." The word came out harsher than I intended.

It was the same *they* Lou had referred to before. Henry and Sloane. He was right, they probably would pay for me to see a shrink. But then they'd *know* I was seeing a shrink. They were nice enough, the Fletchers, but they were my bosses. And very different from me, with their Upper East Side addresses and old money. The gallery had been in their family for almost a century. I was a college dropout from Ohio.

No, Henry and Sloane thought I was enough of a fuckup already. They were too polite to say anything to my face—also they valued Lou too much—but I could tell. Henry often looked mildly incredulous at my presence, as if he had forgotten I worked there and was newly surprised by it each time our paths crossed. I had more daily contact with Sloane, and she was closer to my age, but her lunches at Bergdorf's and her Barneys shopping trips were as foreign to me as my world in Brooklyn was to her.

Besides, I only wanted to forget.

"Guess we'd better get to work," Lou said after a short pause, dropping the subject of therapy. He headed back to our office, and I followed.

Gratitude surged again.

Lou was the only person I really felt comfortable with at the gallery. Like me, he didn't come from this world. Unlike me, he had finished college. And graduate school, falling in love with art history while an undergrad at Brooklyn College, and then earning his PhD. He'd hopped around the museum world for a while but had been curator at Fletcher & Sons for over a decade. At first glance, he was an unlikely fit for the Fletchers. Lou was a little short, a little portly, his hair a little too long, and while his clothes weren't quite mismatched, he was still scruffy and completely lacking in the style department. He had an open, friendly, almost hangdog face that belied his intelligence. But he was very, very good at what he did.

There was a stash of Advil in the bathroom, so I grabbed three of those and a giant glass of ice water before making my way back to my desk. Settling back into the office, I pulled up the document I'd been working on for the last week, a series of catalogue entries on Inga Beck's paintings for our upcoming show of her work. It was a big step for me. Lou was writing the longer essay about her, but even these short entries would count as a publication under my name.

"Give it a try," he'd insisted. "You've got a good eye, and you've pulled and read all the research for my essay. You know more than you think you do about this. You're sharp, Chloe."

The unexpected compliment had made me glow inside. And he was right; the more I did it, the easier it came. Lou was a good teacher and editor. Patient. And maybe more surprisingly, I actually loved the work. It had opened up a whole new world, of artists and movements, of color and light.

I was being extra careful with this essay, checking and rechecking sources, thinking about how I wanted to situate Inga Beck's work. Winning her as a client had been a coup for the gallery, which normally specialized in work dating from around 1850 to 1950: French impressionism, American impressionism, early modern artists. People like Picasso. Sloane had been pestering Henry for years that Fletcher & Sons needed to modernize, take on some contemporary artists, and had somehow signed one of the most prominent up-and-coming painters in the city.

The catalogue needed to be perfect.

The Advil did its job and my headache receded from a roar to a mutter. I soon lost myself in the work, in the words, staring at the board on which Lou had tacked small color copies of all the pieces that would be in the show, tiny replicas of Inga Beck's gargantuan, sprawling canvases. Willa was right: They were full of swirly colors, reminiscent of Abstract Expressionism, but softer somehow. Not as aggressive and textured as Jackson Pollock's drip pour works, but not as fluid and muted as Helen Frankenthaler's stained canvases.

I smiled to myself as I pondered the small cutouts, copies I'd made that were now clipped and tacked to the big bulletin board Lou liked to use to plan his shows. Names I hadn't known a few months ago now felt familiar, thanks to the daily research I did for Lou as his assistant.

Maybe he was right. Maybe I did know more than I thought.

My smile faded as I thought of the huge canvas at the party last night. Inga's painting *Helpless*. Lou had been staring up at it, I remembered suddenly. It was taller than he was.

The loud clack of heels rang on the marble floor of the hallway leading to our space, startling me out of my thoughts. Lou glanced at the doorway as Sloane's sleek figure filled it.

"What's up?" he asked, turning back to his screen.

"Lou," she said. Something in her voice seemed to make him swivel back in her direction.

"Sloane? What is it?" Lou asked.

Sloane paused, her eyes darting between the two of us, then pursed her rosebud mouth.

"The police are here," she finally said, her look settling on Lou.

A chill settled over me. I wanted to cross my arms across my chest but made myself hold still.

Her bright blue gaze shifted to me. It was piercing, pinning me in place.

"They want to speak with both of you."

CHAPTER THREE

The police. An image of the box in my closet nudged at me insistently. I tried to ignore its pull. Nobody knew about the box, I was sure of it.

But why else would the police want *me*? Unless . . .

The black, yawning gap in my memory taunted me. Had something happened on my way home? Is that why I didn't know how I'd made it from the loft to my apartment?

My heart thudded as I followed Lou's short, broad back and Sloane's taller, narrow one up the winding staircase into the bright white lobby, past Carmen, her eyes huge and greedy for gossip, then up another staircase to the third floor of the gallery, which housed Henry's and Sloane's offices. I rarely went up this staircase and didn't like it, its narrowness making me feel like the walls were closing in. I held my breath until we reached the top step. This floor had been renovated but still retained characteristics of the original brownstone, with ornate molded cornices around the doors in gleaming oak and matching window frames. They also kept a bedroom on this floor, a guest space where wealthy out-of-town clients could stay.

"They're in here," Sloane murmured over her shoulder, leading us to Henry's office.

I'd never been inside Henry's office and had only peeked at it through his open door if I was bringing something to Sloane. It was a huge room, dominated by a giant fireplace and richly furnished with antiques and plush patterned rugs. Gorgeous nineteenth-century art graced the walls; one Millet painting of peasants in a field stood on an easel in the corner.

The place looked like a museum. All the art was for sale, of course.

"Here they are." Henry rose from behind his desk and walked around it, gesturing expansively to me and Lou.

Henry was the type of man who often gestured expansively. He was wearing his typical pin-striped, three-piece suit and a tie in a shade just this side of loud. His brown eyes behind round tortoiseshell glasses, normally twinkling, were grave today.

The box. The box the box the box. They know.

A man and a woman rose from the chairs that faced Henry's desk.

"Chloe Harlow, Dr. Louis Stern," Henry introduced us. "These are detectives with the New York City police."

It was obvious Henry had forgotten their names.

The female detective's mouth twitched in a quick, wry smile, there and gone, as she extended her hand. "I'm Detective Anita Gonzales, this is my colleague Detective Harlan Downs." I took her hand, then the male detective's, after Lou, conscious of my sweaty palm.

"You had better sit down," Henry said, still grave, nodding to a seating area in the front of the room.

Lou and I exchanged a look. He seemed in the dark. I wondered if his heart was pounding as fast as mine. My earlier nausea surged, and I swallowed hard, hoping I wouldn't have to run from the room.

We arranged ourselves on the matching antique sofa and chairs. I surreptitiously wiped my palm against my skirt as I sat. There wasn't enough room for Sloane, who stood to the side and behind her father.

"I'm afraid I have some upsetting news," Detective Gonzales said. I blinked a few times, steeling myself. Lou and I had chosen the sofa, which was shallow and uncomfortable, forcing me to sit more upright than normal.

"Inga Beck is dead."

It was the last thing I had expected to hear. The room tilted, objects blurring. I heard Lou's gasp of shock next to me, but it sounded like it was coming from far away, like I was underwater.

"Ms. Harlow? Chloe? Are you all right?" The room snapped back into focus. Detective Gonzales was leaning forward in her seat, staring at me intently.

"I'm sure she's shocked," Lou said, putting a protective hand on my arm. He sounded shocked himself. "We were at a party at Inga's place just last night. She seemed fine. Sloane was there too."

Sloane nodded tightly.

"Yes, Ms. Fletcher told us about the party. It's why we wanted to talk to you. It seems people at this party were among the last to see her alive." Detective Gonzales's face was full of careful sympathy, but her eyes were sharp and watchful. My emotions were a wild pendulum, swinging from relief that this wasn't about me, to utter disbelief that Inga was dead, and back again.

I shot a glance at the male detective, Downs, a tall, lanky redhead. He hadn't said a word so far.

"What happened?" I finally found my voice. "Did she have a heart attack or something?" I regretted the stupidity of the question as soon as it left my mouth.

Detective Gonzales kept those watchful eyes trained on mine. "We believe she was murdered."

The chill I'd felt downstairs intensified. The image of Inga I'd recalled earlier, her face close, eyes growing wide, forced itself into my head again. But I still couldn't remember what had happened next.

"Oh my god," Lou muttered, slumping into the upright seat as best he could.

"A photographer who was scheduled to come to her loft this morning found the door ajar and discovered the body. He called it in."

The body.

I could see the yawning, empty space of Inga's Williamsburg loft. The concrete floors, the giant industrial windows. The noisy space heater that hung in the corner, the massive canvases stacked against the walls. Her futon, upright in a sofa shape, shoved against a wall, the kitchen area against the opposite wall, a hodgepodge of found and reclaimed appliances.

Where had she been when this photographer found her? Her *body*. Unbidden, images flashed: Inga lying face down on the futon, face up near the stove, half in and out of the curtained space that concealed the toilet. In each her pale skin was pristine, free of blood or damage.

Murdered. How?

A shudder racked me, and I shoved the thoughts away.

I didn't need the details.

Detective Downs was leaning back in his chair, a fussy-looking thing with gilding on the arms and legs covered in peacock-embroidered upholstery, his relaxed posture in opposition to Detective Gonzales's tense one.

"You had an existing relationship with Ms. Beck prior to her representation by the gallery, didn't you, Dr. Stern?" Gonzales had produced a notebook from some pocket and was consulting it, glancing between the pages and Lou.

Lou's arms folded over his midsection. "I knew her a little." He sounded bewildered, like he was still processing what he'd been told. "My girlfriend, Debra, knew her better. She's an artist too."

Detective Gonzales made a note on her pad. "We'll need her information. Was she at the party also?"

"No, she has a bad cold, stayed home last night. Oh my god," he repeated.

"Were they close, Ms. Beck and your girlfriend?"

"Not particularly. Inga was one of the crowd, you know? Artists, they know one another." Lou circled a hand in the air, like he was trying to convey a sense of community. "We were all thrilled when she started getting so much attention."

"And you brought her work to the attention of the Fletchers?"

"I did," Sloane interjected. "That was me."

"Yeah, that was all Sloane," Lou said. "Inga mounted a show in a space out in Williamsburg—what, last February?" He looked to Sloane, who nodded her agreement. "Some critics got wind of it, and, I don't know, it just exploded. Suddenly she was the next big thing. Everyone wanted to represent her. Mary Boone, Gagosian. We're not known for contemporary art, I didn't think of her for us." Lou shook his head.

"I saw the show," Sloane said. "The work was brilliant. We'd been wanting to expand into contemporary art for a while, and I convinced Henry we needed to pursue her. In the end, she picked us."

Detective Gonzales twisted her head to look at Sloane. "You call your father by his first name?"

"She does," Henry said in a mild voice. "It keeps things professional."

The detective untwisted and tapped her pencil on her pad exactly one time. "You said earlier Inga Beck has been with your gallery for six months now?" It wasn't clear which Fletcher the question was for, but Henry answered.

"That's right," he said. "We are planning a big exhibition, due to open early in the new year. We've secured space in SoHo for it. The canvases won't fit our walls downstairs."

"And what about you, Ms. Harlow?"

My head snapped up. I hadn't even realized it had dropped, but I'd been zoning out the past few minutes, breathing deeply to help my stomach settle, staring at my fingers in my lap, and letting the others' conversation wash over me.

"I'm sorry, what?" I asked. My voice sounded shaky. I didn't like it.

"How did you know Ms. Beck?"

"Through the gallery."

The detective stayed quiet, her sharp eyes seeming to take in every inch of me.

Was I supposed to say more?

"I went with Lou to her loft after she came on board in the spring. I think it was May. He's writing the catalogue essay for the exhibition. I'm his assistant. Well, I was the receptionist then, but his assistant was out so I was helping. So I went with him and met her then."

Another long silence. I didn't know what else to say.

Detective Gonzales glanced at her pad again. "But you knew her well enough to be invited to this party last night?"

I shrugged a little, glancing at Lou for help. What did the detective want from me? "I saw her around the neighborhood after we met. I live nearby. We were, I guess, friendly acquaintants. Everyone was invited last night, the whole gallery."

"What was the party for?" Detective Downs spoke for the first time, making me start in my seat. His voice was deeper than I'd expected, and harsher. "Looked like a pretty big blowout. It her birthday or something?"

"She had just finished a new series. The pieces for the January show," Sloane answered, sounding a little prim. "She wanted to celebrate."

"Party that wild, on a Thursday night?" Downs's New York accent was thick, much more so than Gonzales's evenly tempered voice. Something about his pale skin and slightly oversized nose gave me the impression of a bookworm, like he should be buried in a library somewhere, but his raw speech was pure cop. He chuckled a little. "We're in the wrong line of work, right, Gonzales? Lotta empties in that loft. Other stuff too." Downs maintained his easy posture, but his eyes, like his partner's, were hawkish.

And trained on me.

I swallowed.

"What time did you all leave this party?" Gonzales had picked up the questioning again. "You didn't attend, Mr. Fletcher?"

"No, no. It was for young people," Henry said, though he was probably only ten years older than Lou.

It was hard to not roll my eyes, despite how anxious I felt. As if Henry Fletcher would soil his suit by stepping foot into a Brooklyn loft party.

"Ms. Fletcher?"

"Around ten," Sloane said. She cut her eyes toward me. "Chloe was just arriving when I left." I nodded my agreement.

Another image from the night emerged: Sloane wrapped in a trim camel coat, sliding out the door moments after I'd come in. Giving me a look I couldn't interpret as she shut the door. "And Dr. Stern?"

"You can call me Lou. I left about an hour later. Eleven."

Gonzales scribbled on her pad. "Ms. Harlow?"

"I'm not sure."

That sharp gaze flicked up to my face and stayed there. She waited.

My palms grew sweaty again, but I didn't dare wipe them.

"It was late." It sounded lame even to my ears.

"Late," Gonzales repeated in a deadpan.

"Yes. Definitely after one. Maybe two? I wasn't wearing my watch. And—well, I'd had a lot to drink." I dropped my head again, not wanting to see how either Fletcher took this.

You didn't do anything wrong, I insisted to myself. *You're a grown-up, it's not a crime to get drunk and stay out late on a Thursday night.* "And how did you get home, that late?" the detective asked after a short silence.

I looked up again. She hadn't asked Lou or Sloane how they'd gotten home.

Did she know? Had this Detective Gonzales, with her slicked-back hair and her stylish, charcoal-gray suit, somehow intuited that I couldn't remember? That I blacked out?

That it wasn't the first time?

That it had been happening more and more?

I opened my mouth, unsure of what I was going to say until it popped out.

"I walked."

An ever so slight narrowing of her eyes. "You *walked*? At two a.m.?"

"I don't live that far. I'm on the north side, Inga is by the river. I've never felt unsafe there."

It was partially true. I had walked around the neighborhood that late at night, plenty of times, but rarely alone. And while I'd never felt threatened, the sheer emptiness of the streets at that hour, the stillness, no sound except that of your own feet, was unnerving in a way I didn't like to think about.

Detective Gonzales eyed me for another moment. I met her gaze, not daring to look at Detective Downs.

Finally, she gave a thoughtful nod. "Did anything unusual happen at the party? Anyone there who shouldn't have been? Anyone who had any problems with Inga?"

Sloane, Lou, and I looked at one another. We all said no, nothing out of the ordinary had happened.

"Know if she had any enemies? Anyone jealous of her success, old boyfriends, something like that?"

Again, no.

Detective Gonzales nodded again, her face impassive. "We're going to need a list of everyone you remember who was at the party. We'll have to talk to all of them."

My mouth went dry.

Who *had* been at the party? I strained to recall, but only came up with the same images.

Vik and Benny laughing. Lou and the canvas. Sloane closing the door.

Inga.

The only other memories I could dredge up were more sensations than images: someone's hot breath on my ear, the whir of the overhead heater as it kicked on, the strident rasp of the shower-curtain-cum-bathroom-door being pushed open.

The detective flipped her notebook shut with a snap.

"That's all we need for now. Thank you all, we'll be in touch."

CHAPTER FOUR

I stared at Lou as Sloane and Henry led the detectives from the office. He held up his hands in a gesture of disbelief, shaking his head.

"I think we should close up for the day," Henry said, once again grave. "I'll tell Olive and Sebastian. Lou, can you inform Douglas?" Douglas was the preparator, who oversaw the packing and crating of the work at the gallery. His office was on the far side of the downstairs, near the kitchen. I hadn't seen him yet today.

It was past lunchtime, I realized with a start. Early afternoon.

"Of course," Lou murmured.

"I don't think we can pull out of participating in the auction tomorrow," Henry continued. He folded his hands and rocked back on his heels, eyeing Lou carefully. "Do you?"

I'd forgotten about the auction. The gallery was planning to attend an important sale at Sotheby's. Sloane and Henry were meant to bid on several major pieces coming to sale on behalf of one member of a divorcing couple, longtime clients of the gallery.

Lou had invited me along to watch. "It'll be good for you, see how these things work," he'd said. "Besides, auctions are fun."

Now, Lou frowned. "You could bid by phone," he suggested. "Instead of being there in person."

Henry thought this over. "No, I won't be able to read the room that way. We'll go ahead. Inga's death is a tragic shock, but we can't inconvenience our other clients."

"Did they say how she died?" Lou asked, his voice low.

Henry's brown eyes flicked my way, then back to Lou. "She was shot," he said, matching Lou's tone. "Twice. Just brutal. Likely a botched robbery, they said. It's not the safest area." Another eye flick toward me, this one apologetic.

Shot. The images from earlier tried to crowd my brain again, only now with blood pooling under Inga in a misshapen oval, now with dark red matting her fine blond hair, now with half her face missing.

They morphed and merged into other bodies, piles of flesh and hair and clothing unrecognizable as human.

Stop it, I ordered myself.

"You still want to come tomorrow?" Lou asked once we were back in our office. My hands shook as I shoved things back into my bag.

"Tomorrow?"

"To Sotheby's."

I stopped packing my bag, my heart sinking. I'd been so excited to go to the auction. Now, I wasn't sure. "You really think it's appropriate for Henry and Sloane to be there and bid on stuff, after what happened?" I folded my arms over my chest to hide my trembling hands.

He shrugged a little. "Henry's right. Our other clients are counting on us. We really can't afford to upset these people."

I frowned. What did Lou mean, we couldn't afford it? "Is the gallery . . . in trouble?"

Lou sighed. "The whole art market is in trouble. It's been volatile since the attacks. This auction, it's a big deal. If it goes well, it could help things. Set the tone for the market, you know. Investors might start buying more art again."

I turned back to my bag. I had no concept of the complex financials of the business, but if Lou thought the gallery needed this auction somehow, I guessed that was that. It still seemed in extremely poor taste, to go bid millions of dollars the day after one of their artists was murdered.

"Can I let you know about the auction tomorrow?" I finally said. "I'm pretty freaked out. I don't know if I can just, you know, pretend like nothing happened."

"Nobody's asking you to do that," Lou said in a gentle voice. "And I'm pretty freaked out too. Oh god. I've got to tell Douglas. Wait for me, we can walk to the train together."

As soon as Lou's footsteps had turned the corner, I grabbed my desk phone and dialed my home number. I knew Vik wouldn't be there—he was in class on Fridays—and listened with impatience to his recorded voice formally asking the caller to please leave a message, my fingers clenching and unclenching the handset.

"Vik," I said into the static silence as soon as the beep ended, "it's me. Something truly fucked-up has happened. Can you meet me at Rosemary's? I'll tell you what's up in person, okay? I'm leaving now." He'd either call our machine and get the message or hear it when he got home. Either way, I was sure I'd see him sooner or later that evening.

Despite the early dismissal, it was dusk by the time I walked into Rosemary's, my face stinging with cold. I was shaken from the news of the day and the lengthy commute had made things worse. Lou and I had trekked the long walk from the gallery's location at Seventy-First Street and Fifth Avenue to the Lexington subway, then we missed the chance to transfer to an express. Lou groused that he should have taken the bus, and I secretly wished he had. I was incredibly fond of Lou, but I hadn't wanted chitchat. I had wanted to allow the anonymity of the city to wrap itself around me, to blast music through my headphones in the packed train car, and to surreptitiously survey the bodies pressed close to mine. Could one of these average-looking people have killed Inga? Someone in this city had done it; someone had walked through her large steel door, pulled out a gun, and shot her. That man, with the hood of his sweatshirt shrouding his face? The woman hunched in the corner seat, muttering to herself?

I left Lou at Fourteenth Street to catch the L but had to let two trains pass that were too full to board. Once I finally did get on a train, it stopped underneath the East River for a long time. I paused the Radiohead CD I was listening to so I could hear the conductor's voice over the scratchy system: We were paused due to train traffic ahead of us, and we'd be moving shortly. I looked around; nobody seemed particularly concerned. People sighed and rolled their eyes, then reburied their heads into books and magazines.

My finger hovered over the play button on my Discman tucked into my bag.

I rested it there, but didn't press it.

We sat in the tunnel longer than usual. After ten minutes, people were shuffling their feet and anxiously checking watches. The conductor's voice came through again, and we looked at the ceiling in unison. The message hadn't changed: Train traffic ahead of us, we'd be moving shortly. The repeated announcement was now met with aggrieved expressions and pursed lips.

I thought of the two trains that had passed by me at Fourteenth Street, bodies pressed so tightly there hadn't been room to wedge myself in. Our car was only half full, some passengers sitting, some, like me, standing and holding a pole. The few available seats were flanked by other people; I'd wanted space around me.

My finger stroked the raised plastic button of the Discman, but I pushed my headphones down around my neck instead.

We sat. We waited. Another ten minutes passed. I could feel my shoulders tightening, creeping toward my ears, and willed them back down. I made myself take a deep breath.

Inhale, exhale.

Unease began to creep through the train car, first barely perceptible, but catching and spreading like dry tinder.

"You think something's wrong?" one Latina woman asked another. The second shook her head strongly, but worry etched her face.

"If there is, they need to tell us," the second woman answered as she pulled her coat tighter around herself, peering at one of the train windows in vain.

There was nothing to see. Just the tight, dark walls of the tunnel. I removed my headphones from around my neck and shoved them into my bag.

Beyond those walls, above our heads, the invisible weight of the East River pressed down.

"What the fuck is happening?" a hipster guy in a Carhartt jacket muttered to nobody in particular.

The unease rippled across the car now. It spun past me and caught me in its wake. What was going on up there, above the river, where we couldn't see?

I wasn't the only one who felt it. I looked around, and it was as though I could read the other passengers' thoughts.

Were we really paused due to train traffic? Or was something happening again? A bomb, another terrorist attack, another skyscraper imploding?

I tried to focus on my breath.

Inhale, exhale.

The train is just stopped. Nothing is wrong.

My breath wanted to come in short, shallow pants and it took all my effort to keep it regulated. All I could think of was being trapped in the stairwell at the North Tower, of the agonizingly slow descent, of wanting to run and scream but knowing it wouldn't do any good.

I closed my eyes and made myself focus on how Maya's hand had felt in mine, in that stairwell. I imagined her holding my hand now, telling me that it would be okay, that we just had to keep moving.

"Fuck this," I heard. My eyes flew open. A large, burly man with a thick Polish accent had stood up. "They can't keep us in the dark like this. I'm going to find the conductor, I'll be back." He stomped off through the door to the next car amid approving murmurs.

"We're just stopped, it's nothing to be concerned about," said an elderly Black woman sitting in one of the designated handicapped seats, clutching a large knit bag on her lap. "Maybe there's a sick passenger."

"Then they'd say sick passenger," rebuked a young Black man. "This is too long, this shit ain't right. If something's going down, I want out of here."

I tightened my grip on my pole. The train car's walls felt like they were closing in along with my throat. I'd lost the feeling of Maya's imaginary hand in mine, and I couldn't get it back.

Inhale, exhale.

The young man pushed on one of the subway doors experimentally. One or two people yelled at him to stop. "You can't go out there," someone said from the opposite end of the car, I couldn't see who. Another few, including the two Latina women near me and the hipster guy, gathered behind him like he was the Pied Piper.

I braced myself for something to happen, though I wasn't sure what that could be. Would they evacuate us and actually have everyone walk down the long, dark tunnel under the river? Would a fight break out between those who wanted to go and those who wanted to stay? Tension in the car was thick, and I wanted no part of it.

I just wanted to get out. I couldn't be stuck, couldn't be trapped here under the river. I gripped the pole tighter, my arms starting to tremble, and right when I thought I couldn't handle being in the train another second, the speaker crackled to life.

"Ladies and gentlemen, we have received the all-clear. This train will be moving shortly. Bedford Avenue next stop, Bedford Avenue."

The train gave a sudden lurch. The group gathered near the door hastily braced themselves, then slid back to their original positions as the lurch turned into smooth motion.

Several of the passengers exchanged relieved smiles. The elderly Black woman tried to catch my eye to offer a reassuring nod, but I looked down, still clinging to my pole with a death grip.

Inhale, exhale.

Less than a minute later we pulled into the station.

Rosemary's too-warm interior was a welcome shift from the cold wind outside as I pulled off my hat, glad that the bar kept the heat blasting. The last vestiges of fear from the stopped train were slipping away, my shoulders receding from my ears yet again, the anticipation of a Big Gulp–sized Styrofoam cup of beer helping move my emotions along.

Still, a slight prickle ran along the back of my neck as I entered. Was the person who had been telling Bo about the party here? I wondered if they knew what had happened last night. But from a quick glance around the bar, there was nobody who had been at Inga's, at least that I could remember. Which, of course, was the problem. I couldn't remember.

I slid onto the stool next to my friend Edward, curled around his cup as he studied its contents with a morose expression.

"Hey," I said. I waved at Rosemary, cigarette dangling from her mouth, and to Frank, another regular, who was in his usual spot halfway down the long side.

"Hey," he said back. He'd been moody ever since his girlfriend, comedian Amy Sedaris, dumped him two weeks prior. Edward was among the more successful of our friends, a writer who regularly had pieces accepted for *The New Yorker* and *Vanity Fair*. He was almost too handsome, all sharp cheekbones and bedroom eyes under a swoop of thick, mussed golden brown hair. We'd never hooked up, but I'd thought about it.

Rosemary slid a beer in front of me without being asked. You could get anything at Rosemary's, but why would you when you could get a massive beer for only three dollars?

Dusk turned to night outside the big plateglass window at my back as the bar slowly filled. More of my friends wandered in: Penny, a fashion designer with her purple-streaked hair tied into Bjork-like knots on her head, and her boyfriend, Calvin, a guitarist in two bands who sometimes played at a bar on the Lower East Side and waited tables on the side, sporting his usual porkpie hat. Lisel, a graduate student at Pratt in 1950s-style cat-eye glasses and one of her signature vintage dresses, found us next, and was soon teasing Edward out of his slump with her big laugh. By the time I was finishing my second beer Bo had arrived, squeezing himself in between Lisel and Calvin so he was pressed against my side.

Rosemary plunked a beer in front of him, its contents sloshing a little on the bar. I studied Bo's profile closely. Should I ask him who he had talked to—god, was it just this morning? I looked over my shoulder, hoping to see Vik behind him, but there was nobody. Where was he? The beer and the company had helped, our crowd taking up the whole short end of the bar, laughing and drinking and smoking, trading stories of our weeks as the big window fogged from our breath and collective heat, but one part of my brain was constantly focused on the door, willing it to open and Vik to walk through.

I had to share what I'd learned today with someone. Someone outside the gallery, and definitely not Bo. Vik was my closest friend, my confidant. He had helped me get my initial job at the gallery, he knew Inga.

A rush of cold air swept in, and I twisted in my seat, heart leaping, expecting to see Vik striding through, concern from my message streaking his face.

It wasn't Vik.

I stiffened on my stool, so much so Bo felt it. He looked at me and then the door in alarm.

"What's wrong? You know those guys?"

I did. One of them.

Or I had met him once, when he was alive.

A ghost had just walked into the bar.

CHAPTER FIVE

I blinked hard and shook myself, goose bumps pebbling my arms. Bo took a step toward the door then looked over his shoulder at me, his eyes hard.

"What do you need, Chloe?"

There was a blond one and a dark-haired one. It was the guy with the dark hair I couldn't take my eyes off.

He wasn't Greg. On some level, I knew that.

Greg McClean was dead. His body was long gone, pulverized under the rubble of the North Tower.

I'd been the last person to see him alive.

But this stranger with the $200 haircut unwrapping his cashmere scarf was nearly Greg McClean's doppelgänger. Sweat began to pool between my shoulder blades, and a familiar tremor shook my limbs.

It's probably nothing. You can go now.

The words rang in my head, an echo from a ghost.

I blinked again.

The mirage vanished, and the guy looping his scarf over his arm morphed into someone else. He was a little shorter than Greg, with broader shoulders and a squarer jaw.

"It's nothing," I said as the two men swaggered past, choosing seats in the center of the bar. I had to choke the words out. "I thought I recognized one of them, but I don't."

Bo frowned at them. "Bridge and tunnel," he muttered.

The guys were obviously not from this neighborhood; not true locals like Frank or the old guy across the bar nursing a whiskey, or newer locals like my bar friends.

These were Masters of the Universe. Like Greg. I'd read *The Bonfire of the Vanities* in high school and the phrase stuck with me after I moved to the city. It was a perfect label. You could spot them a mile off: Finance bros, who all sported the same expensive haircuts, the same conservative gray or navy suits, same suspenders, same smirks. These two were no exception, sauntering in like they owned the place, their mouths forming delighted, contemptuous smiles as they took in Frank's large form, Rosemary's scrawny bare arms, the soused old guy's hand trembling on his fourth whiskey.

I watched them out of the corner of my eye as I signaled Rosemary for another beer and lit a cigarette, trying to hide my disquiet. Bo slid back to his spot pressed against me. He nuzzled my neck a little. I shrugged him off, staring at the newcomers. The blond one was looking around for somewhere to hang his suit jacket.

Bridge and tunnel, Bo had said. Manhattanites were the bridge and tunnel people now, making the trek to Brooklyn. More and more had been coming lately. They'd heard Williamsburg was the next cool place, the new Lower East Side, full of underground parties in warehouses and great bars without signs, places you had to be in the know to find. The curious sometimes rode the L train, poked around Bedford Avenue, ate at one of the few restaurants, and then piled back onto the subway looking vaguely disappointed. They hadn't rubbed elbows with the Beastie Boys, as it was rumored one could.

Bo's hand was making lazy circles against my lower back.

"What brilliant thing did you work on today?" he asked.

I twitched his hand away. "Where's Tanya?" I asked. Tanya was Bo's sometimes-girlfriend.

He flipped his hair out of his face and dropped his hand, picking up his beer instead. "Think we're done," he said. "Her show is going on tour soon." Tanya was part of why I'd stopped sleeping with Bo. They had both assured me it was an open relationship, but two weeks ago I suggested to Tanya we grab a coffee, and she'd said in a bright, brittle voice, "It's really hard to be around you; Bo has such a crush on you."

It had felt like a slap.

After that I'd kept my distance. Even though I liked that Bo was genuinely curious about my job and often told me how smart he thought I was. He was probably just trying to get into my pants, but still, it was good to hear.

"I'm sorry to hear that," I said now.

Another breakup, like Edward and Amy. This was happening a lot now, couples that had seemed solid splitting at the seams. Ever since the towers fell, really. That, or pairs that had been casual got very serious. Vik and Ben, suddenly inseparable. Penny and Calvin actually got engaged.

"Wait, why aren't you at work tonight?" I asked.

Bo shrugged. "Night off."

That didn't seem right for a Friday night, but I didn't press.

I took a breath to ask Bo about who he had talked to, who had seen me at Inga's, but Edward's loud voice interrupted my train of thought.

"You're full of shit, man." He was standing, red-faced, hands clenched in fists, staring hard at Calvin.

"Whoa," said Bo, sliding in between them. "What's up?"

"This asshole," Edward pointed at Calvin, "is talking garbage."

Calvin raised his hands. "I'm just reporting what I read, man." Penny hovered anxiously behind him.

Bo looked baffled.

"He's saying 9/11 was an inside job. That *our government* was behind it," Edward said. He was trembling, he was so angry.

"Look, some people in Europe have made a pretty strong case," Calvin started, but Edward cut him off.

"Who? Some asshole with a blog?"

"You don't find it suspicious? That plane in Pennsylvania? You buy that story about the passengers taking it down?"

"My uncle died that day," Edward said through clenched teeth. Bo held his hands out between them.

"Hey," he said in a warning tone.

"It was fucking al-Qaeda, and Afghanistan is going to be a fucking parking lot soon, so shut the fuck up," Edward yelled.

I felt frozen to my stool, cigarette burning uselessly between my fingers. The others in the bar were looking our way now, their conversation dimming. The jukebox seemed unnaturally loud, blaring one of those '90s boy bands I always mixed up.

"Exactly," Calvin said in a low voice. "That fucker Bush is itching for a war just like his daddy. What better way to ensure it?"

Edward took one step toward Calvin, his shoulders hunched like he was about to deliver a punch. I gripped the edge of the bar.

But instead of hitting his friend, Edward grabbed his jacket and stormed into the night, throwing a "fuck you" over his shoulder.

I heaved a shaky sigh of relief. A few people I didn't know in one of the booths stared at Edward's retreating back. Chatter began to rise, overlaying the music once again.

Rosemary slid the baseball bat she'd been holding back to its shelf behind the bar.

Calvin lit a cigarette as I stubbed mine out. "He's just pissed because Amy dumped him," he said to no one in particular.

Penny shook her head at him. "You shouldn't have said that." She pulled Lisel into a corner and the two of them huddled, whispering.

Cold air blasted as the door swung open again. I turned, half expecting to see Edward stomping back in, ready to grab Calvin by the shirtfront and deliver the blow he'd so obviously wanted to, but it was Vik.

Finally. I jumped from my stool and grabbed Vik's hand before he could settle in, pulling him past the Wall Street bros, past Frank, who winked at me.

"I got 'Smooth' all cued up," Frank called. I gave him a distracted smile and led Vik to the other end of the bar, where we hovered outside the last empty booth but didn't sit.

"Didn't you get my message?" I hissed.

"Yeah, I got it. What happened?" Vik was uncharacteristically jittery, shoving his hands into his pockets then taking them out, eyes darting around the bar.

"I said something really bad had happened. That didn't worry you?"

"I thought maybe Groucho spit up a hairball, or the kitchen sink backed up or whatever." At my look, he shrugged a little. "I'm sorry, okay? Benny and I had dinner plans. I'm here now. What's going on." The statement was perfunctory rather than inquisitive.

I swallowed my own rising annoyance and took a deep breath. "Inga Beck has been killed," I said. *Shot*, my brain insisted.

Vik exhaled loudly, his shoulders hunching. "Yeah, I heard. Pretty awful."

"You *heard*? You knew and didn't think to check in with me?"

"I just heard at dinner. Ben told me."

"How does Benny know?"

"I don't know, he heard. The Yale grapevine, probably."

I was dumbfounded. Not about the Yale grapevine, that actually made sense. Inga had gotten her MFA at Yale at the same time that Ben, Vik's boyfriend, was in architecture school there, and the two had been acquaintances. What rooted me to my spot in disbelief was that Vik had known Inga was dead, had been *killed*, and hadn't thought it was important enough to come find me at Rosemary's right away.

"It's really sad and fucked-up, for sure," he was saying. "I don't want you walking around late anymore, you know? Call a car. You can charge it to me and pay me back, if you don't have money," he added, in a rare moment of generosity. "Maybe it's time you got a cell phone."

I was struggling to keep up. Vik had a cell phone but never used it, why should I get one? "Sad and fucked-up? That's it? Vik, we were there. At the party." I lowered my voice even more, though it was impossible for anyone to hear us over the blare of the music, "California Dreamin'" by the Mamas and the Papas now. "The *cops* came to the gallery; they said the guests might have been the last people to see her alive."

Vik ran a hand over his thick black hair. "Yeah, probably. That's creepy."

I couldn't believe his nonchalance. Didn't he care?

My incredulity must have shown in my face. "Look, Chloe, it's horrible, don't get me wrong. But it doesn't really have anything to do with us, except we knew her a little, went to a party at her loft. I'm more concerned that there was such a violent break-in in this neighborhood. I hope it doesn't make the news—my parents will flip."

"The police want to know who was at the party," I said slowly, ignoring the part about his parents. "I'll have to give them your name."

"That's okay, they'll get it sooner or later. I'm happy to talk to them, I have nothing to hide." Vik seemed to sense I was still concerned. "What?"

I couldn't say what I actually felt, that it was weird he wasn't more upset someone we knew had been murdered. That we'd been at her place, drinking her beer, less than twenty-four hours ago. He was right, neither of us had been close with Inga Beck, but she was someone we knew, and now she was dead.

Again, the image of Inga's face flared, so close to mine. Her eyes widening at something over my shoulder. I willed the memory of myself to *turn around*, see what she was looking at, but all my brain offered was blackness. She had been so close, though. I could see the tiny smattering of light freckles that dotted her pale nose and cheekbones, the fine hairs on her cheeks.

"The Fletchers are still bidding on all that work at the Sotheby's auction tomorrow," I told Vik instead. "Doesn't that seem a little callous?"

"Huh," Vik said carefully. "Are you still going? You were really excited about it."

"Didn't you hear me? I don't think any of it is a good idea right now."

He frowned. "But it's their business. You should go, Chloe. Lou invited you. Ben's sister works there, it's a good place to know people. It would be another step in the right direction."

I bristled. "What do you mean? What direction?"

"Just that this promotion has been good. You were kind of drifting before you started working there, you know? Waiting tables . . ."

"What's wrong with waiting tables?"

"Nothing. But isn't the gallery better? It could keep growing into something bigger, a real career instead of just, you know, a job."

I folded my arms over my chest and looked away. The words stung. I'd come to New York to study acting but had failed out of Hunter at the end of my sophomore year. Too much partying, not enough studying. There was no way I would return to Canton with my tail between my legs, so I started waiting tables in Little Italy, crashing on various friends' couches. Eventually one of my former classmates told me about a friend of a friend who was looking for a roommate, and that's how I met Vik. We'd become close friends since I moved in. Best friends, really.

Vik was always pushing me to do better, be better. It was because of him that I started working at the gallery at all. He was in the art conservation program at NYU, and the receptionist job came across an email list in his department. He'd encouraged me to go for it, even though I knew nothing about art. To my surprise, I got the job. It was easier work than waiting tables, that was true.

And what started as a way to pay the bills had slowly turned into a real love of art. At Lou's gentle urging, I'd even started thinking about going back to college.

"Excuse me, is this guy bothering you?"

It was one of the Masters of the Universe. The blond one.

The Greg look-alike was hovering behind him. I tried not to stare.

"No," I said shortly. The thing that felt like panic, like I'd felt on the train, rose in my throat again at the sight of him. "Come on," I said to Vik, starting back to the end of the bar toward our friends.

"He's bothering me." The Greg look-alike had pushed in front of his friend, sullen-faced and bleary-eyed. They both crowded Vik. My path was blocked.

"Shit," I whispered under my breath. I tried to make eye contact with Bo or Calvin, but our crowd was laughing among themselves, not paying any attention to us.

"I don't have a problem with you guys," Vik said. He sounded easy, but I knew him well enough to hear the wariness lacing his words.

I was wary too.

It didn't matter that Vik was Indian instead of Arabic, and not even Sikh—he didn't wear a turban. He was brown, and that was enough.

"Well, we've got a problem with you," Greg-not-Greg said. He gave Vik's chest a small, experimental push.

Vik raised his hands as he stumbled back a step but his jaw clenched, and fury lit his eyes. "Back off, man."

"Hey," I yelled at the same time, stepping forward. The sight of that guy's, that *ghost's*, hands on my friend scattered my previous panic, replacing it with instant rage.

The blond one was shoved back just as the dark one's fist clenched, then a beefy hand planted square in the Greg guy's chest. Frank thrust himself between the Masters and Vik, his huge frame dwarfing all theirs.

"Now I'm the one with the problem," Frank said, his accent thick as smog. "You two are my problem. Rosemary's too."

The loud, solid bang of wood on wood brought all conversation to an instant halt, and everyone in the place turned, wide-eyed, to Rosemary, who had crashed her baseball bat against the sturdy length of oak that had comprised the bar surface since 1945.

Bo, Calvin, and the others had finally hipped on to what was happening and headed over our way.

"Get the fuck out, you fucking yuppies," Rosemary ordered, pointing her bat.

Seeming to know they were outnumbered, the finance guys gathered their things, chins jutted, staring with derision at all of us.

"Let's leave this dump," the blond muttered, trying to save face.

"You okay?" Frank asked Vik after the guys left.

"Yeah. But I'm going home." I could tell he was shaken. Fuck, I was shaken. "You coming, Chloe?"

I shook my head. "See you later." It sounded weak but I wasn't sure what else to say.

Vik paused for a few minutes to talk to our friends on his way out, and maybe, I thought, to give the finance guys some distance. I was glad to see Calvin and Penny bundle into their coats and walk out with him.

As the heavy glass door swung shut on their departing backs, the riotous opening chords of Carlos Santana's "Smooth" filled the bar.

Frank mutely held out his hand, and I took it. I would always take it when this song came on, it was just what one did at Rosemary's. You drank too much cheap beer; you smoked, even if you didn't; and if "Smooth" came on the jukebox, you danced with Frank. Even though he outweighed me by maybe 250 pounds, Frank was extraordinarily light on his feet, a sheer joy to dance with.

There wasn't a dance floor to speak of, but that didn't matter. We whirled in the narrow space between the barstools and the booths, Frank expertly spinning me under his arms and down into a dip. I stepped and twirled, faster and faster, taking pleasure and refuge in not thinking, in allowing the music and Frank to guide my motions, the world turning light and blurry.

CHAPTER SIX

Vik's words about my job rang in my ears as I checked my coat in the Sotheby's lobby. The girl manning the coat check looked about my age and was expensively dressed. She maintained a professional smile and handed over my ticket, but I inwardly cringed at the state of my beat-up, vintage green corduroy coat. It looked shabby and out of place next to the tailored wool trenches and luxurious furs hanging behind her, a poor relation.

I had more confidence in my outfit. Lisel had loaned me a black-and-white floral Anna Sui dress her mother had bought her to wear to a family wedding earlier this year. It was a little summery, but at least new and trendy, and I'd paired it with black hose and a decent pair of heels. Normally I didn't fit into Lisel's clothes. Even though we were both on the shorter side, I was a lot curvier, all bust and hips to her leaner lines, but I'd dropped some weight in the past few weeks. Food wasn't particularly interesting these days. Even though the dress strained the tiniest bit in the chest, it slid over my lower half without a wrinkle. I'd taken extra time with my hair, too, wrangling it with a dryer as straight as I could. It still puffed up the second I stepped outside in the moist early winter air. Maybe someday I'd invest in a flat iron.

"Chloe, there you are." Lou found me in the crush of people in the lobby. I smoothed the front of my dress nervously. "You look nice. Want to meet some people?"

I went through the motions of smiling and shaking hands as Lou introduced me to an old couple, the man actually wearing an ascot and the woman draped in pearls, and then a couple in their forties, she with that perfectly smooth, straight hair I could never manage—maybe *she* used a flat iron—he clearly another Wall Street guy. I spotted Henry and Sloane in the crowd: Henry, momentarily, appropriately somber as someone whispered in his ear, then joyfully embracing his companion with lots of laughing and backslapping; Sloane, cool and sleek in a black dress that probably cost more than my monthly salary. Lou leaned away from me, straining to hear another elderly woman chatting at him, this one in a classic Chanel suit.

All around me, well-dressed New Yorkers talked and glad-handed and laughed, slowly filtering into the main auction room. I didn't even know if Inga's murder had made the news, if any of these people were aware of it, or if they were, if they'd care. My guess was that to most of them, it would be another one-line tragedy in a city where one-line tragedies happened daily. They might shake their heads at her picture and wonder why such a pretty young artist—and obviously very talented—had chosen to live in such a dangerous neighborhood. And then they'd move on with their day, their minds already forgetting her image, forgetting her death.

Lou pulled me toward the woman in Chanel, who raised a friendly brow and shook my hand warmly, though I didn't catch her name. I forced myself to smile back, remembering Vik's words, about how this gig could turn into a real career instead of just, *you know, a job.*

The crowd in the lobby was starting to thin.

"Let's get some seats," Lou said.

The auction room was filled with a low, anticipatory buzz.

We stepped over a few more elderly auction-goers to get to a pair of empty chairs in the center of the room, Lou murmuring an apology. I smiled weakly at a man in what looked like an honest-to-god smoking jacket as he frowned up at us, clearly disturbed by our passing. His eyes roved over us both before he turned to an equally well-preserved older man sporting an eggplant-colored velvet suit. His *tsk* was loud enough for me to hear even over the lively crowd, and my back stiffened. Were we really that out of place? Lou was wearing a nicely tailored jacket, for once, and I'd thought I'd dressed appropriately.

For a second, an image of my favorite black dress flashed in my head, the one I surely would have worn to something like this a few months ago, now balled up and sealed in two plastic grocery bags in the back of my closet, the bags slumped on top of a gray archival box. I stomped on that memory like it was a lit cigarette butt, extinguishing it before it could grow and fester.

"Those are the phone bidders," Lou said, pointing to a row of people sitting behind a raised dais. I looked in that direction, glad of the distraction. The phone bidders were mostly on the younger side, closer to thirty than fifty, but like everyone else, expensively and tastefully dressed. Most already had handsets pressed to their ears. "They make the bid on behalf of clients on the other end. And over there is the absentee bidder." Lou gestured toward a man behind a laptop seated closer to the auctioneer's podium. "So a client can tell the auction house in advance how high they want to bid on an item, and the absentee bidder will bid on their behalf." I must have looked confused, because he elaborated. "Say someone wants to go up to half a million on the first lot, the Corot," he said, pointing to the open page in the catalogue. "The auctioneer may start the bidding at one hundred thousand, and the absentee bidder will jump in on the client's behalf, up to five hundred thousand."

I looked at the catalogue. It was a pretty painting of a forest scene. Jean-Baptiste-Camille Corot, *La Forêt*, estimated to sell between $75,000 and $100,000. "Someone would bid that much higher than the estimate?"

"No, it's just an example." Lou flipped farther back through the catalogue, showing me a Picasso gouache from 1909, a gray cubist thing I didn't like as well as the delicate dancer hanging back in the gallery. It was estimated to sell between four million and six million. "Say a bidder on this piece only wanted to go to four million. The auctioneer won't start quite that high, probably at around two, and let the price climb. The absentee bidder will participate until he hits the client's limit."

The thought of the amount of money, figurative or not, that was about to fly around the room was a little nauseating. *Four million dollars.* "What's to stop the absentee bidder from just jumping in at the maximum amount, make sure they get the work for their client?"

"It's about trust, right? The client is trusting the absentee bidder to acquire the work for as low as they can."

I nodded as the auctioneer stepped behind his podium and the crowd stilled. Henry and Sloane were a few rows ahead of us, and their backs both snapped to attention. I wondered how much trust the divorcing couple had in Henry to get the works they wanted.

The auctioneer called for the first lot, and two young Black men wearing pristine black aprons over crisp white shirts brought the small Corot painting onto the stage and set it on an easel.

I couldn't help but get excited as the bidding began. Until I'd learned about Inga's death the day before, I had been really looking forward to this, and I found myself swept up in the drama of the process. The auctioneer called out exorbitant prices, looking from the absentee bidder to the phone bidders to participants in the audience. I had been afraid that if I sneezed or tucked a stray hair behind my ear I would accidentally bid, but now saw that would never be possible. Those bidding, whether by phone or in person, took pains to make their intentions clear. Eye contact with the auctioneer, a raised hand, sometimes a call of "bid," sometimes a mouthed amount if they wanted to offer more or less than the auctioneer was asking. The phone bidders would even put their hands over their mouths to mask the conversations they were having, further clarifying when they weren't actively bidding.

The longer the sale went, the higher the prices climbed. "That's typical," Lou murmured in my ear as lots changed on the stage. "The auction house wants to build anticipation to the high-ticket items."

"The next lots, important Impressionist paintings, including property from a Florida collection," the auctioneer, a gray-haired, handsome British man, called. The crowd rustled, and ahead of me, Henry's shoulders straightened even more.

This lot contained the paintings Fletcher & Sons was bidding on. I checked the catalogue. The collection included paintings by Berthe Morisot, Pierre Renoir, and three works by Claude Monet: one of haystacks that glowed pink and orange in a sunset, one of a cathedral that looked like it was melting into lavender slashes of paint, and a large, vibrant canvas of water lilies. This last was estimated to sell for ten to fifteen million.

"Whoa," I breathed. "So, I get how the auction house makes money. They take a commission from both the buyer and the seller, right?" At Lou's nod, I continued. "So how do the Fletchers make money here, bidding for these clients? Do they charge the clients a fee?"

Lou looked surprised. "They don't make money. It's a service they're offering to these people, in the hopes that one of them will eventually use the gallery to resell one of the works, and then they'll make money. Or that one of them will want to build on what they buy today and turn to the gallery to acquire more. It's part of the relationship."

My eyes roved over the crowd as a new painting was placed on the easel. The attendees looked bright-eyed, full of nervous, happy energy, and—if you looked closely enough—relieved. I remembered what Lou had said about the current volatility of the art market.

"It's going well so far, isn't it?" I asked Lou. "Pieces are selling."

He nodded. "Better than expected."

We quieted down as the bidding began on the next lot. Once again, I got a rush out of the spectacle of the rising prices, of a battle between a phone bidder and a gray-haired lady in the audience—the same woman in Chanel whom Lou had introduced me to in the lobby—for an exquisite painting of a pink-cheeked little girl by Renoir. The prices soared to unheard of, dizzying heights, amounts beyond my comprehension: twelve million for the Renoir, nine million for an Henri Matisse. Henry had participated in the bidding for both a Cézanne and the Berthe Morisot but had dropped out once the prices reached over five million.

"Lot 206, Claude Monet's oil *Nymphéas*, circa 1916. An extraordinary masterpiece, long since thought lost in the Holocaust, recently rediscovered. Fit for a palace, it is estimated at ten to fifteen million. Can we start the bidding at seven million?" the auctioneer said as the painting was set on the stage. A murmur ran through the audience. Henry raised his paddle.

The bidding went on and on, first fast and furious among six or seven people, then slowing as the price soared. The audience gave a collective gasp when the work reached its high estimate of fifteen million, the bidding down to three people, Henry among them. The auctioneer called for sixteen million, and Henry leaned his brown, curly head to Sloane's smooth, blond one. They consulted for a moment and I could see Sloane's eyes scanning the room, taking in the phone bidder they had been up against, as well as the tall, dark-haired man in the audience who also wanted the piece.

"Any takers for sixteen million then? Do I have sixteen? Selling for fifteen million to Darla on the phone, fair warning . . ." Henry raised his paddle, and the auctioneer pounced. "Sixteen million in the room. I have sixteen million in the center. Sir, do I hear seventeen? Darla, seventeen?" Heads whipped toward the phone bidder, apparently called Darla, who cupped a hand over her mouth as she consulted with the client. "Seventeen to you, sir," the auctioneer called over his podium toward the dark-haired man in the aisle seat, who cupped his own hands and mouthed something to the auctioneer.

"Sixteen and a half?" the auctioneer responded. "I'll take it. Sixteen and a half million to the gentleman on the aisle. I'm asking for seventeen now. Darla? Sir?" He cut his eyes between Henry and the phone bidder, waiting for a response. "Are we selling at sixteen and a half?"

The audience rumbled as Darla on the phone shook her head and mouthed *We're out.*

"Back to the room, then. Seventeen to you, sir," the auctioneer said to Henry.

Henry raised his paddle.

The bidding continued between the dark-haired man and Henry. My heart was in my throat as the numbers crept up, eighteen, eighteen and a half. At nineteen million, another gasp and low chatter spontaneously arose from the crowd.

"We have a record high price for a Monet now," the auctioneer confirmed. The bid was Henry's. I caught Lou's eye and shook my head slightly. *Nineteen million dollars.* "Nineteen and a half to you, sir," the auctioneer said to the dark-haired man.

The man took the bid, raising his paddle marked "75." The audience murmured again, and every face in the room turned to Henry.

Twenty million now.

The auctioneer asked for the price, holding his gavel, eyes fixed on Henry, then quickly sweeping the room, then back to Henry. "I'm selling for nineteen and a half million to the gentleman on the aisle. Fair warning."

Again, Henry's paddle rose. I sucked in a breath along with everyone else.

Twenty million dollars.

Whoever this client was, they had very deep pockets, divorce or no.

The entire room stilled, attention on the dark-haired man. The auctioneer was asking for twenty and a half million dollars. I looked at the painting, its cluster of grass-green lily pads bunched together on the left side of the canvas, the blue-gray background interspersed with dashes of white, resembling light dancing on the water. It was incredibly beautiful, like a deep pool one could dive into.

"Twenty and a half to you sir. Twenty and a half million to the gentleman on the aisle. I have you at twenty, sir"—the auctioneer indicated Henry—"and I need twenty and a half. Any takers, twenty and a half."

Almost imperceptibly, the dark-haired man—like the Fletchers, he was seated several rows ahead of me, and I could see the barest outline of his profile but mostly just the back of his head—shook his head.

"Twenty million in the room. I'm selling for twenty million to the gentleman in the center. Twenty million, fair warning. Going once, going twice . . ." The hammer fell. "Sold, twenty million, a new world record for Monet, to the gentleman in the center." The crowd broke into spontaneous applause.

Henry nodded genially at those around him. Sloane turned enough that I could see her beam.

"That was . . ." I whispered to Lou. My skin was buzzing, and I hadn't been the one bidding.

"I know," he said. "Pretty wild, isn't it?"

Wild didn't begin to cover it. I could see how the gamble of such high-stakes bidding, the competition of it, could be addictive, even as I reeled at the unimaginable, nearly unconscionable, amounts of money that were being spent.

Lou swallowed visibly, his eyes fixed on the stage as the lots changed. "I think we're going to be okay," he murmured to himself.

His words shook me. Did he mean the art world in general, or the gallery itself? Had we been that close to *not* being okay? It didn't seem prudent to ask.

The rest of the auction seemed tame after that, and even though the prices for the remaining works remained in the millions, Henry's record-setting purchase of the Monet was clearly the highlight of the night.

Well-wishers and friends swooped in on both Fletchers as soon as the sale was over. Lou and I lingered, waiting to say hello before we left. He steered me in their direction once he saw an opening.

"Congratulations," Lou said to them both.

"Thank you. Didn't he do great?" Sloane squeezed her father's arm, flushing with excitement.

"Nerves of steel," Lou agreed.

"What did you think, Chloe?" Sloane asked as someone else occupied Henry's attention.

"It was pretty exhilarating," I admitted. "I've never seen anything like it. And it was recovered from the Nazis?"

Sloane opened her mouth to answer but was interrupted by the man who had been speaking to Henry. "Lou, you old dog, still up to your tricks?" The newcomer leaned over to shake Lou's hand.

"As always," Lou replied. "I didn't know you'd be here, Carl, good to see you. Chloe, this is Carl, Henry's brother. Chloe is my assistant."

Carl turned his attention toward me. His gaze was outwardly friendly, but underneath it was acute and penetrating, and I tried not to flinch. His handshake, too, was just a shade too firm.

"Great to meet you, Chloe." Carl looked around Henry's age, maybe mid-fifties, but he was far better-looking, with a handsome cragginess that reminded me of the actor Sam Shepard from that movie *The Right Stuff*.

"Well, Lou, Chloe, thank you for coming," Henry said, doing the spread-armed, head-tilt gesture he liked. "We have a reservation, so we will see you Monday."

I was ready to say a polite goodbye, but Carl spoke first. "Why don't Lou and Chloe join us, Henry? They're part of the team."

Henry concealed his shock at the suggestion, but not quickly enough. Sloane, too, suddenly looked pinched.

"Well, the reservation," Henry began, stammering a little. He looked from Carl to me with concern. "We are meeting some other clients there, I'm not sure there would be room."

"I'll call," Carl said smoothly, pulling out a cell phone. "Le Charlot, right? I'm sure Michel can squeeze in two more, god knows you spend enough money there."

I didn't know what kind of pissing match was happening here, but I didn't want to be in the middle of it. It was obvious Henry and Sloane didn't want the peons attending dinner, and honestly, sitting in a fancy French restaurant with my bosses sounded like the furthest thing from fun I could think of.

"Thank you, but I can't go. I have plans," I lied.

"I do too," Lou said. "Debra will be waiting for me. But I appreciate the offer."

Carl paused mid-dial. "Are you sure?"

"They can't make it, Carl," Henry said. His tense voice was at odds with his expression, which was utterly relieved. Despite the fact that I didn't want to go, I couldn't help but feel a little insulted. Would it really be that horrific to be seen in a restaurant with me and Lou?

I smoothed the front of my borrowed Anna Sui again and adjusted the strap of my vintage purse. I had thought it looked so chic but was now conscious of its worn edges.

"Another time, then," Carl said, reaching out his hand again. I had no choice but to take it, even though I'd already shaken his hand less than two minutes ago. He increased the pressure, his smile widening as I started a little at the uncomfortable squeezing sensation. "I look forward to it."

CHAPTER SEVEN

"Detectives Gonzales and Downs are here for you, Chloe." Carmen's crisp voice echoed through the receiver.

My stomach jumped in response, then turned a lazy somersault. I'd just talked to them last Friday. What could they want only a few days later?

"The detectives? They're here for me?" From across the room, Lou's head jerked up.

"They are."

I paused, my eyes seeking Lou's. His brow furrowed in question, and I silently shook my head in response.

"Okay. I'll be right up." I replaced the receiver but stared at it for a minute and took a deep breath.

"What's going on? The police are back?" Lou asked, half rising out of his seat.

"Seems so." My mind raced. Did I need a lawyer?

But for what? I'd already told them everything I knew about Inga's murder. Vik had been right, I barely knew the woman.

"Did something happen while I was out?" I asked. I couldn't think what else they wanted to see me for; there must have been some kind of development in the case. It was Wednesday now, and I hadn't been into the office for the past two days. Lou had called Sunday night, told me he was emailing me a list of references on the new Monet, and I was to spend all day Monday and Tuesday at the New York Public Library chasing them down. I loved library days. The New York Public's main branch was all carved wood and old fixtures and a gorgeous, painted ceiling of clouds and cherubs. There was a hushed reverence to the place, even though it was always full of researchers.

Plus, I could come and go as I pleased, taking an extra-long lunch in Bryant Park if it was sunny, or nurse an expensive Midtown cappuccino if I wanted.

"No, nothing," Lou said. He stood up all the way and circled around his desk. "I'm coming with you."

It felt better to have Lou at my back as we mounted the curved marble stairs to the lobby.

The detectives were just as they had been last Friday, both in understated, fashionable suits, her with slicked-back hair and small, tasteful earrings, him with his red hair neatly combed and parted.

"What can we help you with, Detectives? The Fletchers aren't in today," Lou said.

"We're here to speak with Ms. Harlow," Detective Gonzales said. She turned to me. "Is there a place we can talk?"

"Henry's off-site today, we can use his office," Lou said. "I'll take you there. Carmen, do you know if it's locked?"

Carmen handed over the key mutely. I would have never dared to enter Henry's office without him, but Lou was senior staff.

Once Lou unlocked the door, Detective Gonzales turned to him. "Thank you, Dr. Stern, but we really need to speak to Ms. Harlow alone."

Lou hesitated. "I'm not sure that's a good idea."

The detective's brow rose the barest amount. "And why would that be?"

My boss inhaled as though he wanted to say something, then seemed to think the better of it. "She works for me," he said instead. "I feel responsible."

"I'd prefer if Lou stayed," I said. Anxiety was starting to nip at me. I didn't want to be alone in there.

"We just have some simple questions, a few things to clarify," Gonzales said. Her voice was soothing, but also no-nonsense. "You're welcome to wait in the hall," she told Lou. The dismissal was pointed and unarguable.

Detective Downs watched the exchange mutely, hands in pockets.

"I'll be in Sloane's office, right next door. Call if you need me," Lou said to me. He looked slightly worried as he gently closed the door behind him, which only ramped up my anxiety.

I took the sofa again, conscious that the last time I'd sat there I'd had Lou by my side, and the Fletchers nearby. Now I was by myself.

Both detectives settled themselves in the decorative, spindly seats across from me. I folded my hands in my lap, then switched the crossing of my fingers, before forcing myself to be still.

The Monet had been delivered yesterday, I guessed, as it was carefully propped on foam blocks against a bookshelf, looming behind the detectives. I stared at the thick, buttery swabs of candy-pastel paint, itching to run a finger over its surface.

Detective Downs glanced at the painting once over his shoulder. He looked grudgingly impressed.

"Thanks for seeing us again so soon, Chloe," Detective Gonzales began.

"I haven't had a chance to make a list of the people I remember from the party yet," I blurted out, cutting her off. Now both of her brows rose. "I'm sorry. It's been a really crazy weekend, we all went to this big auction on Saturday, really important for the gallery, for the whole art market I guess, and then Lou sent me to the library for a few days to do research, and I just haven't had time." I was speaking a hair too loud, and too fast, but couldn't make myself slow down.

Detective Gonzales held up a hand. "That's not why we're here. We have a pretty good idea now of who was at the party. Your list will certainly help corroborate what we have, and you can get that to us later in the week, no problem." A card appeared in my line of vision, held out by Detective Downs. I took it, the thick paper smooth under my fingers.

"You can call either one of us. Or email it," the male detective said. Gonzales slid her card across the marble-topped coffee table between us as her partner spoke.

"Okay," I said. The trousers I had on, a low-slung black Daryl K pair I really hadn't been able to afford, didn't have any pockets, so I shifted the cards awkwardly in my grasp.

"We want to know why you lied to us, Chloe," Detective Gonzales said, so smoothly that for a second, I thought I'd misheard her.

But I hadn't. My throat went dry. I had to work to swallow a few times before I could speak.

They didn't know about what was in my closet.

Did they?

It had nothing to do with Inga's murder.

"I didn't lie to you."

"You said you met Inga Beck through the gallery, when you and Dr. Stern visited her loft to see the paintings, so you could help with his essay." The detective glanced at her open pad as if confirming what was written there matched what she was saying. "Isn't that what you said?" Her piercing gaze returned to my face.

I opened my mouth and then closed it again, mind racing. "Yes," I said. "Because that's what happened."

"So you never met Inga through your roommate, Vikram? Or his boyfriend, Ben?" She tilted her head, eyes continuing to bore into me.

I let out an involuntary sigh of relief, understanding flooding in. That's what this was about.

"No, no. I never met her before I went to her place with Lou."

"But your roommate did know Inga?"

"Well, yeah. A little, I guess. Ben really knew her better; they went to graduate school at Yale together. Not really together, they were in different programs, but I guess they knew each other." I was talking too fast again, even though their questioning made more sense now. I took a deep breath. "But the first time *I* met her was when I visited the studio with Lou."

Both detectives stared at me. I waited. My stomach started those flips again.

Did this mean they'd talked to Vik? He hadn't said a thing to me.

"So you expect us to believe that your roommate . . . who is a good friend, right? . . ." Detective Downs had started speaking, and now he paused, waiting for my nod of confirmation. "You expect us to believe that he knew Inga Beck, and he never mentioned it? Never thought to introduce you? I mean, with you working in this gallery and all?" He gestured around the room.

Their questions suddenly made even more sense.

But I also now understood something else: They didn't have a clue about how the art world worked.

I almost laughed with relief.

"Oh, no no no. I am not anybody who could have advanced Inga's career, really I'm not. Fletcher & Sons doesn't normally deal in art like Inga's, so no, Vik and Ben wouldn't have thought I could help her." I could hear the eagerness in my voice, my will to help them understand. "Vik knows a lot of working artists, but unless he was friends with someone who had, I don't know, like a Degas painting to sell, I'm not the person to help them out. It's like Sloane told you: The gallery wanted to expand its focus. Inga was the first contemporary artist Fletcher & Sons has represented. And look, even if the gallery did handle more living artists, I'm not a good contact. I'm the bottom rung of the ladder here. Just Lou's assistant."

I didn't even get into the weird dynamics of Lou's position. He was a senior staff member, true, but even he didn't interact with the clients much. Lou wasn't an Upper East Side guy. I sometimes thought the Fletchers, as much as they valued the research he did, were a little embarrassed by him, with his Brooklyn accent and occasionally unkempt hair or dirty fingernails. He and his girlfriend owned a funky row house in Red Hook, a dock-front neighborhood in Brooklyn, and he ran a spoken word workshop out of a warehouse over there every month. I went once, a little stunned to see bookish Lou take the stage and read his own beat poetry.

Rather than try to unpack all that for the detectives, I reiterated what Lou had told them last Friday. "It was Sloane who brought Inga to the gallery. Interacting with clients or artists is not my place, not my job here. Not even Lou's. Vik knows that, so no, he wouldn't have thought to introduce me to Inga. I don't think they knew each other very well. When did you talk to him?"

Neither detective answered this.

"Did you know the bodega across the street from Inga Beck's building has cameras, and one of them captures a partial view of the building's front door?" Detective Gonzales asked instead.

"Definitely the street," Detective Downs chimed in.

"That's right. The point is, Chloe, we're pretty sure we'll have at least partial pictures of people coming and going the night of the party." They both looked at me expectantly.

"Okay," I finally said. "That's good, right?"

"We're still waiting on the tapes. The bodega is temporarily closed, owner's visiting family in Puerto Rico. But we should have them soon."

Another long pause. The relief I had felt was starting to ebb away. They seemed to want something from me, but I had no idea what.

"Okay," I said again. "Good."

"Is there anything you want to tell us, before that happens?" Detective Gonzales watched me keenly.

I looked from one detective to the other. Neither of their faces gave anything away.

Did they know something I didn't?

"Nooo," I said slowly. Then I mustered more firmness. "No. I left late, walked home."

The detectives didn't speak again, but they waited a few more beats. The tension that had built in the room during the past few moments had become an oppressive thing, weighing me down and making it difficult to breathe. I was seconds away from twitching convulsively, just to feel the air move, from screaming that I didn't know anything about Inga's murder, that I couldn't fucking remember that night.

"Okay." Detective Gonzales finally broke the silence. The strain of holding myself still poured out of me, my shoulders sagging. "Thanks for your time. You have our cards in case you change your mind."

They didn't wait for me but stood and strode from Henry's office without looking back.

CHAPTER EIGHT

I couldn't bring myself to get up from the sofa. What had just happened?

On the surface, nothing. But the detectives' questions had shaken me to the core.

Their insistence that I was hiding something.

That they'd spoken with Vik, and I didn't know.

"How'd it go?" I flinched at Lou's voice. He leaned in the doorway, watching me carefully.

"It was weird," I admitted.

Concern wrinkled his forehead. "Weird, how?"

"I don't know. It's like they're trying to catch me in a lie, but I don't know about what. I don't *know* anything."

Lou took the chair Detective Gonzales had abandoned.

"It's what cops do," he said, folding his arms over his chest. His concern turned to disgust. "They don't have anything on this murder, so they're harassing other people."

"But why *me*?"

He shook his head. "Who knows, with cops. I mean, you didn't see anything unusual that night, right?"

I strained my brain. *Had I?*

"I don't think so."

Lou half shrugged.

The feeling that I was missing something, a vital piece of information that I should be remembering but couldn't, gnawed at me. It wasn't just the detectives' leading questions. It was the sensation of something tickling the peripheries of my memory, dancing right out of reach, equal parts tantalizing and tormenting. The harder I tried to capture it, pin it down so I could study it properly, the more liquid and elusive it became. I was sleeping poorly, waking up from dreams that faded too fast, gasping with fright.

I needed to tell someone the truth about the gaps in my memory, before it ate me alive.

"Look, Lou," I said, but then stopped. Maybe Lou wasn't the right person to tell. I didn't want to jeopardize my job.

"What is it, Chloe? What's going on?" Lou's voice was incredibly gentle, and he'd unfolded his arms, leaning forward and looking at me with sympathy.

My lips tightened, but I forced them to relax and took a breath.

"I don't remember, okay? I don't remember much about that night. I don't even know how I got home."

He didn't say anything. I forced myself to continue.

"It happens. Since the towers. When I drink, but not all the time." I was rambling again, like I had with the detectives. "Just sometimes, but I promise I won't let it affect my work."

Lou waved his hand, as if swatting the notion aside. "I'm not worried about your work, but you need help, Chloe. I wish you'd just talk to someone."

"I'm not ready," I interrupted him. The last thing I wanted to do was talk about what had happened on 9/11. About how it felt to be trapped in a stairwell, the scent of fuel and fire filling my nose and throat, about choking on dust and smoke. Why didn't anyone understand that?

"It's not going to get better on its own. Trauma doesn't magically go away by itself."

"So I'll be fucked-up forever?" I meant it as a joke but wound up sounding desperate.

"Not if you get help."

A long pause unfurled, during which I considered and rejected a dozen different responses.

"I'll think about it," I said.

"Yeah?" Lou brightened.

"Sure."

I would not, in fact, think about it. But maybe I would try to drink less.

"Listen, what are you doing for Thanksgiving?"

"I'm not sure," I said. Lou's question caught me off guard. Thanksgiving was the following week, and I didn't have any solid plans yet. "I have a few options."

"Why don't you come to our house? It'll be a good group, some old friends. Debra would love to have you."

I was surprised, and touched. Even though I had only become Lou's assistant a few months ago, I'd known him for two years now, ever since I started working the reception desk at the gallery. We'd become a little chummy, and I'd met his girlfriend a few times, at openings or the one or two times I'd dropped off some documents at his house. He'd invited me to that open mic night he hosted, and I'd joined him and a few of his friends, including Debra, for a drink afterward. We were friendly, but not what I'd call close. Not close enough to be invited over for a holiday.

"You should come," Lou continued, seeming to interpret my silence as reticence. "Debra is a great cook. I buy the pies from this old bakery on East Ninetieth, best in the city. You're probably not going home to Ohio, right?"

He was right, I hadn't planned on going home. I was the only child of divorced parents, and my mom would likely spend the day with her best girlfriend from high school, Sherrie. The turkey would be too dry, they'd drink too many fuzzy navels and spend the whole day complaining about men. My dad would be in his pristine McMansion with his equally pristine new wife and kids. I barely knew my little half brother and sister, who stared at me with a mix of suspicion and wonder the few awkward times we'd met over the years. They hadn't invited me, anyway. Vik had proffered a half-hearted invitation to his parents' house in New Jersey, and while I enjoyed his family a lot, his parents were very traditional and Vik wasn't out to them as gay yet. Once I'd had to pretend like I was the one dating Ben instead of Vik, an awkward experience I wasn't keen to repeat.

"Okay," I said, surprising myself.

"Great!" Lou seemed genuinely pleased, which made me pleased. "Debra will be so happy. She worries about you."

Some of my pleasure dimmed. Was this a pity invite?

I shoved that aside. Even if it was, it would beat fielding questions from Vik's parents about why their handsome son, who was such a good catch, didn't have a girlfriend.

"It sure is something, isn't it?" Lou was looking at the Monet now.

"I can't believe a twenty-million-dollar painting is just sitting there. Why didn't it go to the warehouse?"

Lou shook his head. "I'm sure there's a good reason. It'll get there."

We both stared at the painting for a few seconds. The memory of Lou gazing up at *Helpless* in Inga's loft surged again, then receded. I wanted to stomp my foot in frustration.

What had happened next?

"It go okay at the library?" he asked.

"I found most of the references, yeah. To think it's been missing for so long. And it turned up in an old lady's storage unit in Florida?"

Lou shrugged a little. "It happens sometimes. The provenance we do have is pretty tight."

Provenance, I'd learned, was the history of who had owned a work of art when. As this one had gone missing during World War II, there was a huge gap in its provenance, but apparently the woman who had owned it had been connected to the last known owners in France in the 1930s.

We looked at the painting for a few more beats. I couldn't stand it any longer and nudged Lou's side with my elbow.

"Say it."

He smiled a little. "Say what?"

"You know."

Lou tilted his head to one side, examining the work. I grinned in anticipation.

"He could paint."

I clapped my hands once and laughed. It had become a running joke between us, that the highest praise Lou bestowed on a painting were those three words.

"Tell me more," I said, gesturing to the Monet.

This had become another ritual between us. When a new work came to the gallery, we would stand in front of it, or Lou would pull it out of its archival box in our small collections storage room, and he would fill me in on the basics: The background of the artist, what movement they belonged to, how the work related to the artist's overall output, details about the medium or the subject matter. He was good at conveying complicated ideas and movements in an understandable way; I often wondered why he had chosen curatorial work over being a professor. He would have been a great one.

"That thickness of paint, it's called impasto?" I asked, clasping my hands behind my back and leaning my face closer to the work.

"Yeah. You can almost see where he used his palette knife here, and here," said Lou, his finger hovering above the surface of the painting.

I shook my head in wonder, my fear and discomfort at the detectives' questions temporarily put aside. It would be back later, I knew, but for now it was enough to revel in the fact that I was inches away from a surface Monet had touched, from paint he had manipulated.

Lou straightened up. "Guess that's enough for today. Think you'll be okay for the service?" A hasty funeral for Inga was planned for next week, the Monday before Thanksgiving, and the whole gallery was attending, prior to taking the rest of the week off. She was being buried in a plot in Brooklyn, per her wishes, Lou relayed, rather than her home state of Minnesota. Her family—just a sister, apparently—asked that one of her works be displayed during the service. The Fletchers had chosen *Helpless*.

I followed Lou's lead and stood.

"*Helpless*, really?" I said. "Is that an appropriate work for the funeral of a murdered person, with that title?" Even though the Fletchers were out, I whispered the question in the hallway as Lou relocked Henry's office door. Just saying the word *murdered* sent a chill down my spine.

"I guess that's what they worked out with the sister over the weekend. Maybe because it was the easiest one to get, the one that was still in her loft. The others are in the warehouse."

This seemed a flimsy excuse to me, but I kept that opinion to myself as I trailed Lou back to the lobby, where he handed Carmen the key, and then down the second set of stairs to our office. The climate-controlled warehouse where the gallery kept the artwork there wasn't room for in the town house—which was quite a lot—was in Queens. Its whole purpose was to store art for people like the Fletchers, and it was their job to unearth a piece and transport it to where a client wanted.

Lou was probably right, *Helpless* was likely chosen because it was at Inga's apartment and closest, and therefore cheapest, to get. Moving art around, I'd come to understand, was an expensive business, especially canvases as large as Inga's.

Still, I would bet a month's pay this was also a publicity stunt on the part of the Fletchers. *Helpless* was from the "Less Than" series Inga had thrown the party to celebrate finishing. The first painting in that series, *Careless*, was the one that had brought Inga her initial fame, landing her on the cover of *Artforum* during her warehouse exhibition. The others all had similar titles, *Loveless, Hopeless, Fearless,* and so on. *Artforum* had gushed about *Careless:* "Overwhelming, near panoramic in scope, the viewer drowns in Beck's riotous color and in her wild, almost angry slashes of paint. An important, fresh voice in painting, taking the reins from the Irascibles and piloting abstraction into new territory." *Careless* sold right away, and buyers had been clamoring for more ever since. Once Inga signed with the Fletchers, though, they had her wait to exhibit or sell any further paintings in the series until it was complete. They were meant to be revealed as a set in the big show in January.

The show that was still happening, even after her murder. Only now it would be a memorial show. As we settled back at our desks, Lou filled me in on the other big piece of news: Inga's sister had said the gallery could keep managing the artist's estate, for now.

My mouth dropped open. This was huge. The prices for Inga's paintings would skyrocket: On the heels of the *Artforum* review, to now have a beautiful artist dead before her time, and in such a ghastly way, would make for a near frenzy among potential buyers.

As the Fletchers were handling the estate, they would get a cut of all the sales.

They were sitting on a gold mine.

I'd seen *Helpless* the night of the party. It was a massive painting, nearly twenty feet wide, with dark reds and pinks and oranges violently jutting up against one another, undergirded by formless, thinly articulated dark blue shapes. I remember thinking it captured only one aspect of feeling helpless. Not the despair or anguish or immobility that often accompanied such a state, but the violent anger that was its sister, the rage born of being unable to act, of having all your choices withdrawn against your will.

A memory clinked into place, like a penny dropping into a slot.

Inga, standing next to Lou in front of the giant canvas as I approached them, the party swirling around us. Her lovely pale skin had a pearly glow and there was a slight pink flush on her cheeks, her long blond hair swirled into a topknot secured with a paintbrush.

For a few seconds, I'd been nearly overcome with jealousy of her beauty.

"It finished drying a few days ago," she was telling Lou as I joined them at the canvas. "This was the last one, the last of the series."

Inga's presence merged seamlessly with the same memory I'd had since the party: of Lou looking up at the painting in wonder.

This was a different moment from the one I already remembered, of her face close to mine, her eyes going wide. Why hadn't I recalled her looking at the painting too? Now I remembered her there, standing next to Lou, clear as day. She'd thrown an arm around my neck and half pulled me in for an embrace, her sweet, slightly beer-scented breath warm on my ear.

"I'm glad you're here," she had murmured, and a pleased flush had filled my face, surprised and happy to have been singled out.

But that was it. After that moment, my memory was a frustratingly black wall again.

"There's probably gonna be press around the funeral," Lou said, jolting me back to the present. I blinked at him. "Pictures of the painting will get out there."

"I'm sure that's the point," I said, distracted.

Me, Inga, and Lou, looking up at Helpless.

Inga's arm around my neck.

What had happened next?

Lou's mouth twitched, but he turned his attention to his screen and kept it there.

"We'd better get back to it," he said.

To my immense relief, Lou sent me back to the library on Friday. I was glad to be out of the gallery, in case the police came back. Plus, the gallery felt weird these days, with everyone going through the motions of being devastated by Inga's murder, planning the memorial and all, but I'd overheard Henry and Sloane talking in the kitchen about how much money they'd make off her work. And it wasn't just them; there was a sort of buzz around the gallery's impending good fortune, from Sebastian to Douglas to Carmen. Only Lou seemed truly saddened by Inga's death.

Here at the library, I could lose myself in the anonymity of the other researchers, in the pleasure of being handed bound copies of early-twentieth-century French journals. I turned the brittle pages delicately, finding the page number on Lou's list, and skimmed the review of the Monet Henry had bought before filling out a slip to have a copy made. The dry, appealing smell of old paper filled the air, accompanied by the gentle noise of pencils scratching and keyboards clicking. My French wasn't that bad, another reason I'd gotten the promotion. Eight years of it, from ages six to fourteen at a private Catholic school, had taught me pretty well. After my parents' divorce, there was no money for private school, but I'd been able to take a few more years at the public high school. It was one of the few subjects I'd liked, so one of the few I'd done well in.

It was nearly dark by the time I climbed the subway steps and emerged onto Bedford. Vera Cruz, the bustling Mexican bar and restaurant across the street from Rosemary's, was packed, noise spilling out from its cracked windows onto the street. I thought I spied the shape of Bo's jacket in the crowd, his flipped-up collar, but ducked my head and hurried past. I avoided Rosemary's too. For once, I didn't want to go out. I wanted to be home, see if I could catch Vik.

He wasn't home. Again. It was the fifth night in a row he hadn't been here. I'd left him a message on his cell on Tuesday, asking if he'd spoken to the police, but he'd never answered. Now, the red light was blinking on our home answering machine. I pressed the button, and Vik's disembodied voice piped through the kitchen, telling me he'd be spending the night at Benny's.

He didn't say anything about the police, didn't answer my question.

I bit my lip and stared at the machine. There were no other messages.

Vik wasn't back in the morning, not that I expected him. But I'd hoped. The empty wine bottle I'd drained the night before sat on the coffee table, leaving a sticky dark circle in its wake. I stuck the bottle in the recycling and rinsed out the juice glass I'd used in the sink. My head felt cottony, my movements sluggish.

So much for trying to drink less.

I found the Bustelo I'd finally bought but stared at the coffee maker, can in my hand. The mechanics of opening the can, getting the proportions right, waiting for the elderly machine to spit the coffee into the stained carafe was suddenly more than I could handle.

Besides, I was pretty sure we were out of sugar.

It was easier to throw on warm clothes and walk the two blocks to Ricci's, let Gio or Veronica make me a coffee instead.

"Hey," Gio turned as the bell above the door tinkled, his face lighting up in surprised pleasure. "Haven't seen you much. The usual?"

"Yes, please. And yeah, it's been a while." Over a week, I realized. I hadn't seen Gio since the previous Friday, the day I'd found out about Inga's murder.

"I looked for you at the bar the other night," he said, turning to fix my coffee. Veronica was helping an old lady in a moth-eaten dark blue coat at the other end of the counter, but otherwise the bakery was empty.

"Yeah, I haven't been going out as much." The glass windows warmed the sun streaming in. I basked in it, even though my head still throbbed from the cheap wine. The coffee would set me up right. "Did you hear about that shit at Rosemary's last week?" I filled in Gio on how the Masters of the Universe had accosted Vik.

Gio slid the coffee across the glass countertop toward me, accompanied by a roll wrapped in a square of wax paper. "Even Edward and Calvin got into it," I said as I dug around in my pocket for a couple of singles.

Gio saw me rooting. "Hey, don't worry about it."

"Come on, this is your business." I came up with a handful of detritus and placed it on the counter. Where the hell was my money?

"What were they fighting about?" he asked.

"Calvin was being an ass, spouting conspiracy theories from Europe about the towers being an inside job." I poked at what was on the counter as I dug in my other pocket. A gum wrapper, a receipt from Duane Reade, a random paper clip.

Gio's face darkened. "That's fucked-up," he said in a low tone, glancing at the old woman's retreating back. Gio's brother was a firefighter and had only escaped going to the towers the day of the attacks because he'd been out of town, on a beach vacation in the Bahamas with his then-girlfriend. They'd gotten stuck there for days and had wound up breaking up before they came home.

I found three crumpled dollars in the second pocket and handed them over, gathering up the other odds and ends to toss. "I know. You have a trash can back there?"

"Sure," Gio said, holding out his hand. But as I palmed the bits of trash, a flash of writing caught my eye.

I dropped the gum wrapper and twisted paper clip into his waiting hand but held on to the receipt, turning it over, mildly curious to see what I'd written. Someone's phone number? The name of a band I wanted to check out?

Only it wasn't my writing. It was writing I didn't recognize, spelling out a hasty-looking scribbled address in Queens I also didn't recognize.

My blood ran cold, despite the strong patch of sun pouring through the window.

Under the address was scrawled a single word.

Inga.

CHAPTER NINE

The funeral was the weirdest I'd ever attended.

Granted, the only others I'd been to had been for two of my four grandparents: my mom's father and my dad's mom, one before the divorce and one after. They had both been church affairs, the receptions afterward held in the parish hall in the case of my grandfather, and at my dad's huge, sterile house in the case of my grandmother. At the parish hall, people had brought casseroles and trays of store-bought bakery cookies. Dad had used a caterer.

Inga's funeral was being held in an event space in Midtown on the river, near the United Nations building, the type I guessed was normally rented for weddings or big corporate meetings. There was no preacher, and every seat was full so it was standing room only during the brief service. The range of speakers included a few words from friends, and a lovely, heartfelt eulogy from Inga's former professor from graduate school. The sister didn't speak. Maybe she, like me, was having a hard time with the open casket on the raised platform next to the speakers, the overpowering scent of lilies hanging heavily in the overly heated room.

I kept my gaze trained on whoever was talking. Inga's profile was insistent in the corner of my eye, but I ignored its pull, refusing to turn my head the fraction of an inch I needed to see.

Lou shifted in the seat next to me, a red-eyed Debra on his other side. I had seen Ben as we'd taken our seats. He was near the back, in a group of attractive-looking people, none of whom I recognized. Friends from Yale, probably.

Finally, blessedly, the professor said we were all welcome to a reception in the adjoining room.

I flowed with the crowd into the next room, clutching my vintage purse close. The note with the address and Inga's name was safely tucked into the bag's interior zippered pocket. For reasons I couldn't put my finger on, I felt better keeping the scrap of paper close to me at all times.

It had been burning a hole in my pocket for days.

The address wasn't Inga's, and it wasn't the gallery's warehouse, either, which was in Long Island City, just over the river.

I'd looked up the address on the internet. It was way out in Jamaica, nearly Long Island. There was no indication of what was located there. Someone's house? An apartment building? A bodega? I'd never been that far out in Queens and had no idea what the neighborhood was like.

I assumed it was Inga who wrote the note, but I still wasn't sure. I wouldn't be back in the gallery for another week and would have to see if I could dig up something with her handwriting on it. The contract she'd signed, maybe. But how would I get my hands on that? And whether she'd written the note or not, how had it gotten in my pocket? Who had put it there, and when? I'd obsessed over where I—and my coat—had been over the past week. Had it been at the party itself? The coat check at Sotheby's? In the gallery, when I'd been in the bathroom? Hanging over the back of my chair in the reading room at the library? I couldn't come up with any good answers.

The reception room was even larger, a giant space with corporate, hotel-like carpet lining the floor, one entire wall floor-to-ceiling glass that led to a long balcony, beyond which the East River shimmered, despite the low-hanging gray clouds. *Helpless* hung opposite, several sections of velvet-roped stanchion placed in front of it to keep its admirers from getting too close. Paid guards stood by in tight, ill-fitting uniforms, but they watched the guests like hawks, intervening with a raised hand if someone got too close to the painting with a cup of coffee.

I got separated from Lou and Debra as I fought my way to the bar, where I ordered a mimosa. It was sorely needed. I was out of sorts, and not just from the funeral and the nauseating scent of flowers. I'd finally seen Vik that morning.

I'd been surprised to find him at the kitchen table with his laptop as I headed to the shower. He hadn't been answering my calls and had seemingly been barricading himself at Benny's. I hadn't heard him come home the night before either. I'd gone to Rosemary's and hung around with Penny and Lisel for a while and was sure he hadn't been there when I came back to the apartment.

"I didn't think you were here," I'd said to Vik as he saved whatever he was working on and closed his laptop.

"Just stopped by to drop some stuff off," he'd said.

"So, when did you talk to the police?" I'd pulled my robe, a vintage cotton one printed with a pattern of leaping marlins I liked a lot, tighter around me.

"Uh, maybe last Monday? I don't remember." Vik had then met my eyes for the first time since I'd entered the kitchen. "Listen, are you coming for Thanksgiving?" He had bags under his eyes, and his beard, normally so well trimmed, was looking a little long.

"No, I'm going to Lou's. But thank your parents for the invitation."

Vik then shoved his laptop into his bag. "Okay, no problem. Gotta get to class, see you later."

"You're not going to the funeral?"

"I didn't get an invite. Besides, I have class. Benny will be there."

I'd stepped in front of him as he began to pull on his coat. "Vik, are you okay? Are we okay?"

He'd focused on zipping up his puffy jacket, not meeting my eye again. "What do you mean?"

I'd bitten my lip but forged ahead. "I mean ever since those assholes were giving you a hard time at Rosemary's, I kind of feel like you've been avoiding me."

Ever since Inga was murdered, I'd realized.

"I haven't been avoiding you." He'd rooted around in his bag for his hat, then jammed it on his head. "I'm just busy, it's getting close to finals. Look, I really have to go. Maybe we can hang out before I leave for Jersey, yeah?"

He had managed a tight smile but squeezed past me to the door. I watched it swing shut behind him, confusion and hurt tangling up inside my chest.

At the reception, I slammed my mimosa and ordered a second, looking around for Lou or Debra, or even Ben. I didn't see any of them in the crush of bodies, but I did see Inga's sister, Anne, whom Lou had pointed out during the service. She and her husband had been sitting in the front row with the Fletchers.

She was across the room, close to the door to the balcony where the crowd was a little thinner. Anne looked like everything Inga was not: a little plump, frumpy, frizzy haired and red-faced, the opposite of Inga's effortless, breezy bohemian style and lithe beauty. Anne's husband hovered nearby. He had the appearance of a former linebacker turned accountant who'd gone soft, with small eyes behind too-large, dated glasses. They both seemed a little bewildered, though Henry or Sloane was with either of them at any given time, introducing them to various people in their art world finery.

I supposed I ought to pay my respects.

The small knot of people around the Fletchers and Inga's relatives loosened as I approached. Both my bosses were speaking with a gaunt older man and Anne's husband. Sloane glanced up in alarm when Anne turned to someone new, but she returned to her conversation when she saw it was just me.

Up close, Anne bore the stunned look of someone entirely out of their element. I immediately felt bad for judging her clothes and introduced myself. I said how sorry I was for her loss, before adding I worked for the gallery.

Something twisted in Anne's face. "We don't know anything about all this art stuff. Decided it's better to let the gallery handle it."

"The Fletchers are really committed to Inga's work. They'll do a great job."

"They seem to think we'll make a lot of money." She glanced toward the painting and then away quickly. I saw her suppress a small shudder. "They say Inga had talent. Not my kind of art, but her teachers were always impressed."

I understood this point of view, had shared it myself before I learned more about abstract art. The dismissive undercurrent in Anne's words, the implication that because there wasn't a recognizable subject—a tree or a house or a person—anyone could make art like that, was familiar.

"She was absolutely talented," I said. Anne reminded me of people I'd grown up with, the moms of my high school friends. I found myself wanting to reassure her.

Anne nodded distractedly, looking around at the crowd. Inga's funeral had attracted a range of people, diverse, funky, chic; the people in the reception room were a clash of New York societies and subcultures, but all undergirded by money. "I don't understand what Inga saw in this place," she said. Her voice was sour. I saw her eyes linger and then narrow on a tall, thin white man with a shaved head and two big hoop earrings, who was talking to a woman with light brown skin and a head of short brown curls I was pretty sure was the painter Julie Mehretu. "Never did. Jim and I left the kids at home with his parents. You have kids?"

I almost laughed in disbelief but stopped myself. "No," I said instead. "No kids." I didn't know anybody my age in the city who had kids. But then I thought, again, of the girls I'd gone to high school with back in Ohio. They were all getting married and having babies, one by one, or so my mom informed me during our infrequent phone calls. There was always an undercurrent of disappointment in her voice that I wasn't doing the same.

It would be similar for twenty-six-year-olds in St. Cloud, where Anne and Inga were from, I guessed. Probably everywhere, except maybe here, or LA or San Francisco, Chicago. I tried to imagine life with a husband, a baby. It was nearly impossible. I could barely comanage a cat with Vik.

Anne nodded approvingly. "Not a good place for kids. Especially now. Who knows when those crazies could attack again? Not that anywhere feels particularly safe these days," she said, with a sigh.

As if on cue, my heartbeat got louder in my ears, and my palms dampened.

"It could happen in St. Cloud, too, you know," she continued.

"What could?"

"Terrorists."

I stared at her.

"They could attack St. Cloud," she insisted. "We're all in danger."

It took all my willpower not to shove my hands over my ears and scream at her, *Nobody is going to bomb fucking Minnesota.* I could feel my blood pounding in my temples, and the air in the room was too close, too hot. I wanted to get out but couldn't make my feet move.

"I hate this city," Anne said. She was so quiet I could barely hear her over the rushing noise in my head. "I'm doing this, this circus with these freaks"—she glared at a blue-haired young white man with a giant safety pin in his lapel across the room—"because Inga wanted it. But she's not getting buried here." Anne looked through the open door into the room where the service had been held, directly at the coffin.

It was like I'd lost control of my body. My gaze pulled in the same direction even as every nerve in my being screamed at me to stop. I'd been so careful to avoid the coffin, but now I couldn't look away. Even this far away, I could see it plainly. There was Inga, or a pale facsimile of her, all the vitality and sparkle that had made her irresistible drained, leaving the dry husk of her physical form behind.

"Oh, I misunderstood." My voice sounded thready and a little breathless. "I thought she was."

It was too crowded in here. Noises were too loud. Everything suddenly echoed, and a tight kernel of pain in the center of my chest began to expand, pushing on all sides.

Anne's expression turned mulish. "She's coming home to St. Cloud where she belongs, where she can be laid to rest in the family plot."

Sloane appeared at Anne's elbow. "Let's get you some food," she said to Anne in a soothing tone. Sloane barely looked at me, but for once I didn't care about the slight. I had to get away.

I slipped out to the balcony. It was cold enough that there weren't many others outside, just a few intrepid smokers huddled under hats and scarves. I gripped the railing and breathed deeply, focusing on the calming motions of the East River.

Inhale, exhale.

I made my eyes follow the path of a seagull, watching it swoop and dive. I let the wind whip my hair into a frenzy, let its sound wipe away the memories that had started to encroach, the images of falling bodies and a looming wall of poisonous-looking beige fog. I breathed that river wind in deeply, letting it erase the sensation of my lungs being clogged.

The sky was bruised-looking. The air kept threatening snow, but it kept holding off. Somehow that made it worse. Snow would at least make the city look clean, for a while, a pristine blanket to cover its sins.

"Need a light?"

"Huh?"

I looked up, surprised to see Henry's brother, Carl. He pointed at my hand, and I was equally surprised to find an unlit cigarette there. I didn't remember pulling one out of my bag.

"Yeah, thanks."

I held my hair back from my face as I leaned toward his lighter. He lit one for himself, and we leaned against the railing in a companionable way.

Maybe he wasn't as creepy as I'd thought. He was even kind of handsome in that older guy kind of way.

"How did you know Inga?" I asked. "Through the gallery?"

Carl looked surprised. "I didn't know her. I've been in town for work, so I came today to support Henry and Sloane. They're good at hiding how they feel, especially Henry, but they're pretty devastated by this."

I was glad to hear it. So far, I hadn't seen any signs of devastation from either Fletcher.

"So where do you live?"

"DC."

"Yeah? And what do you do?" I asked, more out of politeness than anything else, taking a deep drag of the cigarette. My head began to buzz. A cup of Ricci's coffee and the two mimosas were all I'd had to eat today.

"I'm a fed."

"What does that mean?"

He smiled. Not his brother's patronizing grin. Carl's smile had a sharpness to it. "Nothing too exciting. I'm with the Treasury Department."

I didn't know what to say to that, wasn't even sure what it meant, so I just nodded and smoked some more. A sudden warmth enveloped me.

Carl had put his jacket over my shoulders.

"Thanks," I said, startled.

But it was a good startled.

I was feeling better. It was good, standing here in the wind, smoking with someone, but not having to talk.

"It's clearing out in there," Carl finally said, glancing through the big window into the reception area. "I suppose I ought to do the same. I've got a car, can we drop you anywhere?"

"No, I'm staying to help clean up."

Carl raised a brow. "You're not the hired help, you know."

A short laugh burst from me. It felt good to laugh too. "I kind of am."

He looked like he wanted to say something else, but he crushed his finished cigarette instead and straightened up from the railing. I did the same, and he held the door for me as we returned inside.

I handed back his jacket, and Carl held my gaze for a few beats too long, his eyes lingering. "You sure, about the ride?" At my nod, he tipped his head in acquiescence, before sauntering through the main doors.

The crowd was much thinner; we must have been on the balcony longer than I thought. The caterers were clearing away the remains of the buffet, the bartenders doing the same. There was no sign of the Fletchers or Anne.

Helpless gleamed at me, its whirling colors nearly hypnotic.

"There you are." It was Lou, rushing in as the elevators *pinged* open. "I've got to run downstairs and deal with parking for the truck, somehow the garage isn't letting them in. It's ridiculous, I mean we're paying enough for this space, our truck needs access to the loading dock."

"We paid for this?"

"Yeah. Inga's sister, she's sweet, but they wouldn't be able to afford a space like this in Manhattan. Sloane arranged it all. Can you stay here with the painting until I come back with the art handlers?"

"Sure. I was planning on sticking around to help out." Now that I was here, though, I wasn't sure what else I could do.

Lou rushed off, throwing a distracted thanks over his shoulder. The last of the guests had departed, and it was just me and the catering staff, cleaning up and quietly talking among themselves in Spanish.

I moved closer to the painting, studying the dips and whorls of paint.

My kindergartner could do that. I could hear Anne's voice, or someone like her, saying those words.

No, they couldn't. The painting was immersive, emotional, the kind of work you fell into. I don't know how much time passed as I stared at it, following the lines and layers of paint with my eyes, watching where they threaded together, trying to find their beginnings and their ends, transfixed.

Out of the seeming chaos, one grouping of the thin, darker lines caught my gaze, familiar shapes emerging. I squinted at it.

The tiny hairs on the back of my neck prickled, then rose. Was that . . . ?

I blinked hard, looked again. Tilted my head and took a few steps closer. The rent-a-guards were gone, and I leaned in close, nose so near the canvas's surface that I could smell the tang of oil paint.

It was unmistakable. Like an Escher print, once you saw the trick, the image hidden within the image, you couldn't unsee it.

And I could see it. A message, right there in the painting. It was on its side, half buried by a sweep of violent orange, but it was there, plain as day for anyone who took the trouble to look.

HELP ME.

PART TWO

CHAPTER TEN

A cold front blew in the night before Thanksgiving, chasing away the clouds that had been hanging over the city like a bad omen, the day dawning fifteen degrees colder but the sky a clear cerulean as bright as a tropical sea.

I'd basically been on my own for the two days since the funeral, all my friends having scattered for the holiday, and I had done my best to be a proper grown-up in Vik's absence. This meant finally washing the excess coffee cups that littered my room, cleaning Groucho's litter box not once but twice, and giving the bathroom surfaces a spritz and wipe-down with the nearly empty bottle of Lysol I found shoved in the back of the cupboard under the kitchen sink.

Help me.

The phrase was a constant companion during these tasks, repeating in an endless loop in the back of my head.

It could mean nothing. An Easter egg, buried in the strata of paint, a tongue-in-cheek play on the painting's title.

Or it could mean everything. A cry into the void, an acknowledgment of an imminent threat, a desperate lifeline cast into an uncaring ocean, hoping a hand would grasp the other end.

It could mean Inga had known she was in danger. That her murder wasn't the result of a break-in, but that she had been targeted and killed, deliberately.

And that she had been afraid.

But of what? Why? Why would anyone kill an artist?

I chose my clothes for Lou's Thanksgiving dinner with care, unsure of what to expect. I considered the floral Anna Sui dress, which I hadn't yet returned to Lisel, but opted instead for something more comfortable: a pair of navy blue Built by Wendy corduroy pants with a fish embroidered at the hip, plus an orange turtleneck topped with a dark gray sleeveless sweater vest. I fingered the mysterious note with the address on it, debating where to stash it for the day. For reasons I couldn't put my finger on, I didn't like leaving it in the apartment when I wasn't home. I slipped it back into my coat pocket.

My eyes watered from the cold as I hurried the few short blocks to the subway. Lou had said to arrive around two, that we'd have drinks before dinner at four p.m. He had offered to send a car to pick me up, but I declined. He was already doing enough for me by inviting me to his house for Thanksgiving, I didn't want him to go out of his way any more than he had to.

"Are you sure?" Lou had asked doubtfully when he'd called me the day before. "You have the address, right? It's a pretty far walk from the subway, and I don't think the buses are running regularly on the holiday."

"I know, and it's okay. I like to walk," I'd lied. His house was almost at the river, and the closest subway stop was nearly twenty minutes away. I could wait for a bus, but he was right, on a day like Thanksgiving with reduced public transit, I might wait longer for a bus than it would take to walk. The route would take me past several rough housing projects, but I reasoned that it would be broad daylight, and a holiday to boot.

The few blocks to the subway were so cold I was now regretting turning down Lou's offer and pulled my knit hat lower, walked faster.

"Chloe, hey wait."

I turned, blinking from the bright sun that was suddenly in my eyes. Gio was running toward me, carrying a white paper box tied with bakery string.

We were stopped in front of Ricci's, but the lights were off and the Closed sign was turned in the doorway. Gio looked nice in a pale blue dress shirt tucked into dark pants instead of his usual white tee and jeans. Sunlight twinkled off a thin gold chain at his neck, glinted off his dark hair.

"Thought you might want to take these to your friend's house," he said, handing me the box. "Cookies."

The box felt heavy in my hand. "Wow, thanks," I said, a little nonplussed. "How did you know?"

He grinned, his white teeth bright against the olive of his skin, and tapped the side of his head with his finger. "Psychic." I must have looked confused. "Nah, I'm just messing," he continued. "Vik put in an order to take home, and I asked if you were going too. He told me you had plans in town. We had a few left at closing last night, so I put some aside in case I caught you."

The gesture was so thoughtful I was momentarily speechless. "I . . . thank you," I said again. The cookies were another specialty of the bakery, traditional Italian ones, rich and buttery. "I can pay you tomorrow."

He waved this off. "Nah, they would have gone bad. And we're closed all weekend. But they'll be great today." The same long finger now tapped the top of the box.

"Well, okay. If you're sure." I had a bottle of not-terrible wine tucked into my bag for Thanksgiving, chosen from behind the scratched, bulletproof glass of the local liquor store—I'd splurged, avoiding the five-dollar bottles of Gato Negro or Yellowtail I would normally buy—but the cookies were an even better offering.

"Is everything okay? You ran off like a bat out of hell last weekend," Gio said.

It was true, I had. Finding that note in my pocket had shaken me to the core, and I'd stumbled out of Ricci's with barely a goodbye. My hands were now occupied with the box so I couldn't grip the note for comfort, to reassure myself it was still there, but I imagined I could feel it, bright as a lit coal in my pocket.

The address. The message in the painting.

Help me.

"Giovanni!" An old woman's gray head stuck out of a window the floor above the shop. A torrent of Italian rained down on Gio, accompanied by enthusiastic hand gestures. Gio looked up and answered similarly. I didn't speak Italian, but caught the gist: *What are you doing talking to a girl on the sidewalk on Thanksgiving Day? Get back up here.*

"My *nonna*. Grandma," he said, grinning even broader as the window slammed shut, loud enough to startle a nearby roosting pigeon into flight. I knew Gio lived with his whole family in the floors above the store, his grandma on the second floor, parents on the third, and he shared the fourth-floor apartment with his brother the firefighter.

"Sounds like you'd better hustle," I said, grinning back.

"Yeah. Happy Thanksgiving, Chloe."

"You too, Gio." I clutched the box of cookies tightly as I descended to the subway, making sure to keep its contents level and unbroken.

It was always a relief when the train shot out of a tunnel and climbed aboveground. Light flooded the car, warming it, beating back the unhealthy glow of fluorescents. I had had to wait a long time for a G train, and had plenty of time to think while on my way to Lou's.

The big questions circled. Would I tell Lou about the note in my pocket? About the message in the painting? I turned the pros and cons of doing so over in my mind. Lou might be able to tell me right away what the note meant, what the address was for, even if it was Inga's handwriting or not. But something told me to hold back. Whoever had written the note, they had left it for me, not Lou. My pocket had been chosen, not his. Once I was back in the gallery next week, I could dig around in Inga's file, see if I could match the handwriting. If it looked like the note was from her, then I could talk to Lou.

As for the message in *Helpless* . . . I decided to wait on that too. What I really wanted to do was examine the other paintings, see if there were hidden words in those as well. But I'd never be able to find any secret messages in the digital images we had; the paintings were so big, and the files so small. I would need to see the works in person, and I wasn't sure that would happen until the January show.

For reasons I couldn't explain, that felt too late. I'd have to find a way to access the paintings in the warehouse sooner.

My fingers were nearly frozen by the time I made it to Lou's. The walk from the subway took longer than I remembered, and I hadn't seen a single bus on my way. The wind from the river was blasting down the empty, cobblestoned streets of Red Hook, and the bright sun did nothing to raise the temperature. American flags hung from nearly every row house, snapping in the brisk wind. My shadow was long and wavery, a mirage accompaniment to the long, frigid walk.

Debra answered the door sporting jeans and a necklace of tiny plastic dinosaurs topped by a vintage apron. I was relieved I hadn't overdressed. She made a satisfying, motherly fuss over me, exclaiming over the wine and cookies, urging me into the small, warm living room, and taking my coat. I had already transferred the note into the zippered pocket of my bag on the train, knowing I wouldn't wear my coat during dinner, but assuming I'd toss my bag into a corner where I could keep an eye on it.

Now that the bag was in said corner and I was settled into an overstuffed vintage armchair with a glass of crisp white wine, I wished I'd worn something with pockets. Not that there was anyone suspicious or odd at the dinner; in fact, everyone was lovely. I had been a little worried that I wouldn't fit in, that Lou and Debra's friends would all be longtime New Yorkers, older than me, married, smarter. And they *were* older, mostly in their forties like Lou, and several were married—one couple even brought their five-year-old daughter—but they were nothing but friendly and welcoming to me.

Still, I wanted the note on my person.

By the second glass of wine I hadn't forgotten about the note, but I was so caught up in lively conversation that it receded to a back portion of my mind.

The evening was a revelation. It was like glimpsing me and my friends fifteen years in the future, of what our lives could be. I hadn't realized until tonight that I couldn't visualize what my life might look like two decades down the line. I knew I didn't want either pole of the suburban existence I'd experienced growing up—neither the cookie-cutter McMansion and conspicuous consumption of my dad and his wife, nor the crumbling brick ranch and soured aspirations of my mom. Here, in Lou and Debra's comfortable, cluttered row house a stone's throw from the river, were gathered an array of middle-aged people who listened to the same music as me, who still went to punk rock shows, who worked jobs like graphic designer, performance artist, magazine editor, and two very chic women—a couple, I realized—were both musicians in the New York Philharmonic. They talked passionately about politics and books and art, all to a background of endlessly rotating jazz records spun by Lou and endless bottles of wine. And Lou's bragging about Debra's cooking hadn't been hyperbole; the dinner was excellent, including a fancy wild rice and butternut squash casserole for the vegetarians.

By midnight I was exhilarated and exhausted. Lou noticed me stifling a yawn. "I'm calling you a car, my treat," he said, pushing himself out of his place on the sofa. About half the guests had left, but there was a cadre of people still going strong.

I didn't argue this time. Lou made the call as I gathered my things and said goodbye to those still left. Debra hugged me tight, smelling of spices and red wine.

"Don't be a stranger," she said, looking me in the eye. "I'm so glad you came tonight. And Chloe, you know we're always here for you."

I nodded, suddenly shy.

"We got lucky, a car can be here in five," Lou said. "I'll wait outside with you."

The sky was still crystal clear, the brightest of stars visible above the ambient light of the city, but the ceaseless wind from the river made the temperature feel twenty degrees colder than it was. I shivered inside my coat and stomped my feet, the sting of wind cutting straight through the thin leather of my boots.

Lou exhaled gustily and looked up, a plume of white erupting into the sky. It was utterly quiet here, not a soul on the street, no cars, no traffic noise. Just the wind, and, if you listened hard enough, the gentle lapping of the river on its pilings half a block away.

"Pretty night," he commented, still gazing at the sky.

I pulled my fingers into the hands of my gloves to make a fist and jammed my fists into my coat pockets. The cold was like a living thing, creeping in between the folds of my clothes, up my pant legs, and burrowing into the small gaps where my coat sleeves ended and my gloves began.

"It is," I agreed. "Cold, though."

"Yeah. Thanks for coming tonight, Chloe."

"Hey, thank you for inviting me. And Debra. This was maybe the best Thanksgiving I've ever had." As soon as I said it, I realized it was true.

"Yeah?" In the glow of a nearby streetlamp, real pleasure lit Lou's face, as it had when I'd first accepted the invitation.

"Yeah," I confirmed.

Tell him about the note, the painting. The thought was sudden and insistent.

"Lou," I started, but before I could say more, headlights turned the corner, approaching us.

"This is you," Lou said as a town car pulled up to the curb. He wrapped me in a quick hug, as unexpected as it was welcome.

Monday, I decided. I would tell him about the note and what I'd seen in the painting on Monday.

I could trust Lou. He would help, help me figure out what the address and the message in the painting meant. Help me figure out if it meant nothing, or if the wisps of dread that had been curling themselves around me, giving slight, insistent tugs on my fingers and toes, were justified.

The car's interior smelled like cigarette smoke and air freshener, but it was warm. The driver confirmed my address in an Arabic accent, and I made sure to smile and nod in a friendly way, eager to show I bore him no ill will, that unlike those shitty Masters of the Universe from Rosemary's, I didn't judge people by the color of their skin.

Lou slipped some money through the driver's window and stepped back on the sidewalk, waving at me through the tinted glass. Even though he probably couldn't see me. I waved back.

As the car started to pull away, movement on the sidewalk caught my eye.

A figure stepped out of the shadows in between Lou's house and that of his neighbor. In the dim light I could tell it was a man, dressed in an indiscriminately colored, bulky down parka and a dark knit hat pulled low. I twisted in my seat to watch, drawing in a breath to order the driver to stop, to throw the car door open and scream at Lou, *Behind you*. But the man must have said something, because Lou slowly turned to face him. All I could see was the silhouette of Lou's back as the car rounded the corner, carrying me home.

CHAPTER ELEVEN

I stopped short in the doorway of my office, trying to figure out what was wrong.

For starters, Lou wasn't at his desk. But on the surface, that didn't mean anything. I was so anxious to talk to him that I'd arrived ten minutes early, rather than my usual twenty minutes late. Maybe he wasn't here yet or was in the kitchen getting coffee.

Then it hit me, all at once: Lou's desk was almost preternaturally tidy.

I slowly finished peeling off my coat and plunked my bag onto my desk chair. As I fired up my computer, I took the note out of my coat pocket and transferred it to my skirt pocket, almost without thinking.

Usually, Lou's desk was piled with stuff: files, messy stacks of paper, half-drunk blue-and-white paper diner coffee cups that Willa would grumble over—unless he was having liquor, I had never seen Lou drink anything other than coffee, not even a glass of water—jumbles of books. But today I could see the desk's shiny wooden surface. The books were in a neat stack on a shelf behind the desk, and the files and papers were nowhere in sight.

I poked my head into the hallway. Had he come in early, or over the weekend, and cleaned up?

I'd left a message on Lou and Debra's home machine on Saturday, thanking them again, and specifically telling Lou I hoped we could have lunch today, that I had something to discuss with him. I planned to take him out, though I would need to use my credit card to do so. Even the less expensive places near the gallery were beyond my means, but I wanted to thank him for dinner.

I was ready to show him the note, ask what he thought it meant.

I crossed back through Sebastian and Olive's office toward the kitchen, hoping to find Lou nursing a cup of coffee. Olive offered a distracted wave but Sebastian ignored me.

Only Willa was in the kitchen, wiping down the countertop.

"Have you seen Lou?" I asked her.

"No," she said curtly, not meeting my eye as she focused on her swishing dishcloth. I frowned. I wasn't Willa's favorite person, but she wasn't typically rude.

The printer across from Olive's desk was just finishing a job as I passed through again. I automatically picked up the pages and started to hand them to her when they were snatched out of my hand so forcibly I got a paper cut.

"Ow," I cried, sticking my finger in my mouth.

"These are mine, thank you," Sebastian said, whirling away from me, the papers tucked close to his chest.

"Sebastian," said Olive in a tired voice. "That wasn't necessary."

"Have either of you seen Lou today?" My finger throbbed and the coppery tang of blood filled my mouth. There were Band-Aids in the kitchen, but I didn't want to see Willa again.

"I haven't," Olive said, concern prickling her face. She checked her watch. "It's not like him to be late."

I made my way back to my office. My head was starting to hurt along with my finger. I stared at Lou's empty desk, wondering what to do.

My shoulders hitched up in surprise as my desk phone rang. I snatched the handset.

"This is Chloe," I said breathlessly, fully expecting Lou to be on the other line, saying he'd finally caught Debra's cold, or he had errands to run and would be in late.

"Hi, Chloe." It was Carmen. "Henry and Sloane would like to see you in Henry's office."

I replaced the handset with more care.

The Fletchers were in the same seating area where I'd been for both visits with the police. I glanced around the room quickly, not sure who else I expected to see—the detectives again? Lou?

But there was nobody else.

"Chloe," Henry greeted me in his too-hearty voice. "Sit, sit."

Both Fletchers were in the gaudy chairs the detectives had occupied, so the only option for me was the uncomfortable, shallow sofa. Spidery fingers of unease traced themselves up my spine as I faced them, just as I'd faced the police.

I wished Lou was with me. Where *was* he?

"Dr. Stern no longer works for the gallery," Henry said, as though he'd read my mind.

"What?" The room contracted for a moment, as it had done when the detectives had told us about Inga's murder. I gripped the edge of the sofa's seat.

"Henry," Sloane snapped. She looked at her father furiously. Her long blond hair, perfectly smooth as opposed to my wild mane, was pulled into an immaculate ponytail. "I'm sorry, Chloe. That was a very insensitive way to tell you."

"What happened? Is he okay?" I looked around the lavish room again. Was this only a place to receive bad news, the worst news?

"He's fine," Sloane said, after exchanging a glance with Henry. "As far as we know. It was a mutual parting of the ways. I'm afraid we can't say more, for legal reasons."

I heard the words, but they didn't make sense, even once I felt a little more in control of myself. I kept wanting to protest as Sloane spoke, to interrupt and insist there had been a mistake, that I'd just seen Lou four days ago and he hadn't hinted that he might not be here today, hadn't said a word.

"We have a question for you, Chloe," Henry said, leaning forward in his seat with intent. My attention snapped back to the room.

"Our question is very serious," Sloane continued. She paused, and anticipation built inside my chest.

Was I about to get fired too?

"Can you take over the Inga Beck exhibition?"

My mouth dropped open. They wanted *me* to curate the show?

"We have seen Lou's files, and the show seems to be mostly complete," Henry said, leaning back again and crossing his legs comfortably. "The checklist is set, the essay mostly finished—Sloane can tie up any loose ends there, if you like—and the entries you were working on are about wrapped up, isn't that right?" He peered at me through his tortoiseshell glasses. "Douglas can take over arranging the transport, and we'll help you with placement of the works in the SoHo space. Really, the editing of the catalogue is most of what's left."

"But you'll still get the credit," Sloane interrupted. "The show will be in your name."

"And of course," Henry continued, "the added responsibilities come with a considerable bump in pay."

They both fixed me with intense looks, and the hairs on my arms prickled.

The realization hit: This was a bribe. As they both said, the show was mostly complete and ready to go, and the few odds and ends left to sort could easily have been managed by Douglas, Sebastian, and Sloane. There really wasn't much for me to do at this point, that's why Lou had had me working on the Monet instead.

"So, will you take over, Chloe? I do hope you will." Henry flashed his bright smile at me, sending the full force of his charm in my direction.

"Of c-course," I said, stammering a little. What the hell else could I say? Relief lit both their faces, wreathing them with smiles.

My returning smile felt wooden. I was still too stunned by the last ten minutes to fully process what had happened.

What was the bribe *for*? What did they want from me?

Only one answer came to mind: to not question the circumstances around Lou's sudden departure too closely.

My mouth suddenly went dry.

"Wonderful." Sloane beamed at me. "Douglas should be in by now; let's go see him together and make sure he's up to speed on the changes."

Douglas's office was as tiny as the one I shared—or had shared, I guess—with Lou, adjacent to a much larger workspace where he could package works for transport, which itself led into an art storage area for smaller paintings and works on paper.

Sloane explained that I would be taking over the Inga Beck exhibition, and the two talked logistics of transporting the works to the SoHo space for a few minutes before Sloane left, leaving Douglas and me alone.

Douglas had been at the gallery a long time, longer than Lou even, and, like many preparators, was a working artist himself. As he rarely interacted with clients, he always dressed casually, in neat plaid flannel shirts tucked into jeans, and between that and his full beard, he looked more like a lumberjack in his Sunday best than an artist. He was friendly enough, but mostly kept to himself.

He tilted his head at me now, rolling his broad shoulders once. "Big opportunity for you."

"Jeez, Douglas, what the hell happened with Lou?" I hissed, mindful that Sloane might still be within earshot. "Do you have any idea? I just had Thanksgiving with him last week."

Douglas pursed his lips and considered me, as if trying to decide how much to say. "Sloane told me it was mutual," he finally said. "I got a call from her last night, giving me a heads-up."

"Nobody called me," I said, mildly offended. As Lou's assistant, shouldn't I have been told in advance too? "I found out a couple minutes ago. I haven't even had a chance to talk to Lou yet. I'm going to try him now."

"If you catch him, tell him I'm sorry. I think he's getting a raw deal."

"What does that mean? How can it be a raw deal, if it was mutual?"

Douglas leaned forward and glanced down the hallway, checking that it was clear, before settling back in his seat. "Lou may not have liked whatever options were presented to him is all I'm saying. So maybe he chose to leave instead. I could see *them* framing that as 'mutual.'"

Them again. The Fletchers.

I glanced down the hallway too. The prickling that started on my arms was radiating across my body.

Douglas held up his hands. "But, hey, that's just a guess, based on what I know about everyone involved. Maybe Lou asked for a raise and they didn't want to give it, is all. I don't really know anything."

The disquiet I felt grew as I returned to my office and again took in the shiny, rarely seen surface of Lou's desk. There was no way I was going to sit there.

I fired up my own computer but stared blankly at the screen as it warmed up. I had to talk to Lou, find out what had happened. I snatched up the phone and tried his home number.

Nothing. It just rang and rang.

I waited for the machine to pick up, as it had done over the weekend when I'd called, as it always did.

But not this time. The phone just kept ringing.

I finally hung up and tried his cell phone.

It didn't even ring. A disembodied, robotic-sounding voice immediately came on the line.

We're sorry, the number you are trying to reach has been disconnected . . .

I hung up and tried again.

We're sorry, the number you are . . .

I slammed down the receiver.

The basement office was cold as always, but my blouse dampened under my arms.

I didn't even know if Debra had a cell phone, let alone what her number might be. I didn't know who I could ask.

I chewed on my bottom lip. There had to be a reasonable explanation for all this. Maybe, if he wasn't working full-time anymore, Lou had had his cell disconnected to avoid the additional expense. Maybe they'd disconnected the home machine to have some quiet and had forgotten to reconnect it.

Neither of these scenarios seemed very plausible.

I opened my gallery email and tried to send a message to Lou's AOL account, as I figured his gallery account wouldn't work.

It instantly bounced back.

What the fuck?

There was only one thing left to do. I couldn't sit around the gallery all day, waiting for Lou to reach out. It would drive me insane, and I wouldn't get any work done anyway, not until I knew what had happened. I had to find him at home. If something shady was going on here, something Lou had big enough concerns to quit over, then maybe I should find another job too.

I packed up my bag, told Carmen on my way out the door I was heading to the library for last-minute research relating to Inga's show, and if anyone was looking for me, I'd be back tomorrow. She nodded in a distracted way, and then I was on the street, trying not to break into a run, calculating the fastest way to Red Hook, my breath coming in hard, fast pants.

It took just over an hour to get there. The trains were on my side today, and as it wasn't a holiday, I caught the B61 bus pretty quickly. It all felt like a good omen. Like the city was urging me forward, wanting me to get to Lou's as quickly as possible.

Once I reached the cobblestones of Beard Street, I did break into a run. The late November wind pressed against my back. I slowed the last few steps as I approached Lou's house, breath labored.

It was broad daylight, the sky an overcast, milky white, but Lou's street felt as deserted and empty as it had at midnight on Thanksgiving. I had been the only person on the nearly empty bus getting off at Beard Street, and we'd barely passed any cars and fewer pedestrians since heading this deep into the neighborhood, so close to the water. The flags along the street flapped with a mournful, eerie noise.

I rang the bell and waited, my heart in my throat.

"Come on, Lou, come on," I whispered under my breath. *Please open the door.* Or Debra. *Someone, please, answer me.*

I rang twice more and knocked loudly. I didn't care if I was being rude, interrupting their private life.

Panic was rising in my throat, lazily at first, but becoming more insistent with each unanswered knock.

They're just not home, I tried to tell myself. They went to breakfast, or grocery shopping. *Calm down, Chloe.*

But I couldn't calm down.

I bit my lip again and winced, tasting blood for the second time today. I'd chewed a spot on the inside of my mouth raw and tender.

Nobody was coming up the street. I took three steps to the right, standing in front of their living room window. There were bars, so I couldn't press my face against the glass like I wanted, and instead leaned my head as far in between two of the bars as I could, the cold metal scraping my cheekbones.

What I saw took my breath away.

The space wasn't entirely empty, but it wasn't the same living room I had drunk wine and listened to jazz in just four nights ago.

A few books listed sadly on the tall, wide bookshelf directly across from the window. On Thursday they had been crammed into the shelves, squeezed together so tightly some had to be stacked perpendicularly on their ranks. There had been knickknacks, trinkets, and artifacts from Lou's and Debra's life scattered there too. Now long, empty stretches gaped at me, like a mouth missing most of its teeth. The mismatched but stylish vintage furniture was mostly gone, though one end table lay on its side in a corner. A bar pressed harder against my left cheek as I twisted my face in that direction, trying to see more of the room. I could just make out a painting still hanging on the far wall, which I knew to be one of Debra's, but otherwise the walls were bare.

My face stung from where I'd squashed it against the rusty bars. I idly wiped at the spots with my gloved hands as I crossed to the other front window, the one that looked into the kitchen, but the miniblinds were closed tightly and I couldn't see in.

The need to sit was overwhelming, and I gave in, plunking down on the second step of the front stoop.

I couldn't deny it or make any more excuses.

Lou wasn't just gone from the gallery.

He was gone from his home. Probably from the city, his whole life.

Why? What the fuck had happened?

A headache was beginning to press at my temples. I looked up and down the street again, hopelessness now fighting with the panic that was starting to consume me. A lone man sauntered down the street on the opposite sidewalk, face turned to the sky as if he didn't feel the cold at all, head moving in time to whatever was coming through his headphones. He didn't look my way.

I sat on the stoop for a long time, long enough that the cold of the stone steps seeped through my coat, my skirt, and tights, chilling the backs of my thighs and my rear to ice. I thought about the shadowy figure of the man calling to Lou as I was being driven away Thanksgiving night, and Lou turning. I remembered the shape of his silhouetted back under the weak streetlight as the town car I was in had turned the corner.

"Who was that, Lou? Where are you?" I whispered to the empty street.

A violent chill shook through me, first one, followed by another. The tremors continued as I slowly put my bag back over my shoulder and stood. It was time to go; I was risking frostbite if I stayed out much longer.

I walked toward the bus stop, the weak sun at my back.

First Inga was murdered. Now Lou had disappeared. The note in my pocket. *Help me* hidden in the painting.

There was no discernible connection between these events, but for whatever reason deep in my bones, I knew each had something to do with the other, that they were part of a web I could feel, but couldn't see.

A bus rumbled to the curb. I climbed on, grateful for the blast of hot air that greeted me in its interior.

The Fletchers would hire another curator soon. Someone more qualified than me, someone with a PhD. In the meantime, in my new position, I had access to the gallery's records, to files.

To Inga's paintings in the warehouse.

I'll figure it out, Lou, I promised silently. *I'll figure out what the hell is happening.*

CHAPTER TWELVE

"How complicated is it to see Inga's paintings in person, at the warehouse?"

I'd found Douglas in the kitchen, stirring cream into a mug of coffee. Willa was washing out a mug at the sink. She shot me a dirty look before resuming her task.

It was hard not to flinch.

We were a small staff at the gallery, and over the past two days it had become obvious that some of my coworkers seemed to blame *me* for Lou's departure. Or they seemed to think that because I was temporarily taking his place, I was happy about it.

Nothing could be further from the truth. I'd spent the past twenty-four hours racking my brain, trying to slot the pieces of Lou's disappearance into a shape that made sense.

It was fruitless. I could think of a few reasons why Lou would quit—or be fired—so abruptly, but none as to why he would pack up his worldly possessions and just disappear.

None that amounted to anything good, that is.

Mostly, I hoped he and Debra, wherever they were, were okay.

I did flinch as Willa brushed past me on her way out of the kitchen, pointedly not looking my way. Her coldness to me the other day was clear now. She'd already known Lou was gone.

"Not very," Douglas said, answering my question. He put his spoon in the sink. "I can call over there and see when they can do it. Did you have a particular day in mind?"

"As soon as possible, I guess," I said, surprised at how easy it sounded. "And then what, I just take the train out there?" I hadn't been to the warehouse yet.

Douglas pulled a face. "No, you'll take a car on the gallery's account."

Right. I wasn't used to being the one in charge, and the perks that came with it—like the warehouse pulling paintings at my immediate request, cars paid for by the gallery.

I stepped out of the kitchen, surprised to find Henry and Sloane filling the narrow hallway. Sloane was whispering furiously in her father's ear but stopped as soon as she saw me. An awkward silence followed.

"Chloe," Henry said with a tight smile. "I didn't know you were in there."

"Just making arrangements to go to the warehouse, see Inga's paintings."

Sloane gave an exaggerated expression of approval, as though I was a kindergartner who had colored inside the lines. "That is a *fantastic* idea, Chloe. Good thinking."

We stood awkwardly in the hallway for another few beats. I couldn't get past them unless they stood single file, and they didn't seem willing to move.

"Um, I'm heading . . ." I pointed down the hall.

Sloane stepped in front of her father to let me pass. The small space felt oddly tense as I squeezed by them. Were they afraid I'd overheard their whispers? I hadn't, but it did make me wonder.

What didn't the Fletchers want me to know?

My next stop was Sebastian for Inga's official file. As registrar, Sebastian kept track of all the artwork the gallery owned, maintaining the records for each piece. As the curator now, I had one filled with research, of course, but his file would include things relating to the business side of the gallery's relationship with the artist. I hoped it would have a sample of her handwriting, so I could compare it to the note I'd found in my coat pocket.

"Whatever you need, *boss*," Sebastian said as he swiveled in his chair to get the file, his voice full of venom. Behind his rectangular-framed glasses, his blue eyes shot daggers at me too. I could smell the gel he used to coax his close-cropped brown hair into gentle spikes.

"Sebastian," said Olive, from the next desk, in a warning tone. As the gallery's accountant, she didn't have access to anything that would help me, but I appreciated her support all the same.

"What? She's the new Lou, so she outranks us both."

"Just for now," I said, attempting a smile, hoping to lighten the atmosphere.

"Yes, for now," he agreed, a brittle smile cracking on his narrow face. "I'm sure they'll start looking for a real curator soon."

Olive sent Sebastian an admonishing glance before offering me a reassuring look. "You'll do a great job, Chloe. You've got this." Olive was a busty, motherly woman, with a cloud of springy curls on her head and two preschool-aged kids at home in New Jersey.

"I'm sure you do," Sebastian agreed with a smirk. There was a nasty glint in his eye as he handed the file, retrieved from one of the drawers in the large cabinet next to him, over to me. I grabbed it and pulled, but he held on for a second too long. "You know where to turn if you need any help. I do have my master's degree, after all." His tone was condescending.

I'd had enough of his bullshit. "Thanks," I said. "But the Fletchers put *me* in charge."

Olive *tsk*ed at both of us, frowning.

I shot her an apologetic look on my way out of their office, slightly chastened. I couldn't really blame Sebastian for being pissy that I'd taken over for Lou. He was right: He did have more education and experience and had worked at the gallery for far longer. On paper, he was the more logical choice.

Another reason that their tapping me to finish out this exhibition—and giving me a huge boost in my career, should I decide to stay in the art world—had to have an ulterior motive.

I paused at my desk, file in hand. It wasn't terribly thick, but its contents felt loaded.

Did they want me to fail, to fuck up something with the show? Was that why they'd given me the job?

I shook off the thought. Speculation wouldn't get me anywhere. I needed answers, hard facts.

Pushing the office door mostly shut, I opened the file.

Inga stared back at me.

The front of the file was all press clippings, pulled from the recent surge of attention she'd gotten, first for her warehouse show, then for her murder.

It was a good picture of her. Inga had that casual blond elegance the camera loved. I doubted any photos existed of her making a stupid face, eyes half closed or mouth open at an awkward angle. In this one, she stared intently at the camera, paintbrushes clutched in one fist, the other hand resting on her hip.

I stared back at her, wishing she would divulge her secrets.

The photograph was cut from a newspaper, the Arts section of *The Village Voice*, I saw, stapled to the rest of an article that must have been on the following page. I skimmed its contents. It was a well-written piece, though mostly a rehashing of what had already been said in *Artforum*, but covering her death also, the overall tone more laudatory than salacious, which I appreciated. I moved it aside.

The next clipping was the *Artforum* article, the cover image, the one that featured *Careless*, attached to the rest of the article with a paper clip.

I devoured the picture of *Careless*.

Were words hidden in there too? What would they say? It was impossible to tell from the photograph in the magazine; it was far too small an image to pick out any letters or words as tiny as the ones I'd found in *Helpless*.

Careless was the one painting from the "Less Than" series not in the gallery's possession, because it had sold from Inga's warehouse show. I stroked the image with one finger, the glossy surface of the magazine slick to my touch. Who had bought it? It was sold prior to the Fletchers' representation of Inga, so there may not be a record of the sale in the file.

But maybe there was. And maybe whoever bought *Careless* would let me come see it, if they lived in the Tri-State area.

I quickly flipped through a few more articles, eager to get to the more official-looking paperwork I could see poking out from under the clippings at the bottom of the file.

Another photograph snagged my attention before I reached the end of the thin pile.

It was a skinny image that had obviously been cut down, on paper that was thicker and rougher than the smooth pages of *Artforum*. In it, Inga looked slender and graceful as a lily, nearly ethereal in a column-shaped, pale pink dress adorned with gauzy matching flowers. It wasn't a posed shot; the camera had caught her just as she turned her head, a glowing smile on her face.

I released the picture from underneath the paper clip and took a closer look. The right edge of the photograph had been cut. It neatly followed the lines of Inga's body around her shoulder and arm, down her side and leg.

It looked as though something was in her hand. I held the photograph under my desk lamp to illuminate it, staring hard.

The thing in her hand was someone else's hand.

Whoever she had been with in this photograph, whoever's hand she was holding, had been carefully cut away.

Some of the caption remained under the cut image. *Artist Inga Beck and—* The rest of the sentence was cut out, in the missing half of the photograph, but partially resumed underneath—*Beswick Gallery, openi.*

The article the image was attached to detailed the opening of a new gallery in DUMBO, one that specialized in performance art. It wasn't from a publication I recognized. I found its website, and it looked more like a zine than a proper glossy art magazine, one that focused on the burgeoning gallery scene in the outer boroughs.

I sat back in my chair, looking at the image. At Inga's radiant face, clearly shining her megawatt smile on the person whose hand she was holding. I didn't know much about Inga's personal life. She wasn't married, and no one—not her sister or Lou or the Fletchers—had ever mentioned a boyfriend or partner. Not at the memorial service, or any time since her death.

Once again, I tried to call up memories from the night of the party. Had Inga seemed interested in anyone that night?

The same frustrating loop of sights and sensations played in my head. Sloane at the door, Vik and Ben laughing, Lou looking at *Helpless* in wonder.

Inga's arm around my neck, her breath on my cheek. A haze of laughter, smoke, the scent of beer, the rasp of the shower curtain bathroom door moving on its bar.

I yanked myself back to the present and looked closer: the cuff of a white shirt, the end of a jacket sleeve.

A man's hand.

The date from the piece revealed the picture had been taken after Inga's warehouse show, but before she had signed with the gallery. She had been gaining enough fame, especially in the art world, for her presence to merit a mention in a publication, even in what seemed like an obscure one.

Beswick Gallery. I'd never heard of it. Curious, I returned to my computer. The gallery's website listed the limited roster of artists it represented, and I'd never heard of any of them either. But I didn't know anything about performance art.

I clicked on the events tab and scrolled down until I found the date listed on the article, from last spring. Sure enough, there was a write-up about the opening, which was also the space's inaugural show, with pictures. The same picture from the magazine was on the website, but this one wasn't cropped as closely. The arm of the person whose hand Inga was holding was fully visible, as was part of their side.

It was definitely a man, a man in a suit.

The caption read, *Artist Inga Beck and guest, copyright Steven Schmidt, 2001, Beswick Gallery grand opening.*

Steven Schmidt must be the photographer.

I put the image aside with reluctance.

Pushing aside a few other articles, all of which I'd already seen during my research for the show, I pulled out the more official-looking papers I'd spied earlier.

First was a bill of sale. It wasn't on the gallery's letterhead, or any letterhead. It was a simple, typed-up document, confirming the sale of *Careless* to a company called Dunbar Capital.

A corporate entity, instead of an individual? Interesting.

I tried to find Dunbar Capital on the internet.

Nothing.

I felt a frown pucker my forehead. Lots of collectors created corporations to purchase their art, some kind of tax shelter. But I wished I could figure out who the real buyer was.

I flipped the page of the bill of sale, and there, toward the bottom of the page, was a line listed "Seller."

I could tell now the bill was a photocopy, the ink of the signatures translated into a matte, muted black. The buyer's name, whoever was behind Dunbar Capital, was completely illegible, a tangle of slashing marks I could not unravel.

But not Inga. As the seller, she had scrawled her name across that bottom line, a large, proud, looping *I*, followed by smaller but legible letters spelling the rest of her name.

My fingers felt icy as I scrabbled in my pocket for the note. I finally plucked it out and smoothed it over the desk. The enigmatic address was first, followed by the scrawl of her signature.

17816 107th Ave Jamaica Queens
Inga

The handwriting was a match.

I carefully laid the two on my desk, keeping the note lined up next to the signature on the bill of sale, my hands now shaking.

Inga's contract with the gallery was the last document in the file, a much thicker and more legal-looking set of pages than her makeshift bill of sale for *Careless*. It was on many pages of thick, creamy gallery letterhead, an original and a copy. I turned to the final page, where the signatures would be.

Henry had signed on behalf of the gallery, his name neatly typed under the appropriate line.

Inga's signature here was the exact same as the other two.

I looked at the address on the note again. *Jamaica Queens.*

The *J* in Jamaica was bold, nearly identical to the capital *I* in Inga. The lowercase *a*'s and *n*'s were the same.

My breath quickened.

Inga had written the note in my coat pocket.

But had she put it there? Had she slipped it in during the party on the night she was murdered, in the stretch of time I couldn't recall? As I had been doing . . . what? Using the bathroom? (Had I used the bathroom? Logic said probably, but I had no recollection of doing so.) Laughing with Vik and Ben? Cozied up with some guy I didn't remember?

Or had someone else placed the note in my pocket? Was someone watching me, tracking my movements, biding their time? And why?

The familiar feeling of encroaching panic began to encircle my rib cage. I closed my eyes and made myself take long, deep breaths.

Inhale, exhale.

It worked, enough. My heart stopped racing, and the feeling that the walls were closing in receded.

When I felt able, I opened my eyes and stared at the three signatures again.

Someone, dead or alive, was trying to tell me something. Someone wanted me to visit a desolate part of Queens, and maybe invoke Inga's name.

The question was, would I do it?

CHAPTER THIRTEEN

My key made a comforting *snick* in the lock as it connected. I'd come straight home tonight, even though the twinkling lights of Rosemary's—she had switched the paper turkeys out for leering elves and Christmas lights—beckoned. I was somehow exhausted from the events of the day, even though I hadn't done much except pore over Inga's file and chase down errors in the footnotes of Lou's essay.

Groucho wove himself around my legs, mewing accusingly. I reached down to stroke his soft head. I had decided on the subway that it was a good night for a container of take-out pad thai and a bottle or two of Rolling Rock from the emergency stash we kept in one of the crisper drawers in the fridge. *The West Wing* was on tonight, and Vik and I generally had a standing date to watch it together, though I had no idea if he was coming home.

I perused the local Thai place's stained take-out menu as I crossed the living room to my bedroom. Maybe I needed an order of spring rolls too. It was a lot of food, but the leftovers could be my lunch tomorrow. Vik usually paid for our take-out nights, but I was making more now as curator and could afford to buy myself dinner.

My internal rambling screeched to a halt as I stepped into my room and flicked on the overhead light.

Someone had been in here.

The menu fluttered from my hand to the floor. I slowly stooped to pick it up, ignoring Groucho, who protested at this lack of attention.

The changes were subtle, things that would be unnoticeable to anyone but me.

The pile of books near my bed was out of order. I knew the battered copy of *Infinite Jest*, one I'd gotten half price at the Strand, was always second from the top, even though it was bigger than some of the others and made the stack precarious. I kept it there, near the top, as a reminder to finish the damn thing, though I'd tried to for over two years and never made it farther than page 153.

But now it was on the bottom of the pile.

That wasn't it. *A Heartbreaking Work of Staggering Genius*, which Penny had loaned me and I was enjoying, hadn't been in the pile this morning at all. I'd read a few pages in bed before forcing myself to get up and shower, and I had left it next to the pile, not on top, where it was now.

I turned a slow circle, seeing other, tiny shifts in my space.

The magazines on the desk were too close to its edge.

The three bottles of perfume on the vintage tray on my dresser were slightly out of order. I always had the Chanel No. 5 on the far right, Clinique's Happy in the middle, and the Bath and Body Works Freesia next. Now the Chanel was in the center.

Fingers of fear crept up my spine.

I opened the top drawer of my dresser, swallowing hard. It was more difficult to tell if anything was amiss here, as the contents were always such a jumble. I had no idea if this drawer, which contained my underwear and socks, had been subject to someone's rooting hands.

The closet.

The fingers turned to palm prints, pressing up my back and onto my neck, until I shook myself physically so hard my foot grazed Groucho's tail. He gave one loud, protesting meow as he shot from the room like a marmalade-colored rocket.

Was someone in there, making themselves small in the cramped space, hiding behind my haphazardly hung dresses and piles of thrift store sweaters?

Or . . . did someone know what I had in there? Had someone broken in, rooted and rooted, until they found the box under the plastic bags that held my ruined dress?

I grabbed my cheap desk lamp, yanking the cord from its plug. It wasn't much of a weapon, but it was better than nothing.

Bracing myself, I flung open the closet door and lifted the lamp over my head, gasping in fear.

The closet was empty.

I dropped the lamp and fell to my knees. The box looked untouched, but I wouldn't know, couldn't know, until I saw for myself that its contents were undisturbed.

Sitting on my bedroom floor, I shoved the bags aside and pulled the box onto my lap, where I slowly, carefully opened the lid. I lifted the cream-colored, hinged mat and placed the thin sheet of protective glassine to one side.

The delicate charcoal drawing was exactly as I'd left it the last time I performed this ritual. I held my breath, my heart in my throat, as my finger hovered just above the smudged lines that formed the image: three trees, gathered together, the limbs of the leftmost tree stretching out toward the paper's edge, almost like the bars of a jail cell.

The woods in the drawing looked dense and impenetrable. But beyond the thickly clustered trees, past the branches reaching like fingers, around the blurred and heavy charcoal, were moments where the page was blank.

Light was in that blankness.

Freedom.

I stared at the drawing, trying to find my way through the trees. Like always, time stopped. My breath slowed. A rare sense of calm washed over me.

Whoever had been here hadn't been after the drawing. It was safe.

But was *I* safe? I didn't know.

My whole body jerked as the front door slammed shut.

"Chloe?"

I hurriedly replaced the glassine over the fragile charcoal surface, put the matted drawing back in its box, and pushed the box back into the nether reaches of my closet before rushing into the living room.

Vik was lifting the messenger bag that held his laptop off his chest, duffel bag at his feet.

"Christ, Vik, you scared me."

He raised his brows. "By walking in the door?"

"Come with me." I pulled him toward my room, even as he protested he needed to take off his coat. "Were you in here? Looking for something, or, I don't know, moving stuff around?"

Vik looked at me like I was crazy. "Chloe, I just walked in the door. I stayed in Jersey a little longer than I'd planned, but came back for *West Wing* night. Why would I be in your room anyway?"

I grabbed at his arm, still in its puffer jacket. "Someone broke in. My things are not where I left them."

I was gratified to see worry flush Vik's face. "Shit," he said, looking around. "Have you checked all the windows?"

"No, I just got here."

Together, we made sure the locks on all the windows were secured, no glass was broken. The window in my bedroom was the only logical place a thief could enter, as it was the one that led to the fire escape; those in Vik's room and the living room faced the building's interior courtyard, and we were on the third floor. Still, it was reassuring to see all the locks securely latched in place.

"I'm going to check my room, see if anything's missing." Vik tossed his coat on the couch as he moved to his room.

I'd been so focused on the drawing, I hadn't even thought to see if anything in the living room was gone. Whirling around I noted the TV and CD player were still there. In my room, my computer, though hardly valuable, was still on my desk. I opened my jewelry box. The only item of any worth, a pair of antique pearl and diamond earrings that had been my dead grandmother's, was still nestled inside, jumbled up against the thrift store stuff I normally wore.

"You find anything missing?" Vik's voice floated through my open door.

"No," I said, meeting him in the living room. "You?"

"Not that I can see. My passport is there, all my CDs. My computer was with me."

I nodded, crossing my arms over my chest, even though the apartment was, as always in the winter, almost too warm.

"What do you think happened? Could Ben have come in while I was at work? He has a key, doesn't he?"

"Ben doesn't have a key." Vik looked almost affronted. "I'd never give someone a key without telling you." He paused, thinking. "My parents have a key, but that's in Jersey, and they'd only use it for emergencies. Have you given a key to anyone? What about Alex?"

Alex was a documentary filmmaker I'd dated for six months last year, until he revealed he had restarted a heroin habit he'd originally claimed was long past. The relationship, such as it was, hadn't worked for months at that point, but I had given him a key in the early, giddy days, when his sleepy bedroom eyes and lazy smile had sent my pulse racing.

Had I ever gotten the key back? I didn't think so. I'd been so pissed once I found out he was using, both at him for doing it and at myself for not noticing, that I'd stormed out of his stale-smelling room in a group house on the south side of the neighborhood and hadn't seen him since. My guess was his parents had thrust him back into rehab.

"Shit. I don't think I got it back," I admitted.

Disappointment filled Vik's face. "Damn, Chloe. He's a junkie. He could have made a copy of that key for anyone, hundreds of times over."

"Okay, okay, I'm sorry. I'll call a locksmith in the morning." My skin crawled at the thought of someone pawing through our stuff. "But are we sure it was Alex, or some other junkie? I mean, nothing is taken. The TV is still there, the stereo, all our CDs. My good earrings too. Wouldn't a junkie be after stuff to steal?"

"I can't think of any other explanation, can you? Unless maybe you're . . . I don't know, misremembering? Maybe you did stack the books that way last night." Vik looked at me carefully. "Had you been drinking?"

This was a rhetorical question, and Vik knew it. I had, of course, been drinking last night. I'd polished off most of a bottle of cheap white wine, enough that I had stumbled on my way to bed.

Doubt crept in. I looked to the open doorway of my room, wondering.

Maybe I was misremembering.

There was a lot I couldn't remember these days.

"Let's forget about it," Vik said in a reassuring tone. "If you can take care of the locks tomorrow, we'll be all set, and we won't have to worry about it any longer." He moved to take his bag into his room. "Are we getting food?"

I followed his lead and didn't bring it up again that night, tried to put the moved books and shifted magazines out of mind. The comforting feel of noodles in my mouth, the swell of music at the show's opening, and the crisp Rolling Rock all helped.

The end credits rolled for *The West Wing*, and Vik began to gather the empty beer bottles and take-out containers.

"Something else weird happened while you were gone," I ventured to say. I was more content now, full of good cheap food and beer and Vik's company, which I'd missed during the past two weeks.

"Yeah?"

I followed Vik to the kitchen as I told him about Lou, how generous and friendly he and Debra had been at Thanksgiving, what a great time I'd had, and then about how he had been fired from or quit the gallery.

"And now he's gone," I said.

Vik's brow furrowed as he rinsed the containers out in the sink. "What do you mean, gone?"

"I mean gone. He's not answering his home phone, his cell has been disconnected, his emails bounce back, and I went by his house—"

"You what? Isn't that kind of stalkerish?"

"I wanted to find out why he left the gallery. What was I supposed to do, if he wasn't answering his phone?"

"Give the poor man some peace and let him be." Vik noisily dumped the containers and bottles into the recycle bin, keeping his back to me. "So what did he say?"

"He wasn't there. Nobody was there; the place was cleared out, Vik."

Vik turned to lean against the counter and crossed his arms. "Cleared out?"

"Yeah. I looked in one of the windows . . ." I began.

"God, Chloe." Vik buried his face in his hands.

His reaction was making me, again, doubt myself. Had it really been extreme to check on Lou at his house?

I forged ahead. "The point is, it was like they'd moved. The furniture was gone."

Finally, Vik seemed to take me seriously. He nodded slowly, looking concerned. "Wow, okay. I guess something really bad happened. Like maybe Lou violated an NDA, that kind of thing." "

"Why would he sign an NDA? I haven't been asked to sign one."

"Well, you're just filling in. Lou, he might have been privy to all kinds of sensitive stuff, information about clients, prices, that kind of thing. The Fletchers said the split was for legal reasons, right?"

"Yeah," I said. "But his house, Vik."

Vik shrugged. "It's embarrassing, getting fired. Didn't you say they have a place upstate? They probably went there for a week to lick their wounds."

"Oh, right." I'd forgotten about their upstate house, hadn't really considered it. "But I think that's more like a cabin, tiny. No heat or anything, a little summer place. Like camping, he's said. And all their stuff was gone. Like they'd cleared out of town."

He shrugged again. "I don't know, Chloe. It's an unusual reaction to leave town, sure, but not totally unreasonable. Imagine it: You work at a place for a long time, you're established, and something happens where you get laid off. Maybe you'd clear out of town too. Besides, you don't really know him that well, do you?"

Frustration bubbled inside me, the same as it had in the bar when I'd tried to talk to Vik about Inga's murder. Whatever he said, it wasn't normal, Lou's moving at the drop of a hat like that.

But underneath my anger, even more uncertainty swirled, pressing the irritation aside. I thought I'd had a connection with Lou, and even Debra, especially after Thanksgiving. Thought he was a mentor, and maybe more, maybe a friend. I thought he'd cared about me. But maybe I'd been wrong.

And maybe Vik was right, and Alex had given a copy of our key out to someone. A junkie had used it to root around our apartment, but hadn't found anything easy to sneak out, no cash.

Or maybe not. The earrings were still there.

And so was the drawing.

I didn't know what to believe. It was on the tip of my tongue to tell Vik about the note, but he'd been so dismissive about my other concerns, I held back.

Just as I did about how "Help Me" was written in *Helpless*, hidden there within the brushstrokes. I had seriously considered telling Vik, had thought of enlisting his help in looking at the other paintings. He was studying to be an art conservator, after all, and probably could see all kinds of things I couldn't in the painting, or maybe tell which part had been painted first. But now I was convinced he'd say it was an inside joke on Inga's part, a little tongue-in-cheek play on words, a message to whoever took the time to look, not a plea for actual help.

And the kicker was, he might be right.

Vik finished wiping the kitchen counter off with a paper towel, balling it up and throwing it in the trash. "Look, if you're that worried, maybe you should go to the police," he said. "Report Lou missing."

As soon as he said the words, I felt ridiculous. What evidence did I have that Lou was even missing? It's not a crime to abruptly move and not tell your assistant.

Vik was right. I really didn't know Lou very well. Whatever connection I'd thought we had, I must have imagined it. I snorted a little under my breath. A shrink would have a field day with me, I was sure, imagining my boss was a kind of parental replacement for my own absent father.

Once I said good night to Vik and shut the door to my room, though, that feeling of foreboding rose again.

I looked at the misaligned pile of books, the rearranged perfumes.

I wasn't imagining things—or misremembering. Someone had been in here.

Someone had been looking for something.

CHAPTER FOURTEEN

"Hey." Douglas poked his head into my office. I shoved the picture of Inga I'd been staring at, the glossy one from the *Artforum* piece, under a pile of other papers. I'd lost track of time looking at it, my eyes drinking in the contours of her face, the line of her neck. "The warehouse staff are a little backed up. Is early next week okay?"

It wasn't ideal. I was itching to see the paintings as soon as possible, but nodded. It wasn't like I had much choice.

After Douglas left, I typed the address on the note into my search browser again. I don't know why I expected a different result or more information, but I hoped that one of these times I'd stumble across something new.

No luck. It was the same, just the location on a map showing me the address was located in Jamaica, Queens. I chewed my bottom lip, thinking. I hadn't spent much time in Queens. I knew Long Island City, where the warehouse was, was right across the river from Manhattan. But this Jamaica neighborhood was almost in Long Island, way out by Kennedy airport.

I could get there. It would take a train—either a really long subway ride, or the quicker but more expensive Long Island Rail Road—and then a bus, but I could get within fifteen blocks of the place. I'd been toying with the idea of making the trek over the weekend, but the idea filled me with dread.

If I went, I wanted to go in daylight. Walking around a neighborhood I knew nothing about after dark, to check out an address left to me by a dead woman, was out of the question. At the same time, I didn't want to be seen, which made daylight tricky. What would really be best was to go in a car, drive by whatever this was. I pictured myself in disguise, a hat and dark glasses, or maybe I could borrow that Elvira wig Penny had, slowly cruising down the street.

But I didn't have a car, nor did any of my friends. And a taxi or car service would cost a fortune, going out that far.

The real truth was, I didn't want to go at all. The thought was terrifying. I don't know what I imagined I'd find—a crack dealer's den, maybe? Thugs with guns, *Sopranos* style? Had Inga stumbled across something she shouldn't, something so dangerous it had gotten her killed?

I pondered, again, telling the police about the note. Detective Gonzales's card was pinned to the bulletin board above my desk, and I'd written her number down in the appointment book I kept in my bag. But I didn't like that idea. Maybe because it seemed the detectives were convinced I had done something wrong. I didn't want to draw any more attention to myself, and if the address was a crack dealer's den, how was I going to explain that it had wound up in my coat pocket? Would they really believe the truth, that I'd just found it there?

I slugged more of Willa's coffee and rummaged through the papers in Inga's file again. Was there something else, some other avenue I could pursue? I didn't know any of Inga's friends, so I couldn't ask them about the address. My closest connection to her was Ben, but because of his relationship with Vik, and Vik's dismissal of my fears, he was a dead end.

I picked up the photograph of Inga at the Beswick Gallery opening, the one where someone had cut out whoever she was with. An idea came to me. I found the gallery's website again and dialed their number.

"Hi, this is Chloe Harlow from Fletcher & Sons," I said when a female voice answered. "I was hoping to speak with Steven Schmidt?"

"Steven doesn't work here, he's one of the freelancers we've used. I can pass along his information, we do recommend him."

I thanked her and wrote down Steven's information.

"Yeah, this is Steven," a gruff voice answered when I dialed.

"Hi, this is Chloe Harlow from Fletcher & Sons. I was wondering—" I began, but the voice cut me off.

"I thought we were done." He sounded a little accusatory, angry even. *What the . . . ?*

"Um, not quite," I improvised, my pulse picking up. I had no idea what he was talking about, but he obviously had some previous relationship with the gallery. "Actually, we need someone to photograph our upcoming Inga Beck memorial show and wanted to talk to you about that. Could I come to you?"

There was a long silence, so long I wondered if he'd hung up. Just as I was about to speak again, a frustrated sigh came through the line.

"Sure, fine. Does two work?"

"That's perfect. Remind me where you are?"

Another silence stretched before he gave me the address, a downtown location.

At two o'clock, I rang the bell on the side of a restaurant in Chinatown with a typed, peeling label taped above it, *Steven Schmidt Photography*. A harsh buzz and a metallic click responded, letting me know the door was unlocked. The stairs were grimy, and the smells from the adjacent restaurant had permanently soaked into the walls and floors of the place, a slightly sickening miasma of old oil and spice.

I carefully pushed open the door on the third floor, which had a more professional-looking sign announcing the business. It had been left ajar, but nobody was waiting for me.

"Hello?" I called.

"Back here."

I followed the voice through a large loft studio space, lights on stands and tripods grouped on one side, huge windows letting the winter light pour in. In a back room I found a tall, rangy man with graying stubble placing unopened boxes of photographic paper on a shelf.

"Hi, I'm Chloe Harlow." I extended my hand, but he barely glanced at it, looking behind me instead.

"Just you?" His tone was cold.

"Just me."

He blew out a breath and leaned back against the counter below his supply shelves. There was a funky-looking couch and a few chairs set up around a coffee table with a thick black portfolio on it. A door on the far end of the room had a light-up sign, dark at present, reading "Darkroom In Use."

"Jesus," he said under his breath, eyeing me. "How old are you?"

I ignored the question. "I'm curating the memorial show of Inga Beck's work," I said instead, trying to establish that I had every right to request this meeting, despite my age. "You were recommended by Beswick Gallery. I'd love to see some more of your photography."

Steven gave me an incredulous look and huffed a small, disbelieving laugh, but he gestured to the portfolio. "If that's what you've gotta do," he said in a sarcastic tone. "Be my guest."

I moved to the sofa. Whatever previous relationship this photographer had with the gallery, it wasn't a good one. *Tread lightly, Chloe. You need this guy's help.*

The portfolio was filled with gorgeous photographs, page after page of shots of gallery openings, artists posed with their work, the work itself. Another thing I'd learned from working at the gallery was how hard it was to photograph art, to get the colors right, to make sure there was no glare, and that large pieces were especially difficult. Doing it well was a skill, and this was obviously Steven's specialty.

"These are great," I said, and I meant it. The pictures of openings were particularly arresting, more than typical posed event shots; somehow, he captured moments of people looking at art that made you want to look at the art too. The wonder and admiration on their faces, the instants of surprise.

"Yeah, well. Didn't think you all liked me." Steven still looked suspicious, but I could sense him softening.

"As I said, Beswick recommended you highly."

"Yeah, but after last time. Well, I appreciate the second chance." He said this as though it cost him something. "Actually, it would be great to photograph Inga's show. She was pretty perfect, you know? An unbelievable artist."

My breath caught a little. "You knew her?"

"A little." Steven moved closer, took one of the chairs across from me. He leaned over to see which page of the portfolio I was on. "We weren't super close, but we always saw each other around, at openings and stuff, you know how it is. Small world."

I didn't, not really. It wasn't my world. I was on the peripheries.

"I have to admit I was surprised she signed with you all," he said, rubbing a hand over his stubble, "but then, given what happened last spring, I guess not."

After what happened last spring? The Beswick opening Steven had photographed had taken place in May. Was that what he meant?

"I know, I know. I'm not supposed to talk about it, I get it. I signed the papers, all that." He leaned back and held up his hands. "Look, I did everything you guys asked. I figured it was okay if I mentioned it to you, but it won't happen again."

I was utterly confused. Other than admitting outright that I had no idea what he was talking about, which would expose me as the impostor I was, I wasn't sure how to get the information I needed.

I chewed the inside of my cheek for a second, then decided. "Can I see the shots from the Beswick opening?"

He instantly went rigid again, looking like he'd been slapped, and stared at me as if trying to come to some kind of decision himself.

What the fuck was happening?

"Okay," he said finally. "But just so you know up front, I kept the original. It's only in my private portfolio; I promise nobody will ever see it. I mean, I don't want to lose my shirt."

"Of course, I understand. That's fine. I just need to check something," I said in a reassuring tone, hoping I was saying the right words when I had no idea what I was talking about.

He shrugged and went to the shelves, removing a different portfolio, which he placed on the coffee table between us. Shots of people in contorted positions flipped past.

"It must be hard to photograph performance art," I said, trying for flattery again.

"Yeah, it is." There was no softening now. Steven's jaw remained clenched.

Eventually, we reached shots of the crowd, people clutching champagne flutes or the necks of beer bottles.

"Here you go," he said in a tired tone, shoving the book toward me. "I did everything you required in your little agreement; this is the only copy left. I even destroyed the negative. As *requested*."

I could pick apart what he was talking about later. Right now, I turned all my attention to the image spread before me.

It was a glossy 8 x 10 color photograph. There was Inga in her pink dress, looking more luminous in the original than in the slightly pixelated version on Beswick's website, or the grainy reproduction in the gritty magazine that was tucked into her gallery file.

Only this image wasn't cropped or cut. The full photograph showed the person she was looking at, the person she had been showering with a gaze full of love and joy, the person on the other end of the arm, holding her hand.

My heart plummeted to my stomach.

The man holding Inga's hand was Carl Fletcher.

CHAPTER FIFTEEN

My head was reeling.

Somehow, I'd made it back to the gallery, though I didn't really remember the cab ride.

I couldn't stop thinking about that picture.

Carl had lied about knowing Inga when I saw him at the funeral. And nobody at the gallery had ever mentioned anything about the two of them being an item.

I sat in front of my computer, staring at the blinking cursor, thinking through the implications of what I'd learned.

It wasn't only Carl who had lied. They all had. The Fletchers, maybe even Lou.

My hand flew to my mouth. Carl had *flirted* with me.

I had to assume the police didn't know about the relationship, or they would have brought it up when they questioned me and Lou. Wouldn't they? And the Fletchers hadn't volunteered the information.

Steven had clearly signed an NDA. Was this why Lou had left or was fired? Was this the kind of NDA Vik had meant? Maybe Lou had signed one, too, and had violated it. Maybe the Fletchers had threatened Lou with a lawsuit, like they'd obviously threatened the photographer, so he'd fled.

Any possible explanation sounded implausible in my brain, like I was nearing tinfoil-hat-wearing territory. But the facts were irrefutable.

Carl and Inga had been an item, at least back in May, when they'd been photographed at that opening. I'd never seen anyone look as besotted as Inga looked in that picture. May was one month before she had signed with Fletcher & Sons.

The relationship explained a lot about how the gallery had landed her.

Shortly after that, someone at the gallery—Henry and Sloane, certainly—had gone to great lengths to make sure the relationship was kept secret.

Had Carl and Inga still been dating when she was killed? If so, surely the police would have found evidence of it, right?

I thought about the papers in the printer Sebastian didn't want me to see. How Sloane and Henry hushed up their whispered conversation when they saw me.

What the hell was going on here?

The cursor pulsed at me.

Quickly, I typed Carl's name and "treasury department" into the browser, shooting a quick look into the hallway first to make sure it was empty.

A couple of news stories piled onto my screen, as well as the Treasury Department's website.

Carl Fletcher worked at a unit of the Treasury called the Office of Foreign Assets Control. There was nothing extraordinary here; he seemed like a regular government drone.

I shook my head at my screen and drummed my fingers on my tiny desk. It was barely big enough to hold my laptop, phone, and one open book. Lou's large, shiny desk gleamed at me emptily. I looked away from it.

Frustrated, I pushed back my desk chair. This was getting me nowhere. It was time to talk to someone who might be able to give real answers.

Two floors up, Sloane looked at me in surprise and annoyance when I appeared in her doorway.

"Chloe," she said, carefully tucking away whatever document she had been studying. "What can I do for you?"

I took a seat without being asked, followed by a deep, steeling breath.

"I know about Inga and Carl."

A flash of real surprise, and maybe even panic, zipped over Sloane's face before she smoothed it into its familiar implacable mask. A few beats passed in which I could tell she was considering whether to lie or not.

"Where did you hear about this?" she said finally, folding her hands over the file on her desk.

"Someone I met at a bar in the neighborhood," I lied. "A guy she was friends with. When he found out I worked here, he asked after Carl. I guess he thought Carl ran the gallery." I was a little impressed with myself, it was a good story.

Frustration flickered across her face, there and gone in an instant. Sloane took a deep breath of her own.

"Look, Chloe, I'm relying on your discretion here. My uncle is happily married, a father of two. He confessed the whole thing to his wife, and she's forgiven him. He has a very sensitive position in the Treasury Department, especially right now. It would be embarrassing for everyone involved if this information became public."

Embarrassing for you, I thought. And Carl. Maybe even of interest to the police.

"Of course," I said. "I don't have anyone to tell. But as I'm in charge of the show now, I want to be prepared in case I get a question about this."

"You won't." Sloane's voice was sharp. "My uncle's affair with Inga was a mistake, they both agreed on that. It was very short-lived. But now, with her unfortunate death, all the more reason we want to keep it quiet. I wouldn't want anyone to get the wrong impression." Now her tone had turned careful, slightly probing.

So the police don't know. I wondered how much the Fletchers had paid Steven to suppress his photograph. Thinking of the auction, and of those improbable-sounding dollar amounts flying around the room so casually, I bet it was quite a lot.

"Yes. I understand, don't worry."

"Good." Sloane plastered on a brittle smile. I could tell, underneath her confidential, reassuring demeanor, she didn't like that I possessed this knowledge.

No, more than that. She was *furious* about it.

"Henry and I feel very lucky to have you on our team, Chloe. I think you're going to make a big difference here."

The weekend passed in a blur of alcohol and late nights, followed by later mornings. On Sunday, the morning after Penny and Calvin's early holiday slash unofficial engagement party, I didn't pull myself out of bed until two in the afternoon and spent what remained of the day on the couch nursing a vicious hangover, only making it as far as the bodega on the corner to get myself a two-liter of Coke. The thought of coffee made my stomach turn over, but I needed the caffeine.

It had been a pretty crazy night. Calvin and Penny lived in an old bar near the river, and they were determined to honor the location's past by throwing parties as raucous as they could. Like any good dive bar, the now-apartment was dark and smoke-filled, with a long wooden bar running its length, and alcohol flowed freely. I didn't remember a whole lot of the night, but it felt more like regular I-drank-too-much memory loss than the other black pockets of time that sometimes happened to me, those terrifying holes in my mind where, try as I might to remember a moment in time, only darkness answered.

I did remember what I'd had to drink, exactly why my head felt like an anvil was hammering away at it and my stomach was ready to dispel the first glass of Coke if I moved the wrong way: beer, far too much of it, followed by shots of Wild Turkey at the bar.

I also remembered Bo pressing against me, already hard in his jeans, his whisper to follow him to the bathroom.

I remembered how I pushed him away, stumbling past him to join Lisel on the couch across the room.

I remembered the look of anger on his face before he flipped back his hair, thrust his hands in his pockets, and casually strolled to the opposite side of the apartment.

By Monday morning, I wasn't 100 percent, exactly, but well enough to get through the day without my stomach turning on me. I looked like shit, though, and I knew it: dark circles under my eyes, my skin yellowed and dried out. I had managed to wash my hair on Sunday night, so at least I didn't smell like the party anymore.

I was scheduled to meet with Ryan Crandall at the warehouse in Long Island City. Ryan, the art handler Fletcher & Sons worked with there, was expecting me. Douglas had prepped me on Friday and promised Ryan would have the works ready and would get me anything else I needed.

"Hi there, Chloe," Ryan said to me now as he ambled out from a security door behind the front desk in the chrome-accented, modern lobby. He was a short, heavyset Black man with powerfully muscled arms and a head of dreadlocks that reached just past his shoulders. "Come on back."

I followed Ryan through the security door and into a maze of hallways that ended in an elevator, where we rode up one flight. He used a key card to buzz us into another space, and I gasped.

We stood on a balcony inside an enormous warehouse, surely as big as an aircraft hangar. It was lined floor to ceiling with crates of varying sizes. It went on so far, I couldn't see the other end of it.

"Oh my god."

"Go ahead." Ryan grinned. "Say it. Everybody does."

"It looks just like the closing scene of *Raiders of the Lost Ark*."

"Damn right it does."

"I had no idea it was this big in here. You cannot tell from the outside."

"Yup. We stretch two full city blocks. This area is a mix of works we store for galleries, museums, and private owners. Fletcher & Sons has its own space, I'll take you there."

I followed him again down the long balcony space, past rows that branched off with shelves covered by long, heavy pieces of archival drapery or metal cabinets. I itched to know what was hiding inside.

Eventually we reached another security door on our left, and Ryan buzzed us through. We walked down an interior corridor with doors about every thirty feet. He finally stopped in front of one marked 210 and opened the door. "This is you."

It was a large, utilitarian storage space, absolutely spotless, lined on one side with hanging metal racks that could be pulled outward. I could see canvases of different sizes hanging on them. The climate- and humidity-controlled space was safe for the art, and I'd been surprised when Lou had explained that there was less potential for damage if the works were stored this way.

Lou. It was December now, and still no word. Where could they be? Why hadn't he gotten in touch yet?

I forced myself to shove thoughts of Lou away. I had to focus on what was in front of me.

Inga's paintings. One was leaning against the outer edge of the racks, another on the blank wall opposite. A third was leaning against the wall that held the door we'd come through. All three were up on foam blocks.

I knew the pieces by sight but had never seen them in person.

Loveless. Hopeless. Fearless.

"Do you need a restroom before I go?" Ryan asked. At my head shake, he continued. "I'll leave you to it. The door will automatically lock behind you, so if you need anything, press that call button by the door and I'll come. You won't be able to get through the doors without a key."

"I should be fine. I'll call you when I'm ready."

"By pressing that button, remember. Cell phones don't work in here."

"I haven't got a phone anyway."

"Keeping it real, huh?" He threw a wink at me as he walked out the door.

I smiled into the now empty space. It was always fun when a cute guy flirted.

Ryan had placed a folding metal chair in the middle of the room facing *Loveless*, so I decided to start there. I pulled the chair closer, took a seat, and let myself get lost in the churning, hypnotic swirls of color. *Loveless* was all pinks and purples, sardonic valentine colors in a painting about the lack of love.

I followed the lines with my eyes, tilting my head this way and that, for what felt like hours. When I finally found what I'd been looking for, I had to remind myself to breathe. That I was safe in a secure, locked building.

I checked my watch. Twenty minutes had passed.

I repeated the act with *Fearless*. This painting was predominately bright red, the bursting, boastful tone associated with bravado. There were bright blue streaks interspersed, but the work was saved from feeling overly patriotic by an underpainting the color of bile, as though betraying the real insecurity that lurked under false flag-waving.

I was starting to get a feel for how Inga thought now. I was learning which lines of paint to follow, how she'd hidden her messages like a trail of oil-based breadcrumbs embedded into the canvas.

This time I found it in under twenty minutes.

I had just moved the chair in front of *Hopeless* when the door buzzed, making me jump.

Ryan poked his head in. "You doing okay still, Chloe?"

I managed a smile. "I'm good. Thanks for checking."

"Okay. You know what to do when you're ready, but take your time. I'm here all day."

The knowledge of his presence, out there in those empty, endless corridors, somewhere in that huge warehouse, was a relief.

It was creepy, tracing a murdered woman's thoughts.

"One more, Chlo. You got this," I whispered to myself as I settled in front of *Hopeless*. This was my least favorite painting in the series, but not because it wasn't good. It was brilliant. That was the problem, it captured the feeling of hopelessness almost too well.

Hopeless consisted of languid strokes of dour green, puce, and gray, swirled with sickly looking yellows. The whole painting was reminiscent of a bruise, of the hollowed-out, nauseous feeling of knowing there were no more options, that all hope was gone.

This message took longer to find, the paint itself seemed heavier somehow, applied more thickly maybe. When I did find it, it was nearly illegible, but it was there.

I wrote it down on the pad on my lap, then physically picked up the chair and turned it away, so I was facing the shorter, empty back wall of the space.

My eyes needed a break.

The pad had only three lines written on it. I studied them, forcing myself to breathe slowly, even though fear was creeping its way up my spine and down my limbs.

Loveless: Carl

Fearless: Afraid

Hopeless: Too late

The door clicked again, and I turned, ready to tell Ryan that I needed a minute to pack up but otherwise was ready to go.

A man walked through the door, letting it close behind him.

It wasn't Ryan.

CHAPTER SIXTEEN

"Hi, Chloe. I'm sorry if I startled you." Carl Fletcher's smile was still sharklike, all teeth in his handsome, craggy face.

The fear that had been slowly moving through my veins began to rush, erupting into my limbs, filling every inch of me. "What are you doing here?" It was hard to get the words out, my mouth was suddenly so dry.

"Sloane told me you'd be here, gave me her key." He held up the piece of white plastic.

I frowned at the card. I hadn't thought anyone had their own key, for security reasons. I thought everyone had to be escorted anywhere in the facility.

"I'm sorry if this seems like an ambush," he said. *Seems?* I wanted to yell. *What else would you call it?* "But I wanted a chance to talk in person."

"I thought you lived in DC." My voice sounded frail and distant. At some point I'd stood up, and I now grabbed the back of the metal chair with one hand to steady myself. In my other hand I clutched the pad of paper, the one with his name written on it, for dear life.

"I come and go a lot," he said, still showing me his teeth. "The shuttle is very quick. But listen, Chloe. I'm sorry I lied about Inga. You understand now why I couldn't tell the truth."

"Sure," I said. God, why did I have to sound so wimpy? I made my voice stronger. "Of course, I do."

Carl moved into the room. Only three steps, but they turned my insides to ice. All I could think of was how he had a key and I didn't. That even if I could get past him somehow, rush out the door, there was nowhere for me to go. I would be trapped in that hallway.

I eyed the button next to the door. How could I get closer to it without raising his suspicions?

"Inga was such a bright spirit," he said. "We were all devastated by her loss. Even though our relationship ended months ago, I mourned her, Chloe. I still do."

He advanced another few steps. I retreated behind the chair, keeping it between us. I was past caring how it looked. I felt better with the chair, flimsy as it was, in front of me.

"Okay," I said. "I understand." I could feel my breath shortening, coming in fast little pants.

Come on, Chloe. Inhale, exhale. You can do it.

"She was so full of life," Carl said, placing his hands on the chair back and leaning into it. I backed up another step. "You remind me of her."

"Me?" Confusion cut through my wariness, the panic attack that was encroaching.

What did he mean? I was nothing like Inga.

"Yes, you. There's an energy about you, a passion. Frankly, it's intoxicating."

I didn't want this, I didn't want any of this. Another moment of fear, of panic and claustrophobia, began to overlay with the present one. A moment of screaming and the sky filled with dirty dust and the sickening sound of bodies hitting pavement.

I began to shake.

It's probably nothing. You can go now.

"Chloe?" Amused concern laced Carl's face. He stepped around the chair toward me. I was frozen, unable to move, only aware of my shaking and filled with the knowledge that if he touched me I would start screaming and maybe never be able to stop.

Carl took another step closer.

The door buzzed, and whatever spell had me locked in its clutches broke. I was still trembling but stepped around Carl and toward the door, which closed with a soft click.

Ryan held a box cutter in one hand, casually. But its blade was out.

He gestured over his shoulder with it. "I was unwrapping some stuff that came in, just wanted to check on you, see how it's going with the paintings." His eyes slid between me and Carl. "You doing okay, Chloe? Getting what you need?"

"Yeah, I'm good." I glanced nervously at Carl, who had silently stepped closer to both of us.

"It was good to see you, Chloe. I'm glad we were able to talk. If you need me, Sloane has my number."

He stepped forward again and I involuntarily tensed, resisting the urge to grab Ryan by the arm. Out of the corner of my eye, I saw Ryan shift his grip on the box cutter.

But all Carl did was rest a hand on my shoulder. It was heavy, not pushing into me but nearly so.

"Take care," he said, flashing me his teeth one final time. "Excuse me," he said to Ryan, gesturing at the door.

"I'll take you back," Ryan said. "Gotta follow protocol." Carl nodded, amiable.

"I'll be right back, Chloe. You okay by yourself for a few?" Ryan looked between us again.

"I am," I said. Though really I wasn't.

Once the door closed behind them, I buried my face in my hands, pressing the heels of my palms into my eye sockets. I was trembling so hard I could barely see the paintings anymore.

It's okay, I told myself. *It's okay. Inhale, exhale.*

I stayed that way for however long it took for Ryan to come back.

"You okay?" he asked, looking at me with real concern. I noticed his box cutter was put away, stored safely in a utility belt slung around his hips.

I blew out a breath, trying to get my tumbling thoughts in order.

"Yeah. I didn't know people had individual keys."

Ryan frowned at me. "They don't. Nobody does but people who work here. We don't even let the director of the Met have his own key; it compromises the security of the other clients. Are you telling me that guy was able to get back here on his own? I thought he came with one of my coworkers."

"No," I said quickly. Whatever was happening with Carl and Sloane, and however he got his hands on a key and back here without an escort, I didn't want to make trouble for the gallery. I had to keep my job until I got to the bottom of whatever was going on. "He just surprised me, is all. I didn't know he was coming."

Ryan looked at me a long minute. "All right. Hey, did you want to see the other painting? It wasn't on your list, but I had it uncrated and put on a rack just in case."

What other painting? There were only the five, as far as I knew: *Careless, Loveless, Helpless, Hopeless,* and *Fearless. Careless* was in private hands, and *Helpless* I'd already seen, at the funeral.

"Which painting do you mean? *Helpless?*" We'd sent the painting here after the memorial service. Or maybe the owner of *Careless*, whoever was behind Dunbar Capital, stored that work here also?

"No, you said you didn't need that one." Ryan moved the chair out of the middle of the room and told me to stand back. He pulled out one of the racks, one of the front ones that wasn't supporting *Loveless*. It stretched out in front of us, all the way to the opposite wall, almost, but not quite, touching *Helpless*. "This one."

I gaped, my stress and fear over Carl's menacing visit momentarily shoved aside.

The painting was clearly part of the "Less Than" series: same size, same large, frenetic brushstrokes, layering over smaller, more delicate lines that slipped in and out of view. It was dark, angry-looking, but a muted fury, rather than the howling rage of *Helpless*. Dark purples, midnight blue, and some intertwining moments of a surprising periwinkle threaded throughout. The undergirding lines were an evil-looking yellow.

"I didn't know about this work. It's not on my checklist; it's not going to be in the show—" Was this what the Fletchers were trying to do? Keep a painting back, embarrass me with the oversight?

But no, Lou had made the checklist, and he hadn't included it.

"When did this arrive?" I asked.

Ryan checked his file. "November 8." I gasped again before I could stop myself.

It was the day of Inga's death, the day of the party. I went from too hot, flustered, and charged from my encounter with Carl to too cold in an instant. A shiver ran down my spine.

"The gallery sent it?"

"No, we picked it up in Williamsburg." He looked up from his file. "See?"

Ryan held a clipboard out to me. The delivery form featured Inga's signature, now familiar to me, that bold, looping capital *I*, the other letters following in neat succession.

Inga must have arranged for the transport herself, either that or the Fletchers had felt they didn't need to tell Lou.

"Can I see that?" I took the clipboard and studied the form. If I could figure out who had paid, it might explain why we didn't know about the painting. The warehouse probably assumed we did; it wasn't their job to let us know if an artist dropped off one of their works.

Date: November 8, 2001. The address was Inga's, close to the river. Transport of one canvas sized 12 x 22 to ArtSmart storage facility, Long Island City.

My eyes roved over the details, then snagged on the painting's title. *Lifeless.*

The fear that had been waning filled me again, so much so that I thought I'd drop the clipboard.

Lifeless. The day she died, Inga had sent to storage a painting called *Lifeless.*

"You want some time with it?" Ryan looked at me curiously.

I couldn't speak but managed to nod and smile my thanks as he slipped out again.

The folding chair seemed tainted somehow, now that Carl had touched it. I sat on the concrete floor instead.

I stayed there, staring at the painting, trying to get a feel for it, for a long time.

Hunger began to gnaw at my insides, but I ignored it. I could eat later. This might be my only chance with the paintings.

With *this* painting.

Now that I knew about Carl and Inga, and after Carl's impromptu visit here, I had a feeling the Fletchers would let me go as soon as the show opened.

Which was fine. Whatever the hell was going on there, I didn't want to be part of it any longer.

But I did want to find out what happened to Lou, to make sure he was okay.

And to Inga.

She had given me the note. It was a sign, a direct plea from her, to help. To make sure whoever killed her didn't go unpunished.

Maybe the answers were here, right in front of me. Hidden in the depths of *Lifeless.*

I scanned the work from top to bottom, side to side, looking closely and carefully at all the thin yellow lines, trying to find the ones that would create a message, the letters so tiny but the impact potentially gargantuan.

Lifeless.

What was in there? I thought of the other messages, my eyes never stopping their journey.

Carl.

Afraid.
Help Me.
Too Late.
What did it all add up to?

I was terrified I already knew the answer, but I had to keep looking. I had to see it for myself.

Finding the secret word was taking a lot longer with this one. I scootched back, so I was almost against the door, changing my perspective. What was I missing?

I stopped following the yellow lines and took in the whole, the strokes of purple and blue somber and resigned.

When I found it, I was glad I was already sitting down, because I don't think my legs could have held me.

There it was. Proof that Inga's death hadn't been the result of a break-in. Proof that it had been planned. At least, enough proof for me.

The lines in the painting spelled *Murder.*

They weren't small letters, this time. That's why it had taken me so long to find them. The seemingly random yellow lines that turned this way and that, like a worm burrowing under soil, formed the word across the giant sprawl of the canvas.

Everyone knew Inga had been murdered. The police knew it, too, nobody doubted it.

What this told me was that Inga knew it had been coming.

CHAPTER SEVENTEEN

After my run-in with Carl at the warehouse, I'd had the car take me home to Williamsburg instead of back to the gallery. The driver dropped me at Rosemary's. It was almost five o'clock anyway, the long shadows of dusk making their way toward true nightfall, the sun having just slipped past the skyscrapers and over the horizon.

I couldn't stop thinking about the words I'd found in the paintings. About Carl's fingers curling over the back of the metal chair as he bared his teeth at me.

Did Carl kill Inga or have her killed? But why? If what Sloane had said was true, if his wife already knew about the affair, surely it wasn't worth murdering Inga to keep it secret. I wondered if he could lose his job over the affair, but probably not. Men more powerful than him had been called out for having mistresses, very publicly, and kept their jobs. Just look at Bill Clinton. Or Clarence Thomas, who didn't have an affair but had sexually harassed a woman and still got appointed to the Supreme Court.

If men were powerful enough, they generally could survive any kind of scandal, it seemed. Even if it hurt women. It might be a little embarrassing, but if news of Inga and Carl's affair did get out, it would probably blow over.

I settled myself into our gang's usual corner. It was quiet tonight, a Monday, but I was sure somebody would show up sooner or later. Probably Calvin, as the restaurant where he worked was closed on Mondays, and Penny would join him.

Rosemary dropped a beer in front of me.

"Doing okay, hon?" She squinted a concerned face at me. I guess I looked as wrung out as I felt.

I took a foamy sip before answering. "Bad day at work."

She grimaced in sympathy. "Chin up."

As Rosemary moved to the other side of the bar, I took another sip, briefly hit by a shot of cold as the door opened.

Calvin plopped onto the stool next to me with a grin. "Pretty crazy party on Saturday, yeah? Did you have fun?"

"It took me all day Sunday to recover," I admitted. "Hair of the dog here, but I can't do more than one tonight."

He gave me a knowing look.

"Okay, maybe two. But really, it'll be an early night. I just need to take the edge off work."

"Oh yeah? What's going on?" Calvin accepted his own beer from Rosemary with a smile and nod of thanks.

I couldn't get into it: the messages in the paintings, Carl's non-specific creepiness.

"Nothing I want to talk about. Just some guy being a little shady." A half-truth was always better than a full-out lie.

"To you?" Calvin frowned. "Does your boss know? Or, shit, *is* it your boss?"

"My boss's brother. He doesn't work at the gallery, he works for the government."

Calvin snorted. "All those guys are shady. What area is he in?"

"Treasury, I guess. Something about Foreign Assets. I can't remember the whole title of his department."

"Office of Foreign Assets Control? Huh." He looked thoughtful.

"What?"

Calvin considered me, then waved his hand. "Nah, you don't want to hear all this stuff."

"No, what?"

"Penny told me to tone it down, you know, after what happened with Edward."

I agreed with Penny but wanted to hear what Calvin had to say.

"Tell me."

He blew out a breath, pitched his voice low.

"Well, like what I was saying to Edward that time, there are these people in Europe who think the attack on 9/11 was an inside job. There's some things that don't add up, you know? And someone at a place like that, like OFAC, I mean, they'd be in the thick of it."

I was bewildered. "What is it? Foreign Assets Control?"

"Yeah, the guys who put sanctions and stuff on our so-called enemies' money. It started after World War II. But, like, how did these terrorists from 9/11 *get* all that money? Why wasn't OFAC keeping track of that? Why isn't our high and mighty government investigating who is behind the attacks?"

I blinked. "I thought it was the Taliban, al-Qaeda?"

He snorted again, took a deep drink of beer. "But who *funded* them? That's the big question, but that asshole Cheney claims it will take resources away from that asshole Bush's *war on terror.*" Calvin used his fingers to create air quotes around the phrase. "Bunch of fucking fascists. Edward should be angry with them, not me. They're why his uncle died."

"But . . . who would do such a thing? I mean, an American, help out with attacking their own country? Why?"

Calvin lifted an eyebrow at me. "Money, probably. Why else?"

The images and sensations were starting to crowd in again. Trying to breathe and sucking in dust. Walking blindly in the beige fog, the feeling of brick and glass and siding sliding under my fingertips, guiding me. The sound of screams slowly replacing the steady chatter and jukebox of the bar.

My chest was beginning its familiar tightening. I forced myself to slow my breath.

It's probably nothing. You can go now.

"I know I brought it up, but let's talk about something else, okay?"

He held his hands up. "Yeah, yeah. Of course." Calvin picked up his beer and gazed across the bar, a tiny muscle working in his jaw. "You asked."

"I know. Thanks for explaining it. Hey, how are the wedding plans coming along? Did you find a Justice of the Peace in Jersey?"

Calvin and Penny were getting married on a beach in New Jersey later this winter, which I thought would be beautiful but cold. Calvin let the conversation shift, and we finished our beers while talking about less stressful things: the music he was planning for the wedding, the house they'd rented for everyone to share. Eventually Penny showed up, her nose pink, and convinced us to get a six-pack and head to Bean for burritos for dinner.

By the time I got home it was already ten. Vik was nowhere to be seen, and the red light on the answering machine was still, indicating no messages. A vague hitch of disappointment rose inside, as it always did when another day passed and Lou hadn't made contact. I changed and climbed into bed, ready to read a few pages of my book, but couldn't focus.

What Calvin had said kept bubbling into my head every time I tried to read.

I stared at my computer across the room. I pictured myself settling into the chair before it, firing it up, connecting to the internet, and chasing down those blog posts Calvin had talked about. The ones that said people in our own government were responsible for the attacks.

I'd avoided the news as much as I could in the past several weeks. The subject of 9/11 hit too close to home whenever it came up—and it always came up. It was everywhere in the city, unavoidable. How could it not be, when the skyline was irrevocably altered? When Ground Zero was still burning?

I swallowed, putting my book down and swinging my legs out of bed, eyeing the computer.

It wouldn't hurt to do a little cybersleuthing.

As soon as my toes touched the cold floor, I snatched them back up.

When I was little, I had been convinced a witch lived under my bed and if I put my feet down at night, she would grab my ankles and pull me under. I hadn't thought of that in years but just now, I felt the same sensation. The same utter certainty that icy fingers would wrap around me and I'd get yanked under the bed, where unfathomable, unspeakable things would happen.

I tucked my feet back under my sheet and comforter, safe.

There was no witch under the bed, of course. I knew that. But the last thing I needed to do was read crazy conspiracy theories about what happened at the towers. The city—really the whole country—was already swarming with rumor and uncertainty. Would the war on terror evolve into an actual war? And with whom? How would we punish those responsible? And yes, even I had heard whispers, not that the attacks were an inside job per se, but that we as a country had brought it upon ourselves, due to years of mismanaged policies.

Just thinking about it was enough to shorten my breath.

No, I wouldn't do any digging online. What I really needed was sleep.

Turning my back on the computer, I rolled over and shut off the light.

The next morning, I woke feeling simultaneously doubtful and determined, my moods swinging like a pendulum. The sky out my window was that bright shade particular to winter, cloudless but so pale it was nearly white. The bright sunshine made me doubtful that the words in the paintings added up to anything. Yet in the next moment I'd find myself thinking that if they did have a deeper meaning, I would find out what it was.

Inga had picked me, after all. She'd left that note in my pocket. I could do this for her.

My computer sat harmlessly on my desk. It was an old desktop. I'd made a smart decision, not to go chasing ghosts and half-cocked truths last night, working myself up over nothing.

I was relieved to find coffee in the cupboard, then emboldened as I recalled I had bought it. That I'd remembered to pick some up, that I did normal things like buy coffee and have dinner with friends, and that all these unconnected things were just that, unconnected.

As the calming aroma of coffee filled our tiny kitchen, I allowed myself to continue this train of thought.

Yes, I'd probably worked myself up over nothing about all this. The words in the paintings were just words. The note with the address had probably gotten into my pocket somehow by mistake at the party. I'd accidentally shoved it in there when pocketing a tissue, or, I don't know . . .

This was where my internal pep talk faltered.

Inga was still dead.

My memory of the party at her loft was still mostly a giant blank space.

I had no idea how I had gotten home that night.

And the police seemed to think I knew something. *Careless* could prove to be the key. I needed to see it. I was still the show's curator, for now. I could ask the Fletchers if they knew where it was. I'd only ever seen it in reproduction, and it was the first of the series.

Would it also have a message? Or were the messages only incorporated into works Inga made *after* she signed with the gallery? I was certain Lou hadn't known about the messages, or he would have written about them in his catalogue essay. I wished I could talk to him about it.

Knowing about *Careless* might help me put Inga's messages into perspective. Maybe it was something she did with all her art. Maybe the words were just responses to however she was feeling at the time, and there was no deeper meaning, no bigger picture.

I put extra care into dressing, taking time with my hair and makeup. I'd never achieve the slick, straight look that was popular right now, the one Sloane pulled off so effortlessly, but I put in a defrizzing product and carefully dried it with a diffuser, then twisted the pile of dark blond curls into a knot at the nape of my neck. I found a slightly more conservative navy blue–collared shirt and paired it with a vintage beige pencil skirt, dark blue tights, and boots. It was way more corporate than my normal look, but I wanted to be taken seriously.

As I exited the subway at Sixty-Eighth Street and began to walk north, I pulled my thick pink scarf tighter around my neck, almost up to my ears. I turned west. My boot heels made a satisfying, purposeful clang on the sidewalk I felt all the way up my legs. I turned the volume up on my Discman, Sleater-Kinney today, hoping to channel their powerful chords into decisive action when I met with the Fletchers.

I would go straight to Henry as soon as I took off my coat. They had to let me see *Careless*, and I wouldn't take no for an answer. The Fletchers were the ones who put me in charge, after all, and if they wanted me to be thorough then I needed—

"Ms. Harlow? *Chloe.*"

The determined monologue in my head was cut short as the sound of my name filtered through the wall of music. I whirled around. Who was calling to me on East Seventieth Street?

Detective Gonzales stood next to a silver four-door sedan, her hand resting lightly on the driver's-side door handle. My shoulders instantly clenched and I clutched the strap of my bag, like I was about to get mugged. The passenger door opened and Detective Downs's head and chest rose into view, tall and spindly like a wading bird, his eyes hidden behind a pair of aviator sunglasses.

"Would you come with us, please?" Detective Gonzales said. "We need to ask you some questions."

CHAPTER EIGHTEEN

It didn't hit me that we were going back to my own neighborhood until the unmarked car inched its way down Delancey Street, toward the on-ramp of the Williamsburg Bridge.

"We're going to Brooklyn?" My voice sounded high and thin, almost panicked. The Fletchers were going to wonder where I was. I took a deep breath.

Detective Downs glanced over his shoulder at me from the front passenger seat. I could see my face, white and pinched, in the reflection of his sunglasses. "Yes. We're headed to our precinct."

"Oh." My response was so faint I barely heard it. Downs didn't seem to care or need a response. He turned forward again.

I hadn't asked where we were going when I'd gotten in the car. I had asked, instead, if I had to come. Detective Gonzales had said no, I didn't have to, but it sure would be helpful. And I wanted to help them find whoever had murdered Inga, didn't I? I couldn't think of a good answer to that, so had climbed into the back seat. Of course, I wanted the police to find Inga's killer.

It had taken me over thirty minutes to get to the Upper East Side that morning on the train, and now it looked like I'd need to make the trek all over again as soon as I was finished talking to the detectives. I had had a vague idea they were taking me downtown, but I realized now it was based solely on stereotypes in television shows and movies.

Going back to Williamsburg made the most sense, though. It was where Inga had died, so the detectives assigned to her case would be stationed there.

The river glittered in the cold sunshine as we crossed the bridge. Once in Brooklyn, we drove deeper into the neighborhood than I normally went, crossing under the Brooklyn-Queens Expressway and turning south down Union Street. Eventually the car pulled into a spot next to some squad cars in front of an ugly, gray square building at a busy intersection of two main roads. A few tattered "missing persons" flyers about people who had probably died in the towers were stapled to a telephone pole outside as we made our way inside. I looked the other way, quickly.

"Can I call the gallery?" I asked as I followed the detectives inside. The interior was as utilitarian and unimpressive as the exterior. "Let them know why I'll be late?"

Downs had taken off his sunglasses. He raised a brow at me. "You couldn't do that from the car?"

"I don't have a cell phone."

"You can use the phone from my desk," Gonzales said, leading me past a harassed-looking front desk officer. She led me into a large, windowless room with white painted cinder block walls and a drop ceiling, sickly looking fluorescent lights overhead giving the space a greenish glow. Gray metal filing cabinets lined the walls, a TV propped on top of one turned to Fox News, its low volume filtering through the smoky air. The bright, crisp winter day outside may as well have not existed; it was impossible, in here, to tell if it was night or day, summer or winter. Two men in white dress shirts and dark ties sat at a long desk filled with computers and phones, sucking on cigarettes. Both glanced up at me trailing Gonzales as we passed.

We stopped at a phone in front of an empty chair at a second long desk. Gonzales picked up the receiver and handed it to me, pressing a button until I heard a dial tone.

"You can dial out now."

The shrill ring sounded louder than usual.

"Fletcher & Sons, this is Olive." For a split second I wondered where Carmen was—probably getting coffee or in the restroom—but then was relieved. Carmen reminded me sometimes of a cat, not an amiable furball like Groucho, but a sly, watchful caricature of one.

"Hi, Olive, it's Chloe. Can I speak to Henry or Sloane? Whoever is available, it doesn't matter which."

"Hey, Chloe. Neither are here. Do you want me to take a message?"

Embarrassment filled me at the thought of telling Olive I was at a police station, even though I hadn't done anything wrong. I was being helpful, I reminded myself. Just answering questions.

"Could you let them know the detectives working Inga's case had more questions for me? I'm with them in Brooklyn right now, so I won't be in until later." I glanced quizzically at Gonzales, wondering if I would, in fact, be back at work later, but she wasn't looking at me, instead intently reading something in an open file in her hands.

Olive sounded suitably impressed by the gravitas of the situation and promised to relay the message. I could only imagine Sebastian, listening in at the next desk, eyes narrowed. He and Carmen were peas in a pod.

"All done?" Gonzales asked once I hung up the phone, closing the file with a snap. We exited the dark squad room and she led me down a grim hall and into something that more resembled the TV-influenced idea of a police station I'd pictured: a rectangular interview room, with a mirror on one side that I assumed was two-way, and a table surrounded by three chairs. Detective Downs was already there, fiddling with the bulky television sitting on a metal stand with wheels on one end of the room.

The TV made me even more nervous, for some reason, even though it was turned off. Downs stepped away from it and sat down, a closed file on the table in front of him. Gonzales nodded her head at the empty chair across from them, indicating I should sit.

"Thanks for agreeing to come with us, Chloe."

"It's fine," I said. I squirmed out of my coat and hung it over the back of the chair. It was much hotter in the interview room than it had been elsewhere in the station. "I want to help. But, uh, do I need a lawyer?"

Gonzales raised an eyebrow. "Why would you need a lawyer, Chloe?" Downs looked at me without expression, but tilted his head to one side, like he was considering my question.

"I don't know." I fiddled with my own hands uncertainly, unsure of how to put my anxiousness about being here into words. "Because I'm in a police station, being questioned about something when I've already told you everything I know."

"You can call a lawyer if you want, sure." Gonzales's tone was easy.

They both stared at me, waiting. I suddenly felt stupid. I didn't even know any lawyers, let alone have the money to pay for one.

"Am I . . . under arrest?"

"You're not under arrest. You're free to go whenever you want," Gonzales said. Her tone stayed easy but her eyes pinned me in place. "But you came all the way down here with us, so we'd appreciate it if you stayed. And we do need your help with something here. About Inga Beck's death."

"Shouldn't you be talking to people who were closer with Inga? I barely knew her."

Detective Gonzales looked thoughtful. "We've tried to reach Dr. Stern but can't seem to get hold of him. Do you know anything about that?"

"He doesn't work at the gallery anymore." My nervousness increased, morphing into something bordering on guilt, even though I didn't have anything to do with any of this.

"Did he get fired, or quit?"

"I don't know. You'd have to ask the Fletchers that."

"You don't know? I got the impression you two were pretty close."

"No, not really. He was just my boss."

A long silence stretched. I thought of Debra, pink cheeked, a few frizzy strands of hair wild around her face, as she pulled a casserole from the oven. Of Lou, staring up at the stars outside his house, the way the white of his breath had dissipated into the dark sky.

"And where is Dr. Stern now?" Gonzales finally asked.

"I don't know."

"You don't know." It was a statement more than a question.

The repetition of what I said was starting to get under my skin, nearly making it itch, which I'm sure was the intention.

Downs, who still hadn't spoke, inclined his head the other direction.

"No, I don't know," I said. I couldn't keep the irritation from my voice. Why didn't they believe me?

Another long silence.

"If you hear from him, let us know, okay? He's not in any trouble, we just want to ask him a couple questions."

"Uh-huh. Okay." There was no way I'd rat out Lou, even if I did know where he was. God, I wished he'd get in touch.

I wished he would tell me the truth, what was really going on here.

"Let's get to why we really want to talk to you, Chloe. We want to show you something."

Downs leaned over to the TV and pressed a button. I noticed for the first time that it had a built-in VCR in its bottom section.

The screen came to life, a frozen, grainy image. It was a partial view of a street, and most of the front entrance of a convenience store. Downs pushed another button, and dark gray lines looped up the screen in a pattern.

"Remember how we were waiting on video from the bodega across the street from Inga's building?" Gonzales said quietly.

The dark lines continued to loop, indicating the video was playing, though nothing happened. A date and time floated in crude, boxy white numbers on the lower left of the screen.

Cold settled over me despite the stifling temperature in the room as I realized it was the date of Inga's party. Or the following morning, really, 3:10 a.m., November 9.

I drew in a breath to speak, to ask if something was going to happen, when there was movement on the screen. A dark town car pulled into view and idled in front of the bodega. I watched, holding my breath, as the back door opened and a man wearing jeans and a nondescript hoodie got out. Though it looked like a streetlamp just out of frame illuminated this section of street, the man's hood was pulled forward enough that it was impossible to see his face.

The minutes ticked by on the bottom corner of the screen. My heart began to race and my palms started to sweat as we waited. I was aware of my breath, how it sounded too shallow and fast and loud in the small, enclosed room. I could feel both detectives' eyes on me.

Take a deep breath, I commanded myself. *Inhale, exhale.*

Was that Inga's killer, who had crossed the screen? That hooded man?

I stared at the TV, willing the person to show themselves again. The horizontal line ran up the screen, disappeared at the top, reappeared at the bottom, and climbed upward again and again, a nauseating loop.

The date and time stamp in the corner of the screen taunted me. It was like watching a horror movie, when you knew the ax-wielding killer could jump out at any minute but it hadn't happened yet. Tension filled the room.

3:23 now.

I couldn't take it any longer. "Is that it?"

At some point both detectives had also turned their attention back to the screen. Gonzales's eyes flicked toward me, then back to the TV. "Just wait," she said, her soft words a pointed contrast to my loud ones.

At 3:25 a figure appeared, walking from the left side of the screen to the driver's-side back door of the waiting car. It was, I assumed, the same hooded figure, only now seen from the back. Same build, same indistinctly colored hoodie.

Only now, he wasn't alone.

He was carrying someone.

The man had one arm under the person's shoulders, the other under their knees. The carried person's head was dropped forward toward their own chest, and you couldn't see their face.

But I knew right away.

The coat on the woman being carried matched the one hanging on the back of my chair, its wooden toggle buttons pressing into my back. The boots were the same ones I was wearing now.

The man set one foot on the tire well of the town car. He adjusted the body in his arms so the person's legs briefly rested on his propped knee, freeing up his left hand to open the car door.

I watched, horror-struck, as the head of the woman being carried lolled back, her face fully exposed to the bodega camera.

No. Don't let it be true. Don't let it be me. No.

There was no denying it, though. Not at that angle.

The unconscious woman being maneuvered into the back seat of the car on the night of Inga's murder was me.

CHAPTER NINETEEN

I wanted to gasp but was frozen, locked in place. The sight of my body, there on the screen, was deeply disturbing. I looked as floppy as a doll, obviously unaware of what was happening to me. After shutting the door, the hooded man circled around the back of the car, got in the passenger-side rear door, and the car drove away.

Downs pressed the pause button before the car could fully exit the screen. Both detectives turned to me expectantly.

"What the fuck was that?" I could barely speak.

"You tell us, Chloe."

"I don't fucking know." My voice was shaking, and the rest of me followed suit. It didn't matter that the room was so hot sweat had begun to gather under the arms of my blouse, I was now shivering uncontrollably.

Who was that? Who had picked me up and carried me, so drunk I was obviously passed out, to a waiting town car and drove away with me?

I strained to recall any part of what the video showed, or rather, didn't show. Of drinking so much I blacked out.

I didn't remember. Those same fragments of that night were all my mind would offer: Benny and Vik laughing in the smoke; the scrape of the shower-curtain bathroom door on its rod; Lou looking up at *Helpless*. And the new memory: the warmth of Inga's arm around my neck, the scent of her breath in my nostrils.

I'm so glad you're here.

The next morning, waking up naked in my bed, with no idea how I'd gotten home.

Gonzales rewound the tape a few seconds. I stared at the wavering, black-and-white image of the sweatshirted figure carrying me.

"Who is that?" I whispered.

"We were hoping you could tell us," she said.

I absently shook my head, my eyes glued to the screen. The man was of average height, average build. Half the city wore hoodies. He was maybe a white guy, but with the black-and-white imagery, it was hard to tell by just his hands. He could be a different race but light skinned.

My gaze roved over the paused frame, taking in as many details as I could, hoping against hope to jog my own stubborn memory. My fingers were still gently pressed to my lips. When I noticed Downs looking at them, I forced my hand down to the table.

My eye snagged on something else.

The car didn't have a license plate.

Another disturbing thought hit, unrelated to the license plate.

If I was that passed out, how did I get into my apartment? Was the hooded figure Vik, or Ben?

"How did I get into bed?" I wasn't aware I'd voiced the ominous thought aloud until Detective Gonzales answered me.

"We've talked to Vikram and Ben. Vikram swears he and his boyfriend were home and asleep by one thirty a.m. Ben does recall hearing a key in the lock around three, and noise of someone entering the apartment, but he assumed it was you and fell back asleep."

Did the police believe that? Did *I*?

Someone had carried or maneuvered me up three flights of stairs, into my apartment, and into my bed without my knowledge.

They must have undressed me too.

The cold that had settled over me began to turn to nausea.

"Does anyone else have a key to your apartment, Chloe? Anyone who could have let themselves—and you—in?"

I started to shake my head, then stopped.

"I don't know."

"You don't know." This time, the detective's eyes looked angry, instead of mildly curious.

I released a shaky sigh and explained about Alex, keeping it as simple as I could. I pushed my arms back into my coat as I talked, its weight a comfort, despite the dissonance of seeing the same coat on the screen in front of me.

"I had the locks changed recently, but after that night." I gestured at the picture of me being carried on the screen. "That night, it was the same key Alex had. Or if he'd given it to someone, made copies."

"And what made you recently change the locks?" she asked.

I felt like I was being cornered.

"Um, I felt like someone had been in the apartment around Thanksgiving."

"Did you report this?"

"No, no. There were no signs of a break-in. Nothing was taken. But stuff was moved around."

Did Detective Gonzales flick her eyes to Downs for the quickest of seconds?

She nodded slowly, her gaze back on me.

"We heard the same information from Vikram, yes."

A sudden surge of anger filled me. Why were they asking me this stuff if they already knew it?

"And we've checked on Alex Thompson," she continued. "He is in the Sunrise Harmony recovery center in Arizona, where he's been for nine months."

"So, someone he gave it to . . ."

"He has no memory of making a copy of your key, but of course it's possible. We're chasing down a few associates."

The information slowly seeped through my shocked and befuddled brain. What it meant.

They'd already talked to Alex.

The feeling that I was two steps behind in this conversation was pervasive. They clearly knew something I didn't and were trying to needle me into admitting whatever that was. The problem was, I had no idea what they thought I knew.

"I just don't know," I said again. My voice sounded scratchy. I tried to swallow.

Detective Downs hadn't said a word so far. He leaned back in his chair now and folded his arms over his chest.

I cleared my throat. "Could I have some water?"

He didn't look at Gonzales but kept those light blue eyes on me as he slowly rose, the harsh scraping of his metal chair legs against the rough concrete floor making me start.

Gonzales was quiet until Downs came back with a paper cup of water. I drank several grateful swallows, even though it was room temperature and had a faintly metallic aftertaste. I hoped it had come from a water fountain rather than a bathroom sink.

"Thank you," I said, wiping my mouth with the back of my hand.

The TV was paused on the moment of the video when my head had tilted backward, catching full view of my slack, lifeless face. I didn't want to look at it, it was so unsettling, but my eyes kept sliding in the direction of the screen almost of their own accord, just as they had done with Inga's body at the funeral.

On the TV, my mouth was hanging open, my eyes shut. My head dangled. The sight of it made my skin crawl. Gonzales and Downs watched me look at myself, not speaking. Gonzales's expression was careful and neutral, but Downs's was like a hawk, sharp and cold. My mouth was suddenly dry again. I brought the paper cup to my lips but only drops remained.

"The thing is, Chloe, it seems you were the last person to leave the party."

I blinked at the detective, trying to hold back the tears that were ready to spill. My tongue felt like sandpaper. I tried to swallow but couldn't, my thoughts chaos. My own lolling face wavered on the screen, taunting me.

A short silence stretched.

"Which means," she continued, "you were the last person to see Inga Beck alive."

"Except for whoever killed her," Downs added. His unexpected voice was a shade too loud. It felt like a slap.

"That's right. Except for whoever killed her," Gonzales repeated.

I wrenched my attention away from the screen and looked between the two detectives. The nausea in my gut intensified.

Did they think I killed Inga?

I wiped at my eyes and finally managed to swallow. "I don't . . ." The words came out as a croak, and I don't know what I would have said next, but at that moment the interview room door banged open and a robust man with a florid face over a navy suit stormed in.

"Jonathan Marz, legal counsel for Ms. Harlow," he announced, standing behind me and placing a hand on my shoulder. "Detectives, please refrain from asking my client any further questions. Ms. Harlow, let's go."

I jerked in surprise but wasn't about to argue. I needed to get out of this room, away from the image of myself on that TV, alone somewhere to organize the torrent of emotions and thoughts cascading through my head.

Downs didn't bother to conceal his huff of frustration as I stood and gathered my bag, but Gonzales remained perfectly poised.

"Contact my office if you want another interview with Ms. Harlow. No more approaching her on the street," Marz clipped out. I had no idea who he was but assumed the Fletchers had hired him.

"We'll be in touch," Gonzales promised as I followed my new lawyer out the door.

I could feel her dark eyes boring into my back before the door shut behind me, mercifully blocking their weight.

CHAPTER TWENTY

I had never seen Henry Fletcher so angry. All his usual charming bonhomie was gone, replaced by a white-faced fury as he watched me get out of the back of the car Jonathan Marz had had waiting outside the Ninetieth Precinct. It had been a tense ride back to the Upper East Side, with me sitting shell-shocked, still trying to wrap my head around what I'd seen in the video, and the lawyer I'd never met silently fuming beside me. We had only spoken when he reiterated to me what he said to the police: that I wasn't to speak to them again without him present. I nodded to show I understood, and he passed me his card.

"My office, cell, and car phone numbers are all listed there," he'd said. "If it's an emergency and you can't reach me directly, leave a message with my secretary at my office and she'll find me right away. I'll answer myself on a weekend or late at night."

"Okay." I was too dumbfounded by this turn of events to say much more. That video did not seem to bode well for me. I didn't know why the Fletchers thought they needed to protect me, but I found myself very, very glad of Jonathan Marz's presence.

We'd pulled up in front of the gallery to find the Fletchers waiting outside.

I exited the car and stood before them. Noticing my discomfiture, Sloane said, "It's not you Henry's angry with, Chloe."

Henry glanced my way. "No," he said shortly. He leaned into the car after I got out. "Jonathan, you made it clear to the detectives they are not to contact Chloe again without going through you?"

"Of course," Marz replied. "She has all my numbers now."

"Good," Henry said. "Let's talk upstairs," he continued as Marz's car pulled away.

Once we were in his office, Henry's expression shifted. Not entirely back to normal, but a closer approximation of his usual genial self.

"I am sorry about that, Chloe. Sloane is right, I wasn't angry with you, I was angry at the situation."

"Okay," I said, as I had in the car to Marz. Which situation did Henry mean?

Did he and Sloane know about the video somehow?

"Those detectives never should have taken you to Brooklyn," Sloane said. "You have nothing to do with Inga's murder, and it's obvious they're just rattling cages, hoping to turn over something."

It seemed they didn't know. Or if they did, they weren't mentioning it.

"What kind of something?" I asked.

"There's nothing to uncover, of course," Henry said, his voice returning to a snap. He seemed to catch himself. "It's about money, Chloe," he continued in a gentler tone. "You know we have it, and the gallery has it. These officers see the price tags of our inventory, how much Inga's art is worth, and try to find a connection. They're badgering you because, frankly, they see you as the weak link here."

I startled at that, unsure if I should be insulted or not.

"All Henry means is, you haven't been here very long," Sloane interjected again. I noticed, not for the first time, how often she served as her father's interpreter.

"It's been over two years," I said.

"But you were our receptionist. I meant in a *meaningful* way."

I wasn't sure her distinction made sense, but let it go. "I don't know anything, anyway. Not about the gallery's finances, or . . . anything." I did not mention how Lou had told me how badly the gallery needed the auction to go well, how he had hinted at money troubles.

And now Lou was gone.

Henry opened his arms in a "there we are" gesture, all good humor instantly restored. "Exactly. So the police have no reason to harass you. Don't worry about it any longer, Chloe. Mr. Marz is on your side, as are Sloane and I."

He offered a beatific smile and then turned to his computer, dismissing me.

"Thank you," I said over my shoulder as Sloane walked me to the door.

"We're so sorry it wasted a whole morning of your time. Totally unnecessary," Sloane said. We stopped on the landing after she closed Henry's office door behind us. "How was your visit to the warehouse?"

"It was fine. Good. Great to see the works in person." After being taken to Brooklyn and shown that security camera footage, my time at the warehouse had been shoved aside in my head. It flooded back now.

Carl showing up, claiming Sloane had given him the key card.

The painting *Lifeless*, with its terrifying hidden message: Murder.

I waited for Sloane to mention either, but she just smiled.

"I'm glad." Sloane turned to her own office, obviously about to dismiss me the same way Henry had, when I remembered the determination I'd woken up with that morning.

"What about *Careless*?" I said.

She stopped. "What about it?"

"Shouldn't it be in the show? So the series is complete?"

Sloane pursed her lips. I could tell she was thinking about it.

"I saw in the file that a group called Dunbar Capital owns it. It was Inga's bill of sale; there wasn't an address." I was sure I was telling Sloane things she already knew but wanted her to realize I'd done my homework. "It really would be best to exhibit the whole series at once," I repeated. "I'm pretty sure that was Lou's plan."

I didn't say anything about *Lifeless*. I didn't know if the Fletchers even knew it existed.

"Let me see what I can do," she finally said. "But good thinking, Chloe. You're right, all the paintings together would make the greatest impact."

"There's room in the space we rented, from what I can tell by the floor plan."

"You haven't been there yet? Let's go later this week. And I'll see what I can do about *Careless*." Sloane's perfectly painted pink mouth stretched into a warm smile. "This shows initiative. I like that. Henry will too." Her smile broadened as she turned her back to me, but not before I saw that the smile didn't reach her eyes.

I went through the motions of work for the rest of the day, but it was useless. I kept seeing the picture of myself being carried, looking lifeless, and put in a car. The knowledge that whoever that was had somehow gotten into my apartment, seen me naked.

That whoever it was may have been the person who killed Inga.

At 4:30 I gave up, shut down my computer, and made my way back to Brooklyn.

It was dark by the time I emerged from the Bedford Avenue station. Ricci's was shuttered, and the street was weirdly empty. Lights and music poured through the windows of Vera Cruz, though, offering a measure of comfort. I peered in the windows from the street and didn't see anyone I knew at the bar, so I popped my head into Rosemary's instead.

Lisel was there, a fresh beer in front of her, in a green-and-white polka-dot dress from the 1940s. I had no idea if Vik was home or not and couldn't bear the thought of sitting alone in my empty apartment, replaying the image of myself being carried into a waiting car over and over and over in my head.

I took the stool next to her.

Calvin and Penny didn't show up that night, but Edward did. He was still nursing his heartbreak but was in better spirits than the last time I'd seen him. I bummed a cigarette off him and ordered. One beer turned into many, the oblivion I craved slowly creeping through my bloodstream along with the alcohol, the music and laughter a balm.

I didn't tell my friends about going to the police station. I didn't tell them about getting so blackout drunk I didn't remember being carried from a party and deposited in my apartment. I didn't tell them about the trail of messages in Inga's paintings, or about Carl showing up at the warehouse.

I didn't want to talk about any of it. I wanted all of it to not be true, so for a few hours, I pretended like it wasn't. Like none of it was happening. I danced with Frank twice. I flirted with the cute guy who showed up on the stool next to me until it was clear he was more interested in Lisel, and then I happily left them to it, filled with drunken warmth for them when they started making out around eleven. Edward called in an order of Chinese food from three blocks over and braved the cold to pick it up for us; we cheered its arrival and filled ourselves with greasy noodles and pork fried rice. As I ate, I dimly realized it was the first food I'd had all day.

"I am drunk," I declared, leaning against Lisel.

"Me too," she giggled. The cute guy, whose name I couldn't remember though I knew he designed websites—Tom? Todd?—had gone to the bathroom. "I think I'm going home with him," she whispered in my ear. "Will you be okay?"

Edward had left a few minutes ago, saying the Chinese food had given him indigestion. We'd teased him about being old—Edward was a good decade older than the rest of us, pushing forty instead of thirty—which he had accepted good-naturedly.

"I will be fine, it's just a few blocks. You have fun, and be careful," I mock-whispered back as Tom or Todd returned. Lisel slid an arm around his waist and they bundled themselves into their coats. She gave me a little finger wave over her shoulder, and they stumbled into the night, pressed against each other's side.

I smiled into my empty cup and considered getting another beer. I checked my watch, stunned to find it was one in the morning, and decided against it.

"You okay?" Frank's voice rumbled at me as I moved toward the door. "Want me to walk with you?"

"I'm good," I called back, full of alcohol-fueled confidence. "Thanks, though." I was sure I'd be fine; like I'd told Lisel, it was only a few blocks to my building, a route I'd taken countless times before.

The cold air pressed on me from all sides, as shocking as a slap after the warmth of the bar, the minute I stepped outside. I shivered, pulled my hat lower, and shoved my gloved hands into my pockets. Across the street, Vera Cruz was closed, its windows dark. The street was empty and silent except for the quiet rustling of the giant tinsel snowflakes that had been recently attached to the streetlights.

My footsteps rang loudly on the pavement. The sound was an echo of that morning—god, had it been less than twenty-four hours ago?—when I'd walked with such purpose and confidence on my way to the gallery. I shuddered, both from the cold and from the rushing memory of all that had happened since then.

I was suddenly desperate to be home, curled up under my thick down comforter with Groucho. It had been a mistake to drink so much, stay out so late. I knew I was risking a massive headache in the morning and could already feel its beginnings pressing on the edges of my skull, but maybe if I took a few Advil with a big glass of water I could stave it off.

A sound crept through my consciousness, just as I was considering pulling out my headphones for the last few blocks of my walk. It was another set of footsteps echoing in the still night.

They were behind me.

My back muscles tightened in response, but I didn't look over my shoulder. It was just someone else coming home late from a bar, or someone who'd worked a night shift. Still, the sound was unnerving. Anywhere other than Bedford was strictly residential around here, not a single business or storefront between there and my building, save the tiny bodega on my corner. I was pretty sure they would be closed at this hour, anyway. The siding-covered row houses were uniformly dark, their occupants fast asleep.

There wasn't another soul on the street.

Despite my assurances to myself that whoever was behind me was just another neighborhood resident making their way home, I began to walk faster.

The footsteps got faster too.

Shit.

Why hadn't I taken up Frank on his offer to walk me home? I knew I was overreacting but couldn't help it. All I could think of was the sight of my own body, frozen on the NYPD's cheap TV screen, hanging limply in a stranger's arms.

What if whoever was behind me was the person from the security footage, come to finish the job?

My heart rate spiked.

I started to run.

The footsteps ran too.

My breath became instantly labored, and a stitch formed in my side. I hated running.

A hand clapped on my shoulder and I hitched a breath, preparing to scream.

"Jeez, Chloe. It's me."

I whirled to find Bo, collar turned up, a lit cigarette dangling from the hand that wasn't on me.

"What the hell, Bo? You scared the crap out of me."

His shoulders hunched in apology. "Sorry. I didn't want to yell and wake anyone."

It was too late for apologies, my fear had shifted to white-hot anger. I was suddenly fed up with all this: tired of being confused, tired of being terrified, tired of feeling like things were happening around me and to me that were part of some big picture I didn't understand, that I was a pawn in someone else's massive game of chess.

Tired of not being able to remember.

Tired of the little probing questions my brain kept serving up, whispers of doubt about my own sanity.

"You don't sneak up behind a woman on a dark street in the middle of the night, Bo!" I was yelling but didn't care.

"I said I was sorry. Keep it down, someone's gonna call the cops."

Hysterical, enraged laughter bubbled out of me. "Bring 'em on. What's one more conversation with the police?" I turned on my heel. I was going home.

"Chloe, wait. What do you mean? You've been talking to cops?"

I whirled again, suddenly ready for the answer to the question I hadn't been able to ask for weeks.

What did I have to lose at this point? Knowing might even help.

"Who was in the bar with you that morning, Bo? When I saw you on the sidewalk the morning after Inga Beck was murdered, and you said you'd heard I had a wild time the night before at her party. Who told you that?"

Bo turned his head, studying the empty street. He took a deep drag of his cigarette. The tip pulsed bright orange for a brief moment, illuminating his sloped brow and calculating green eyes, then went dark.

My heart continued to thud, but from anticipation now instead of fear.

"Come to my place," he said, dropping his cigarette stub and grinding his heel on it. "Let's talk where it's warm."

CHAPTER TWENTY-ONE

"I feel like I'm going insane, Bo."

The words were dramatic, but true. It was both a relief and terrifying to say them out loud. I hadn't realized how cold I'd been until we were inside. Bo's apartment was good and warm, my fingers were slowly thawing. It was quiet, too, now that Tanya had moved out. Something about being indoors, in that quiet—not at the gallery, not at a bar, not surrounded by people—loosened a tide of words from me. I was sitting on the vintage turquoise couch he and Tanya had salvaged from a street corner, Bo in an armchair across from me.

He lit another cigarette and offered me one. I shook my head.

"You have no idea," I continued. Bo abruptly got up and went into the kitchen. I heard the refrigerator door open, then close. He came back and handed me a bottle of Corona, tucked his own into the cushion of his chair next to his side. I knew I shouldn't drink anything else but took a long slug anyway. My hand shook, sloshing a little of the beer onto the front of my shirt.

Bo watched me. His eyes were sympathetic, but he also looked wary.

I didn't blame him. I was babbling, the stress of the past few weeks since Inga's murder pouring out of me.

"Something's going on, Bo. Something fucked-up is happening and I feel like I'm in the middle of it, but I don't know how or why. There's huge chunks of that night I don't remember, but then from time to time I do, you know? Like a puzzle piece will drop into place, and I remember a fragment, a moment. And sometimes it fits the puzzle and sometimes it doesn't, to the point that I don't know what's real or not. Like, am I just making stuff up because I want to remember so badly? Or am

I remembering what actually happened? It's like I'm one step away from making a crazy chart on my wall with red string connecting dots that aren't there. But Vik is being super distant and crappy and weird, and my boss at work just disappeared, like into total thin air. It's been almost two weeks and nobody's heard a word from him." Nobody at the gallery, at least. Or if they had, they weren't talking.

I paused and took another sip of beer, smaller this time. My hand still shook, but I managed not to spill any.

"The police took me to their precinct today, Bo. I got in the back of an unmarked car, and they drove me to Brooklyn and they seem to think I know something, but I don't know anything." It was on the tip of my tongue to tell Bo about the video they showed me, but over his shoulder, something caught my eye.

Something that made me freeze, but only for a second.

I carefully set the bottle on the coffee table.

"What did they ask about?" Bo asked. He was trying to sound casual, but there was a new tension to his shoulders, his voice. "Like, what specifically? Chloe?"

I barely heard him. My entire self was focused on what I'd seen. I tried to tear my eyes away and did so long enough to take in Bo, now sitting upright instead of slouched. He set his own bottle down and followed my gaze as it returned to over his shoulder.

Dread crept from my center down my limbs. The walls felt like they were contracting. It was hard to breathe.

Casually flung over the back of Bo's desk chair in the corner was a dark gray sweatshirt.

It was an ordinary sweatshirt, no patterns or marks, nothing distinctive about it, one of a million just like it. One that zipped up the front and had a hood. I'd seen Bo in it before, plenty of times.

But that was just it. I had seen him in it before. I'd put down the sickening, nagging familiarity of the figure in the surveillance video to the fact that it was me on that screen, that I was responding to my own image, to seeing myself being carted around like a sack of flour.

And it was that, but it hit me that it was something more too.

I had recognized not only myself, but also the person carrying me.

I had recognized his swaggering walk, the set of his shoulders.

My eyes flew back to Bo's face. Whatever he saw in me made his own expression fall, and then change. Wariness and fear and an underlying hardness I'd never seen in him before combined in a way that sent terror shooting down my spine. I grabbed my coat and bag and tried to stand on clumsy legs.

Bo stood first, very slowly, and before I could make myself move, he positioned himself in front of the door to the kitchen.

In front of the only way out of the apartment.

I swallowed hard. There was a noise in my head, a loud buzzing.

"Chloe? *Chloe.*" Bo waved a hand in front of my face, trying to get my attention.

I backed up a few steps until my calves bumped his coffee table.

I was trapped. A whimpering sound filled the room, and I was horrified to realize it was me. I shook my head in denial, clutched my coat closer to my chest like it could protect me somehow.

Bo held out his palms like he was calming a wild animal.

"I can explain."

"What the fuck, Bo?" My voice trembled so badly I barely recognized it. I could feel my heart in my ears.

"Let me explain. I promise I can explain."

"You were there," I said accusingly. I scooted around the coffee table to the other side of the room. There was nowhere to go in that direction, only the tiny bathroom and the bedroom Bo had previously shared with Tanya, the bedroom I'd been naked in, plenty of times. "You lied and said someone at the bar told you about the party, but you were there." The shock of it, that it had been Bo, Bo, who carried me out of Inga's loft and into a waiting town car, reverberated through my bones.

"Just at the end. Just to get you and bring you home." His own voice shook slightly. I didn't know if that was a good or bad thing.

"Oh my god," I said. My shaking hand covered my mouth.

Was it Bo? Had he killed Inga? It made no sense, he hadn't even known Inga.

Had he?

"That guy you were making out with called and told me to get you. That you were on the verge of passing out."

"What? What guy?"

I remembered Vik, the morning after the party. *You were getting awfully friendly with some guy when I left . . . I don't blame you; he was cute.*

I pressed my hands to the side of my head. I couldn't bring to mind a single image of a guy from the party, other than the people I knew: Vik, Ben, Lou.

Nobody I would have been kissing.

"Yeah, Liam." Bo had lowered his hands a little and was eyeing me cautiously.

Who the hell was Liam?

"Sometime in the night you two figured out you both knew me," Bo continued. He was talking more slowly now, but he still sounded a little shaky. "You got so wasted you passed out. Liam didn't know where you lived or what to do, so he called me. I told him never mind, I'd get you."

I shook my head. I didn't have any recollection of that. Not a shred. I couldn't even picture this Liam guy.

"You were pretty wasted, Chlo. Liam had bailed by the time I got there."

"I don't even know who that is. How do you know him?"

"I don't know him well. He was in that off-off-Broadway thing with Tanya last year, we met a couple of times over the show's run. He does stagehand work when he's between gigs, so we exchanged numbers."

"But . . . where was Inga when you got to the party?" This changed everything. Bo had seen Inga after me. *Bo* was the last person to see Inga alive.

Detective Downs's voice rang in my head: *Except for whoever killed her.*

"I didn't see anyone else. You were alone."

That didn't make sense. I shook my head again and clutched my coat tighter.

"Look, the door was open, you were by yourself, passed out on that girl's futon. You were already in your coat. Maybe she went to take the trash out, I dunno. She wasn't there, it was just you, and I got you home." He pointed at his chest as he said this, as if he deserved a reward or something.

"You need to tell the police," I said. I took a step, around the coffee table, farther away from him. I wished he'd move away from the door.

"Shit, Chlo, I can't do that."

"Why the hell not?"

Bo pushed his bangs off his face and blew out a breath.

"Because I have a record, okay? For dealing. Just little stuff, you know. Some weed, some pills here and there. They find out I was last on the scene where a girl wound up dead? Who knows what would happen to me."

"To *you?* They seem to think *I* had something to do with this. Bo, the cops know someone was there. They have you on *video*. Jesus, why didn't you tell me this before? When I saw you the morning after the party?"

"What, when you were on the street with Gio? You really wanted me to spill you'd been making out with a random dude and had gotten so wasted I had to carry you out of there, in front of the guy who thinks you shit gold?"

"What are you talking about?"

"Come on, Chloe. Gio's got it bad for you."

"He does not," I said automatically.

Did he?

Bo carefully reached down and picked up his package of Marlboro Reds, the last one having burned down in the ashtray where he'd set it after he saw me notice the sweatshirt. He shook one out and offered me the pack.

I hesitated, still unsure. But what was I thinking? Bo was a fuckup, but he wasn't a killer. I dropped my coat and bag on the couch and leaned across the coffee table, taking one, and accepted a light.

Bo pulled on his cigarette. "What are you, blind?" he said as he exhaled a cloud of smoke into the apartment. "The guy thinks you're God's gift to women. And look, he's a nice guy. Maybe you should go for it." He gave me a look under half-lowered lids that didn't match the underlying aggression in his voice.

I shook my head again, this time to clear it. The headache I'd felt on my walk was returning and intensifying. Bo sounded . . . jealous. Which was insane, as he'd been the one with the girlfriend the whole time we were hooking up.

"Can we get back to the party?" I said, eager to get back on track. I shoved what he'd said about Gio aside. "How did you get me in my apartment? And you undressed me?" The thought of Bo taking my clothes off my limp, unresponsive body made my skin crawl. Just because I'd slept with the guy didn't make his actions any less intrusive.

"I have a key to your place, Chlo." He looked at me like I was nuts for forgetting.

I stared at him. "No, you don't."

"Uh, yes, I do. How else do you think I got in?"

I racked my brain. I couldn't remember ever giving Bo a key. "When did I give you a key?"

"You didn't. Vik did, like a year ago."

"He did?"

"Yeah. To feed Groucho. Last Christmas, I think. When you both went home. Or maybe Vik gave it to Tanya, I don't remember. But we fed your cat."

I strained my memory for an indication that I knew this, that this wasn't information I was hearing for the first time.

Nothing.

I hadn't been home for Christmas for very long last year, just a long weekend, the expensive holiday season flight courtesy of my dad. It had been two strained days in his immaculate house, and two more in my mom's messy one, each atmosphere thick with tension for different reasons. I'd spent a lot of time with Becky, one of my few friends who was still in Canton. She was engaged, and we'd passed much of our time together in a sticky sports bar, poring over wedding magazines, postseason college football blaring in the background. It had been such a miserable four days I hadn't made plans to return this year. Dad hadn't offered a ticket, anyway.

I suppose it made sense that Bo and Tanya fed Groucho. Vik usually went home for a good three weeks around the holidays, during his entire school break.

But if that was the case, why hadn't Vik mentioned that Bo had a key when we thought we'd had a break-in? What the hell was going on? Vik and Bo didn't even *like* each other that much. Vik thought Bo was an asshole, and he kind of was, and Bo thought Vik was a snob, which he also kind of was. But somehow they'd exchanged a house key?

"And you undressed me?"

Bo shrugged a little, inhaling on his Marlboro Red. I did the same. It was making me feel a little lightheaded; I normally smoked Marlboro Lights. "Nothing I haven't seen before," he said. "I thought I was doing you a favor. Wait, you don't think I'd try anything while you were passed out, do you? Come on, Chloe. You've gotta know me better than that." He looked horrified at the thought.

"No, no, I don't think that." At least I didn't think I did; Bo wasn't *that* big of a creep. I didn't like that he'd left me totally naked, though. I felt a little sick to my stomach, and the headache was worsening.

"God, Bo." I stubbed out my cigarette in the overflowing ashtray and plopped onto the sofa next to my pile of things, burying my head in my hands. "How am I supposed to keep this from the police? None of this rings a bell, I have no recollection of this Liam guy. I don't know about any of this."

Bo gave me strange look from under his too-long bangs. It took me a minute to decipher it.

He was looking at me with pity.

"Just because you can't remember it, Chloe, doesn't mean it didn't happen."

CHAPTER TWENTY-TWO

I spent the night at Bo's. I'd made so many bad decisions in the past few months, what was one more? Besides, despite Groucho's presence, I couldn't face my empty apartment. Bo's body was like a lifeline, something I could hold on to in the midst of the raging storm that was happening all around me and within my own head.

The sex was good—it was always good with Bo, part of why I'd traditionally had a hard time saying no to him—but when I woke to thin sunlight streaming through his cheap vinyl pulldown blinds, I instantly regretted having stayed over. I never did have that Advil and my head was pounding. I gathered my things and crept out of the apartment, leaving behind the musky, sweaty scent of Bo's overheated room and his oblivious sleeping form.

I blinked against the sun, brighter out on the street, as I walked the two blocks home, where I showered away the scent of my nighttime activities. The Advil was in the back of the bathroom cabinet, and I made a mental note to buy more as I swallowed the last two left in the bottle with the bitterly strong coffee I'd made.

Caffeinated and clean, I leaned against the kitchen counter in my still apartment and sipped the brew in the "I HEART NY" mug, wishing I had a little milk to lighten it up. I missed Gio's coffee. I hadn't been to the bakery or seen him around since Thanksgiving, when he gave me the cookies to take to Lou's.

That felt like years ago.

What Bo had said surfaced in my mind. *The guy thinks you're God's gift to women.* I thought of Gio, chasing me down the street to give me the cookies. Of all the free cups of coffee he handed my way.

I pushed the thought aside, for now. It didn't feel like the right time to be pursuing anything like that. I wasn't even sure Bo was right.

Still, I let my gaze slide into the window of the bakery as I passed it on the way to the train. I didn't see Gio behind the counter. An unexpected disappointment rose in my throat.

Once at the gallery, Sloane cornered me in the kitchen, where I was stirring my cup of coffee, grateful Willa had a full pot waiting when I arrived. Hers was so much better than mine.

"I talked to Henry about *Careless*, Chloe. Oh, are you all right?"

My headache had only partially abated—too little water and Advil, too late, they were no match for the amount I'd had to drink on an empty stomach the night before, not to mention the late night. Sloane's question confirmed I looked as crappy as I felt.

"Yeah, I'm okay. Just need this." I held up the coffee.

"Are you upset about meeting with the police yesterday? I can absolutely have Jonathan file a complaint. They had no right." Sloane seemed to be gearing up for a rant, so I interjected.

"I'm okay, really. Had a hard time sleeping, is all."

"If you're sure." She looked at me closely.

"Yup." I gave what I hoped was a reassuring smile. "So, you talked to Henry about *Careless*? You know who owns it?"

"Yes, we do," she said. I was pleased my hunch that the Fletchers knew the painting's location had been correct.

"Great. Do you think they'll let me see it? Maybe borrow it for the show? It would only increase the painting's value, I would think." I took a big gulp of coffee, excitement along with the extra caffeine making my blood sing.

I needed to see that painting. I wanted to know if Inga had left another message in it.

Sloane offered a strange little smile. "Yes to both, I think."

"Awesome. So who is Dunbar Capital?"

"Actually, Chloe"—Sloane's smile turned conspiratorial—"Dunbar Capital is us. We own *Careless*."

The "we," it turned out, was the Fletchers. Henry and Sloane owned the entity Dunbar Capital, and they co-owned the painting. It was in Sloane's apartment, a massive, sprawling affair also on the Upper East Side, but farther east than the gallery and close to the river. As we entered the hushed, elegant lobby of her building, I remembered that Sloane had been in the midst of a nasty divorce when I'd first started at Fletcher & Sons, and Lou had said something about how Sloane had gotten the apartment in the settlement.

Several of us trailed Sloane into her home: me, Douglas, and Sebastian. The space was airy and bright with natural light. I had expected the same heavy, patterned rugs and antique furniture that decorated Sloane's and Henry's offices at the gallery, but the apartment was all sleek neutral tones with modern furniture. I had to stifle a gasp at the view, it was so stunning. A wall of windows looked to the East River, Gracie Mansion's grounds on one side and Queens on the other.

Careless was hanging directly opposite that view. It was rare to find an apartment in the city that had a wall large enough to hold a painting so big. I hadn't seen the work in person yet, and I moved closer, standing next to Sebastian, who was examining the painting closely, his nose inches from its surface, making notes on a clipboard.

"Can you move?" he asked, suddenly a bare inch to my right.

I hastily took a step back, and he moved into the spot I'd occupied, muttering under his breath. I knew Sebastian was making a condition report, noting the exact state of the work before it was crated for shipping, and he would check it again once it arrived at the SoHo space where the show would be held. "I didn't realize the painting was leaving today," I said. "The exhibition isn't for a few more weeks."

He heaved a lusty sigh as if my ignorance was painful. "The shipper we use happened to have an opening in their schedule today, a cancellation of another pickup, so we jumped on it. Otherwise they're booked for weeks. This is why we normally plan these things months in advance." Sebastian gave me a withering look over the rims of his glasses. I resisted pointing out that if I'd known *Careless* was here, I might have asked to have it added to the exhibition sooner. I still didn't understand why the Fletchers had never told me they owned the painting. "They'll take it to the warehouse today. We may have to use a different shipper to get it to the exhibition space."

I took a few steps back to let Sebastian do his job. Sloane had retreated into the depths of the apartment after saying she'd get us some coffee, the thought of which—Sloane brewing coffee herself—took a stretch of the imagination. Douglas was across the room, securing a thin padded moving blanket around the edges of the front door with painter's tape, so as not to risk bashing the doorframe with the crate once the painting was boxed up. Farther back was better for my purposes, anyway. I didn't know if the hidden word in the painting would be written tiny, as in some of the other works, or huge, as in *Lifeless*.

Where was it? I deliberately took a deep, calming breath and tried to tune out Sebastian and his snide comments. Instead, I let my eyes rove over the painting as I had done with the others in the warehouse, not following any particular pattern, but hoping by not doing so I'd find one. The work was a bright, discordant array of color: vibrant, cheerful yellows and parrot greens, mixed with candy-hued pinks and blues. It was a wild, joyful work, but at the same time a little unhinged, as if all that elation was on the cusp of tipping into hysteria. My gaze caught on a thin, sneaky line of turquoise that danced its way in and around the other, larger strokes of paint, disappearing and then reappearing.

I stepped back again.

There it was. Half hidden, peeking out from behind the other whirling, looping brushstrokes.

Be careful.

My breath caught.

Was this message less clear than the others? I squinted and moved three big steps to the right, trying to see the words from a different angle.

From this direction, they vanished. The connections between the lines of paint were gone, and the turquoise lines were just that, marks made on a canvas with paint on a brush.

"What are you *doing*?" Sebastian's nasty drawl broke my scrutiny.

I hesitated. Sebastian was the last person I wanted to share a secret with. But was it a secret? He didn't have to know about the mysterious note with the address I still kept in my pocket, or about the messages in the other paintings. And even if he did know about the other messages, I didn't have to voice my suspicion that they were connected to Inga's murder.

That maybe, somehow, they even explained it.

"Do you see anything in this painting?"

Sebastian narrowed his eyes at me, then looked at the canvas. "Like what? I didn't find any damage." He sounded both defensive and accusatory.

"Not like that. A word? Or phrase?"

He wrinkled his nose at me but looked at the painting again, more closely this time. I moved us three steps back to the left and pointed.

"See there? That turquoise? Follow it all the way across the canvas. Doesn't it spell something out?" I deliberately didn't tell him what I thought it spelled. I wanted to see if we'd find the same words.

Sebastian was quiet for a long time. I watched his eyes move, saw them tracing the line I had shown him. I was surprised to find how badly I wanted him to see it. No, how I *needed* him to see it.

I needed someone to see what I saw, to confirm this wasn't all in my head.

Sebastian inhaled as if to speak, an unusually thoughtful expression on his face.

"Coffee, anyone?" A small woman of Asian descent, maybe Filipino, entered the living room carrying a tray loaded with a ceramic pot and mugs. She was wearing black pants and a loose floral top rather than a uniform but was obviously a housekeeper or maid. Sloane trailed after her.

"Justina, you forgot the sugar," Sloane complained, eyeing the tray.

"I'd love a coffee," Sebastian said, turning his back to me. "Thank you."

"Sebastian," I said. "Wait. Do you see it? You do, right?"

Sebastian paused and looked over his shoulder. "No. There's nothing there."

I was dumbfounded. "Really? You can't see—" I started to point at the line again, but his ice-cold, derisive voice stopped me.

"Whatever you're seeing, Chloe, it's all in your head."

CHAPTER TWENTY-THREE

I came home to the sound of the shower running, an unexpected and welcome surprise. The shower on meant Vik was home for the second night in a row. The night before, Wednesday, Vik had shown up with a bagful of takeout, grinning, saying he was ready for *The West Wing*. I hadn't expected him, resigned to my night alone with my bottle of cheap white. I hadn't had the energy to haunt any of the bars last night, or tonight, for that matter, and had walked the slightly longer way home instead of straight down Bedford, avoiding the commercial strip of the neighborhood altogether. I'd been pondering the take-out menu when Vik arrived. We'd spent a fun, laugh-filled night, sharing drunken noodles and chicken satay, and I'd been able to push the previous night with Bo and visit with the police out of my head for a few hours, before falling into bed in a tipsy, deep sleep. I recalled feeling full and grateful as I dropped off, wondering if maybe I could put the past few weeks behind me.

A delicious smell filled the apartment now. Another happy surprise: Vik was cooking. It was chicken curry by the smell, bubbling away on the stove, the dial set to low. Cooked rice filled the steamer on the counter. I smiled to myself; Vik home two nights in a row was a rarity and a treat these days. I assumed he was spending most of his nights at Benny's, though maybe he'd gone to his parents in Jersey for a while too. But here he was, and maybe he, too, was ready to put the past few weeks of tension behind us. I could maybe forget about the messages in the paintings, forget about the note in my pocket, the hurt of Lou's disappearance—

I stopped in the doorway to my bedroom in shock.

Ben was in my room, frowning into the messy contents of an open dresser drawer.

"What are you doing?" I asked.

Ben started, grabbing his chest as he spun toward me.

"I didn't hear you come in, Chloe. You scared me."

Obviously, he hadn't heard me. "Why are you going through my things?" I dropped my bag at my feet. The dresser drawer was still open in front of him, sweaters and T-shirts in a wild heap.

Ben pushed his strawberry-blond hair away from his forehead. For a moment he looked like a cornered animal. Then a calculating, sly expression passed over his face, there and gone so fast I wasn't sure I'd seen it.

Something in my memory jolted. Something about that look on Ben's face.

"I was looking for the menu to the Thai place. Vik said it was probably tucked away in here."

"You thought it was in with my sweaters? And Vik's cooking. Why would you want takeout?"

There it was again, the same look, skipping across his handsome, boyish face.

"I know. For the weekend, *silly*. Vik's always going on about how great it is, I thought I'd check out the menu while he showered." Ben shoved the drawer shut and pushed past me into the living room, saying in a nonchalant voice as he passed, "No big deal. Just hand it over when you find it, I want to take a look."

It was the *silly* that did it. That, combined with his fleetingly canny, shrewd expression.

The memory snapped into place, so vivid it was like being transported back in time.

Vik and Ben laughing in the smoke. Only now I recalled shot glasses in their hands, filled to the brim with pale liquid. And Inga next to them.

Next to me.

"Ready?" she said, a devilish glint in her eye. Around us the party swirled. We were standing at the kitchen counter, holding shots in one hand and making fists with the other. A plate of lime slices sat before us.

"One, two, three!" On Inga's command, all four of us licked the salt sprinkled on the backs of our hands. The salt burned my tongue, followed by the different hot burn of the tequila, searing its way down my throat. I groped for a lime and shoved it in my mouth, sucking hard, its tartness merging with the other tastes, mellowing them.

Ben whooped as he slammed his shot glass down. There was a whole cluster of them, evidence of the many shots we'd taken together.

The room spun gently, once. I closed my eyes and giggled, gripping the countertop.

"Are you okay?" Inga's voice was soft and breathy in my ear.

I opened them again to find her face inches from mine. "I'm great," I said. And I meant it. "But I do need the bathroom."

She laughed lightly, a musical sound, and took half a step back. I stumbled toward the only door I saw, closed, back by the futon.

"Not that way, silly," Ben said, taking hold of my shoulders and gently turning me in the direction of a yellow shower curtain in the opposite corner of the kitchen. "That's a closet. This way."

"I'll show her," Inga said, taking my hand. An appraising look I didn't like crossed Ben's face as she led me to the curtain, glimpsed but just as quickly forgotten.

Whoosh. Inga drew back the curtain, revealing a toilet that had a jam jar filled with bodega flowers sitting on its tank. She closed the curtain again, its metal rings sliding along the bar, enclosing both of us inside. The makeshift bathroom glowed yellow, and while the chatter and noise of the party rose above and through the thin barrier of plastic curtain, the rest of the guests felt very far away. I was suddenly too aware of my breath, which was coming in quick, shallow pants.

I wobbled a little again, and Inga held my arm and pulled me closer, laughing some more.

"Sure you can manage?" Her voice was a whisper.

She was so close. I could smell the lime from her last tequila shot. I suddenly wanted to taste it, wanted to know what those pink lips would feel like against my own.

As if reading my mind, Inga closed the scant distance between us and gently pressed her lips to mine. An unexpected jolt of desire shot through me.

I'd never kissed a girl before. Inga's kiss left me weak-kneed and trembling.

She pulled away, smiling, her eyes searching mine. As if satisfied with what she read there, Inga gently slipped out between the folds of the curtain again. "There's hand soap by the kitchen sink," she said as she departed.

I turned and looked at Ben now. He was puttering around the living room nervously. The shower had turned off. "You knew," I said. My voice sounded wooden. I held on to the doorjamb, afraid my legs would buckle as they almost had the night of the party, but for a different reason.

I'd come out of the bathroom that night and washed my hands. When I rejoined the group, Vik and Ben had their coats on. Ben whispered something in Inga's ear, making her blush a little and laugh yet again.

And Ben gave me that same look. The one that had shown up on his face tonight, unconsciously, I was sure.

"Knew what?" he asked, flopping onto the couch and pretending to look at a magazine.

"You knew I kissed Inga. Vik said there was a guy, but there wasn't a guy, was there? That's why I can't remember any guy, any Liam. It was Inga I kissed."

Ben sat up straight on the couch. "I don't have any idea what you're talking about, Chloe."

"Yeah, what are you talking about?" Vik padded from the kitchen to the living room on quiet, bare feet, his hair damp but neatly combed. He was wearing sweatpants and a T-shirt, obviously ready for a night at home with his boyfriend.

"Both of you," I said. My mind was racing, putting pieces together. "But you, Ben. You were whispering to Inga when I came out of the bathroom, whispering and laughing. You two were friends, I *remember* you doing that. She told you we'd kissed, didn't she? Why did you make up some story about a guy, Vik? And what the hell were you doing in my room just now, Ben?"

If Vik had lied about my making out with a guy, then Bo was lying too.

And if Bo was lying, then there was no Liam, no excuse for Bo to have picked me up at the party.

I gripped the sides of my head. *Remember*, I wanted to scream. *Remember more, remember it all.*

Were Bo and Vik in on something together? I couldn't begin to fathom what such a thing could be. Why would they lie to me?

"I don't think this is the best night for me to stay over, Vik," Ben said in a regretful tone as he gathered a few things. "I'm sorry I'm missing your curry, but if she's gonna have another episode, I should probably not be here."

He gave Vik's cheek a quick peck and hastily left, his coat dangling from under his arm, backpack slung over one shoulder, boots barely laced.

Vik looked stunned, then furious.

I was furious too.

"Another *episode?*" I asked. "What the hell does that mean?"

Vik blew out an angry breath, placing his hands on his hips.

"It means you've been acting insane, Chloe. For weeks now. Months, at this point. And you refuse to get help and the people around you can't take it anymore."

"I haven't been acting insane," I said automatically, instantly defensive.

"You absolutely have. Freaking out because Ben was in your room? Don't you think your reaction was a little oversized? I could hear you in the *shower.*"

I gaped at Vik. "He was going through my drawers."

"And I don't know if you kissed Inga. I don't know *what* the hell you get up to half the time, Chloe. When Ben and I left that party you were all over some guy."

That was not what I remembered. "No."

"*Yes.* And all this nonsense thinking something nefarious happened with Lou, that someone broke into our apartment, or that Inga's murder had anything to do with you or me. I've tried to be patient but it's got to stop. You have to get help. There are no connections there, no bigger picture. Lou got fired and skipped town to lick his wounds. Inga's death is terrible but who knows what she was involved with, or maybe it was just dumb bad luck. Bad shit happens sometimes, Chloe. That's all any of this is. Shit happening. Do you know why I haven't been around much lately? Why I've been avoiding you? Because of this." He swept his arms around the apartment, indicating Ben's absence, the ruined curry, the recycling bin full of my empty wine bottles, in one swoop. "Because it is hard to be around you these days. You numb yourself with booze and one-night stands and it is *hard* to stand back and watch when you seem so determined to destroy yourself."

He paused, breathing hard.

I, on the other hand, could barely breathe.

"I know it's been hard for you," Vik said in a gentler tone.

I finally found my breath, drew in a big one. *Don't go there, Vik.*

He held up a hand, as if sensing my imminent protest. "No, I will say this. I can't pretend to know what it was like for you, being there when the towers fell, but maybe I would have a better sense if you'd talk to me, or anyone, about it."

I couldn't form words. I spent all my energy focused on keeping the memories from rushing in.

"I think maybe being at that party the night Inga was killed triggered something in you, Chloe. Something about death, from your own near-death experience that you haven't dealt with yet. You don't want to admit it, but you have PTSD. The whole city has PTSD, but you were there, so of course you're more traumatized. And now you're jumping at shadows."

I didn't know who to believe. Vik, who'd been cagey since Inga died? Bo, who had lied about why he'd carried me out of that loft? Or was Vik *not* being cagey, and just avoiding me, like he said? And what if Bo was telling the truth, and there *had* been a guy named Liam? Maybe I hadn't kissed him, I'd just talked to him, and Bo had a few of the details wrong.

Maybe I hadn't kissed Inga at all but had been obsessing about her so much lately, getting lost in staring at her picture, that my brain made it up.

Or should I believe my own gut, which told me strongly that the memory of kissing Inga was true, which told me there was no Liam, which told me something was deeply, powerfully off in my world but I had no idea what or why?

I was still hovering in the doorway of my room, still in my coat. I felt in the pocket of my skirt for the note with the address. Even though I was still too afraid to check out the address on my own, I always had it on my person. It felt like a talisman.

"I'm sure you're right," I said. Instinct told me to tread carefully. "I'm sure I do have PTSD, and I probably would benefit from therapy. I know I drink too much and hook up with too many guys. But none of that changes the fact that something weird is happening here, Vik." My voice started to shake as I tried to explain. "Lou disappearing like he did is *weird*, don't try to tell me it isn't. Someone *did* break in here, I'm sure of it. Maybe it was Bo, since I guess he had our old key. I *did* kiss Inga, and I think . . . I think she's trying to tell me something."

Vik closed his eyes and shook his head. "Chloe. She's dead."

"I know she's dead, but I think she knew she was going to die. That she was going to be killed. She left messages about it, Vik, I'm sure of it."

"Do you even hear yourself? You sound like a crazy person on the street corner."

"And you," I went on as though he hadn't spoken. "You're *lying* to me. All of you are: you, Bo, Ben, the Fletchers, even Lou. I know it. Why, Vik? What's going on?"

Vik's eyes had opened, and he looked at me with a mix of wariness and regret. "Nothing. Nothing is going on, Chloe. Whatever you think is happening, it's all in your head. Please, let me help you."

I *almost* believed him. Almost.

But I had seen something else in his eyes too. Mixed in with the other emotions, and quickly hidden, but it had been there.

Vik was afraid.

Which was enough to make me afraid, nearly as afraid as I'd been in the warehouse with Carl.

Panic began to crowd in alongside my fear.

I couldn't stay here. I didn't have a plan, or any idea of where else I could go, but I knew it couldn't be here.

I pushed past Vik and ran toward the door. My terror spiked as he reached for me and called my name, but I had the element of surprise on my side and made it past him, through the door and out into the night.

CHAPTER TWENTY-FOUR

I ran for four whole blocks before the stitch in my side forced me to stop. I had run south, not really knowing why. Now that I stood with my hands on my knees, panting, I realized it was probably because it was the opposite direction of where Vik might look for me.

If he came looking.

I straightened quickly and checked behind me.

Nobody.

Or no Vik. Just a short white guy with curly hair sticking out from under a hat with flap ears, shuffling down the opposite sidewalk.

I bit my lip. Where could I go? I'd left my bag in the apartment and didn't have any money on me, or my MetroCard. Rosemary's was out of the question, if I wanted to stay away from Vik for now. So was Vera Cruz.

And I did want to stay away. I needed a place to sit and try to organize my thoughts and decide what my next steps should be.

I had to do something, though I had no idea what. All I knew was that I was sick of things happening *to* me, of feeling like I was in an elaborate game where everyone else knew the rules but me.

The streets were dark and mostly empty. There were intermittent streetlights, but they didn't help much, casting greater shadows rather than providing extra light. My own shadow wavered, elongating then shrinking, as I slowly walked toward the river.

There was one other place I could think to go within walking distance.

The interior of Diner glowed warmly. The low, curved ceiling of what had originally been a train's diner car made the long space feel cozy and intimate. I had been a regular when the restaurant first opened. It was great to have a neighborhood spot that served the kind of bistro fare you normally had to go to places like Balthazar in Manhattan to find. That had been when I was still dating Alex, and his trust fund had helped offset the cost of Diner, which, while cheaper than Balthazar, was still a little rich for my blood. I loved it so much, though, I still managed to swing by at least once a month. I'd have a cocktail and burger at the bar, or steak frites if my bank account allowed it.

The restaurant was almost directly under the Williamsburg Bridge, and the only other business for blocks was the Peter Luger Steak House, which had been there for almost a century. The fear and tension I'd felt walking the desolate streets to get here instantly eased as I stepped inside.

"Hey, Chloe, long time no see." Andrew was one of the restaurant's owners and often tended bar too. He immediately began making me a cosmopolitan.

"I left my wallet at home," I admitted, sliding onto one of the round, vinyl-covered stools at the bar.

"That seat is taken," a girl on the next stool told me in a snippy voice. She had long, dark, very straight hair, bright red talons for nails, and a thick Staten Island–sounding accent. Diner was a mostly local joint, full of grubby tattooed musicians and artists, and she stood out like a sore thumb.

"Sorry," I said. I slid one over, the only other free spot at the bar, and raised my brows at Andrew. He gave a slight shrug back, shaking a cocktail mixer with vigor. I hung my coat on one of the hooks below the bar.

"Don't worry about it, you can pay me next time," Andrew said, sliding the drink across the bar at me.

I smiled my thanks and took a grateful sip, letting Andrew move down the bar to attend to another customer. The place was busy tonight as always, the booths and bar full.

It was time to review my options. *Did I even have any?* I wondered, taking another sip, the alcohol coursing through me.

I did. I *had* to. The alternative was that I could do nothing and continue being batted around like a piece of driftwood in low tide, subject to the whims of unseen forces.

What did I know?

I knew that Inga had left messages in her paintings.

Leaning over the bar, I grabbed a napkin and fished a pen out of an empty check sleeve. I wrote out the messages in the order in which I knew the paintings had been completed:

Careless: Be Careful
Loveless: Carl
Fearless: Afraid
Hopeless: Too late
Helpless: Help Me
Lifeless: Murder

I found myself chewing the end of the pen, realized how gross that was with a pen from a bar, and quickly took a drink. The booze would kill any germs.

Despite what I'd said to Vik, I knew Inga hadn't had me in mind when she added these hidden words to her paintings. This wasn't a code written for my eyes only; she had probably been using the words to underscore how she felt at the time she created the works, an extended expression of her art.

But, now that I remembered that moment behind the shower curtain, I was sure Inga had put the note with the address in my pocket. I was also sure that whatever was at that address was related to the messages in the paintings. And I was pretty sure she'd hoped I'd find the words, hoped I'd make the connection.

I rewrote the words on the napkin, without the painting titles.

Be Careful. Carl. Afraid. Too Late. Help Me. Murder.

It was a chilling combination.

I downed the rest of my drink.

Andrew was still at the other end of the bar. I waited for him to come back my way, reading the words on the napkin over and over again. Suddenly, the hair on the back of my neck rose.

I snapped my head up.

It felt like somebody was watching me.

Andrew pointed to my empty glass as he walked by, silently asking if I wanted another. I nodded and took the opportunity to carefully look over each shoulder, pretending to casually scope out the other patrons.

Before I could take it all in, the air to my left shifted as another body sat in the empty stool, the one I'd tried to sit in first. I moved a little to the right to give the newcomer some space.

"Chloe?"

The sound of my name made me jolt.

It was Gio. He'd taken the stool next to the dark-haired girl. She stared at me from behind him, her eyes narrowed in suspicion.

He looked good. I didn't usually see Gio out of what he wore to the bakery. He was more dressed up tonight, in a dark burgundy button-down shirt and a stylish pair of jeans, hair slicked back.

"Hi, Gio." I slid my hand over the napkin I'd been writing on, hiding the words, and moved it to my right, away from him. "How's it going?"

"Real good. How about you? Haven't seen you since Thanksgiving." The mention of the holiday, the memory of Debra's joyful expression when she'd opened the box of cookies, sent a twinge of sadness down my spine.

"That's right. Thank you again for the cookies. They were a huge hit."

"Aw, no problem, I told you. It was my pleasure." He'd turned his back almost completely on the dark-haired woman, who elbowed him a little now and gave him a loaded look.

"I'm sorry," he said, "this is Stacie. She's an old friend of my cousin's, lives in Staten Island." I experienced a trill of satisfaction that I placed the accent correctly. "Stace, this is Chloe. She's a friend from the neighborhood."

Stacie extended her long-nailed hand across Gio. Her handshake was unpleasantly limp, like holding a dead fish. "Nice to meet you," she said, though her face said the exact opposite.

"You too. But don't let me interrupt you guys, I'm just hanging out, you know. Gathering my thoughts." I managed a small smile.

A fresh drink appeared in front of me. Andrew turned to Gio and Stacie. "You all ordering?"

Gio looked at Stacie. "See anything?" he asked, picking up the menu.

She wrinkled her nose, just a little. "There aren't many choices," she said in a loud whisper. Andrew tactfully moved away again, letting them decide. Diner's menu was sparse, but the food was outstanding. "Can't we go to the steak house?"

I pretended to turn to my drink but was eavesdropping shamelessly. I guessed Stacie meant Peter Luger's.

"Nah, not without a reservation," Gio said. "You don't like it here?"

She looked around, her face a mask of disapproval. "It's not very fancy, is it? I thought we could go to a club or something."

Out of the corner of my eye, I saw Gio smile thinly. "I ain't much of a club guy. You want a cosmo, though? Andrew makes a really good one. Chloe, you having a cosmo?"

"Uh, yeah. Best in the city," I said, flashing them a quick smile before turning back to my napkin. It was one thing to eavesdrop, another to be put in the middle of what was obviously a bad date.

Why was Gio even on a date with this girl? He could do better than her.

I shifted a little on my stool, uncomfortable with my own train of thought. I'd never considered Gio in that way before, but ever since Bo had said Gio liked me I'd been wondering if it was true.

If maybe I liked him back.

Stacie flashed me a dirty look before she leaned in and began to furiously whisper to Gio, low enough now that I couldn't hear.

That tingling sensation on the back of my neck started again.

There was no denying it; it definitely felt like someone was watching me.

I tried the casual, look-over-my-shoulder thing again.

Nothing unusual. There was nobody else I knew, and nobody was paying me any attention. The row of diners in their booths were looking at each other, their drinks, their food, menus, normal restaurant things.

It was the same with the people at the bar. Nothing and nobody stood out.

Except . . . I frowned.

There was a man by himself at the end of the bar. He had a bottle of beer in front of him, a knit hat pulled low, and his coat collar turned high. A little dark hair poked out from under his hat, and he wore chunky, black-rimmed glasses.

I couldn't put my finger on it, but something about him looked familiar.

Where had I seen him before? I searched my memory. It came up blank.

I was sure our paths had crossed at some point. I just didn't know how.

As I watched him, he raised his eyes and looked directly at me. I jerked my gaze back to the napkin. My heart rate spiked.

Next to me, Gio and Stacie had finished their whispered discussion. A bright pink cosmo sat untouched on the bar in front of her. Gio worked at the label on a beer bottle with his fingernails, pulling long strips and letting them fall to the bar's surface.

I risked a glance toward the man in glasses.

He was gone.

There was no empty bottle, no stack of bills hastily left to pay for his drink, no sign he'd been there at all.

Had I imagined him?

My heart thudded as I brought the cosmo to my lips, drinking more slowly now.

I stared at the words on the napkin. The last one, especially, seemed to vibrate with intensity.

Murder.

What the hell was I doing?

It hit me with a sharp, knifelike clarity: I was in way over my head. The only option was to go to the police.

As soon as I made the decision, relief swept through me. My shoulders loosened, and I let out an involuntary sigh.

The cosmo tasted better, the air seemed lighter. I would finish my drink, I decided, and go home and call Detective Gonzales immediately. Or Downs, whichever one I could get. I knew the Fletchers and Jonathan Marz didn't want me talking to the police, but I could call Marz too. He could come with me.

The thought stopped me cold.

And say *what*?

That Inga had worked some words into her paintings? That her married ex-boyfriend, my boss's brother, had acted a little creepy? That I'd drunk so much I'd blacked out and my friend had been called to take me home?

None of that was illegal. None of that suggested murder. And then I could get in trouble: with the Fletchers for pointing an unnecessary finger at Carl, with the police for wasting their time, with my friends for turning in Bo when he'd done nothing wrong.

I needed more proof before I went to the police. Proof for them that something was going on, or for myself that nothing was.

There was only one place I could think to get it. Whatever lay at the end of the address Inga had left me.

My glass was empty again.

Andrew raised a brow at me but I shook my head. "I'll come by tomorrow to pay you," I told him as I slid off my stool.

Gio noticed me putting on my coat. "You going? You'll be okay?"

"Yeah," I lied. I wasn't actually that comfortable walking home by myself. It was late and Diner was in a pretty isolated spot. But I was even less comfortable breaking up Gio's date. Stacie's eyes were shooting daggers in my direction again, she obviously couldn't wait for me to leave.

There wasn't a single car on the road, and nobody else on the streets. The moon was a thin white sliver in the sky. I walked straight north on Berry Street, under the creepy darkness of the Williamsburg Bridge overpass, hands shoved deep in my coat pocket. My gloves had been in my coat pocket when I ran out of the apartment, as had my house keys. I was grateful for both. The temperature seemed to have dropped even more while I'd been in the restaurant, and I was glad I wouldn't have to wake up Vik to get in if he'd already gone to bed.

At first, I thought I was hearing things, because just as I'd been thinking of Vik, I heard his voice calling my name. But when I turned, there he was, halfway under the overpass behind me. I recognized his familiar puffy coat and bright orange knit hat.

He must have come into the restaurant to look for me right after I'd left. It was dark under the overpass and I couldn't see his face, but Vik raised his hand and waved, starting to jog in my direction.

Four men melted out of the gloom.

I screamed Vik's name, pointing.

He whirled, but they were coming from all directions. I couldn't see what was happening, it was a blur of punching fists and kicking feet as the men descended on Vik, who crumpled under their assault.

I screamed again.

One of the men stopped pummeling Vik and turned. He saw me and started to run.

Not away from me. Right at me. He emerged from under a streetlamp like a bridge troll in a fairy tale, all bared teeth and fists smeared with blood. He was hatless, his shaved head gleaming, and for a split second I got a clear look at his furious, determined face.

I sprinted as hard as I could.

CHAPTER TWENTY-FIVE

Buildings blurred as I raced up South Fifth Street. I was running blind again, not thinking about where I was going, just hoping to get away.

Men's voices were loud behind me, their harsh cries carrying through the night. I couldn't make out what they were saying, but it felt like more than one was behind me now.

Vik.

The thought of his body collapsing under the onslaught of fists and feet forced a sob from my throat but also broke through my unthinking panic.

I needed a phone. I had to get Vik help.

There were no businesses here, no storefronts, no other restaurants except Diner and Peter Luger's, and I couldn't double back in that direction. Should I bang on the door of one of the houses? Start ringing apartment buzzers?

I saw myself in a flash, standing on a stoop ringing doorbells and shouting, when the men behind me caught up and pulled me down, screaming.

No. Too risky. What if nobody was home, or they didn't want to answer the door? I'd have wasted precious minutes waiting on help that would never arrive.

It was getting harder and harder to breathe. I didn't dare stop.

The smell of burnt molasses hung heavily in the air, mixing with the salty tang of river water.

The sugar factory.

I cut a hard right on Kent Avenue, hoping I had enough of a head start to evade detection.

I didn't. There were definitely footsteps behind me, thudding loudly.

The streets were barren of any life, like a movie set gone quiet. But to my left, lights glowed in the factory's windows, and metallic clangs of industry rang in the air.

There were people in there.

"Chloe, stop." The harsh voice rang in the night, with an accent I couldn't place. They were maybe half a block behind me and gaining.

They know my name. I'm not crazy. They know my name.

I pulled at the handle of a glass door in the middle of a brick building. Locked. I banged on the door with my fist but knew I couldn't be heard over the sound of the machinery.

A few steps away was a gate in the middle of a short wire fence between the low, industrial building and the massive brick processing plant. I slipped through.

The interior grounds of the Domino Sugar Refinery were a maze, a tangle of buildings and equipment and trucks. Orange light surged from some of the windows, but others were dark. I could hear noises in there but saw no doors other than the locked one that I'd already tried. I had no idea how to get inside.

I kept running. Surely there would be another door, and if not, then a place to secrete myself away until a worker passed by, or daybreak came.

Massive conveyor belts crisscrossed overhead as I slowed to a jog between the buildings, frantically scanning left and right. I couldn't run anymore. My side was screaming, my breath coming in short pants.

"Come on out, Chloe. There's no place to hide." The voice was farther away than it had been. They were inside the plant grounds, too, but didn't know where I was.

That was good.

I saw the crane as I rounded the corner around the back of the main processing plant. There was a line of trucks parked in cargo bays on my right, the river on my left. I darted between the silent trucks, trying to not be seen or heard.

Were the men still there or had they given up?

"Chlllloooe." The voice drew out my name in a terrifying sing-song. It was closer now.

There was nowhere to go after the crane. The building on my right ended at what was almost a pier.

It was as good a hiding spot as I would get. Maybe they would think I was crouched behind a truck or had managed to make my way into a building.

I darted out from the deep shadows and climbed up the steel ladder of the crane as quietly as I could, cringing each time the soles of my boots made contact with metal, praying I wouldn't be heard. The ladder ended in a small square platform, the cab where the driver sat taking up most of the room. I wedged into a corner, trying to make myself small.

I convulsed as the sweat from my sprint began to cool.

There was no way I could hide here until morning. I'd freeze to death. My best hope was for a shift change, for one of the unseen doors below to open, for a worker clocking out of the sugar factory to stumble outside. I could scream then, tell them to call the police.

It was a slim hope. The factory ran on a skeleton crew since their union strike ended last winter.

A blast of wind picked up pieces of my hair and tugged. I curled tighter into myself.

I tried to control my shaking and strained to hear something, anything, over the noise of the factory and the lapping sounds of the river.

I had no idea how long I huddled there. Long enough that I thought maybe they were gone. Maybe they'd given up and left.

I cautiously unfolded myself, my spent muscles screaming in protest. My boot scraped noisily on the rusted surface of the platform.

"Up there."

Shit. The noise had seemed small, but they'd heard me. Or seen me move.

It didn't matter, they were coming.

Panic exploded in my chest.

There was nowhere left to run, not that I was capable of running anymore anyway. The arm of the crane extended over the river, but I couldn't shimmy up that. The only way out was down.

I was out of fuel. Out of breath.

Out of time.

The decision was easy, once it was made. No matter how much it terrified me.

There was no other choice.

I could hear them coming up the ladder already.

I unzipped my boots and kicked them aside, the icy metal platform seeping through the soles of my tights, burning my feet with cold, shards of peeling paint poking.

I'm not crazy.

The staccato rhythm of the phrase pounded through my skull.

I'm not crazy. I'm not crazy. I'm not crazy.

I could barely undo the wooden toggle clasps of my coat, my fingers were trembling so hard.

"Come on," I muttered. "Come on come on come on."

The sounds of their climbing grew louder. A sob escaped my throat, but I finally jammed the last sleek button through its loop and shoved the beer-scented, dark green corduroy coat off my shoulders.

But not before pulling Inga's note from its pocket. I shoved it into my bra, wincing as cold fingers brushed bare flesh.

The shivering was constant now, my whole body shaking uncontrollably, making it hard to keep my balance as I climbed over the railing of the platform, rusted flakes of paint fluttering away on the wind when my hands dislodged them.

"There's nowhere to go, Chloe." The voice was deep and harsh. And very angry.

I risked a quick glance over my shoulder. I couldn't see them yet, but by their voices they were almost at the top.

I'm not crazy.

The thought was oddly comforting, a warm blanket against the icy wind that pulled my skirt up with an insistent tug.

I was up maybe three stories. Or four. The water was a long way down. Was I far enough from shore to avoid the rocks? Light emanated from the factory at my back, but not enough to tell.

I scrambled up the last two rails that surrounded the platform as quickly as I could. My feet slid, but I managed to hold on.

One leg over the top rail. Then the other.

I stood, holding the top rail at my back. In the one precious second I had before I jumped, I soaked in the brilliant skyline of Manhattan, spread before me like a glittering feast, the silent river a dark snake between us. From this angle, if I looked uptown, the city still seemed miraculously whole. You could forget about the gap downtown, where the towers used to be.

Just for that one second.

The memories rushed in fast. How the bodies had hung suspended for a moment, nearly weightless, and then how they'd flown. How their horrific, twisting descent had been nearly graceful.

"There she is."

The memories scattered as I shot a glance to my left.

A head popped up from the top of the ladder.

Don't look down.

I finally understood how they felt, those who had flown. Knew it deep in my bones, my skin, the inevitability of the choice that wasn't a choice, because there were no other options.

Jumping was safer than staying.

And then I, too, was flying.

Fingers grazed the back of my sweater but couldn't catch.

My stomach dropped with my body.

Don't look down.

I looked up. The dim stars grew more distant the farther I fell.

And then black water rushed over me, welcomed me with its frigid embrace, and the world went dark.

PART THREE

CHAPTER TWENTY-SIX

My first sensation was one of motion. I blinked. The tops of siding-covered row houses glided past.

I was lying in the back seat of a car.

The second was pain, followed closely by cold. The two feelings were almost interchangeable. Everything hurt, and I shivered in wet clothing, despite the heater I could hear blasting from the front seat.

Memory rushed into place, and terror set in. The silhouetted men attacking Vik. Running through the lonely streets. The game of cat and mouse under the shadows of the sugar factory.

The black water of the river, rushing to meet me.

The jump had been for nothing. They'd found me, and now were taking me to god knew where.

I had to get out of this car.

By what I could see from the window, we were still in Brooklyn. That was good. Keeping my motions as slow as possible, I stretched my hand to the door handle at my head. I silently placed my fingers on the hard plastic, ready.

The car began to slow. We must have been approaching a light or stop sign. My head was behind the driver's seat, legs stretched out. I had a clear view into the front passenger seat and was relieved nobody was there—that meant there was only me and the driver.

That was also good. One person I could maybe outrun, if I could get out.

I strained my ears for a whisper, a rustle of movement, any noise from the front seat.

Nothing.

The car stopped. I waited only a breath, then grasped the handle and pulled, ready to fling myself onto the road, even though every muscle screamed in protest.

The handle pulled uselessly.

Fuck. Child locks.

Hysteria started to creep into the edges of my brain. I had inhaled deeply to scream, when a voice from the front seat stopped me.

"Chloe?"

The welcome sight of Gio's anxious face peered between the front seats. I flopped back down, breathing hard.

"Okay, you're awake," he said. His voice was shaky. He sounded terrified. "That's good. Hang tight, we're on our way to the hospital." The car began to edge forward again.

"No!" I cried.

I jolted forward as Gio slammed on the brakes. He twisted in the front seat again. "No hospital? You jumped from what must have been thirty feet at least. You're lucky you didn't die."

I shook my head. A hospital meant police, and I wasn't ready to talk to the police yet. "I'll be okay. But Vik is hurt. Those guys beat him up."

What if he was more than hurt? I pushed the thought aside.

Gio's Adam's apple bobbed as he swallowed. "A bunch of police cars and an ambulance raced by right when I saw you go into the sugar factory. I bet they were going to him." He ran a trembling hand through his hair. "Who were those guys, Chloe? They didn't seem local. I mean, there aren't that many muggings and stuff around here. Some, but not with guys like that. They seemed . . . professional."

I knew what he meant. Especially on the north side, the neighborhood was relatively safe. Desolate at times, but safe.

"It wasn't an ordinary mugging, was it?" Gio's dark eyes scanned the street outside the car, as if looking for the men who had been chasing me to return. They slid back to me, held me in an intense stare. "I saw you go in the water. I was on the pier, and I saw you. Jesus, Chloe. The guys, they ran. I yelled I was calling 911, and they ran."

"Did you? Call, I mean?" A shiver racked my whole body.

"No. I jumped in after you."

I pushed myself upright. Every movement made me wince; I felt like one giant bruise. I saw for the first time that Gio was wet too. His hair was plastered to his forehead, the burgundy shirt he'd worn for his date sticking to his chest. I briefly wondered what had happened to Stacie.

He turned forward again, gripping the steering wheel hard with both hands. "What the hell is going on, Chloe?" His voice was nearly a whisper.

"I'll tell you," I said, wrapping my arms around my body. Suddenly, I was desperate to tell someone everything. About the note I now had tucked into my bra, about the words in the paintings, Carl in the warehouse, Bo carrying me away from what might have been a murder scene. About how I was sure someone had broken into my apartment, about how I was afraid Vik and Ben were involved. "I'll tell it all. Can we go to your place? I don't want to be alone in my apartment. And I need to find out what happened to Vik."

There was a long pause. Maybe Gio, like me, was remembering the last time I had been in his apartment.

"Yeah," he said finally. "Of course. Mateo's on a twenty-four-hour shift, won't be home for a while. You can sleep in my bed, and I'll take his."

Gio's apartment that he shared with his brother was as I recalled it, a remarkably clean, nearly spare space for two single guys in their twenties. The kitchen was spotless, which maybe wasn't that surprising for someone who worked in the restaurant trade. I caught a glimpse of Mateo's room through a partially open door, and it was a little messier, with a small pile of clothes on the bed and knickknacks cluttering a bookshelf. Gio's room, though, was almost bare of personal items. What looked like a 1930s advertisement for espresso was framed and hung on one wall, and an unframed poster of an Italian soccer team was on another. He had two photographs sitting on his dresser—I recognized his grandmother in one and assumed the other group was also family—and a small dish where he deposited his keys and damp wallet. Otherwise, the surface was clean.

Gio handed me an equally clean set of sweats and socks before he gathered clothes for himself. "Go ahead and take the first shower, I'll call some local hospitals and look for Vik while you're in there. There's clean towels in the cupboard."

Even the bathroom smelled nice, like pine and lemon. The water was good and hot, and I finally began to warm up as I washed away the river. I scrubbed my skin, even though it hurt, and shampooed my hair twice, trying not to think of how polluted the East River was. When I emerged in a cloud of steam, I smelled like Gio's body wash.

In the living room, Gio presented me with a cup of herbal tea and two ibuprofen. Out of habit, I was tempted to ask for a drink, but I held back. Liquor was the last thing I needed, and the hot mug felt good in my hands. I curled up on the couch, exhausted.

"It took a few tries, but I found Vik," Gio said. "I thought he'd be at Presbyterian in Park Slope but turns out he's at Maimonides in Borough Park." He looked and sounded as tired as I felt.

A wave of relief passed over me. Vik wasn't dead. He had lied to me, which suggested he was somehow involved in all this, but I didn't want him *dead*.

"He's not in great shape, Chlo. Broken ribs, a concussion, a broken jaw, fractured one arm, and he's in a coma."

"A coma?" I set my tea on the coffee table and sat up.

"They think from being kicked in the head."

My heart contracted. I wondered if his parents knew. I had their phone number back at the apartment.

"The nurse I spoke with said next of kin were on their way," Gio told me when I asked if I should get their number from home. "The head injury is what they're most worried about, the other stuff can heal. The police got there pretty quick—someone in one of the nearby houses called 911—and that may have been what saved him. They'll know more in a few days."

I buried my head in my hands.

Gio was beside me in an instant. His hand hovered close to my shoulder but didn't quite touch it. "It's gonna be okay. Whatever is going on, I'll help, okay? We'll deal with it together."

The words were a blanket of comfort. I nodded, unable to speak, overcome by his kindness. Maybe he was only being so nice to me because he harbored a crush, like Bo said, but I decided I didn't care.

Gio had saved my life. I had no memory of being in the East River, everything from the moment I jumped until waking up in his car was blank. I'd probably knocked myself unconscious. If he hadn't pulled me out, I would have died.

I'd take any other help he wanted to give, never mind the reasons.

"You take those, I bet you hurt like hell," he said, wrapping my fingers around the painkillers. "I'm gonna take a shower now. Knock on the bathroom door if you need anything, okay?"

I swallowed the ibuprofen and checked out Gio's bookshelf while he showered. There were some Dan Brown novels, a couple of Fodor's guides to Italy and France, a few accounting textbooks. I wondered which books were his and which were his brother's.

Gio came out of the bathroom in a similar cloud of steam to mine, rubbing his damp hair with a towel. "You hungry? I could make eggs and toast. Got some good sourdough from downstairs."

"Actually, yeah. That sounds great, thank you." I couldn't remember the last time I'd eaten, lunch probably. "Guess you and Stacie didn't get dinner, huh?"

He shrugged a little, collecting pans and eggs and bread in the kitchen. "My cousin set us up. She's a nice girl, but not my type. Wants one of those slick city boys, I think."

"What's your type, Gio?" It came out flirtier than I intended. What was up with that? I had jumped from a crane to escape skinhead-looking thugs, every inch of me ached as a result, I was wearing a gray FDNY sweatsuit four times my size, and yet I was flirting with the guy who supplied my morning coffee.

He ducked his head and waved the question away, but he smiled. "Stacie and I were walking to my car, the date was kind of a bust, as you probably know," he said, his smile fading, "when I saw you come tearing down the street, and that guy behind you. Then another one. I yelled after them but they didn't hear or didn't care. Luckily there was a town car right there, and I shoved Stacie into it, threw some money at the driver, and took off after you. I saw you go into Domino's. I didn't want to follow and risk them ganging up on me, so I went around the distillery to the pier to call the cops. That's when I saw you jump."

My heart had accelerated during Gio's tale, but now it seemed to still. I could still see the water far below, feel the wind flinging up my hair as I flew through the sky.

"I was lucky you were there," I said quietly. I wrapped my hands around the mug more tightly.

"I was a lifeguard for the city in high school. Got some skills." The delicious scent of butter sizzling filled the apartment as Gio cracked eggs into a bowl.

Once the food was ready, we sat on the couch opposite each other with plates in our laps.

"Tell me," he said simply.

So I did.

Between bites, I told Gio everything. He listened, nodding, making noncommittal noises as we ate.

I ended the story by telling him why I didn't want to go to the police yet, that I felt I needed more proof. He frowned at that but kept quiet.

I put my empty plate down. The food had been just what I needed. "Let me get the note."

The piece of paper I was sure Inga had left me had been stuck to my skin after I'd been in the river. I'd peeled it off and laid it on the top of Gio's dresser to dry out. It was creased, and the ink had faded, but it was still legible.

Which didn't matter. I knew the address by heart now.

Gio took the note and studied it carefully, before placing it on the table between our plates.

"Not gonna lie, it seems kinda dangerous to be your friend right now, Chloe."

I should have laughed at the quip, or been annoyed, but instead all I felt was relief.

Gio believed me. He, too, could see that there was some unseen web at work here, and that somehow, *I* appeared to be at its center.

It was people close to me, or people I'd recently spent time with, who were winding up gone, hurt, or dead.

"I don't understand how it all fits together," Gio admitted. "It feels like this Carl guy could be the key. He was the closest to Inga and has ties to the gallery. And maybe some of the other stuff is coincidence."

I relayed to Gio what Calvin had said about Carl's job, about the Office of Foreign Assets Control, and about how the government apparently wasn't investigating who had funded the terrorists who took down the towers.

Gio's brow furrowed. "That sounds like a crazy Calvin theory."

"I know, but he's got a little bit of a point, doesn't he? Why isn't the government investigating where the money came from? Why don't we know more about the attacks, and more importantly, why didn't they know before they happened? I mean, maybe Carl is a traitor, working with terrorists somehow, and Inga found out, and then Lou . . ."

It seemed insane.

But was it any less insane than what had actually happened? Any less insane than downtown reduced to a gaping, smoking hole?

Just thinking about 9/11 made my gut clench. I took a deep drink of my now-cold tea.

"Maybe. But Vik doesn't know this Carl guy, right?"

I put the tea down and gingerly flopped back on the sofa. "I feel like I'm losing my mind." The words came out in a whisper. "But you believe me." It was a statement, not a question. I could tell he believed me.

"Something weird is going on, yeah. I saw those guys chase you, Chloe. That wasn't a coincidence. They weren't junkies after your wallet. They were out for blood."

I shivered, suddenly cold again.

"Hey, we're not going to figure any of this out tonight. We can't do anything else for Vik right now either. Let's reassess in the morning, okay? Including that maybe we should go to those cops. But first, I think we should check out this place." His long finger tapped the note on the coffee table.

"You'd go with me?"

"Yeah. I'm invested now. Gotta see how it ends."

A smile tugged at the corners of my mouth. "Okay."

"Get some sleep, Chloe. I'll see you in the morning."

I slept more soundly that night than I had in a long time.

CHAPTER TWENTY-SEVEN

The feeling of contentment and security I'd gone to sleep with was still with me when I awoke, sunlight streaming through the curtains in Gio's room. I checked the bedside clock; it was past noon. Yawning, I wandered into the living area in search of coffee. There was a Bialetti ready to go on the stove, and in the bathroom I could hear the shower running. Gio had left the TV on, turned to the midday news on NY1. I used the landline to call in sick to work.

"Hold on, Sloane wanted to talk to you if you called," Carmen said, putting me on hold.

I lit the burner under the coffeepot while I waited, tinny Chopin playing in my ear.

"Chloe? Is everything okay?" Sloane said when the call connected. "We were worried when we didn't hear from you, and nobody answered your home number."

"Sorry, I had the ringer off," I improvised, a little thrown that the gallery had tried to call me at home. I made a mental note to stop by and feed Groucho later. "I think what I have is just a bad cold, but I don't want to give it to anyone, so figured I'd stay home. I slept really late, my body must be fighting it off."

There was a pause. "Are you sure that's it? You seemed fine at my apartment yesterday."

A tingle of suspicion danced across my shoulders. What did she mean, was I sure that was it?

"I actually felt pretty lousy, and it got worse once I got home."

There was another long pause, though I could hear Sloane's deep intake of breath.

"Okay. Well, get yourself to the doctor if you feel worse. Oh, and *Careless* made it safely to the warehouse last night. I thought you'd want to know."

Be Careful, Inga had written in that painting.

It seemed a good time to heed the warning.

"That's great. I'm sure after a weekend of rest I'll feel better and be in on Monday."

"Yes, rest up. See you then."

Had her voice grown colder during the phone call, or was I imagining things?

We hung up. Gio came out of the bathroom with a towel wrapped around his middle and made a beeline for his bedroom. I hastily turned my attention to the hissing coffeepot but not before I caught a glimpse of his wiry but surprisingly well-defined chest.

Dang. Gio worked out.

Smiling to myself, I rooted around in various cupboards until I found the mugs, picked a stained but clean FDNY one, and poured the coffee. I was just reaching for the phone to dial information for the number for the Maimonides hospital to check on Vik when the words of the news anchor stopped me cold.

"As the holidays approach, Ground Zero is becoming more and more of a tourist destination, even though the site is still smoldering. We go now to our correspondent, live on the scene."

I told myself not to look but was unable to help it. I set the coffee down and walked into the living room, transfixed.

There it was. The sight I'd worked so hard to avoid for the past two months, right there in front of me. The camera panned the steel remains of one of the towers, stripped to the point of resembling a scaffold, silhouetted against nothing but sky. Rubble and debris were heaped in front of the structure, a bulldozer moving giant piles of it around. The camera cut to the exterior of St. Paul's Chapel. The wrought-iron face was plastered with faded, xeroxed missing-person posters, home-made memorials on pieces of cardboard, signs and prayers and stuffed animals and mementos and letters, all dedicated to the people who had died across the street.

Those hand-crafted signs and flags were what did me in.

It's probably nothing. You can go now.

The room began to lazily spin. I dropped to the floor, shaking, unable to catch my breath. A surge of nausea rose in my throat and my heart hammered, sweat trickling down my face. I don't know how much time passed before Gio's voice broke through the fog in my head.

"It's okay, Chloe. It's okay. It's only a panic attack. You're okay, I'm here with you. This will pass. Try to take a breath for me, okay? Can you take a breath? You're safe. Come on, take a deep breath with me. Inhale, exhale. Inhale, exhale."

The words wrapped around me like a blanket. I focused on them, willing my way back to the present, to see the clean, orderly room around me instead of the approaching cloud of brown smoke, rolling toward me like something out of a horror film.

After a few torturous minutes, my heart began to slow again. The dizziness and nausea abated, and I could take a deep breath.

Inhale, exhale.

Gio led me through a dozen more breaths, until I pulled back slightly, embarrassed.

"I think I'm okay now."

He looked at me closely. "This one was shorter than last time."

I sucked in my breath, then caught myself and let it out slowly. "Yes. It was."

"How often do you have them?"

"I don't know. The last time I was here, after you found me in the street, that was the first. After that one, every few weeks, I guess. Until all this stuff started happening. Now it feels like one comes on every few days."

The first time I'd had a panic attack, I'd truly thought I was dying. It was only two days after 9/11, and I'd been at Rosemary's with Vik and a few of our friends. You'd think the city would have been in mourning, and it was, but the bars and restaurants were consistently packed from the afternoon of the eleventh onward. It seemed people wanted, maybe needed, to be together, even if it was with mostly strangers. The two televisions Rosemary had mounted in the corners were playing, as always. That night every channel showed how the guards at Buckingham Palace played the American national anthem. The entire bar went still to watch. Almost every single patron, and Rosemary herself, was openly weeping.

I had begun to feel awful. My heart was racing so fast I thought I was having a heart attack. I felt nauseated and sweaty and, convinced I was about to throw up, I'd run from the bar into the street to be sick. I found out later Penny had tried to follow me but Vik, thinking I was just upset, had told her to give me a minute. Gio found me instead, huddled in a terrified ball on the opposite side of the street from the bar, practically on his doorstep.

He'd done the same thing for me then that he'd done today. He'd taken me upstairs, held me close, and told me it would be okay. He'd helped me slow my breath.

Inhale, exhale, he'd said, over and over.

It had helped.

Afterward, I'd fallen asleep on his couch. A thunderstorm rolled in that night, and I'd woken up, screaming and banging on his closed bedroom door, the noise of the thunder convincing me we were being bombed.

I'd spent the rest of the night in Gio's bed. Nothing had happened, but I could still feel the warmth of his body next to me.

That same warmth encased me now, enveloping me like a quilt, sitting on the floor with Gio. He'd turned the news off, and for a few minutes the only sounds were distant traffic noises and our conjoined breathing.

"I think I need to tell you what happened to me that day," I said finally. I hadn't expected to say those words. I hadn't thought I'd ever be ready to talk about how I almost died in the attacks. But something about the way the sunlight made a rectangle on the floor next to us, about Gio's patient silence, about seeing those images on the TV, made me want to unburden myself. That maybe, finally, talking about it would help.

"If you want to, then I want to hear."

I leaned my back against Gio's chest and started talking.

CHAPTER TWENTY-EIGHT

My story wasn't particularly unique. There were thousands of us in One World Trade Center, the North Tower, that morning. Secretaries, food service workers, cleaners, people who worked in finance, insurance, transportation, all kinds of industries. Regular people going to work.

I was there to deliver a drawing to a client of Fletcher & Sons.

The day started almost like any other, but prettier. There wasn't a cloud in a sky so blue it qualified as azure.

It was also an earlier day for me than normal. I'd gotten a late call the night before from Lou, telling me the gallery needed an urgent favor. They wanted me, the receptionist, to make a delivery. It was a perfect storm of nobody else being available: Douglas was supposed to do it, but he had come down with a vicious stomach bug and was bedridden. Henry and Sloane were in Europe to see a collection they might acquire, Lou and Sebastian were in Los Angeles at a conference, and Olive was home in New Jersey with a sick kid (probably the source of Douglas's stomach bug).

"There's no one else, and the client says he has to have the drawing tomorrow," Lou told me, distressed.

"I can do it," I said. In truth, I was terrified of handling something so valuable. But all that year I'd kept surprising myself at how much I liked my job. Lou had been giving me more and more assignments. I thought I was good at them—and it had been so long since I felt I was good at anything. I wanted to keep at it, so if they needed me to get in a car and drop off a Georgia O'Keeffe drawing to somebody down at the World Trade Center, I'd make it happen.

"You've already got the keys. Douglas has the drawing all packed and ready. It's small. It's on his desk in his office, and he has a car arranged. It'll be easy, Chloe. You can do it. But the guy wants to meet at eighty thirty, so with traffic, you might want to be leaving the gallery by eight," he said.

I'd set my alarm for good and early—normally I didn't have to be at work until 9:30—and put on the outfit I'd laid out the night before: my favorite black vintage dress with the Peter Pan collar and the pleats in the skirt that Sloane had once said looked like a Prada design. I made it to the gallery right on time, full of nervous anticipation. Everything was exactly where Lou said it would be. The neatly boxed drawing was easy to carry, and I slid the file of paperwork into my messenger bag. I felt self-important and grown-up as the waiting car began to make its way downtown, like I was part of the cogs that made the city turn.

The sky was so, so blue.

Despite seeing the tops of the Twin Towers almost every day from across the river in Brooklyn, I had never visited the complex itself. The place was a maze, but since I was going to one of the towers, my entrance was easy enough to find in the end.

One WTC was intimidating. Dozens of people in suits walked purposefully with briefcases across the white marble lobby to rows of chrome-doored elevators. I had to remind myself that I had a purpose here, too, that I was bringing a $50,000 drawing to somebody in this building.

I shared the express elevator to the seventy-eighth floor with several of the suit-clad folks, all of whom either sipped their take-out coffee or tapped on their BlackBerrys, then transferred to an elevator to the seventy-ninth floor on my own. It took a few moments of wandering before I found the offices for Dryden Investments, where the client, Greg McClean, worked. They apparently ran a hedge fund, whatever that was.

A pretty receptionist with long red hair made a phone call while I waited. There were rows of offices extending behind her, walled with glass. I was itching to see into one, to catch a glimpse of the view through one of the exterior windows. I'd never been in a building this tall.

"You're from Fletcher & Sons?" A short, middle-aged woman in neat navy slacks and a beige sweater with black hair pulled into a bun appeared. "I'm Maya, Mr. McClean's secretary. Come with me."

As she led me down the hall, I got my wish. Through the glass wall I caught glimpses of the windows on the other side of the offices. The other Twin Tower loomed back at me, and the whole of Manhattan unfolded below. The scene was breathtaking, and, honestly, a little freaky. We were so high up.

"Mr. McClean, the girl from the gallery is here," Maya said as I followed her into an airy office. A dark-haired man in a crisp white shirt and striped suspenders held up a finger, indicating we should wait while he finished a phone call. I paused on the threshold, unsure if I should enter or not. Greg McClean was younger than I thought he'd be, closer to my age than the silver-haired Master of the Universe I'd expected. He was good-looking, too, with a chiseled jaw and piercing blue eyes.

"I don't give a fuck what the analyst says, I say to buy," he yelled into the phone before slamming down the receiver. The noise was so loud I took an involuntary step backward. He caught sight of me and scowled. "Who are you?"

"Chloe Harlow, from Fletcher & Sons." I was proud I didn't allow my voice to tilt up at the end, like I was asking a question, but instead drew myself tall and held out the box containing the drawing. "I have your O'Keeffe."

"You're not who I was expecting. Where's the blonde?"

I blinked, uncertain. I had blond hair.

"Come on, come on, the blonde. The pretty one, who runs the place?"

That seemed to mean he didn't think I was pretty. I tried not to let the insult bother me.

"You must mean Sloane Fletcher," I said. "She's in Germany right now. Our preparator, Douglas Curt, was supposed to make the delivery, but he came down with the stomach flu." I wasn't sure why who delivered the work was so important. "I have all the required paperwork right here."

He sighed gustily and stood, indicating I should put the box and file on his desk. "Whatever. Let's take a look at this."

To his credit, Greg was careful as he undid the string Douglas had secured around the box, and he lifted the lid gently. The delicate charcoal drawing was encased in an archivally appropriate, cream-colored mat, itself nestled in a perfectly cut archival foam nest. Three trees clustered together, suggesting a larger forest, and almost spiky branches reached for the left side of the drawing. It was a unique piece, Lou had told me on the phone. Not like her well-known floral or cow skull paintings, but a private drawing from one of her sketchbooks. We both looked at it for a few beats.

"It's beautiful," I finally said.

"Yeah? Not totally my taste, but it's a wedding present for my fiancée. Georgia O'Keeffe is her favorite artist."

This seemed a surprisingly touching—and expensive—gesture. "What a wonderful gift."

Greg replaced the lid. "Just glad it's not one of those vagina flowers she painted," he said, smirking.

The bald, casual drop of the word "vagina" stunned me. "Here's the bill of sale," I said, trying not to sound as flustered as I felt. "There's two copies to sign, one for you to keep and one I'll take."

He quickly scanned the document before scribbling his name on both pieces of paper.

"And this is for you." Greg handed me a thin envelope. I carefully tucked it into the file, and the file into my bag.

There was a $50,000 check in that envelope. More than I'd ever made in a year. By a lot. Whatever a hedge fund was, it paid well.

I was reaching my hand forward to shake Greg's when a muffled explosion sounded and the building rocked. I stumbled, thrown off-balance, and held on to one of the chairs in front of Greg's desk for support.

"Sorry about that," I gasped, more embarrassed than frightened.

Greg had swayed a little also and had grabbed the edge of the desk, which he now let go. A quick spasm of concern crossed his face, and he looked out the window, frowning, before his features settled back into contempt and disappointment.

"Maya? What the hell was that?" he yelled through his open door.

She poked her head through the door, holding the end of a phone on a long cord. "I don't know. I just dialed building security, but it's busy."

Greg moved closer to the tall, floor-to-ceiling windows that comprised one entire wall of his office. I looked out, too, from behind him.

There was nothing. Just the blameless, cloudless sky in a blue so intense it made my eyes water. Greg had an enviable south-facing view, and the tip of downtown lay before us, far below and encased by the sparkling harbor.

He rolled his neck, then turned with irritation back to his desk.

"Just what I need, a drill or some such shit. We're done here," he said this last to me. "I'll call the owners if there are any problems." And with that, I was dismissed.

Before I turned, something floated past his window. It was so incongruous at this height that for a second I had trouble comprehending what I was seeing.

It was a piece of paper, floating lazily along.

"What's that?" I asked stupidly, pointing, even though I knew what it was. Greg was in the midst of picking up his phone, but followed my finger out the window.

"What the fuck," he muttered, before bellowing. "Maya? What is going on?"

"Still don't know," she called back.

Behind Greg, more paper fluttered, and other kinds of debris I didn't recognize: metal, plastic, shapes I couldn't make out. My eyes traveled to the ceiling, and the first shard of real fear poked its way into my belly.

What was happening above us?

Greg brushed past me, striding into the hallway. "It's probably nothing," he said without looking at me again. "You can go now."

I stared, stupefied, at the drifting debris out the window. A distant alarm began to sound, not within the suite of offices itself, but maybe out in the main hallway.

Maya appeared in the office doorway. Our eyes met.

She was afraid too.

"Come on, grab your things, we need to leave." Her voice was quiet and full of fear. She glanced upward at the ceiling, as I had done moments earlier. "I got kids, you know?"

I didn't know. I didn't have kids. But I didn't feel safe, even if I wasn't sure why.

A woman in a navy suit rushed past us, her cell phone pressed to her ear. She glanced our way. "It's a fire, Maya," she said, breathless, before hurrying on her way.

Fire. I looked at the archival box on the desk.

"Where's Greg?" I asked.

Maya had retreated and was silently packing her bag. She shook her head. "Don't know. Let's go." She slung the bag over her shoulder and gestured for me to follow.

I didn't even think about it. I scooped up the box on the desk that held the Georgia O'Keeffe drawing, shoved it into my messenger bag, and followed Maya back to the main reception area.

Others in the suite of offices were making their way toward the front reception desk too. Nobody was panicked, but they all looked as concerned as I felt. The sound of the alarm was louder here.

I joined the half dozen or so office workers gathered at reception where the red-haired woman was corralling everyone.

"Why are the lights out in the hall but not in our suite?" a tall guy in glasses muttered to nobody in particular. He cradled a laptop to his chest like it was a baby.

I looked through the glass wall to the main hallway where the elevators were. He was right, it was dark out there, the dim glow of an emergency light the only illumination.

The fear in my stomach climbed into my chest. I remembered how high up we were, so far up the city looked like an architect's miniature model.

The red-haired woman looked at Maya. "Where's Greg?"

Maya shook her head. "He's still trying to work, I think."

A thin, wiry man with salt-and-pepper hair furrowed his brow at this. "You all go ahead. I'll get him."

"Okay, everyone," the red-haired woman said. "The elevators are out, we need to take the stairs."

"The stairs weren't lit in '93," the laptop guy said as we followed the woman into the dark hallway. "Maybe the express will be working when we get down a floor."

My nose instantly filled with the smell of smoke, and something like gas. I looked around the darkness but didn't see any fire, didn't hear anything unusual over the insistent blare of the alarm. My eyes traveled to the ceiling again.

Something up there was burning.

I pressed closer to Maya, the only person whose name I knew in the small crowd. A rectangle of light shone into the hallway as the red-haired woman, who had become our leader, opened the door to the emergency stairs.

"The lights are on, Eric," she said in a mild voice. He smiled thinly but held the door open for the group as we filed past him.

The stairs were narrow, and we made steady progress down a flight. The red-haired woman—someone called her Jeri, and I was happy to have a name to go with the face—poked her head into the sky lobby and reported back that the express elevators were out too.

We kept going.

The only thing keeping me from panicking was that everyone else was calm. Quiet, and scared-looking, but calm. Nobody ran, or yelled, or shoved or pushed, and we made a fairly quick and orderly procession down for about ten floors.

I kept my eyes fixed on the stairs, and the back of Maya's beige sweater as she descended before me.

I thought about Greg, and the man who had gone to get him. So far, nobody seemed to be behind us. It was as though our little band had the staircase to ourselves.

Eric must have thought the same thing. "Are we the only people stupid enough to be walking down seventy-nine flights of stairs?" he grumbled. "I have a conference call to London in an hour. Someone upstairs probably put metal in a microwave."

I remembered the explosion, how the building had shaken. How pieces of metal and paper and chunks of plastic I couldn't recognize had drifted through the sky.

Whatever was happening, it wasn't a small office fire.

No sooner had the words left his mouth than the stairwell door opened a few floors down and dozens of people began pouring into the stairs below us. Our progress slowed, then halted. About five minutes later we moved forward a few steps, then stopped again.

I risked a look over the smooth metal banister into the bottomless chasm of the stairwell.

An endless sea of the tops of people's heads greeted me.

I twisted my head and looked up.

Equally endless faces peered down at me.

Had Greg finally left? Was he up there somewhere?

Rumors began to filter up and down the stairs as we snaked our way down. It was a bomb. No, it was a plane. The White House was hit. A second plane had crashed into the South Tower.

"I was here in '93," Eric said loudly over the intermittent chatter, insistent in his experience. "This is probably a small bomb again. We still have electricity so it can't be as bad."

"No, man," a voice from behind us floated down. "We're with the Transportation Authority here, I heard it on our radio. Tower Two was hit by a small plane. They're saying it's terrorism."

Maya looked over her shoulder and our eyes met again. She must have seen the worry on my face. "We just keep moving, we'll be fine," she said.

I nodded.

We descended another few floors.

At one point Maya turned again and handed me several bottles of Snapple. "Want one? They're passing these around."

I took a diet peach flavor and stuck it in my bag as I passed the rest back. Once my hands were free I unscrewed the lid, savoring the cool, sweet liquid as it poured down my throat.

At the forty-fifth floor we moved as one herd into the second sky lobby. A crowd of people were waiting to traverse down a second, separate set of emergency stairs.

Maya stopped, so I did too.

"You don't think we should take those stairs?" I asked.

"I don't know," she said. Fear creased her face as she looked between the two exit doors. Eric stood near us, still clutching his laptop. Jeri caught sight of us hovering in the middle of the lobby and gestured frantically.

"I'm going back to these," Eric said, taking a few steps back toward where we had just exited. "You all should come too. There's too many people on those stairs."

He turned his back on us.

Panic began to set in. "What do we do?" I asked Maya. I didn't know the building. The smell of smoke was stronger here.

She bit her lip.

"Maya," Jeri called urgently, once, before moving with the crowd through into the second stairs.

"I think these stairs are bigger," Maya finally said, pointing to where Jeri had gone. "We maybe can get down faster."

"But if there are more people, maybe it'll take just as long."

Maya swallowed. "I think this way." She joined the crowd waiting to exit down the second staircase.

I paused for ten seconds, torn by indecision, then followed. I sent a silent prayer to whatever higher power was there that I'd made the right choice.

I wormed past a few people, muttering an apology under my breath, pointing at Maya like I was trying to reach my best friend. She had become a lifeline for me, and maybe I was for her, because when I finally reached her side she grasped my hand silently.

Like I said, what happened to me wasn't unique. There were hundreds, maybe thousands of us descending that staircase.

One foot in front of the other, one step more. Again and again and again. It seemed Maya was right, this staircase was moving more quickly than the one we'd left. The crowd was not fast, but we moved down at a consistent, steady pace.

At one point injured people were passed down, and we all squeezed to the right to let them pass. I caught a glimpse of a horribly burned, disfigured body being carried past us.

"Don't look, *mija*," Maya said. "Just keep moving."

Somewhere around the thirty-first floor, the pounding of heavy treads echoed up the staircase. We collectively squeezed against the wall again as firefighters, in full gear and carrying heavy equipment, ran up the stairs. They were already red-faced and drenched in sweat.

But they kept running.

One looked right at me as he passed. He looked no older than nineteen, and the terror in his hazel eyes was palpable.

The crowd stayed quiet until the firefighters passed, and in silence, we started moving down the stairs again. The sounds of both open and muffled weeping rose, and I blinked back my own tears.

I knew how many more floors those firefighters had to climb.

I already knew, somehow, that they might not be coming back.

We all knew it, those of us on the stairs.

Maya whispered under her breath, a long, melodious string of Spanish. I guessed she was praying, but didn't want to interrupt her to ask. Instead, I gave her hand a squeeze.

She squeezed it back.

Water appeared under our shoes around the twelfth floor. It got a bit deeper the lower we descended, and suddenly we were moving faster. There was a collective urgency to the crowd now, a quick forward momentum, like a horse straining toward water.

We were close to the exit. Close to being safe.

Finally, Maya and I passed through the main doors into the lobby.

It was unrecognizable.

The electricity was out and water sloshed the floor. One elevator door was blasted in, so mangled it looked like a giant had picked it up and twisted it. Firefighters and other emergency personnel were scattered around the lobby, frantically directing us into the open plaza.

It was chaos. People were screaming, debris was falling everywhere. A guy in what looked like an EMT uniform screamed at us to run, and everyone around me complied, except Maya. We clutched each other's hands like children and stared up, horror-stricken.

The upper sections of both buildings were consumed by orange fire. People were flying through the air, one after another. Falling like rain. Ties and skirts flying upward as their bodies descended. I didn't want to look but couldn't turn away. It was the most shocking, terrifying sight I had ever witnessed. It was suddenly impossible to breathe.

Maya's hand shook in mine. She was saying her prayers again, out loud now, as she turned and pulled me by the hand along with her. My legs couldn't move. My brain screamed at me to run, but I was transfixed with dread, tears streaming down my face.

Then my hand was empty. I turned, but Maya had been swallowed by the screeching, rushing crowd.

"Run!" A man in a bright yellow hard hat had appeared in front of me. He, too, had tears streaming from his eyes. "Get the fuck out of here, lady, run!" He physically turned me and gave me a little shove. Later I would realize he'd pointed me north, a lucky thing. "Don't look left. Don't look left."

My eyes skittered left, then snapped forward again. My mind didn't want to comprehend that the pile of bloody clothes and hair on the ground had been a person.

Another small shove propelled me forward, and my body suddenly caught up to my mind. I started to run, as fast as I could, in the direction I was facing. The need to get as far away as possible from the hellscape that had blossomed around me rose swift and urgent.

I made it past Vesey Street, past Park, and was out of the Trade Center complex. People on the street were either staring, open-mouthed and crying, in the direction I had just come from, or were moving purposefully forward like me. I couldn't run anymore. I stopped to catch my breath, noticing for the first time I was barefoot. The trendy loafers I'd worn with my best dress were half a size too big and had slipped off as I'd run.

The sidewalk was rough under my feet, and I looked around, trying to figure out what to do. Should I go back to work? Try to get home? The thought of getting on the subway with bare feet was disgusting. My bag was still slung over my shoulder, and my ragged breath caught as I remembered what was in there.

A rare Georgia O'Keeffe drawing. Plus a $50,000 check.

It would all get sorted out later. Right now I needed to get out of here. Maybe there was a bodega where I could buy a cheap pair of slippers or flip-flops to get home.

As I peered around at the shops on the block, the earth began to rumble under my feet. *What the fuck?* New York didn't have earthquakes.

Screams filled the air. I whirled back toward the complex.

The South Tower was falling, not outward but straight down, consumed by flames as it descended.

Suddenly everyone was running. A huge, billowing wall of beige smoke rolled between the buildings, rushing toward me.

Then I was running, too, but I wasn't fast enough.

Nobody could be fast enough.

The cloud enveloped us all. I was blinded, the bright day instantly transformed to darkness. The entire world was reduced to a filthy brown, debris-filled smoke. It was like being in the middle of a tornado or a volcano eruption. I couldn't breathe. Every time I tried I only got a mouth full of ash.

Someone crashed into me, and I stumbled. All I saw was a human-shaped form emerge from the smoke and then disappear again. Something sharp pierced my arm but I couldn't even cry out, couldn't speak, I was choking on the smoke. I continually stepped on things I couldn't see, poking and tearing my feet open, the ground a minefield.

I lurched forward, arms stretched out like a zombie, feeling bodies rush past but unable to see anything. My hands hit brick. Somehow I had gotten turned around and had walked into a building instead of up the sidewalk.

The brick was rough but comforting under my fingertips, grounding me. I moved forward, hoping I was heading north, using the building as a guide. The brick changed to metal, then glass.

The whole world was silent. No alarms, no voices, no traffic, no sirens. No birds.

Distant voices occasionally carried through the mist. I heard muffled fragments of someone calling out, but I remembered what Maya said and kept moving.

The fog became brighter. I could see people and the surfaces my hand traced as I walked more and more clearly, until finally there was no longer a cloud.

I kept going.

People stared as I passed, their faces horror-struck. Many asked if I was injured, if I needed help. I shook my head at them, numb, unable to speak, but I did accept a bottle of water thrust into my hands by a stranger, using it to rinse my mouth and spit out as much ash as I could.

I moved on autopilot, heading toward the Canal Street subway station, assuming I could climb aboard a train and get home.

My path was blocked by a soldier with an automatic weapon.

"Subways are closed." His mouth was a tight line.

Tears sprang into my eyes. "But I need to get home."

He took in the sight of me, covered in ash, and his mouth softened. "Where is home?"

"Brooklyn."

"No traffic allowed until we're sure it's over," he said. I'd been so focused on walking, on getting out of the cloud and putting one foot in front of the other, I hadn't noticed there weren't any cars or trucks at all. "But I think the bridges are about to open to pedestrians."

I nodded and swiped at the tears on my face. The Williamsburg Bridge wasn't far, just a few blocks east, and from there a short walk home.

I walked more.

A block later, a Chinese woman wordlessly pressed a pair of sequined plastic slippers into my hands. They were too big but I put them on anyway, grateful. My feet stung and ached from stepping on countless pieces of debris, unseen and unknown.

There was a backup at the entrance to the bridge, hundreds of people milling around empty Canal Street waiting to cross. 1010 WINS radio blared out in unison from a parked car, an open window, and a shop that sold knockoff designer handbags. The word *terrorism* reverberated over and over in the air. A group of people huddled around the parked car, listening, shaking their heads, and talking in low voices.

After around five minutes soldiers began letting people pass. As on the stairs, everyone was calm. There was no outright panic, no mad rush to the bridge, no shoving or pushing. Just a long, stoic mass of haunted-looking people, some like me so dust-covered we resembled ghosts. Many of the women, like me, were wearing sparkly plastic slippers that kind vendors on Canal Street had given to those who'd lost their shoes, incongruous with their business suits.

Every person in Brooklyn, it seemed, was standing on their stoop holding out cups of water as we passed, like it was the marathon. I was so close to my apartment, so close. Once I was in front of my own door, the key was barely in the lock when the door flung open. Vik grabbed me and held me close, sobbing, and I blessedly, finally, collapsed.

CHAPTER TWENTY-NINE

I don't know how long it took me to tell Gio everything, but the shadows in the room had shifted by the time I was finished. He hadn't interrupted me or asked a question once.

We were quiet for a long time, sitting on the floor. Gio was holding me, and we leaned up against his couch. It slowly dawned on me I was crying—the first time, I think, I'd cried since that day. He didn't say anything, and I wasn't embarrassed. I couldn't be, because it was impossible to stop. I cried and cried: for the firefighters, especially the one with the hazel eyes. For all the people behind me on the stairs who didn't get out in time. For those who had jumped. For everyone in the missing-person posters and their families.

And I cried for Maya, whose last name I didn't know and who I wished I could thank in person.

When my sobs subsided to hiccups, I told Gio one last thing.

"That guy Greg didn't make it. One of the people at work told me." It had been Sloane. She seemed to think I'd want to know.

I didn't want to know. I would have preferred to have imagined him alive, the pretty little drawing hanging in his bedroom somewhere. Maybe the Upper West Side. Maybe Connecticut.

But it wasn't. Sloane had let me know Greg McClean was among the missing. The gallery had, of course, shredded the check I had kept safe in my bag. Insurance paid out the cost of the work.

Greg was dead, and the drawing lived in the back of my closet, under my balled-up, dust-covered vintage dress that looked like Prada, sealed up tight in plastic bags to keep the smell contained. To keep as much of that dust encased as possible.

The fact I had an actual Georgia O'Keeffe drawing in my closet was the one thing I didn't tell Gio. I couldn't explain why I hadn't been able to give it back, not even to myself. But I couldn't. The Fletchers assumed the work was gone, and I never corrected them.

"My guess is he waited too long to leave," I said. "We were up so high, among the last floors where people made it out at all. Some people were still coming down, or got caught in the concourse under the buildings, when the first tower fell. I think a few got out of all that, but a lot didn't."

Gio still didn't say anything. He just held me, resting his chin on the top of my head.

A long moment passed. I had one more thing to say, and I didn't want to look at him when I said it.

"Why me, Gio?"

He pulled back slightly and twisted to look at me.

"What do you mean, why you? Why were you there that day? Just bad luck." His calloused fingertips brushed a strand of hair off my face, tucked it behind my ear.

"No, why didn't I die? I wasn't even really hurt, just a cut on my arm that didn't need stitches and torn-up feet. Why do I get to live?"

It had been a near thing. I understood that now, and I'd probably understood it in the moment but hadn't let myself think it. That I had survived and others hadn't, coming from those upper floors, was down to a series of choices. That Maya and I took the wider staircase instead of staying with the narrow one. If we'd walked out of the building one minute later, we would have been in there when the first tower fell. That I ran when the EMT screamed in my face, that I'd been those precious few blocks away instead of still in the plaza, where I probably would have been crushed by falling debris.

"Honestly, Chloe? You made it out for the same reason you were there in first place. It was just dumb luck. Good luck, in this case, but that's it."

I let that sink in for a minute.

"Look, I'm not going to pretend that the people who survived deserved it and those who died deserved that," Gio said. He swallowed. I wondered if he was remembering how his brother normally would have been at work that day, if he hadn't been traveling. "Nobody deserved to die like that. It was pure luck you survived. But it's okay. And I'm glad. And it's okay for you to be glad too."

The silence wrapped around us again like a quilt. I thought about what Gio said for a long time.

"I'm also glad you told me about it," he finally said.

"Me too." I was surprised to find how glad I was. I'd avoided talking about my time at Ground Zero for so long, and getting it out had been as hard as I'd imagined, but I was also glad I'd done it.

"And I don't think you didn't die because you were destined to help figure out this artist's murder. But since you didn't die, you know . . ." He trailed off.

"It's something good I can do?"

One shoulder lifted and his lips turned up in a slightly rueful smile. "Kind of." The smile faded. "I don't know you that well, Chloe. But I've felt for a while that you're not very happy. And I don't mean the panic attacks. I mean in general."

My heart seized, then calmed. I fought the urge to wrangle myself out of Gio's hold, to tell him I was perfectly happy.

I fought the urge to run out of there and straight to Rosemary's and drink three giant beers in quick succession until the world became pleasantly blurry.

"And I don't think you should go turn into Nancy Drew," he continued when I didn't speak, "but maybe, telling me what you just did, and maybe if we can figure out this thing with the paintings, maybe after all that it could be kind of a fresh start, you know?"

If *we* can figure this out. The relief of not being alone in whatever crazed funhouse was happening was nearly overwhelming. I sank deeper into his chest in response.

"Are you hungry?" he said, when I still didn't speak.

"Actually, yeah." Another surprise.

"Wanna get pancakes?"

Pancakes suddenly sounded like the best thing in the world. "Sure. And do you mind swinging by my apartment with me after? Poor Groucho must be starving. Ah shit, I don't have my keys." They had been in my coat pocket, and I had left my coat on the platform of a crane on the grounds of the Domino Sugar Factory. The thought of calling the factory and trying to explain what happened, of asking if they had a lost and found, forced a short, slightly hysterical laugh from my throat.

"You got a super?"

"Kind of." Technically, a leering, aggressive stoner named Jake was our super, but he only did the most basic of maintenance, uniformly refusing tenants' requests to fix minor leaks or broken cupboard doors.

Gio rolled his eyes at my description. "We'll get you some keys."

Gio's presence shamed Jake the super into giving me his copy of my apartment key, and we'd driven to a local hardware store to get a copy made. It had been less than twenty-four hours since I'd run out of my home after fighting with Vik, but the apartment felt like a time capsule from long ago, closed and shut like a relic. The congealed, ruined curry still sat on the stove. Groucho jumped down from the top of the fridge, making me yelp in surprise.

I'd told Gio about it the night before, but being there, it all came rushing back: How Ben had been rooting through my drawers. How Vik had yelled that I sounded like a crazy person, but how he had been lying to me for weeks.

And how I'd seen something else in his eyes.

Vik had been afraid.

Images of my friend filled my mind: Vik stirring countless curries in that pot over the years, laughing at a well-written line on *The West Wing*, sitting on the couch and holding my hand in those long days after 9/11. And now, of him lying in a hospital bed somewhere. My heart clenched.

Groucho wove around my legs and complained loudly. He allowed himself to be petted on the head once, then shot away like a cannonball at the sound of Gio putting food into his bowl.

The lines of paint, twining like a cat's path through Inga's giant canvas.

Afraid.

My bag was still slumped in the doorway of my bedroom where I'd left it.

Be Careful.

The red light on my answering machine blinked. I made myself press play.

A long, silent pause sounded, punctuated by one audible intake of breath.

Then a click, and the message ended.

"Who do you think that was?" Gio was at my side. "Wrong number?"

"I don't know." Sloane had said she'd tried to call the house line this morning, maybe it had been her.

But even as I thought it, I knew I didn't believe it.

"You still wanna head to the address on that note? In Jamaica?" Gio asked. He looked at the answering machine like he didn't trust it.

"Yes," I said with more conviction than I felt. "It was just a wrong number."

Back in Gio's car, I dictated the directions he'd printed out from MapQuest. We came to a standstill on the Brooklyn-Queens Expressway due to construction. I'd had too much coffee at the diner where we'd gotten our pancakes, and I was a jittery mess, my stomach slightly sour.

"So are *you* happy?" The question blurted out of me before I could stop it.

Gio looked surprised, then thoughtful. "Mostly. I love the bakery. My grandparents worked hard to build it, and I like that I can keep it going." He maneuvered past a slow-moving construction vehicle and we sped up a degree, then met another wall of brake lights.

"So that's it? You'll run the bakery forever?" Gio must have been around my age, maybe a little older. I pictured him in the same apartment, twenty years from now, horsing around with a couple of teenaged kids while a Stacie look-alike smiled from the kitchen. Mateo would be doing the same thing downstairs, in the apartment now occupied by their grandmother.

He gave the road a wry smile. "I didn't say that. I was a business major at Baruch. I've got ideas about expanding the bakery, opening another few branches, maybe even one in a different city." We finally inched past the construction and traffic opened up. "Here we go," Gio muttered.

There was more to Gio than I'd assumed. "I dropped out of Hunter," I admitted. My knee jittered up and down, up and down. It was driving me insane, and I put my hand on it to help it slow. "Really, I failed out."

Out of the corner of my eye I could see Gio shrug a little. "College isn't right for everyone."

"But I'm good at the research I do at the gallery." There wasn't much to see in the late-afternoon light, but I kept my eyes out the window and watched the ugly apartment buildings and stunted trees, many with plastic grocery bags caught in their bare branches, whiz past. We were getting closer. "Lou said so, at least."

"Then maybe the timing wasn't right."

"Maybe."

"What's our exit?"

I read out the exit number, and soon we were taking a series of turns through confusingly numbered streets.

"107th Avenue at 180th Street," I said, shaking my head. "What's up with that, Queens?"

"Okay," Gio said, pulling over and parking. He pointed. "That's it."

"That's the address?"

"Yeah."

The building was a long, low warehouse, nondescript, surrounded for blocks by other long, low warehouses. The one we were parked in front of had a sign declaring it Franklin's Glass and Metal. Minor graffiti graced some of the others, but the one at the address Inga had left was unmarked.

"I don't get it," I said slowly. "I thought that whatever was here would tell me something. That it would offer a clue about why Inga put that note in my pocket." *And about why she ended up dead.*

The light was fading, but it wasn't gone yet. Gio put his hand on the door handle. "Let's go check it out."

My stomach lurched. "I don't know." It was Friday afternoon, still business hours. A guy in a bulky canvas jacket came out of the glass and metal place and walked past the car. "Someone could be in there." Images of the skinhead-looking guys flashed in my head. What if one of the guys who had chased me last night was in there and recognized me?

As if reading my mind, Gio said, "I'll go see what's what. You stay here."

I bit my lip. "Okay. But be careful."

From the warm interior of the car, I watched Gio amble across the street and casually walk the sidewalk in front of the warehouse. He looked up at the glass block windows, then back at the car, and shook his head slightly. I understood; the windows were way too high to see into, big, long rectangles at least eight feet off the ground.

Gio's head snapped left, and he hurriedly walked away from the building, gesturing downward with his hand once. What the hell did that mean?

The warehouse door swung open.

Fuck.

I pitched forward, ducking below the dash, the sound of blood rushing to my ears.

A few tense seconds passed. I was convinced I was about to hear a loud pounding on the window of the car.

Or worse, the door opening, a hand grabbing my hair and dragging me out, determined to finish what they'd started last night.

To do to me what they'd done to Inga.

Murder.

I waited, breath held. Who was out there? Who had been in that warehouse?

Curiosity won over fear, by a hairbreadth, but enough. I slowly raised my head, just enough to peer out the driver's-side window.

A man in a long overcoat and leather gloves was securing a padlock on the warehouse door. He didn't wear a hat and his back was to me; his dark hair looked slick and well groomed.

Gio was nowhere.

It was dusk now, the shadows growing long and the sky glowing orange. The man turned, cupping his hand to light a cigarette, then shook out the match. There was just enough light for me to make out his face.

My breath caught.

I had seen the man somewhere before, but couldn't quite put my finger on where.

He unlocked a silver Mercedes parked next to the warehouse and climbed in. Once his profile was illuminated by his car's interior light, it hit me. The tilt of his head, at that angle, was what clued me in.

It was the man from the auction. The one who had bid against Henry, his competitor, there at the end, for the Monet.

All the saliva in my mouth seemed to dry at once.

I had no idea who the man was, but there was only one obvious connection between him and Inga.

The gallery.

CHAPTER THIRTY

I leaned back in the faded gray rolling chair and rubbed at my aching eyes. When I opened them again, the microform no longer swam on the screen. I sighed, turned the knob on the side of the machine, and continued scrolling.

The skills Lou had taught me were coming in handy today.

Aesthetically, the microform reading room of the New York Public Library was the exact opposite of the main reading room. There were no painted ceilings or gorgeous old wood fixtures here. Instead, it was an industrial, gray room, bright with fluorescent lighting, bulky reading machines hunched in grim rows. I'd been sitting at one for almost two full days now, all day yesterday, Saturday, and for most of today. Gio needed to do some bookkeeping at the bakery, so I was by myself.

Which was fine. It was sort of a one-person job anyway. I had a pile of reels stacked next to me, as I looked for each article written out on a sheet I'd prepared.

It was how I researched a work of art for Lou, like the Monet. He'd find the references, then give me a list of publications and dates and page numbers, and I'd hunt them down. Sometimes, for the older stuff, the library pages would hand me a hard copy of an old journal.

But I wasn't researching nineteenth-century art today. I was chasing more recent articles, the list of which I'd found indexed in the subject card catalogue.

I was researching the Fletchers.

My eyes skimmed the date of the microform. It wasn't quite where I needed it, so I turned the knob. The film whirred in the machine, fast-forwarding to the date I wanted.

Thank god the Fletchers were wealthy, the kind of wealth that brought a certain amount of fame, and therefore publicity, so there were actual references to chase. More articles had been written about Henry, of course, as he was older, but Sloane had her fair share as well. Pieces about New York society, philanthropy and charity events, articles from art publications.

There was also the obituary for Henry's wife, Sloane's mother.

A notice about Sloane's marriage. Three years later, a short mention of her divorce.

I didn't know exactly what I was looking for. Something that might link the Fletchers to the dark-haired man. Some sign of impropriety, of illegality. Something I could give the police, and then let them figure out how the web was spun.

But after two days, there had been nothing.

Earlier that afternoon, I'd moved on to Carl and was slowly working my way through the list of references relating to him. Mostly they were short, dry notices about a graduation, or a new job. Carl had worked in finance before his time with the government. I had paused on the *Washington Post* article from the late 1970s detailing his wedding, staring at the grainy photograph of the young, pretty woman with the feathered bangs.

I covered my mouth with my hand, trying and failing to hide an enormous yawn. That was it, I was done for the day. This would be my last article; I could chase down the rest tomorrow after work. It was late, I was starving, and felt seriously cross-eyed.

Finally on the correct date, I turned a different knob to bring the words into greater focus. It was a short article, more about the bank Carl had worked for at the time partnering with the Saudi National Bank, and then a lot of financial talk I didn't understand. Carl wasn't mentioned in the article, which confused me for a hot second until I saw he was in the accompanying photograph. Sighing, I zoomed in on the picture.

And my stomach dropped.

Two men were shaking hands, each flanked by a row of mostly unsmiling subordinates. Only three people in the picture were named. The president of Carl's bank, accompanied by Carl, and the president of the Saudi National Bank.

And standing in the row of Saudis was the dark-haired man from the warehouse.

Detective Gonzales was waiting for me when I emerged from the Sixty-Eighth Street subway the next morning, leaning against a newsstand with a blue-and-white take-out coffee cup in each hand. I walked around a man in a Santa hat who was clanging a bell for the Salvation Army, not even pretending like I didn't see her.

"I thought you weren't supposed to approach me on the street," I said.

She raised a brow. "I was just standing here; you approached me. Coffee?"

She was right, of course. I could have kept walking, could have ignored her fashionably long, black-wool-coated figure the entire way to the gallery, where I could have called Jonathan Marz, the fancy lawyer I wasn't paying for and could never afford. Hell, I could have walked to the phone booth on the corner and called Marz.

But I didn't. I accepted the proffered cup, instead. The coffee was just how I liked it, lots of sugar.

"How'd you know how I take my coffee?"

"Lucky guess." Gonzales took a sip from her cup. "I'm sorry about Vikram."

The wind stung my eyes, making them water. I blinked fast and took a too-quick swallow of coffee, burning my tongue.

"Hate crimes against brown people are skyrocketing across the country. My colleagues working Vikram's case believe that's the motive for the attack on him." She looked at me carefully. "Would you agree with their assessment?" she asked.

The coffee made my burnt tongue tingle. There were so many answers I could give her. If I told the detective that the attack wasn't random, that I'd been pursued and had narrowly escaped Vik's fate, would she believe me?

And would it cast more suspicion on Vik, if he was involved in . . . something?

I couldn't do that to him. Not until I knew what was happening myself. I'd seen the fear on his face, plain as day, when we'd last spoken. My anger at Vik for lying to me was tangled up with my concern for him.

Until the last few weeks, Vik had been the most loyal, devoted friend I'd ever had.

"Are you any closer to finding Inga's killer?" I countered. The clanging bell was making me twitchy.

The detective tilted her head to one side, a move her partner normally did. Where was Downs? I glanced around the street and didn't see him, but that didn't mean he wasn't nearby.

"Look, Chloe, I'm sorry if you felt ambushed the last time we talked," she started.

"Carl Fletcher," I interrupted. My heart was pounding. I slugged more coffee anyway.

Now both brows hitched up. "Excuse me?"

"Carl Fletcher. Henry Fletcher's brother. He was having an affair with Inga. You should look into him."

Gonzales took a slow, careful drink of coffee, eyeing me over the white plastic lid. When she finally lowered her cup, she said, "We know. But he's not a suspect. He was seen by at least a dozen people the night Inga died."

I tightened my grip on my coffee cup. "There's more. There's this guy, I don't know his name, but I think he's involved with the Fletchers, including Carl, and there's a warehouse in Queens—"

"*Chloe?*" Even Detective Gonzales flinched a little at the harsh bark calling my name, loud enough to be heard over the Salvation Army guy.

Jonathan Marz slammed the back door of the town car and marched over to us. "Were my instructions not clear, Detective?" Gonzales raised both hands in a gesture of surrender.

"I approached her," I said quickly.

"Chloe, come with me." Marz ignored me and grabbed my upper arm, hauling me toward the car, where I meekly climbed into the back seat, guilt roiling up my throat. "I was on my way to the gallery anyway, I can take you there."

I expected the lawyer to yell some more, but once we were fighting the morning traffic—it was ridiculous to drive, the gallery was three blocks away—he gave a lusty sigh instead, rubbing his forehead.

"I shouldn't have to tell you to not talk to the police alone, Chloe. They have no leads in Inga Beck's death and are grasping at straws." I was surprised by how gentle Marz's voice was now. "You don't want to be one of those straws, do you? Have the police turn your life inside out, looking for proof of your involvement in this crime, proof that doesn't exist?"

I sank a little deeper into the leather seat. No, I didn't want that. Not at all.

"I know how persuasive a good detective can be. They can make you feel like they're on your side, that they only want what's best for you. But remember, Chloe, the police are not your friends in a case like this. They suspect everybody. Your employers, every single person who works at the gallery, every single person who was at that party, everybody."

I nodded to show I understood. We were pulling up in front of the gallery's gray stone facade.

"Will you let me do my job? Which is to keep you safe? And yes, the Fletchers, too, but you're the one they seem to have targeted, Chloe. I don't know why, but those detectives have put a bull's-eye on your back. So please, don't talk to them again without me present. Okay?"

"Okay." I sounded as chastened as I felt.

"Okay," he repeated. "I won't tell Henry about this. We'll keep it between us, yeah? But you have my number. Call if you see either of those detectives again."

Carmen eyed me narrowly as I walked in. "Henry wants you," she said, picking up the phone. "Fletcher & Sons." She placed a hand over the mouthpiece and hissed, "*Now*," when I didn't move.

I went to my office to deposit my coat and bag. I wasn't about to jump just because Carmen said so, but I didn't stop to admire the Picasso. The paper cup of coffee was still in my hand. I set it carefully on my desk.

"Chloe! I thought I heard you." Henry suddenly filled the doorway, beaming at me from behind his tortoiseshell glasses. I paused in the act of removing my scarf.

"Carmen told me you wanted to chat. I was just taking my coat off."

"No rush, no rush." He folded his hands over his stomach and smiled comfortably.

I rushed anyway, placing my coat and bag on my desk chair. Henry frowned at Lou's big, empty desk, then at my tiny, messy one, but he didn't say anything.

"I was hoping you could share with me your write-up on the Monet," he said, as soon as my scarf had joined the pile on the chair.

"Oh, sure." I'd been so busy with Inga's show I'd forgotten about the Monet. "It's almost done. I can finish it up today and bring it up to you." The Fletchers had a one- or two-page write-up on every piece they had in their inventory, complete with provenance, exhibition history, and sometimes a publication history, for any prospective clients.

"Excellent. I'd love to see what you have so far."

"Okay." The request had me suddenly flustered. I strained my memory, trying to remember how complete the essay was. "It'll take a minute to start my computer and print it out . . ."

"Bring it up right away, will you?" He left without waiting for an answer.

I did as requested, finding both Fletchers in Henry's office five minutes later when I handed over the incomplete document.

"Hold on a second, Chloe," Sloane said as I turned to go, skimming what I'd written over her father's shoulder.

Nervousness pooled in my stomach as I watched them read it. I wasn't the scholar Lou was, though I thought I'd done a decent job with what I had so far.

"All these references, you've checked them personally? Found them in the library, made copies?" she asked.

"I did." It was hard not to twist my fingers together, but I forced myself to keep them still.

Henry leaned back and caught his daughter's eye. The two shared a look I couldn't interpret.

"This is a sensitive work of art, Chloe. You know it disappeared from public view in the 1930s," Sloane said.

"But reappeared in Florida just last year," Henry added. "We've checked with the appropriate databases, and neither we—nor Sotheby's—believe it was stolen by the Nazis. The seller claims it was bequeathed to her by her mother, who received it as a gift by the last known owners shortly before she fled France."

"So what we're saying is, even though we know this isn't a looted piece, this document," Sloane pointed at the piece of paper in Henry's hand, "needs to be airtight."

"It has to be perfect," Henry added.

"I understand," I said. "It's not finished yet."

"What you have is quite good, so far," Henry said, handing the paper back to me. Again, their eyes slid toward each other, then back to me.

"We may have a buyer for it," Sloane said.

"For the *Monet*?" I was flabbergasted. The Fletchers had broken a world record with what they'd paid for that painting, on behalf of their client. Someone was willing to give them more than twenty million for it?

A Cheshire-cat-like smile began to curl the corners of Sloane's mouth. "That's right."

"What about the client? The one you bought it for?"

"Actually, this is exactly what he wanted. That someone would offer to buy it privately after the auction, and we both make a profit."

"So . . . why wouldn't this buyer just bid at the auction?"

Sloane shrugged. "Some people don't want the publicity." I thought of the phone bidders, the absentee ballots. There seemed to be plenty of ways to bid if you didn't want to be seen. "Also, often people don't realize how badly they want something until it's out of reach." Her smile widened, completely self-satisfied.

I swallowed.

Was the buyer the runner-up at the auction? The dark-haired man from the warehouse, the one from that newspaper photo with Carl?

"Thanks, Chloe," Henry said in dismissal. "I'd love to see the finished product as soon as you've got it. You won't mind a few editorial notes?"

My mind was swirling as I made my way back to the office. Sure, maybe some other random person decided they needed a Monet painting of water lilies for over twenty million dollars, but the way Sloane had phrased it, that often people don't realize how badly they want something until it's out of reach, made me almost sure this buyer was the man they'd thwarted at the auction.

The auction.

Sotheby's knew who the dark-haired man was. He had to register in order to bid. If I could find out the identity of the man who held paddle 75, I could give that name to Detective Gonzales and let her and Downs look into it.

What Jonathan said about the police not being on my side rang in my brain.

But surely, if they had a better lead, they would focus on that and leave me alone?

Whoever this guy was, he could be the key. He had bid on a painting the gallery now owned. He was connected to Carl. It couldn't be a coincidence that he also had been at the warehouse where Inga had sent me.

Now all I had to do was identify him.

CHAPTER THIRTY-ONE

The pleasant buzz of nicotine wafted through my veins as I took a deep inhale of my first cigarette of the day. The streetlights were already on, even though it was only five o'clock, that early onset of a winter night.

Next week the solstice would arrive. Longest night of the year.

I took another grateful suck on my cigarette. I'd been trying to cut back, move toward quitting. I knew it was bad for me, not to mention expensive.

I waited for the last customer to leave the bakery before stubbing out my half-smoked Marlboro Light, trading the biting breeze of the street for the fragrant warmth of inside.

"You mind grabbing that broom?" Gio asked, pausing from counting out the register.

I didn't. I began to sweep the spare dust and crumbs up, creating a small, neat pile. I'd begun to help Gio here and there, cleaning up, or arranging rolls in the display case. His parents did all the baking with a small crew at an industrial kitchen deeper in the borough, and I'd never been there, but I enjoyed the retail end of the business.

I hadn't spent a single night in my apartment since Gio had fished me out of the East River. We stopped by daily to feed Groucho. The cat let me know in no uncertain terms that he was angry about Vik's and my absence, but as bad as I felt about leaving him alone, I couldn't bring myself to stay the night there.

Instead, I had curled up next to Gio for the past four nights.

And while we slept in the same bed, we hadn't slept together. No sex. I was bemused but also touched. I could tell it wasn't from lack of interest on his part—and not on mine, either; I would find myself drifting off into daydreams thinking about his well-defined chest—but rather from a sense of respect.

It was a new feeling, getting close to a guy without immediately getting naked. Most of the guys I dated really were interested in just sex, even though I convinced myself over and over that this time it would be different.

Only *this* time, it seemed, it was.

And I liked it.

More than liked it.

I felt safe, and cared for, sleeping curled up next to Gio. I was finally feeling less like one giant bruise from my jump and was enjoying taking the physical part of whatever was developing between us slowly. And I liked being part of the rhythm of his daily life, of folding myself into it. Mateo, Gio's brother, had so far taken my presence in stride, automatically making an extra coffee for me in the morning, or making sure there was enough of whatever he was cooking for dinner.

The floor looked clean, so I put the broom away and helped myself to a predinner cranberry muffin, peeling away the paper wrapper.

"I still think you should call that detective and tell her to contact Sotheby's," Gio said after he'd finished closing out the register. He leaned against the display case.

The muffin was amazing, tart cranberries exploding in my mouth, perfectly contrasting with the crunch of walnut pieces. I waited to swallow before responding, even though we'd had this conversation several times already.

"But what will I tell them? That a guy who knows Carl tried to buy an expensive painting?"

"You tell them that a dead girl left you an address and that guy does business there."

I shook my head. "But none of that is a crime. I feel like I need something more concrete. And maybe that lawyer is right, and I shouldn't trust the police. I mean, why are they so hell-bent on questioning me? I don't *know* anything." Even as I said the words, though, I wondered if they were true. The same images and sensations from the night of the party tried to rear up in my head. I shoved them away, for now.

"Besides," I continued, "there's all that stuff Calvin was saying."

Gio folded his arms across his chest and gave me a look. "Chloe, come on. Not everyone from Saudi Arabia is a terrorist, and you know it."

I popped the last of the muffin into my mouth. "I know, of course. Jeez, I'm not like those guys at the bar." More images tried to force their way in, that of the Greg McClean look-alike shoving Vik, quickly followed by Vik disappearing under a hailstorm of fists and feet. The muffin stuck in my throat, and I took a swig of now-cold coffee to wash it down. "I know not everyone from Saudi is a terrorist, okay? But he was at the auction. And he knows Carl. That's a lot of weird connections. Given Carl's work, what if—just what if—Carl is somehow in league with terrorists? I mean, there aren't that many reasons to kill Inga, right? Not unless she knew something she wasn't supposed to know."

Gio blew out a breath. "I still think you should talk to them. Let the cops figure out the weird connections."

Yeah. It was sounding like a better and better idea. "I don't want to get Vik in trouble, though. Whatever is going on, he may have been involved." I still couldn't wrap my head around the idea that maybe my arty, sophisticated, intelligent best friend was so deep in something shady that he'd almost been killed. Even though he'd lied to me about who I'd been kissing in the loft, I just couldn't bring myself to throw him to the wolves until I knew the truth. "Or even Bo."

A hard look crossed Gio's face. "Bo's a grown man, even though he acts like a toddler. He can handle himself. Carrying you down some stairs isn't a crime."

As if summoned, the door to the bakery swung open and Bo sauntered in, holding a lit cigarette.

"What the fuck, Bo?" Gio asked angrily, eyeing the cigarette.

"What? Nobody's in here."

"It doesn't matter, you know we don't allow smoking in the bakery." Gio pointed at the prominent sign posted next to the door.

Bo rolled his eyes, yanked the door half open again, and tossed the cigarette through the opening, where it smoldered on the sidewalk.

"Happy now? Hey, can I get a coffee?"

"We're closed," Gio said, moving to behind the counter and making a show of taking off his apron, turning off the light in the back room. "On our way out the door now."

"Aw, come on. Just one coffee." Bo waved a dollar bill in the air.

"I already dumped it. You'll have to come back tomorrow." Gio retrieved our coats from the hook behind the counter and handed mine to me.

Bo watched the exchange, his hands stuffed in his coat pockets.

"What, you a barista now?" he asked me. "Gonna put on a green apron?"

"Just helping out," I said, pulling on my red wool coat. It was too lightweight for the weather, but I'd lost my good heavy green one on the grounds of the sugar works and wasn't about to go back for it. The last thing I needed was them calling the police because I'd been trespassing.

"Hey, I heard about Vik," Bo said, removing his hands from his coat and leaning against the counter. Gio scowled at him, obviously not wanting Bo to get comfortable. "How is he?"

My heart gave a squeeze. "Holding steady, I guess. Still in a coma, but the doctors are hopeful." I'd finally called Vik's mom the day before, asked if I could bring anything from the apartment to the hospital. She said no, that they'd already been there. I was glad I'd thrown out the curry and cleaned Groucho's box.

There had been two more hang-ups on the answering machine.

I still hadn't been to see Vik. I wasn't sure I could handle it but knew I needed to go soon.

"Hey, come to Rosemary's," Bo said. He stepped closer, ignoring Gio entirely, and leaned in, his nose grazing my neck. "Let's get a drink. I called you a bunch, where have you been? Get a cell phone, woman."

I took a half step back, glancing involuntarily at Gio. He had refolded his arms and was as stone-faced as I'd ever seen him.

"No, I can't." Bo had called? Was he one of the hang-ups on the machine?

"Come on," he wheedled. "I bet it's hard being in the apartment without Vik. I can keep you company if you want. Or you know you're welcome to stay at my place. Besides, I wanna talk."

I tried for lighthearted. "We can talk here." I shot another look at Gio. What the fuck was Bo doing?

Bo followed my gaze, understanding dawning across his face.

"Okay." He took three steps back himself and flipped his hair out of his eyes, looking inexplicably hurt. "So, uh, I got Liam's phone number. You know, the guy you were all over at Inga's party?" His words came out clipped and biting, a verbal slap in the face. "So you can call him, and he'll confirm he asked me to come get you that night. You seemed a little concerned that you couldn't remember the guy you'd been making out with, because you were so blackout drunk. So I thought you might want to talk to the man himself."

Over Bo's shoulder, Gio's jaw tightened. He narrowed his eyes at Bo's back.

Because I'd told Gio what I remembered. That I hadn't been kissing a guy named Liam that night.

I'd been kissing the woman who was murdered, it seemed, shortly before I'd left her loft. Before I'd been *carried* out.

Bo thrust a ratty piece of paper into my hand. A number was scrawled on it.

I had no choice but to take the paper. It was that or let it drop.

Gio silently shook his head at me, warning me not to say anything. My fingers curled around the paper.

"Hey, can I get a thank-you? I had to talk to Tanya to get that. Would that be so hard, to say thank you, Bo?"

His eyes locked with mine, fury and jealousy and a small, cruel delight dancing in them.

"Thanks, Bo," I said in a wooden tone. He was such a prick. Why were the men I slept with always such pricks?

"It's time to go now." Gio's voice was loud and forceful. He marched from behind the counter and held open the door. "We're closed."

"See, they're closing, Chloe. Let's go to the bar." Bo started to walk. I nearly gasped in surprise at his bravado.

"We're not closed to her," Gio said.

Bo looked over his shoulder, eyeing both of us coldly. He gave one derisive snort before walking out, shoulders hunched against the wind.

Silence fell between me and Gio once Bo had left. I was mortified about what Bo had said, even though I knew he'd only said it because he was angry I was . . . well, whatever I was with Gio now.

"What sounds good for dinner?" Gio finally said in a light tone. He turned off the other lights and moved toward the door. "I could make gnocchi."

I swallowed, fighting back the shame that was rising in my throat. He paused at the door and looked at me questioningly, illuminated only by the streetlamp light streaming in through the front window.

"I'm sorry," I said miserably. I wasn't even sure what I was apologizing for; I hadn't said anything rude. But I was sorry, for all of it: that this kind, smart, funny man was involved in any of this, that he had jumped into the East River because of me, that I was fucked-up and suffered panic attacks and had a past with assholes like Alex and Bo. "I'm just so sorry." A sob rose where the shame had been, and I choked it back. I'd cried more in the past four days than I had in years.

Gio crossed the room and pulled me to him in what seemed like one quick motion. I buried my face in his coat, reveling in the feel of his chest through the layers of fabric.

He kissed me, once, on the top of my head. My scalp tingled from the contact, and I imagined tilting back my head, giving him access to my mouth.

But I didn't.

It was enough, for now.

"I always thought that guy was an asshole," Gio said into my hair.

That was enough to make me stop crying and start laughing.

"Okay, let's go upstairs and have some food. You've got a big day tomorrow."

"Yeah?" We made our way toward the door, arms linked. "What's happening tomorrow?"

"You're going to see Vik."

I pulled my arm free and stared up at him, my heart already starting to accelerate. "No, Gio, it's too soon."

"It's time, Chlo. You'll never forgive yourself if you don't."

He was right. I hesitated, then nodded, and took a deep breath.

"Okay."

CHAPTER THIRTY-TWO

Lights pulsed and machines whirred and beeped in Vik's hospital room, the infrastructure that was helping return him to us. Vik's father, Darsh, pulled me into a brief, tight embrace when I walked in. I was momentarily shocked, as the man had only ever formally shaken my hand in the past.

His parents had not thought it at all appropriate when I moved in. For weeks Vik's mom, Indira, insisted on speaking to my mother, though eventually she'd given up after I'd stonewalled her long enough. Vik had appeased her that I had a boyfriend (I hadn't at the time, not really, though I suppose the bartender I'd been sleeping with intermittently could be called that if one squinted hard enough), and after six months or so she seemed to accept that I was not going to make her son "fast"—her words, according to Vik, who thought it was hysterical. I'd been mortified and faintly crushed that this elegant and polished woman, who was a doctor no less, thought so little of me.

Over the years Indira had become more motherly toward me, especially once Vik brought me home for a holiday or two. I think she pitied me more than a little, which was also crushing, but not enough that I declined invitations. They had tried desperately to get Vik to move home after the towers fell, fearing just the type of attack that had landed him in the hospital now. Ironically, their mostly Indian community in New Jersey had seen more vandalism and hate than Vik had experienced in the city, despite the neighborhood's deliberate and prominent display of American flags. My own parents hadn't asked if I would move back to Ohio. My mother did pointedly tell me about a guy from high school who enlisted in the days after 9/11, and I got a rare call from my dad, who cleared his throat a lot during it, asking if I shouldn't find some nice girl like me to be roommates with, instead of a guy named Vikram. I could hear my stepmother prompting him in the background.

That was as far as their worry went.

Vik had nice parents.

"We could use a little break," Indira said, pulling a more reluctant Darsh out of his chair and herding him toward the door. "And a touch of tea from the cafeteria. Can we bring you anything?"

"No, thank you," I said quickly. "Please, can I go to the cafeteria for you, bring you some tea?"

"You take a moment with Vikram," said Darsh, catching on. "That boy, he'll be running the Metropolitan Museum one day, I keep telling the nurses." I smiled and nodded. Darsh was a professor of physics at Rutgers, and neither of Vik's parents really understood why he had chosen art conservation as a field, but they were determined if that's what he wanted, then he would be the most successful person in the art world.

The room was quiet in their wake, the humming and chirping machines my only company.

That, and Vik, bandaged and puffy, a lump under a crisp white hospital sheet. What skin peeked through the gauze and wires was covered in small cuts and massive bruises.

Guilt tore through me. I moved closer to the bed, staring at the tubes disappearing into the back of Vik's left hand. Until recently, Vik had been a rock for me, an anchor, making me laugh and keeping me from spinning into complete chaos.

The words he'd flung at me the night of our fight loomed in my head. I realized, though, that aside from whatever was prompting him to lie about the night of Inga's party, he'd spoken the truth. With a little distance, I could see how hard it must have been for Vik to carry me for all those months.

"I'm sorry," I whispered. Just as I had with Gio. I didn't even know what I was apologizing for, really. That he had been brutally attacked, yes. But also for whatever role I might have unknowingly played in it.

Apparently, Vik was improving. He was no longer in a coma, but slept most of the time. He'd been responsive to simple instructions, which the doctors said was a great sign for his recovery. Staring at his inert, battered form, I found it hard to believe he was getting better, though I desperately wanted him to.

"What's going on, Vik?" I whispered. "If you could, would you tell me the truth now?"

I wanted to whisper more, to lay it all out for him: the mysterious note, the words in the paintings, Carl Fletcher, the dark-haired man, but I couldn't bring myself to do it. The very thought was overwhelming.

So I simply kept vigil. Watching the gentle rise and fall of his chest under the sheet.

Minutes ticked by.

I didn't hear anyone come in, so I jumped almost a foot when a voice asked, "How is he?"

I whirled, almost knocking over a standing IV drip, even though I knew who it was.

I recognized his voice by now.

Carl Fletcher grabbed the metal pole holding the IV and straightened it before it fell. "Careful. Why are you so jumpy, Chloe?" His light eyes glinted in the green glow of the nearest machine.

"What the fuck are you doing here? I'm calling the police."

But the phone was on the other side of Vik's bed, and Carl was between me and it.

Carl raised an eyebrow. "And tell them what?" He asked as though he were genuinely curious. "That I had an affair with Inga Beck? The police know that already, because I told them. I'd prefer it not become public, but if it does, it does." He shrugged. "My wife already knows. We decided to stay together, work on our marriage."

"You're stalking me," I blurted out. "You followed me to the storage warehouse and you followed me here."

He proffered another look of mild curiosity and surprise. "Am I? I was at the warehouse that day to see some artwork a friend had said he'd loan me. And I'm here to visit a sick colleague. If you want to mention those two coincidences to the police, go ahead." He shrugged again, smaller this time, and put his hands in his pants pockets. "My stories will check out."

I darted a look at the phone, then at the door.

Carl stood between me and both.

"My stories always check out, Chloe," he continued when I stayed quiet. "I was in DC when Inga died. Dozens of witnesses can place me at a restaurant with my wife and several colleagues that night."

He wasn't advancing on me or making any particularly threatening gestures. Yet I felt unmistakably threatened. I quickly scanned the room for some kind of weapon, but other than the IV stand, which I wouldn't use as it was attached to Vik, I didn't see anything.

"I didn't kill Inga, Chloe. But you, you seem to be grasping at straws that aren't there, seeing things that aren't real. I know your history. I know you were at the towers when they fell." My heart plummeted to my stomach. How did this man know anything about me? "I also know you often—oh, so often—drink to excess and then can't remember what happened," he continued. Now he did advance a step. Fear spiked uncontrollably. "All totally understandable, given what you experienced. But who do you think the police will believe, you or me? Your crazy theories and drunkenness, against my airtight alibis and, other than an ill-advised fling with a beautiful woman, impeccable reputation?"

The police. Detective Gonzales. She must have circled back to him after I saw her on the street.

Carl smirked, closemouthed this time, keeping his teeth hidden for once.

"You really think my brother and niece don't notice how you come in late, leave early, and how you're typically so hungover you can't think straight? They feel sorry for you, so when Lou skipped town they decided to throw you a bone, make you curator. But you're not up for this, Chloe. This isn't your world. My advice is you quit while you can, before you make an even bigger fool of yourself than you already are."

The words were like bullets, each one finding home and leaving indelible, painful welts. They were the words I'd said to myself in the middle of the night, the words I drank to erase.

This was the same man who, a few short weeks ago, had told me he thought I reminded him of Inga. That I was full of life and promise, just like her.

I knew at the time he'd only been trying to endear himself to me, but I didn't know why then.

Now I did.

He was up to his neck in whatever was going on somehow, and he didn't want the police looking any further into him.

That knowledge didn't make the words any less hurtful. Or him any less terrifying.

I had backed away as far as I could, but Carl took one more step toward me. I was about to push past him, physically shove him aside to get to the door and start screaming as loud as I could, when the door swung open.

A nurse padded in. I must have looked as terrified as I felt, because a frown ripped across her face in an instant. "How can I help?" she asked in a no-nonsense way.

Now the teeth appeared. The nurse looked taken aback at the sight of them. "Thank you, but I was just leaving," Carl said.

"Are you okay, miss?" The nurse cast a worried look between me and the door through which Carl had left. "Should I call security?"

"No. No, I'm fine."

I whispered a hasty goodbye to Vik and stumbled out of the room, the nurse frowning after me.

The elevator ride to the lobby was a blur. I only wanted to get away from the overpowering scent of antiseptic cleanser and the hum of machines and take the deepest breath I could of cold city air.

But in the lobby I ran smack into Ben.

He looked awful, white-faced and wide-eyed, not at all the urbane preppy I was used to.

We stared at each other awkwardly, he clearly as surprised to see me as I was him. The last time I'd seen Ben, he'd been rifling through my dresser drawer.

"This is pretty fucked-up," he finally said.

I wasn't sure if he meant running into me here, or that Vik was lying in a hospital bed upstairs, or something else.

I chose to believe it was something else.

"Yes, it is." I was still shaking from my encounter with Carl. He wasn't anywhere in the lobby that I could see. "I can't take anyone else lying to me, Ben. What is going on? I know about the Saudi guy. I know about the warehouse."

Ben shook his head at me, but he had a hunted look I didn't trust. "I don't know what you're talking about. *I* don't know anything. Just that Vik was messing around in something he shouldn't have and he nearly died. Saudi guys and warehouses? Jesus, Chloe. Whatever you two are doing, leave it alone."

"I haven't done anything, but whatever you all are involved in, I am too now. Tell me." I kept my voice to a furious whisper, mindful of the people entering and exiting the huge revolving glass doors, those coming in clutching bouquets of flowers as they squinted up at the wall directory, those leaving looking either hopeful or shaken.

"I'm not involved in shit. Inga, yeah, maybe she was. Vik had a secret, but I didn't pry. Honestly?" Ben pushed his hair back and blew out a frustrated breath. "I thought you were in on it too. I didn't ask because it was better if I didn't know. And see? I was right. It was the right move. You want to end up in a hospital bed next? Or worse? Look, I'm leaving New York, Chloe. I got a transfer to our Boston office."

Ben was leaving?

Just like Lou.

"Is that why you were snooping around my room? Because you thought I was caught up in whatever is happening?" At Ben's nod, I shook my head. "I'm as in the dark as you. And now you're bailing because the shit is hitting the fan, and abandoning Vik? What about him?"

Ben bit his lip. "He's got his family. They don't even know about us, you know? It's not like I'm going to out Vik to his parents while he's fighting for his life. Once he recovers"—a hitch entered Ben's voice—"I can hopefully convince him to move to Boston with me. If he agrees he's done with this bullshit. Because whatever Vik was up to, it wasn't my scene. I just introduced him and Inga."

My mind whirled again. Was Carl some kind of kingpin of . . . what? Guns? Drugs? Money laundering for terrorists? Was that why Inga was dead? How and why would Lou be involved? Or Vik?

"I'd better get up there," Ben said. "Vik's parents know I'm coming. They think I'm such a devoted friend, though they don't understand why I dumped you." His mouth tightened.

Jesus, what a mess. I was on the verge of letting him go when something occurred to me.

"Ben, wait. I need you to do something for me."

"What?" His voice was wary.

"Your sister works at Sotheby's, right? Vik said so." I rooted around in my bag until I found a receipt for cigarettes I'd bought on the way to the hospital. Turning it over, I wrote the date of the auction I'd attended and the paddle number of the dark-haired man.

"I need to know who this bidder is." I thrust the paper at him.

He looked incredulous. "You know she can't tell me that."

"Convince her. I think whoever that is had a connection to Vik's attack. I could go to the police, tell them, but I feel like I need a name."

Ben looked unconvinced but took the receipt with obvious reluctance. "No promises."

"Come on, help me. Help Vik." When he still looked uncertain, I dropped a trump card. "You owe him that."

I didn't wait for an answer but ducked through the revolving doors, desperate to get back to Gio's.

That night, I dreamt of Inga.

We were facing each other, the same as in my memory. My lips stung in the pleasantly bruised way of someone who has been kissed, hard, and has kissed back. A kernel of desire glowed in the pit of my being, expanding in all directions.

I wanted more.

Of the kissing.

Of *her*.

Inga's face was so close, I could get lost in her freckles.

And then it happened. What always happened in this moment, when I remembered it.

Inga's gray eyes widened at something over my shoulder.

Turn around, Chloe. Look, goddammit it.

And, finally, I did.

The industrial metal door was gone, as was the entire interior of Inga's loft. Where it had been was an empty, endless space filled with a toxic beige cloud roiling toward us. I gasped and looked back to Inga, but the cloud had already swallowed us. She was barely visible in its gloom, then absorbed by it completely. I could hear screams and the sound of falling debris and the sickening, more visceral thud of what could only be a falling body, but they were all muffled, as if I were deep underwater.

"Inga?" *I screamed, reaching blindly forward.* "Inga, where are you?"

"I'm here," *a voice answered through the ash.*

Only it didn't sound like Inga. The voice was more guttural.

More greedy.

"Where?" *My words came in a shaky rush. I groped in the fog, trying to find her, for what seemed like eternity, those horrifying noises distant but still audible and real.*

"Here," *she called. I reached, and my hands hit yielding flesh.*

"Inga." *I nearly sobbed with relief.* "Come on, we can walk out. I'll *show you. I did it before, I know the way."* I curled my fingers around her hand and began walking blindly, pulling her with me.

"But I have something to show you," came the now-terrible voice.

Despite its awfulness, I couldn't let go of her hand. We all sounded awful now, it was okay. We needed to stick together, it was the only way out of the cloud.

And we did need to get out. I realized I couldn't breathe, that my mouth was full of unspeakable grit.

The figure holding my hand came closer, a faint wraith taking shape in the blur. Somehow, I was living and surviving despite not being able to breathe, but the panic was beginning to set in, the desperation for air.

I couldn't make out Inga's shape until she was so close she was already upon me, and in a heart-stopping instant I realized my mistake. This wasn't Inga at all, or at least not anymore. I was holding hands with a creature that was mostly fangs and claws and terrible red eyes, its mouth gaping and descending. I tried to scream but couldn't—my lungs were too clogged with the poisonous smoke—so I was silent when the yawning, bloody mouth with pointed teeth captured mine.

I woke up screaming.

CHAPTER THIRTY-THREE

"Just quit, Chloe." Gio put down a spoon and stared at me, concern all over his face. "That place is fucking miserable, and you don't have to go. We'll hire you at the bakery, I could use an extra hand."

"I do have to go," I said, gratefully accepting the small cup of espresso he passed me. I'd been staying at Gio's for a week now, and it already felt more like home now than my own apartment, except without Groucho. I had only finally stopped aching from my jump from the crane, and we'd fallen into an easy rhythm, me and Gio. Mateo was back on a twenty-four-hour shift and watched us with a bemused yet pleased expression when he was around. "Okay, you're right. I don't have to. But I need to. Does that make sense?"

Gio blew on his own coffee before sipping some foam off the top. We were in the kitchen, leaning against the Ricci brothers' pristine counters. "It makes sense, but I don't like it." Gio had been almost as perturbed by my dream two nights ago as I had been. Not about the kissing-a-girl part—I'd already told him that, and he had rolled with it—but about how it had freaked me out so much I'd woken up shrieking. He'd sat bolt upright, pulling me close, even as Mateo leapt into our room with a baseball bat.

"I never finish anything," I said, swirling my espresso around a little. "I dropped out of college, I stopped acting. I need to see this through. I feel like I owe it to Inga." Staying at the gallery was out of the question, but I was starting to think the kind of work I did there was something I could do elsewhere, in time. Maybe this was the thing that would stick.

"At the expense of your safety?"

I bit my lip. "I'll be extra careful. Make sure I'm with people all the time, won't walk alone at night. I really feel like I'll have something for Gonzales soon." I kept my other thought—that I wasn't sure I could trust Detective Gonzales, not after she'd apparently ratted me out to Carl—to myself.

Gio drained his cup and turned to the sink, shoulders tense. "You're getting a cell phone this weekend, okay?"

"Okay."

"Are you sure you won't come tonight?" Gio was going to a big family dinner at his grandmother's. They normally did it every other Sunday, but with the Christmas rush at the bakery, they were doing it on a Thursday night instead.

"I'm sure."

He looked doubtful, and maybe a little disappointed.

"I want to. I really want to meet them more properly." I'd seen Gio's parents on occasion at the bakery but realized I didn't even know their first names. Gio did most of the front-of-house work. "Let's, you know, keep taking it a little slow. We'll get there."

On the surface, this was a ridiculous thing to say. I was living with the guy these days, sleeping in his bed every night.

But we were taking it slow in a way. We still hadn't had sex. We hadn't even kissed.

And even though we'd had dinner at his apartment every night, we hadn't, I realized, ever been on a proper date. I thought of Gio sitting on a stool at Diner, the gold chain winking at his neck, his soft burgundy shirt unbuttoned one button lower than usual.

I wanted to be the girl on the stool next to him, a sudden, desperate urge that hit deep in my bones.

"Maybe we should go on a date," I suggested, trying to keep the deep need out of my voice. "Before I meet your parents."

A slow smile spread across his face.

"Yeah. Maybe we should. Chloe Harlow, would you go to dinner with me this Friday?"

An answering warmth exploded in my middle, and I had to smile back.

"Yes, Gio Ricci. I would love to."

The happy, satisfied feeling that encased me on my whole commute evaporated the second I walked into work. Carmen spared me one quick, disgusted look before returning to her work. I instinctively checked my watch, confused; I wasn't *that* late.

The glistening colors of the Monet stopped me in my tracks. The show on dance had come down, and the painting had been moved from Henry's office and installed on the main wall of the exhibition space. I moved past it, admiring the pale greens and blues and pinks, the flecks of white meant to represent glittering sunlight on water.

My own office remained lopsided, the empty surface of Lou's desk a dark sheen, mine cluttered with piles of books and papers.

I hated being here now. The only reason to come, to not quit as Gio had urged, was access to Inga's files and paintings and the free internet. Carl's ugly words in Vik's hospital room floated into my brain and squatted there, pulsing. That I didn't belong. That I wasn't up to this.

I will prove you wrong, I vowed in my head as I fired up the computer. I meant it for Carl, the Fletchers, my dad, my professors with their indifferent head shakes as they failed me, even Vik and his doubts.

Henry and Sloane were in and out, brushing past me with barely a hello on the few occasions our paths crossed.

Carl must have told them that I'd said his name to the police.

The slights would have stung me before, but I didn't care. I was getting closer to the truth, I could feel it.

"They're frantic, trying to get everything ready for this potential buyer for the Monet to visit," Olive told me in a low voice as she handed over a file I needed.

"I still can't believe they found someone so fast." I was whispering too.

"The buyer came to them, they didn't even have to try."

"And they'll make a profit on a twenty-million-dollar painting?" I still couldn't believe anyone would pay that much for a piece of art. I tried to stretch my mind, think of what could be worth twenty million. A midsized island nation? A castle formerly occupied by royalty?

Sebastian snorted at the next desk. "If they sell it for twenty-two million, duh."

"But doesn't their client own the work, and he'll get the two million?"

"Unbelievable," he muttered, then raised his voice like he was explaining something simple to a child. "Because they charge their regular commission, dummy. They'll still make at least a million off this deal."

"Someone must really want that Monet," I said, ignoring Sebastian's insult. "Any idea who it is?" I tried to keep my voice casual.

He glared at me. "Yes. But that's my job, not yours."

Sebastian was a dead end, unless I could sneak a peek at his files, but he always made a show of locking his file cabinet every night. Also, the potential buyer for the Monet might not be the dark-haired man from the warehouse. It could just be some rich person with a spare twenty-two million lying around.

I wove my way through the crowds back to the subway at the end of the day, frustrated that I hadn't made much progress. I needed a new tactic. Maybe it was time to head back to the warehouse, poke around over the weekend? I mulled this over as I slipped in between other quickly moving pedestrians, mindful of my promise to Gio to stay around people and to go straight back to his apartment.

The sound stopped me short, causing the man walking behind me to nearly bang into my back. He scowled at me, muttering something about tourists as he passed.

You give us twenty-two minutes, we'll give you the world.

The familiar *tick tick tick*, 1010 WINS's signature background noise, filled the sidewalk, louder than the chatter of pedestrians, louder than the tinny holiday music wafting from stores as customers came and went, louder than the incessant clack of shoes on pavement.

A cab had pulled over, idling at the curb, its light off, the driver smoking out his open window. He was blaring the radio, loudly.

And I was there again, for just a flash, but so vivid it felt real: covered in toxic dust, gripping a bottle of water, hearing the radio blasting out of apartment windows, parked cars, boom boxes, all in unison up and down Canal Street. Feeling people's stares, mutely shaking my head at the offers of help. The rough texture of the sequins under my fingers, the slippers the shopkeeper had pressed on me.

Now, on Lexington Avenue, my steps slowed and my body tensed. I waited for the inevitable surge of nausea, the accelerated heart rate, the feeling that the world was closing in.

I waited for Greg McClean's voice to reverberate through my head, taunting me, telling me I could go now, that it was probably nothing.

But none of it came. The images from the past receded, and the warm September day of three months ago was replaced by the cold December street of today.

Inhale, exhale. Gio's voice in my head instructed. *It's just a radio.*

I followed the instructions, taking a deep breath of chilly air, letting it go slowly.

My calm only lasted for a count of three.

A firm grip closed around my upper arm from behind, forcing a short scream from my throat before I could stop it. I wrenched my arm away and whirled, fast.

It was Ben, looking shocked. People eyed us warily, a few slowing or stopping to see what would happen, if they needed to intervene.

"Hey, Chloe, didn't mean to startle you." Ben's voice was unnaturally loud. "How've you been?" He leaned forward and kissed both my cheeks, European style.

"Uh, fine." My heart was still hammering. Seeing that the man who'd grabbed me was someone I knew, the people who had gathered moved on.

The cabbie playing 1010 WINS tossed his cigarette butt out the window and pulled away from the curb, taking the sound of the radio with him. It got fainter and fainter and then disappeared.

"So, remember you were asking me about that restaurant from last week?" Ben's eyes were wide and exaggerated. God, what a terrible actor.

"Uh, sure." I lowered my voice. "Is this really necessary? You think someone is watching us?"

"Pretty sure I've been followed a few times lately." His voice was quiet and fast.

Now the edges of panic did start to set in. "What?"

"So glad I caught you," he said, back to his pantomime. "Here, I'll write down the name. La Venezia, down in the Village." Ben pulled a small leather-bound notebook out of his coat pocket, along with a pen, and scribbled something on a clean white page. "I'm going home to Connecticut tonight, having my things shipped to Boston once I get settled," he said under his breath as he wrote.

I glanced around. Nobody was paying us any particular mind. People were walking past briskly, many carrying brightly colored, glossy shopping bags. It was the middle of Hannukah, and twelve days until Christmas. The door of the expensive shoe shop we were standing in front of opened, sending a wave of warmth and the trilling of the Ray Conniff singers into the street.

Ben grabbed my upper arm again and pulled me closer to the shop's window, away from the door. He pressed the paper into my hand. "Best squid ink pasta in the city. Though this is it, I can't give you any more restaurant recommendations. I'd get in so much trouble with my sister for sharing this one, it's her favorite place and she wants to keep it secret." A forced laugh, slightly manic. I understood—no more favors from the sister who worked at Sotheby's. I realized with a jolt I didn't even know her name. "Take care, Chloe. It was great to bump into you."

I automatically started to say, *you too*, when Ben pulled me into an unexpected embrace. "I'm sorry." Ben's breath was hot in my ear as he whispered, reminiscent of how Inga's had been on my cheek the night she died. "Tell Vik I'm sorry too. And I'm sorry I snooped in your room a few times. I made a copy of Vik's key and looked around when I knew the place was empty, to see if I could figure out what he was involved with. I was worried about him, and I thought you were involved too." He pulled back and looked me in the eye. "Have a great holiday, Chloe."

"You too," I said automatically, but it was too late. Ben had disappeared into the crowd.

CHAPTER THIRTY-FOUR

I didn't dare look at the neatly folded square of thick paper there on the street. I carefully tucked it into my wallet, trying to look pleased I'd gotten the name of the restaurant with the best squid ink pasta in the city.

The skin between my shoulder blades prickled. I looked up sharply, scanning the street again.

Had someone been watching us?

Was someone watching me now?

I hurried to the subway entrance. The rest of the commute flew by in a blur. Only once I was safe in Gio's apartment, behind his locked front door, did I take the paper out of my wallet. I didn't open it yet, though.

Nobody was home. I remembered: Gio and Mateo had family dinner tonight.

My breath quickened as I unfolded the note.

A name was scrawled on the paper: Amin Noor.

The name meant nothing to me, but at the same time it could be everything. A key, a cipher, to the insanity that had been happening.

I needed more. Who was this person? What was his link to Carl and the rest of the Fletchers?

There was no way to find any further information in Gio's apartment. A newish laptop sat on a desk in his bedroom, but I didn't know the password, and there was no way I was knocking on his grandmother's door downstairs in the middle of their dinner. I bit my lip, deciding.

I had to go to my apartment, use my own computer. The tug to find some kind of proof was urgent, and I couldn't wait for Gio to get home. Besides, I reasoned as I picked up the purse I'd just dropped on the floor, I could feed the cat, get more clothes.

Groucho leapt onto the kitchen table at my entrance, meowing furiously. I flung my coat over a chair and picked him up, taking comfort in his thick orange fur before filling his food dish.

Even though I'd only been at Gio's for a week, the apartment felt more like a time capsule than ever, full of stale air. I didn't like being alone here.

My computer hummed loudly as it warmed up. Groucho abandoned my lap once he realized he didn't have my undivided attention, jumping onto my bed and stalking away, tail in the air.

I took advantage of the time it took for the computer to wake up to check on the O'Keeffe. The drawing looked the exact same as always, nestled in its bed of foam. Just seeing it calmed my nerves, which were on edge being in the empty apartment. I tucked the drawing away, thinking about when and how I would tell Gio about it. Maybe during our first official date on Friday.

Would he think less of me, having not returned the drawing? I didn't think so. I thought he would understand how it felt like mine now, a talisman, a good luck charm against the evils of the world.

"Come on," I muttered at the computer, back at my desk. The loud tone of the modem dialing into the internet filled the room. Finally, I was able to type *Amin Noor* into the internet's search bar.

A soft thump made me jump in my seat.

I leaned back in my chair to peer into the living room. I'd only turned on a light in the kitchen, and the living room was shrouded in darkness.

Nothing. Just the musty, empty room, the furniture shadowed lumps, recognizable to me only because of their familiarity. A feather of fear tickled my belly, any calm from seeing the drawing dissipating in an instant. Why hadn't I turned on a light when I came in? It was fully night now, and I'd have to cross the dark room to hit the light switch on the far wall.

I turned back to the computer, shoving my unease aside.

The search hadn't turned up much. There were two or three recent articles relating to Noor's work for the Saudi National Bank, all within the past five years. I clicked on one, from Al Jazeera, my eyes automatically skimming the words. It was a dense piece about the financial world and yielded nothing helpful. I moved on to one that looked more interesting. This was a lifestyles-of-the-rich-and-famous-type blog, but it was based out of Europe, and the names were unfamiliar.

One thing was obvious. Amin Noor was very, very wealthy. He seemed to live a completely Western lifestyle, having nothing in common, on paper at least, with the religious extremists who had taken down the towers. He looked to be quite the jet-setter, or was in 1999, when he'd been dating a random French model. I looked closely at the picture. The woman was gorgeous, all tawny skin and perfect body, and Noor looked like a model himself, flashing a muscled bare chest at the camera. The two were snapped on the deck of a yacht moored outside Monte Carlo.

I sat back in my chair and gnawed a thumbnail absently.

Why was a Saudi playboy lurking around a decrepit-looking warehouse in Jamaica, Queens?

Thump, from the direction of the living room. I whirled around in my seat, heart pounding.

Again, nothing.

It was probably just the cat.

I turned back to my screen slowly, scanning the room as I did. An undulating mound of orange fur caught my eye.

Groucho had half buried himself under a pillow on my bed. I watched as he stretched out a hind leg to wash.

The fear curdled in my belly and rose to my chest.

If Groucho was in here with me, what was making that noise?

Or who?

I held my breath for a few beats to listen as hard as I could, waiting for something—a creak of floorboard, a too-loud breath, a rustle—to break the now foreboding silence.

There was nothing. Only the slight whisper of Groucho's tongue moving down his own fur.

It was Vik and Ben who had been moving my things around before, according to Ben.

"Ben?" I called into the silence. "Are you here? It's okay, just let me know."

Nothing.

The apartment was now *too* quiet, almost preternaturally so. Even Groucho was still.

I could reach the door to my bedroom from where I sat. I could twist fast in my chair, slam the door shut, and jam my desk chair under the knob. My bedroom window was the one that accessed the fire escape. I pictured myself opening the window, stepping into the frigid night, my breath bright white in the darkness. How cold the rusty iron would be under my hands as I climbed down three flights. It would be an easy run back to Bedford, back to where there were more people.

To Gio.

Time seemed to stop as I considered this plan, prodded its pros and cons in my brain. All the while my heart thudded and my breath came in short, rapid pants. I stared blindly into the living room, waiting for one of the shadows to move, to form a body uncurling from a crouch, for a shaft of light to shine on a face.

Inga's words danced in my head.

Be Careful. Help Me. Afraid. Murder.

The panic was closing in, fast. I forced myself to take a deep breath.

Inhale, exhale.

I was being ridiculous. Nobody was here except me and Groucho.

Inhale, exhale.

I repeated the breathwork ten more times, then blew out one final, deep breath, before turning back to my computer.

Just one more article, then I'd let myself leave.

I clicked on a slightly more recent article, this one from 2000. It was another foreign site, either European or Arabic, and seemed devoted to horse racing.

My hard-won breath suddenly left my body again, leaving me gasping. The room tilted slightly, then righted itself.

It was both the photograph and the caption that left me shaking, gripping the edge of my desk like a lifeline.

In the photograph, Amin Noor posed with a glossy black horse.

Saudi Arabian financier Amin Noor with the newest addition to his stables, Midnight Silk, a serious contender for the Saudi Cup. Noor co-owns the stallion with American investment group Dunbar Capitol.

Dunbar Capitol.

The writer must have meant Dunbar Capital.

Dunbar Capital was the Fletchers.

The writer had obviously misspelled *Capitol*, meaning *Capital*. There were one or two other typos in the write-up, as if English wasn't the writer's first language. The mistake must be why the article hadn't come up when I'd searched for the term before.

Amin Noor wasn't just associated with Carl Fletcher. He had a connection to Henry and Sloane too.

But what really left me reeling was the picture.

In it, Noor was wearing a pair of trendy, heavily rimmed black glasses.

With the glasses, I recognized him immediately.

Amin Noor had been the man sitting at the bar in Diner the night the thugs attacked Vik and chased me into the sugar factory. The night I jumped from the crane.

Those men had almost killed Vik.

Those men had known my name.

And this man, this Amin Noor, had been there.

CHAPTER THIRTY-FIVE

The shrill ring of the phone made me scream. I actually clutched my chest like a heroine in an old movie.

I sprinted through the living room as fast as I could and slammed the light switch on. Warm light from the two table lamps connected to the switch flooded the room, chasing away the shadows that had freaked me out only minutes earlier.

The phone rang two, three more times. I stared at it like it was a live, dangerous thing, chest heaving, waiting for the machine to pick up. After four rings, Vik's greeting floated into the room, followed by the loud beep.

A slight crackling told me that someone was on the other end. A barely audible intake of breath confirmed it. The noise made me draw my breath in too. I clapped my hand over my mouth before I remembered that whoever was calling couldn't hear me.

But they were there. I could feel them. Whoever they were, they were hungry for me to pick up the phone.

I let my hand hover over the receiver. The air in between my palm and the hard plastic felt full of electricity.

Another soft breath on the machine.

I snatched up the handset.

"Hello? Who is this?" My voice sounded high and uneven.

The flat monotone of the dial tone was the only response.

Whoever was there, they had hung up.

I whispered a frantic apology to Groucho, snatched up my coat and bag, and fled into the night.

Cold air snapped around me, and I thrust my hands deeper into the pockets of my too-thin coat, walking as fast as I could, not even bothering to pause to light a cigarette. It was dark and so freezing my shoulders hunched up around my ears. I ducked my head against the night air, ignoring the few other people on the street, desperate to get back to the warmth of Gio's.

As I turned right onto Bedford Avenue, my shoulders softened a little. There were more people here, more light. The pharmacy had just closed for the evening, but Vera Cruz was still open, laughter from behind its window spilling onto the street.

I paused in front of Gio's, my finger hovering over the buzzer, and turned toward Rosemary's. I hadn't been there for over a week, but it felt like months. I could see into the big front window, right where my crowd normally gathered. Sure enough, there they were. Calvin and Penny, Edward, Lisel.

From this distance, I could see the slightly manic look everyone had. The determination to party away their fears. Edward and Calvin, downing shots of Wild Turkey, their faces contorted with anticipation as Rosemary poured out two more. They must have made up. Lisel had an arm slung across the shoulders of a shaggy-haired hipster type I didn't recognize—it wasn't the same guy from the last time I'd seen her, whose name I couldn't remember. Penny was talking animatedly to yet another stranger, a woman with a short, bleach-blond pixie cut, who was nodding sagely at whatever was being said.

It hit me, watching them, how we were all hanging on by the barest of threads. More than that, really; how we were, collectively, careening. None of us knew when the next plane might fly into our skyscraper, or when the next bomb might rock the very ground beneath us. As a city, we'd been upended, torn from our roots, and we were all coping in the only ways we knew. Some people got tattoos, some like Bo rushed to finish that novel they'd always wanted to write, some fled the city; others doubled down on staying and bought up real estate in remote neighborhoods like Ditmas Park, then complained when their friends wouldn't visit.

We swung between extremes, from despair to a near hysterical optimism. Lisel clinging to whatever warm body she could find, Penny clinging to Calvin, Calvin to his crazy conspiracy theories.

Only right now, the idea of a conspiracy didn't seem quite so crazy.

I was tempted to join them. The thought of the cold foaminess of cheap beer in a giant Styrofoam cup was so, so tantalizing. I could drink one, and then another, Rosemary would pour for as long as I wanted, and I could lose myself in the words and laughter of my friends. I could dance with Frank. I could forget about Amin Noor and about how Vik's hands looked in his hospital bed and how Lou was gone, and I could forget about how gritty the horrible beige smoke was as it coated the inside of my mouth.

"Chloe?"

The call made my breath catch.

It was Gio, leaning out his front window, three stories up.

"Hey, did you buzz and I didn't hear you? I'm coming down to let you in." His head pulled back in.

I took one last look at the fogging window of Rosemary's, then turned my back, and waited for the door to open.

"I don't understand," Gio said, popping the cork out of a bottle of red wine. "I thought Dunbar Capital was your bosses."

"They are."

Gio placed a glass of wine next to a plate of manicotti his grandmother had sent up for me. It smelled divine.

"So why would this Amin guy be bidding against them? Isn't that like he's bidding against himself?"

"I don't know," I admitted, spearing some pasta with my fork. It tasted as good as it smelled. "It doesn't make sense."

"To raise the price," Mateo called over his shoulder.

Gio's brother was playing *Madden* on their PlayStation, one of the few nods, along with the bottles of Moretti in the refrigerator, to typical guyhood in the apartment.

"What do you mean?" Gio asked, twisting in his chair at the tiny café table in their kitchen to face his brother. I turned too.

Mateo shrugged, keeping his eyes on his game. "Happens sometimes when we do charity auctions at the station, you know? Suddenly there's this intense bidding between two people for one basket, and the price is getting high, and then everyone thinks, hey, what's so good about that basket? Turns out it's two cousins bidding on their other cousin's basket of wine to drum up interest in the cousin's new shop, you know?" Something happened in the game, making Mateo twist and grimace. "They ain't supposed to do that, but sometimes it slips in.

Basic value manipulation. *Aw, man.* You're fucking useless, Manning," he yelled at the game, shaking his head in disgust.

I gaped at Gio, who stared back.

That was it. That was what the Fletchers had been doing. They had artificially raised the value of the Monet.

One of Lou's favorite answers, when asked how much a piece of art was worth, was *however much someone is willing to pay.*

A deep pang went through me.

Had Lou known?

Had Inga?

"You think that's why . . ." Gio asked, clearly thinking the exact same thing as me. He had lowered his voice, even though Mateo's attention had fully returned to the game.

"It makes the most sense. Sebastian said the Fletchers were making about a million off the sale of the painting."

Gio frowned. "A million? Don't get me wrong, that's a lot of money, but like, is it enough to murder over? You think?"

"Maybe, if they were really going broke. And maybe they were. And what about Vik? And Lou?" I shook my head. "Can you take tomorrow off? I think I should go back to my place and search Vik's room. And if you're up for it, maybe we could go to the warehouse again."

Gio blew out a breath. "Yeah, I can get Veronica to cover for me. But on one condition. This is our last investigation, Nancy Drew. We don't find anything, you take what you do know to the police. Deal?"

I reached across the short distance of the table and wrapped my hand over his, squeezing his fingers, enjoying the mild pressure when he squeezed back.

"Deal."

The next day, I called in to work to say I wouldn't be in but would be at the library to finalize some research on the Monet. Then Gio and I went to my apartment, where he insisted on going in first, checking closets, flinging back the shower curtain. "You said there was a noise," he said when I argued.

Truth be told, I didn't argue very hard. Other than the presence of the drawing, I was creeped out by my own apartment now, though I hated leaving Groucho alone so much. I waited in the hall outside the open door, fidgeting with the strap of my bag.

Maybe Gio would take in the cat too. The thought of Groucho and me as a pair of strays, like Holly Golightly and her no-name cat, made me sigh. How much more could I ask of Gio?

"All clear," he said, poking his head out the door. "But you've got a message."

My stomach dropped. I slowly walked through the kitchen to the living room, stopping short at the sight of the answering machine perched on a side table.

The red light blinked accusingly at us.

"It's just a message. Go ahead, play it. I'm right here," Gio said.

I took a deep breath and pressed the play button.

Tears sprang into my eyes as Lou's voice rushed into the room.

CHAPTER THIRTY-SIX

"Hi, Chloe. It's me." I took a stumbling step toward the machine, as if Lou himself might rise out of the impersonal black box. He talked quickly. "Look, I'm sorry. I'm sorry I didn't get to say goodbye. I hope everything is okay, but I think you're too smart for that to be the case." A horn blared in the background, and Lou gave an impatient huff. "I can't tell you what I want to tell you. I can't tell you where I am. All I can tell you is, he could paint. Remember? *He could paint.* And so could she. She really could. Remember, Chloe? Try to remember."

The message ended abruptly.

The relief at hearing his voice was nearly overwhelming. I wanted to pick up the phone and demand he tell me where he was, what was going on. I wanted to tell him I was afraid. Mostly, I wanted to be sure he and Debra were okay.

I hit the play button and listened to the message again.

And again.

"What does it mean?" Gio finally asked after the fourth replay.

"I don't know." I shook my head in frustration. What did Lou want me to remember? Did he know something about what happened the night Inga was killed, something I saw?

"What does he mean about being able to paint? Who could paint?"

"He said that all the time, about any of the artists he liked," I said. "It was his ultimate compliment, and I thought it was funny because it was such a generic thing to say. It became kind of a joke between us." Hearing his voice, processing that message, was sending a riot of emotion through me. The relief, yes, but also sadness, and confusion.

The message was a kind of code. Lou was obviously trying to tell me something, but what?

Try to remember.

I did my best to recall that night again, but only the same images and sensations I'd already dredged up returned, playing on a loop in my mind: Lou dwarfed by *Helpless*, knocking back shots of tequila, the scent of Inga's breath on my cheek, the rasp of the shower curtain closing.

The feel of Inga's mouth on mine.

"Hey, let's look in Vik's room. That's why we're here, right? Maybe something in there will help," Gio said.

"Yeah, okay. Good idea." It *was* a good idea. I was on the cusp of screaming in frustration that I couldn't remember, that my head wouldn't offer up the information I needed as soon as I asked for it.

Vik's room was dark, the windows covered in light-blocking curtains. I pushed them back and let sunlight flood the room, dust motes swirling in its beams. He kept his space neat and tidy, especially compared with how messy my room normally was. It was a bigger room, too, but that had never bothered me; it was his place to begin with, after all. The room was so minimalist it was almost spartan, the bed made with a navy blue quilt, a wooden bureau, his laptop on a small desk with a compact stack of files and papers next to it. No milk crate bookshelves for Vik; he had a proper bookcase filled with a small collection of art-related books organized according to color and size, all titles on art history or art conservation.

I opened the files while Gio poked around in the closet. It felt like an intrusion, and it was, but it was necessary. The files were filled with handwritten notes, I assumed from his classes, the paper lined with complex chemical equations.

"I didn't know Vik painted," Gio said, holding up a box of metal tubes of paint that was sitting on a shelf in the closet.

"He doesn't. Not his own work, anyway. But he repairs paintings, or he's learning how to, so I guess that's why he has some."

Gio gazed at the tube of paint in his hand. "That seems really hard. Like, getting the colors right. I mean, didn't they use different paints back when, I dunno, Michelangelo was painting? How do they make sure it's gonna look the same?"

I grinned up at him from the files. "Michelangelo, huh? I didn't know you were into art."

"I'm Italian, I know all those Renaissance guys. Plus the Teenage Mutant Ninja Turtles were awesome."

I snorted out a laugh, but something he'd said niggled at the back of my brain.

Shuffling back through the papers, I flipped them over until I found the one I was looking for. Dread began to seep into my bones.

"Oh no," I whispered, trying to make sense of what I was reading.

But really, there was only one explanation.

"There's nothing much in here," Gio said, not seeming to have heard me. "Other than the paint, it's just normal closet stuff."

I swallowed, tapping the paper.

"What is it?" Gio asked, leaning over to look.

"Probably nothing," I said, even though I knew it was a lie. It was most definitely something. "It's just . . . Vik made a note about Monet here. I skimmed over it before, but now that I'm looking more closely, I think this might be a formula for the kind of paint Monet would have used. It even says *Nymphéas*, water lilies. And the date, 1916."

The dread had coalesced into the pit of my stomach.

I thought about the casual mentions Vik had made about money. How he'd worried about paying for his expensive NYU program when he first started, how he'd agonized over taking out student loans when he had no existing debt—his parents had paid for his undergraduate degree, but they'd made it clear they would only pay for graduate work if it was medical school. But I'd never heard him talk about it since. In fact, he'd started picking up the tab for our Wednesday Thai food nights, had casually paid for more around the apartment, like toilet paper or the electric bill, without making a big deal out of it.

I'd assumed his parents were paying his tuition after all.

These notes suggested maybe he'd found another way to finance his education.

Gio's brow furrowed. "What, like the painting the gallery jacked the price on? *That* Monet?"

My legs were suddenly unsteady. I collapsed into Vik's desk chair with a plop.

"I mean, Monet's not an obscure artist, and it's a famous series, the water lilies. Maybe this is just an exercise Vik was doing for school." I tried to make myself believe it.

Gio furrowed his brow. "So . . . what?"

"I think," I swallowed, fighting to get the words out that I didn't want to believe. "I think the painting might be fake."

"The twenty-million-dollar painting? That one, that's a fake?"

I nodded mutely, and Gio whistled low. He looked at the paper on the desk.

"Vik?" He sounded as incredulous as I felt. "You think Vik painted it?"

Remember, Chloe. Try to remember.

"No," I said slowly. "No."

Lou wasn't telling me to remember something about the night Inga died.

He could paint.

Lou was telling me to remember the things he had taught me, about how artists like Monet painted. How the invention of flexible metal tubes for paint was a game-changer, how it made them go outside, paint what was around them.

My eyes flew to the tubes of paint resting on the shelf in Vik's closet.

He could paint.

The last time Lou had said that to me was about the Monet. I could hear him saying it, recall the exact cadence of his voice.

And so could she. She really could.

"Vik didn't paint the Monet." I raised my eyes to Gio's. "I think Inga did."

CHAPTER THIRTY-SEVEN

"You're telling me that not only did these people jack up the price of a painting so some poor slob is paying over twenty million for it, but that it's not even real? Jesus, what a racket." Gio's voice was light, but he was pale and looked visibly shaken. We were once again sitting in construction-related traffic on the Brooklyn-Queens Expressway, heading to the warehouse one final time. I assumed, now, that the warehouse was where the fakes were made. One of us had to get a peek inside to confirm, and then I was going straight to Detective Gonzales.

"It looks that way." My mind was racing, even as my heart ached. It was going to kill me to tell the police Vik was maybe involved in all this, but hopefully doing so would expose the whole thing and keep him safe. Maybe not from jail—I had no idea what the legal ramifications were for creating and selling fake art at high prices—but from whoever was behind all this. Whoever had hurt him.

So much made more sense now, like Sloane and Henry's insistence that the Monet essay and provenance were airtight. How the painting disappeared during the war but magically reappeared in an attic nine months ago.

"I don't even know that there is a poor slob," I continued. Gio sharply veered into the left lane, and we were moving again. "Or if it's more smoke and mirrors from them."

Them. The Fletchers.

They had seemed so elegant, so chic, their lives so foreign to mine, with their old money and expensive wardrobes and their houses in the Hamptons. And it was all a ruse. They were con artists, pure and simple.

And Inga knew. But something scared her. I thought of the words in her paintings, growing increasingly desperate:

Be Careful.

Afraid.

Help Me.

Too Late.

Finally, *Murder.*

"She knew she was in over her head," I murmured as we drove deeper into Queens. "Inga."

"Twenty million. I could imagine someone killing over that. I saw those guys, know what they did to Vik," Gio said. "Someone's got enough stake in this to have brought in some serious muscle."

"But who? The Fletchers are grifters, but I can't see them paying for murder." *Could I?*

"What about that Carl guy, the brother?"

Of course, the other message in Inga's paintings: *Carl.*

I sighed. "Maybe. I just don't know. That's why we have to at least try to see what's at the warehouse. Once we see that, I can talk to Gonzales."

Gio shook his head slightly. He wanted me to go now. But what was I going to say? My ex-boss left me a rambling message on my machine? My art-conservation-studying best friend had jotted down a few chemical formulas that may as well have been in another language?

"I can't send the police after Vik unless I have something more definitive."

"You realize you keep moving the bar for when you'll talk to them," Gio said quietly.

He was right.

"They're my friends," I said quietly. Vik, Lou. Even Bo. I kept telling myself I owed it to them to make sure they were guilty before I threw them to the wolves.

But it was more than that. Inga had left me the note, had trusted me. I needed to see this through for her.

And, maybe, for me. To finish what I started.

Gio navigated his way through the streets of Jamaica, until we were parked across the street and about half a block down from the warehouse. Luckily it was a sunny day, the winter light streaming in through the windshield, so our sunglasses didn't look out of place. Gio had a black knit hat pulled low on his forehead, and I'd tucked my hair up into one of Mateo's with a NY Giants patch on the front. As disguises went, they weren't the best, but Gio kept the engine running so we could peel away if need be.

There was no sign of Amin Noor's fancy car, and other than a few guys moving in and out of Franklin's Glass and Metal, the street was deserted. We sat for about a half hour, sipping coffee from the bakery in take-out cups with the radio on low, not saying much.

After another thirty minutes I was deflated. This was clearly a wasted trip; whoever had been operating in this warehouse with Noor was obviously long gone. I was about to suggest we leave when the warehouse door swung open.

I gripped Gio's hand.

A man emerged, smoking a cigarette. He wasn't Noor, or anyone else I recognized. He was wearing a pair of blue coveralls, squinting down the street in our direction. I instinctively flinched, but Gio shook his head.

"He's not looking at us," he said. "With the glare on the windshield, I don't think he can see in here." He twisted in his seat and looked up the street in the direction we'd come from. "Look at this."

A battered white van drove past us and parked in front of the warehouse. Despite what Gio said, I hunched lower in my seat. Two more men emerged, then circled around and opened the back of the van.

They came out balancing a large wooden box between them.

"That's a painting crate," I said.

Gio nodded. We had a plan for if we saw someone. "Okay, hold on. Yeah, stay low, that's a good idea." I swallowed, nervous because he was nervous, but he was out the door before I could question whether our plan was still a good idea.

I kept my head just high enough to see what was happening.

Hands shoved in his pockets, Gio ambled up to the man with the cigarette, who was holding the door open for the guys carrying the crate.

"Hey," Gio called, loudly enough that I could hear him through the shut car windows. "This Franklin's? 17812 107th Avenue, yeah?" He put on his Brooklyn accent extra thick and had worn a Carhartt jacket, trying to look like a laborer at one of the nearby warehouses.

The two men carrying the crate paused, looking to the cigarette guy.

I held my breath.

The cigarette man shook his head and said something I couldn't hear, but he jerked his chin to the right. Gio swiveled, pretended to notice the glass and metal place for the first time, then nodded his thanks.

"Come back now," I whispered.

But he didn't. He turned back to the cigarette guy and held out one of his own. I could tell by his gestures he was asking for a light.

An annoyed look crossed the face of the guy in coveralls, but he held the door open with his foot and held his lighter out to Gio as the men with the crate moved inside.

Gio lit up, then handed the lighter back and ambled toward the glass and metal business. The guy with the cigarette stared after him, his gaze hard.

"Keep going," I muttered. "Don't look back, just keep going."

Once Gio walked into Franklin's Glass and Metal, the man in the coveralls stomped out his cigarette. He gave one final look where Gio had gone, then went back inside, the door crashing shut behind him.

I began to count under my breath. There were no low windows in the warehouse, so I wasn't worried about Gio being seen coming back to the car as long as nobody came out again.

When I hit thirty-three, Gio came back out of the glass place. He made a show of shaking his head up at the sign as he walked away, like he was pissed off about an encounter he'd had. He made his way with studied nonchalance back to the car.

"Stay low," he muttered out of the corner of his mouth as he pulled away.

My heart rate spiked. "Is someone there?"

"The door is opening."

At the first stop sign, Gio turned left, out of sight of whoever had come out of the warehouse.

He pulled his hat off and threw it in the back seat, forehead sweaty. His hands were shaking again.

"You were right," he said as we wove through the streets, heading back to the BQE. "Jesus, Chloe, I think you were right. There were easels in there, and more painting crates, and some that were stacked against a wall but they were turned backward, and . . . Jesus. Can you call that detective now, please?"

"Yes," I said, pushing myself upright. A feeling more intense than relief that I couldn't quite label infused me. It was maybe the satisfaction that I'd been right. That it hadn't all been in my head.

What we had was enough, for me. I could put it down now, turn it over to someone else. I didn't know Vik's involvement, I didn't know the extent of the Fletchers' involvement, but I knew something illegal was happening and people were dying.

I didn't want to be next.

"Where's your cell?"

"There." Gio pointed to the cupholder next to his seat.

I picked up the phone and pressed the power button, but nothing happened.

"I think it's dead." I showed Gio the blank screen.

He let out a groan of frustration and smacked the steering wheel. "Mateo. He borrowed it and then didn't charge it. Okay, I can get off the highway and find a pay phone."

"It's okay, we can call once we get back."

It was fully dark by the time we pulled up in front of Gio's building. Ricci's was closed tight.

"Why the hell aren't there any parking spots?" he muttered, slowing down.

"Friday night, I guess."

"Fucking bridge and tunnel. Look, I'll double-park here and walk you up, then park."

"It's okay, Gio. I can walk in on my own, the door is right there."

"Nah, I'm a gentleman." He grinned as he threw on his hazard lights and got out of the car.

I was just closing the passenger door when a siren bleeped. A cop had pulled up behind us.

"We got emergency vehicles coming through, move your car," the officer yelled out his window.

As soon as he said it, sirens sounded in the night.

"Yo, I'm just walking her up," Gio yelled back.

"Move your car, *now*."

The sirens grew louder.

"It's fine, let's just get back in the car," I said.

"No, you go up, here's the key. I'll be there in a few." Gio wrested a key off his ring. The cop car blared its siren once more, insistent. "All right, man, I'm going," he called.

A fire truck appeared down the street.

Gio jumped back in his car and drove off, the cop following. No sooner had they turned the corner than two fire engines raced by at top speed, sirens blaring. I clapped my hands over my ears, the noise making me uneasy.

As I turned to open the door, a shadowy figure appeared down the street.

I froze, key in hand.

Another slipped out of the shadows and joined him. The streetlights shone off their shaved heads.

Fuck.

I tried to thrust the key into the lock, but I was moving too fast, and it slipped from my cold hand, clattering to the pavement.

Risking a look over my shoulder, I saw they were getting closer. They weren't running, but walking very purposefully.

And staring straight at me.

I crouched over, bile rising in my throat, my hand groping for the key.

I couldn't outrun them again, but I could run across the street to Rosemary's, to where people were. I was uncoiling to stand when a hand fell on my shoulder.

"Jesus, Bo." I gasped in fright, then grabbed his arm. He was holding a half-full Styrofoam cup and a lit cigarette, and for a moment time contracted again, to that morning after Inga's party, when he'd been standing on the street holding the exact same things.

"Those guys, Bo, they're after me. They're the ones who hurt Vik, help me, please." The words spilled out, one long nonsensical string.

Bo looked sharply to his left. Something shifted in his face, and he dropped the beer and cigarette and grabbed my hand.

"Come with me. *Now.*"

CHAPTER THIRTY-EIGHT

We didn't run at first. Bo's apartment was only around the corner, so we didn't have far to go. But as soon as we turned left onto North Sixth Street, Bo sped up, pulling me along, racing for his front door, and we ended the short journey in an all-out sprint.

He slipped his key into the lock with a practiced gesture and shoved me inside his building, pulling the door shut behind him. I was herded up the stairs at a similarly fast clip, Bo glancing over his shoulder once or twice.

"Are they coming? Can they get in?" I was winded and terrified.

Bo unlocked the door to his apartment. I hustled in.

"No, they can't get in," he answered once the door was shut behind him. He added the chain for good measure.

"I figured it out, Bo." I was babbling, adrenaline and relief at the near miss pumping through my veins. "It's an art forgery ring. I don't have all the details, but fuck—someone big is involved, and they killed Inga, tried to kill Vik and me. She warned me, Bo. She left messages in her art warning me, or anyone, somebody who would listen."

"Hey, slow down, take it easy. Stop, Chloe, stop." Bo made soothing gestures with his hands but I was having none of it.

"I have to call the police. No, shit, let me call Gio first, he'll be worried when he sees I'm not home. Damn it, no, the police." Tremors were running through me, and I couldn't stay still, pacing around Bo's tiny living room.

"Hey, you call Gio, I'll call the police, okay?"

I was already picking up his handset. "Yeah, okay. Thanks. The local precinct. Tell them Chloe Harlow has to talk to Detective Gonzales right away. Um, is it okay if you tell her to come here?" My hand hovered over the buttons, anxious to dial. I was aware of what a big ask that was, given Bo's record.

"Yeah, yeah. Of course."

Gratitude surged in me, and I closed my eyes for a second before pressing the last button of Gio's landline, as I knew his cell was dead. "Thank you, Bo."

The answering machine picked up. "Hey, it's me. You must still be parking the car," I told the machine. "Those skinhead guys were coming after me, and I dropped your key—I'm sorry, it's probably right in front of your building. Bo was there, and he brought me to his place. We're calling the police. Be careful, Gio. They might recognize you by now."

I wanted to say something more, something about how I cared about him, about how much he had come to mean to me. But I couldn't leave that on the machine. "I'll let you know when the police get here," I finished with instead. "Talk soon."

As I hung up I heard the last of Bo's conversation on his cell. "Yeah, Chloe Harlow. Okay. Okay." He rattled off his address and his landline number. "We'll be here."

Bo faced me, running a hand through his hair, then peeling off his jacket. "Okay, they're contacting the detective, she'll come right away. You must be on a special list because they knew your name. So, we'll wait." He stretched, revealing a sliver of taut stomach as his shirt rode up. It was the kind of sight that might have tempted me to take things further in the past, but I was no longer interested, and not just because of how I felt about Gio. Deep down, I knew I hadn't been interested for a long time. I'd only been sleeping with Bo to cling to some kind of human connection. To remind myself that I hadn't, in fact, died in that toxic cloud of smoke.

He wandered into the kitchen. I flopped on the couch and wrestled off my coat while he rummaged around in there.

"Want a beer?" Bo was back, holding up two bottles of Sierra Nevada, both already open.

"I'm good. But I'll take a cigarette if you have one."

"You sure? They're open." He waggled the bottle at me, but I was way too keyed up to drink.

"I just want the cops to get here."

"I don't think I've ever heard anyone say that out loud in my life," Bo said in a wry tone, leaning forward to light the cigarette he handed me.

I took a deep inhale, the buzz of nicotine racing into my system. "I'm sorry, Bo."

He raised a brow, taking a swig of his beer in between pulls on his cigarette.

"What for?"

"For not trusting you."

Bo tapped some ash. "Didn't know you didn't."

"Well, I didn't." I swallowed. This was hard to say, but Bo was helping me so much right now, I felt compelled to get it out. "When I saw that video of you carrying me out of Inga's loft, I thought you were involved somehow. In her murder."

He slowly nodded but eyed me in a considering way. "It's okay. I get it. I mean, it's the logical conclusion, and you're smart."

That made me smile. "You always say that."

Bo pointed his cigarette at me. "Because you are, Chloe. You underestimate yourself too much."

My own cigarette was calming me down. "So we're cool?"

"Yeah." He quirked a smile at me that was almost a smirk. "We're cool."

"Even though now you'll have to talk to the police?"

"I'm not worried about it. We're cool."

It was oddly peaceful, sitting on Bo's couch, finishing our cigarettes. Maybe because I knew the whole confusing ordeal was nearly over.

Inga's murder would be solved.

"Sure you don't want a beer?" Bo asked.

"No thanks."

"Did I tell you I finished my book?"

"What?" The abrupt topic change made me sit up straighter, but it was a welcome one. "No, you didn't."

"Yup. Three hundred fifty-three pages, read 'em and weep."

"Wow. That's huge news." And it was, Bo had been working on this novel for as long as I'd known him. "Congratulations. I hope it's a huge bestseller, and you can take us all out for drinks."

Bo barked a short laugh. "Yeah, well. Maybe." He took a deep inhale, burning his cigarette almost down to the filter. That considering look had come over his face again. There was something about it I didn't like. "Wanna know what it's about?"

This was big. He had never told any of us, ever, the plot of his book. Lisel even said she doubted he was writing one at all, he could get so cagey about it, saying he had to leave this or that early to go home and get some writing done. She swore he was going home to jack off instead.

"Sure." I leaned forward eagerly.

"Us."

A prickle of unease replaced my enthusiasm. "Us? What do you . . ."

"Not you and me, us. Though you're in it. All of us." The lit tip of his cigarette swirled lazily, before he crushed the filter in the ashtray.

I took a deep drag. "You mean, our friends?"

"Them, sure. And some others. Really, it's about this whole place."

The prickle didn't grow, but it didn't go away either. Bo's look had changed, no longer one of solely consideration. I tried to pinpoint it. Was it craftiness? "What place? Williamsburg?"

He nodded, but didn't say anything else.

"So what happens?"

Bo lit another cigarette and inhaled deeply. "We all die." It came out in a plume of smoke.

My stomach flipped, and I crushed the cigarette I'd been smoking. Where were the police?

"Wanna know how?" he asked.

I didn't.

Bo continued as if I'd answered in the affirmative. "Serial killer," he said in a satisfied tone.

"How Bret Easton Ellis of you." I tried for teasing. It came out flatter than I wanted.

This made him smirk again.

"Wanna know how you die?" Bo's voice had dropped so that he was speaking barely above a whisper. I swallowed and looked at the door. What the fuck was taking them so long?

"Uh, not particularly, no."

"Why don't I tell you anyway?"

Bo's look had shifted to one of disdain. I drew in a breath to protest—I was far too unnerved to hear details of my own fictional death; this whole conversation was creeping me out—when a loud pounding sounded at the door. I started and half rose from my seat.

A strange smile lit Bo's face. "The cops."

"Chloe? Chloe, are you in there?"

Not the cops. It was Gio pounding on the door.

I ran through the kitchen and flung open the apartment door. Gio's fist was poised to bang again, but he dropped it and stepped inside, pulling me close in a one-armed hug. "Hey, you okay? You all right? I was worried."

He was holding a baseball bat in the hand not hugging me. I gave a relieved huff of laughter at the sight of it.

"Just like Rosemary, huh?" I pulled Gio into the living room, nearly giddy at the sight of him. Whatever weird tension had been building between me and Bo had vanished.

I could hear the sound of Bo shutting the front door again, and I sagged against Gio's side.

"Jeez, Gio, is that really necessary?" Bo asked, gesturing to the bat.

"Chloe said those skinhead guys were around again, so yeah. When do you think the detective will get here?"

"I really wish you hadn't brought that bat," Bo said in a rueful tone. Something about the way he spoke snapped both my and Gio's attention away from each other and toward Bo.

The shiny, blank eye of a gun stared back at us.

My heart contracted. Gio's arm was instantly in front of me, his body half shielding mine.

"Bo, what the fuck?" he said.

"Drop the bat, and kick it under the table," Bo ordered.

Somewhere I registered the wooden *clack* of the bat being dropped and kicked, but it was peripheral, like hearing sounds though a layer of cotton.

It was seeing Bo with the gun that did it.

Everything that happened at Inga's party came flooding back.

CHAPTER THIRTY-NINE

It was an unstoppable tide.
 He had been wearing a ski mask. But I knew Bo's body, his stance. I probably recognized it then, too, even though I had been so full of tequila I couldn't stand up straight.

I remembered it all so clearly now.

I'd pushed open the shower curtain bathroom door, leaving behind the glowing yellow interior. The first thing I'd seen was Vik and Ben with their coats on at the door, waving goodbye to me.

The next was Inga, wrapping her fingers through mine as we leaned against the kitchen counter again.

Her industrial steel front door slid shut as a few more people left, calling out thanks over their shoulders. I dimly wondered what time it was, and how I was going to get home now that Vik had left.

"Was that okay, what happened in there?" She indicated the curtained-off bathroom with her chin.

"It was," I said, my voice dropping to a whisper.

That slow smile spread across her face, wrinkling her eyes. I was fascinated by her small white teeth, by the tiny freckles on her nose.

"So this is okay, too?"

Inga's mouth was on mine again, hungrier than before, more tooth and tongue than I expected. But it was good and relit the desire that was already kindled deep in my stomach. I traced the line of her jaw, surprised by its delicacy under my fingers.

After some time, I pulled away with a gasp, suddenly conscious of our surroundings, of the strangeness of it all.

"We're all alone," she said.

I looked around and realized the loft was empty except for us. How long had we been making out? My lips tingled.

Inga smiled again, pulling me around the counter toward the futon, where she turned, eyes alight.

"I like you, Chloe," she breathed against my cheek. "You seem honest. Real."

I didn't know what to say to that, so I didn't say anything. But I wanted more of her.

I was leaning my mouth back toward hers when she jerked her head back, her gray eyes widening in—ah, I knew what it was now—both surprise and fear.

I whirled so fast I stumbled, but I caught the edge of a chair and managed to not fall. The room had begun a lazy spin. I couldn't comprehend what I was seeing at first. Three men stood just inside the door, which they'd managed to open silently. Or maybe it had been left open by the last departing guests.

They all wore ski masks, and two held guns.

It was turning quickly that did it, moving so fast after all that booze. That, and maybe the shock of having a gun pointed at me. My vision blurred and the spinning grew faster, before the floor rushed to meet me.

"You were there," I said now, staring at the gun in Bo's hand. I clutched at Gio's sleeve for support. "It was you, I remember now. There was no guy, no Liam. I was kissing Inga, and you came in with a gun."

Bo gave a half smile, shockingly familiar. "See, Chlo? I told you you were smart."

"So you're in on this? God, you and Vik, and who the fuck else in my life? Did you kill her?"

The smirk faltered. "I got you out of there, is what I did. I made sure you weren't killed too. I told the guys you were too drunk to remember any of this. I convinced them to let you *live*, Chloe. I put my ass on the line for you and now you've nearly fucked it up for both of us."

He hadn't answered my question. "So you did kill her." A wave of nausea overtook me, and if I hadn't been clutching Gio's arm I might have fallen. "Why?"

"She wouldn't do it anymore, right?" Gio asked. His voice was harder than I'd ever heard it, his accent stronger. I shot him a look. It was clear the gun was the only thing holding Gio back from flattening Bo. "She wanted out?"

Bo flipped his hair off his forehead, but he kept his eyes trained on us. He, too, could probably sense Gio's fury. "I don't make the calls, man. I just follow orders."

"From whom?" I asked. My voice was shaking along with my body, but I didn't care. "Who is in charge of this shit?"

Bo gave a tiny shrug. "Questions like that get you killed. Look what happened to your friend."

"*Which* friend, Bo? The one who died, or the one who's in the hospital fighting for his life? Or the one in hiding?" The shock was still there, but white-hot anger was rushing in fast, pushing it aside. "It's Carl Fletcher, isn't it?"

"Only partly," drawled a new voice.

Sebastian stepped in from the kitchen.

I took an involuntary step back. If Bo holding a gun was a shocking sight, seeing Sebastian walk out of Bo's kitchen was almost incomprehensible.

"You?" My disbelief was obvious in my voice. Snarky, shitty *Sebastian* was the ringleader of all this?

"I thought she would be knocked out," Sebastian said to Bo.

Bo shrugged again. "She wouldn't have a beer. I tried."

Sebastian gave an exaggerated eye roll I knew well. Seeing it here, in Bo's apartment, with a gun pointed at me, was entirely dislocating.

"Maybe we'll get lucky and she'll black out on her own again," Sebastian said, eyeing me with something akin to disgust.

"I don't think she's been drinking," Bo said.

Another eye roll. "Of all the nights for you to stay sober, Chloe. And this guy? What the hell are we supposed to do with him? I didn't bring Ivan because I thought we'd just be carrying her out again."

I gripped Gio's sleeve tighter. Carrying me out.

To kill me.

Just like Inga had warned.

Be Careful.

Murder.

"The Fletchers," I began, but Sebastian flicked a glance my way and cut me off.

"You think Henry and Sloane are smart enough to think of something like this? No."

"But Dunbar Capital is them. And Amin Noor, at the warehouse."

He pursed his lips.

"Yes, they thought they were so clever with their little scheme to inflate the price of their own works. Other gallerists were starting to catch on, though. They were going to get caught in a matter of time. But about my operation? No, the Fletchers had no idea. They thought that Monet was real."

Something that wasn't quite relief temporarily overrode my fear. The frisson of being right, maybe.

"But it was a fake," I said. "Right? Inga painted it, and Vik helped get the paint formulas right to fool the experts. But Vik . . ."

"I've known Vik for years," Sebastian said. He pulled a cell phone out of his pocket. "Made him promise never to let on to you when you took the receptionist job that he and I were acquainted. And he brought in Inga. I've got this brilliant painter, he told me. She could do it, needs the money. And how right he was."

"For how long?"

Sebastian was punching some buttons on his phone. "Long enough. There are fakes everywhere," he said, glancing up from his phone and smiling. "You have no idea. Nobody does. Every auction house, every major museum. It was easier for us to stick to an international market."

"You and Carl," I said, putting the pieces together. It was only a small relief that at least one instinct had been right, that Henry and Sloane weren't killers. "Carl wasn't selling guns or state secrets, he was selling fake art. With Amin Noor."

Sebastian gave a short laugh. "What, you thought Carl and Amin were *terrorists*? Jesus, Chloe. Yes, me and Carl. Or Carl had the idea, but he couldn't execute it without me. Amin was the moneyman, who found clients among his wealthy friends abroad. Certain other parties became interested, and it grew from there."

"What other parties?" I had no idea what Sebastian was talking about.

"He means the mob," Gio said, his voice grim. "Probably the Russians. That's where the muscle comes from. And the killing."

Sebastian raised a brow. "You got a cute and smart one, Chloe. *Quelle surprise*. I'll just say we have a lot of clients in that part of the world."

I looked at Bo in confusion, not understanding his role in all this, and Sebastian gave an exaggerated sigh. I could tell one part of him was loving this. I'd always assumed his cruel streak was simple bullying, but no. It was deeper than that.

Sebastian wanted, maybe needed, for me to know he was the mastermind here. It really had infuriated him that I had been given the job he thought should have been his.

That was the only reason he was telling me this. So he would have the satisfaction of knowing that I knew, before he had the mob goons kill me.

And now Gio too.

"Bo here is simply an associate of my associates. Vik brought him in, too, when I told him we needed someone to do a little dirty work. We've never actually met before. Hello." Sebastian nodded in Bo's direction.

Bo still hadn't taken his eyes off me and Gio. "Like I said, I just do what I'm told. Got some debts to pay, this is the price."

"Killing someone, Bo? Is that the price?" I whispered. And another betrayal of Vik's. Did it ever end?

He swallowed once. "I didn't actually pull the trigger. That was someone else."

"But you were there."

His eyes flared under his bangs. "I got you *out*. I even got them to let me use the fucking car, nearly got a broken neck once they learned there was video of that. These guys don't owe me anything, Chloe, do you understand that? I owe them. And for what it's worth, I didn't have anything to do with the art forgery shit. I didn't even know it was one of their angles; it wasn't why I was brought in. Vik just thought I could use the extra cash. I usually work on other matters."

"Other matters? You mean drugs, right? That's how you got indebted to the fucking mob and went from what, dealing to being a hit man?"

"They needed someone to clean up some shit. I didn't ask what that shit was." Bo shrugged, a shrug I'd seen thousands of times. His way of handing off his problems, his responsibilities, of absolving himself.

"Can you handle them?" Sebastian asked. "I'm going to call Ivan. I'm not worried about her." He flicked his eyes toward me dismissively. "But I don't like the looks of that one." He pointed at Gio. "We need backup."

"I can handle them."

Sebastian turned his back, dismissing us, and punched some numbers on his phone.

I didn't want to die like this.

I wasn't sure how they were going to do it. Overpower us, take us to a deserted stretch of Brooklyn or Queens—hell, maybe even to that warehouse in Jamaica—and shoot us there? Or tie a cinder block to our feet and throw our unconscious bodies into the river? Scenes from every mob movie I'd ever seen flashed before my eyes, before being quickly replaced by another scene.

It's probably nothing. You can go now.

The building shook, debris fell, I held Maya's hand tight as I walked down endless stairs, then into the bright day turned dark with smoke, littered piles of blood and hair and clothes that were bodies, with people screaming and running as the very earth shook and I ran, harder and faster than I'd ever run but it wasn't fast enough, and the cloud caught me.

I didn't want to die that day either.

And I didn't.

That day vanished in a blink and I was back in Bo's sour-smelling living room.

I gave Gio's arm a squeeze.

He didn't look at me, but out of the corner of my eye I saw his head give one small nod.

"Bo," I hissed, making my eyes turn desperate, which was not very hard to do. I let go of Gio and took a few steps closer to him, hands out and pleading. "Please, Bo. Help us. You did it before, do it again. Help me."

"Can't," he said. I could see the indecision and regret on his face. "It's too late for that. You should have left it alone, Chlo."

"Come on, it's me," I said, skittering to my left a little to give Gio the space he needed. I forced out some tears, also not super hard to do. "Please, put the gun down. I'm so fucking scared."

The word *scared* was still leaving my mouth, Bo's attention diverted toward me, when Gio lunged.

One hand grabbed Bo by the throat and the other grabbed the hand holding Bo's gun. A shot fired as they fell. I ducked and screamed, clapping my hands over my ears.

The bat.

It was under the kitchen table. I dove for it.

There was no time to register what was happening with Gio and Bo, who were wrestling on the floor, a pool of blood spreading beneath them.

Who was shot?

Sebastian was almost on me, but I scrambled up, gripping the bat in both hands, and swung as hard as I could. The sound of wood hitting bone cracked louder than I would have thought, and Sebastian dropped to the floor in an instant.

Another pool of blood began to form.

I was gaping at the dent in the side of Sebastian's head, horrified, when a heavy mass surged into my side and knocked me to the ground. The bat, which had been hanging limply by my side, flew out of my grasp and rolled away.

Suddenly there was no air.

"I didn't want it to end like this, Chloe." Bo was straddling me, sitting on my chest and pinning my arms down with his legs. His hands were around my throat. "I liked you."

I was desperate for air and writhed and jerked furiously in an effort to get him off, but Bo was so much bigger and stronger.

His grip tightened. The edges of my vision began to blacken.

"This is how you go in the book too." He was leaning close, his breath foul on my cheek. "Kind of ironic."

The darkness was closing in, everything narrowing to a pinpoint.

All I could think was *no. No, not like this, not yet, no no no.*

And then the pressure was gone, Bo's body off mine. Air rushed into my lungs again and I rolled over, away from him, gasping and gagging and taking in huge, greedy sucks of breath.

"It's over, Chloe."

Now Detective Gonzales's face was next to mine. I could hear footsteps and the static of police radios and Bo's incomprehensible shouts and the sounds of scuffling.

A warm, firm hand closed around my fingers. I panted, staring at Gonzales, slow to comprehend. How had she known where I was?

"It's over."

CHAPTER FORTY

Nine Months Later

I handed a bag of crusty rolls to the customer, a middle-aged Polish lady who smiled in return. The door tinkled at her departure, and I inhaled the scent of fresh bread and sugar and hot coffee, feeling perfectly at home.

I would miss this shop. I would miss my neighborhood. But Gio and I were moving to Chicago next week. He'd finally convinced his parents to let him open a branch of Ricci's elsewhere, and he and I, along with Groucho, were heading to the Midwest so he could set it up.

And I was going back to college.

To my absolute shock, I had been accepted at the School of the Art Institute of Chicago to finish my BA. I would major in art history, theory, and criticism. I deferred my matriculation until the spring semester, to give Gio and me time to settle in.

"Babe, you got the counter? I'm heading out for PT." Gio had his jacket on, a lightweight one. It was September again, one of the first real crisp days we'd had.

It had been Gio who called the police, after he'd received my message and before he came to Bo's, baseball bat in hand. "I never trusted that asshole," he'd rasped from Bo's dirty kitchen floor as EMTs swarmed over him and I grasped his hand. Gio had been shot while he and Bo fought for the gun, the bullet going clean through his left shoulder. It had taken months of physical therapy for him to regain most of the use of that shoulder, and he still went once a week.

"Don't worry, you go on. See you at family dinner?" I said.

He planted a light kiss on my cheek. "See you then."

I resisted the urge to turn the lock in the door after his departure. Detective Gonzales had assured me repeatedly that I wasn't in any danger, that since I hadn't known anything specific about the art forgery ring and which pieces were sold to whom, the mob wouldn't be interested in me.

"They really want Carl and Amin, probably," she had said. Both had fled the country soon after Bo's arrest and the joint police/FBI storming of the Jamaica warehouse. Gonzales said she assumed they were living under false identities somewhere in the Middle East or Russia by now.

"Though maybe Carl is on a beach in the Caymans." She shrugged. It was estimated the forgers had made millions, maybe even billions, selling the fake paintings. "He's more the FBI's problem now."

Vik, though, did have reason to worry. He'd pled guilty to multiple charges of fraud and chosen to serve a longer sentence rather than say anything he knew about the Mafia's involvement with the ring, even though it likely didn't amount to much. Bo had done the same, and, as an accessory to murder, would be in jail for a long time. Vik's parents were so mortified by his arrest they had moved back to India, rather than continue to face their tight-knit community in New Jersey. Vik told me in a letter he planned to join them once he was released.

I wasn't sure I'd ever see him again.

He'd apologized, at least. *I needed the money*, he wrote in a hand that was as tidy as he'd kept his room. *And, to be honest, I liked the intellectual challenge. I thought Sebastian and Carl were in charge, that it was just some white-collar stuff more or less; I had no idea any of it would lead to anyone's death. I told Sebastian I was done with all of it, but all I did was bring harm to myself and to you. I'm sorrier than I can say.*

He also let me know that he had, indeed, given Bo a key to our apartment, and that was when he'd asked Bo if he wanted to make a little extra money. He claimed he didn't know it was going to be drugs, or that Bo would get in so deep.

I hadn't written back yet, but thought I might soon.

Henry and Sloane, too, faced charges. They were involved in a complex legal battle, where they were being sued by Sotheby's and multiple private clients, and in turn were suing Amin Noor, if he could be found. The Manhattan district attorney had found shell company upon shell company owned by the Fletchers, a complex chess game of transferring ownership of works of art and borrowing against them to remain liquid. They maintained their ignorance of the art forgery ring, a claim validated by Vik.

The New York Times reported a week ago the gallery had declared bankruptcy and was filing for dissolution of the century-old business.

I knew now, after months in therapy, that it wasn't my fault I didn't see what was happening right under my nose. That Vik and Sebastian had been friendly since they went to summer camp together in middle school, that Henry and Sloane were neck-deep in fraud.

"That's progress, kid," Lou had said when I told him I finally accepted there was nothing I could have done. "I worked there for a decade, and I only figured out how shady it was those last few weeks before Thanksgiving. How do you think I feel?"

It was a document Lou had taken from Sebastian's desk—a rare misstep for Sebastian, not to have locked it away—that had first alerted Lou something might be amiss. Lou had mostly stayed out of the gallery's financial dealings, sticking to research, but the way an Edward Hopper painting had transferred from Dunbar Capital to another financial entity, then back to Dunbar, didn't sit right with him. He had figured out Amin Noor's connection after the auction, having gotten Noor's name from the old lady in Chanel, and then dug around on his own, probably finding the same article I did about Noor and misspelled Dunbar Capitol on the horse racing site. That had led him to look more closely at the Monet itself, double- and triple-checking the articles I'd copied for him at the library.

"The description was just a little off from what we had," he had told me over lunch last spring. He was working now as a curator at a museum uptown, though was seriously considering retiring early and moving upstate. "Small things, you know? We only had black-and-white photographs of the real piece from the 1920s and 1930s, but what the articles said about some of the colors just didn't add up. I first thought it was a different water lilies piece, but the more I looked, the more it didn't seem quite right." He had sighed and put down his fork, taken a huge slug of his coffee. "I confronted the Fletchers about it right before Thanksgiving, told them I thought we had a fake. It happens, and look, if Sotheby's was fooled, there was nothing to be embarrassed about. But they doubled down, *insisted* it was real. And now I know why, because they had that scheme to inflate the price."

Henry, we found out later, confided in his brother that Lou believed the Monet to be a fake. Word of this must have gotten from Carl to his contact in the mob, who sent someone to threaten Lou to keep his mouth shut. That was the man I'd seen approach Lou as I drove away on Thanksgiving.

It scared them enough that Lou and Debra spent the weekend frantically throwing all their belongings into a storage unit, then they took off for Arizona, where they hid out with Debra's sister.

"I called the Fletchers from the road, told them what happened. They fired me." He had picked his fork back up and ate another bite of his salad, shaking his head. "Still can't believe all this. It wasn't until we were out west that I put it together about Inga and the Monet. Can you believe it, two cons going on at the same time?" Lou looked sad as he remembered. "She really could paint. What a shame."

Nobody knew for certain why Inga had been killed, but the general consensus was what Gio had conjectured: She had wanted out, and they—whatever shady consortium of mob figures and international financiers put together by Carl—didn't want her to go. I remembered what she said to me, that night in her loft. That I seemed real, and honest. My strong hunch was that Inga, like so many of us, reevaluated her entire life after the towers fell and decided she was done with married men and fraud and being told what to paint. Her work was starting to sell, and she didn't want to be involved with the forgery ring anymore.

But they wouldn't let her leave.

I thought of her often. Of the messages she left in her paintings, and of how afraid she must have been, but how she must have felt she couldn't confide in anybody.

But in her own way, she had. She had confided in me, by leading me to the warehouse.

The exhibition of Inga's paintings was never held, and even though collectors were clamoring for her works, her sister, Anne, had retaken possession of all Inga's canvases. Last I heard, she was talking to other galleries about taking on the estate.

She would make a fortune.

The FBI was trying to track down the forgeries, but as most of them had been sold overseas, it was apparently going to be a long, slow process. Most of the main players who knew the ins and outs of the business had either disappeared, like Carl and Amin, or were dead, like Inga.

And Sebastian.

He hadn't survived being hit with the baseball bat.

Another thing I worked on in therapy. I'd killed him.

The DA had declined to press charges, seeing as how I was being held at gunpoint at the time.

I could still hear the exact sound of the bat making contact with Sebastian's head. I would probably hear it for the rest of my life.

But there were things that helped. Being with Gio. Our plans for the future. The smells of the bakery.

The Georgia O'Keeffe drawing.

I'd finally told Gio about it, once he was out of the hospital, even though he was still recovering from his gunshot wound. He'd nodded and said he wanted to think about it for a few days. A pit had formed in my stomach, even though I had said of course, I understood, and I was willing to do whatever he recommended. Give it to Jonathan Marz, give it to the police.

For three days I'd been miserable, convinced Gio was through with me, sure that this infraction was the last straw. He'd been shot because of me; of course he wouldn't want a girlfriend who had also, in essence, stolen a $50,000 drawing.

On the morning of the fourth day after I'd told him about the drawing, we'd been sitting on the couch flipping channels, trying to find a good movie to watch. I was about to suggest I go to the local video store when Mateo walked in, carrying two things—a flat brown-paper-wrapped package under one arm, and a cat carrier in the other.

Groucho peered suspiciously from the carrier, but eventually emerged, ignoring us all, to inspect his new surroundings.

"I'm gonna treat him to a new litter box and food dish," Mateo smiled, running his hand along Groucho's silky back. The cat arched up to meet him, then rubbed his head under Mateo's palm. "See you two in a bit."

"Got you a present," Gio said, once Mateo had left.

I stared at the wrapped package, which Mateo had left leaning against his closed bedroom door. "Gio, you've given me so much. I don't need anything."

Gio waved this away. "Come on, open it."

I took the package into my lap and carefully peeled back the brown paper. The familiar strokes of charcoal emerged, and tears sprung to my eyes.

He leaned over to get a better look. "I had Mateo get it from your closet and have it framed."

"You don't think I should give it back?" I whispered. The drawing looked beautiful in its simple black frame. I couldn't take my eyes off it.

"No, I don't," he said simply. "It belongs to you now."

It wasn't an argument that would stand up in a court of law, but I decided that didn't matter. I had earned that drawing, it was mine. The same sense of calm that came over me whenever I looked at it descended again. The light between the branches didn't seem so far away anymore.

I could reach it, if I wanted to.

Until a week ago, the drawing had hung on the wall of Gio's—and now my—bedroom, where I could look at it every day. Last week we'd taken it down and packed it in a box of things that would ride with us in the car to Chicago.

At the bakery, I smiled at the thought of how the drawing would look in our new apartment. I was on my way to the storeroom in the back to get more sugar to refill the canister on the counter when the door tinkled again. I came out, wiping my hands on my apron, to find a short, dark-haired woman nervously holding her purse in front of her body like a shield. She was matronly and a little plump, wearing a sensible cardigan over dark work slacks.

Time stopped.

"Chloe?" The woman swallowed. She, too, seemed frozen in place. "I don't know if you remember me."

Of course, I remembered her. She was another thing, a better one, that I would never forget.

Maya.

"I'm sorry I didn't come before. I knew where you worked, but I just couldn't, you know? We lost a lot of people at Dryden." She nodded to herself. "It was hard."

She waited a beat, but I still couldn't speak. My heart thudded and swelled.

"Then I saw you in the papers, and you didn't work at the gallery anymore, and I didn't know how to find you. You're not listed." She was right. I had given up my old home phone number after the story about the gallery broke, after getting inundated with calls from the press. I'd given up the apartment too. "I pestered the police finally, explained about that day. The nice lady detective—she wouldn't give me your phone number—finally told me to come to this bakery. So I did."

My mouth opened, but still no words would come. All the things I wanted to say were jammed in my throat, blocking it.

Maya finally looked away, casting her eyes down. "I'm sorry," she repeated. "Maybe I should have called first. Maybe you don't want—"

I didn't let her finish. My throat wouldn't work, but my feet did. Within seconds I was around the counter, and leaning into her, and with a small sob she clutched me back.

We clasped each other and cried and didn't speak. We didn't need to. Finding each other was enough.

ACKNOWLEDGMENTS

Like Chloe, I was in New York on 9/11. Also like her, I lived in Williamsburg, Brooklyn, and commuted to a job at a rather posh gallery on the Upper East Side. This is where the similarities between myself and my protagonist end, but it is also where the glimmer of the idea that turned into this book germinated. I was hunting for a setting for a new thriller, and was thinking about times in my life that felt particularly fraught. Those months after 9/11 topped the list. As I explored the idea of writing a book set in that particular moment, I couldn't stop thinking about how, in those few weeks and months after the attacks, everything felt like a conspiracy theory. This was probably true everywhere in the US, but felt particularly so in New York City. What if, I wondered, you unwittingly became entangled in an actual conspiracy in such a time? How would you tell truth from fiction?

Warning: Spoilers are ahead! If you haven't read the book yet and want to be surprised, I suggest you stop here.

But what would that conspiracy be? To answer that question, I turned to my own field of art history. A few years after I left the posh gallery, a different posh gallery in the same neighborhood was rocked by scandal. It was accused of having sold fake paintings, for years, for millions of dollars. That story gave me the inspiration for the scandal Chloe uncovers, though, of course, to much more violent ends. For those interested, the Netflix documentary *Made You Look: A True Story About Fake Art* is a good watch on the subject. While, as I mentioned, I was in New York on 9/11, I was not at Ground Zero (in fact, I was commuting to said gallery when the second plane struck the South Tower of the World Trade Center). To create Chloe's experience of that day, I read countless survivor accounts, preserved in digitized newspapers, in early blogs, and in later reminiscences. The episodes of Spike Lee's *NYC Epicenters: 9/11–2021½* that treat 9/11 were also helpful resources.

The journey from idea to published book is a long one, and one that doesn't happen alone. Huge thanks are due to my agent, Danielle Egan-Miller, who encouraged me to run with the idea. She and the whole team at Browne & Miller Literary Associates, in particular Mariana Fisher, made the story shine with their early feedback and astute edits. Lara Jones, senior editor at Emily Bestler Books/Atria, took a chance on this book and graciously allowed me to make it better. I send more thanks to her, and to everyone at Emily Bestler Books/Atria for all their hard work and support. These include Libby McGuire, publisher of Atria Books, for her cheerleading, and Emily Bestler, editor in chief of Emily Bestler Books, for also taking a chance on my work. Other invaluable team members include Dana Trocker, Karlyn Hixson, Abby Velasco, Sierra Swanson, Aleaha Renee, Paige Lytle, and Shelby Pumphrey. James Iacobelli and Kelli McAdams are responsible for the beautiful design of the cover and Davina Mock-Maniscalco for the interior.

Thanks and hugs to Juli for the beta read and the response that made me cry (in a good way!), and to Chrissy for every second of encouragement and love and the much-needed spontaneous trip to Paris. Special thanks to Celeste for the daily minutiae. A woman hopes she did our past proud. Mountains of love and gratitude to the rest of my family and friends, I am wildly fortunate to be abundant in both, and you are too numerous to name. All my love as always to Marc and Roy, for making me laugh, keeping me sane, giving me space, and then coming home.